Dear Reader,

What you have in your hand are two of my favorite books I've had the privilege to write. They were certainly two of the more emotional books I've written. They're very different stories in some ways, but at their core, they're both about finding love and redemption.

A Hunger for the Forbidden, is the final book in the Corretti Dynasty series (if you've been following the whole series, that's amazing. And I hope this is a satisfying conclusion!) Fair warning, Matteo and Alessia have a hard road ahead. Forbidden desire, family feuds, an unexpected pregnancy and dark secrets are all in the way of their happily-ever-after.

In *The Highest Price to Pay* Blaise and Ella don't have secrets between them. Or so they think. They believe they already know the worst about each other. But it's not about the pain on the surface, or Ella's physical scars, it's about the deep pain they hide from the world.

Matteo and Blaise both feel beyond redemption for very different reasons, but with the same result.

I think that everyone needs love. And who better to appreciate the beauty of love than a man who's resigned himself to living without it? A man who believes he isn't worthy of it?

These stories are about the real power of love. About how love can pull a person from the darkest of places and bring them into the light.

I hope you enjoy my two damaged heroes as much as I did.

All the best,

Maisey

The more powerful the family...the darker the secrets!

Introducing the Correttis—Sicily's most scandalous family!

Behind the closed doors of their opulent palazzo, ruthless desire and the lethal Coretti charm are alive and well.

We invite you to step over the threshold and enter the Correttis' dark and dazzling world....

The Empire

Young, rich and notoriously handsome, the Correttis' legendary exploits regularly feature in Sicily's tabloid pages!

The Scandal

But how long can their reputations withstand the glaring heat of the spotlight before their family's secrets are exposed?

The Legacy

Once nearly destroyed by the secrets cloaking their thirst for power, the new generation of Correttis are riding high again—and no disgrace or scandal will stand in their way....

Sicily's Corretti Dynasty

A LEGACY OF SECRETS—Carol Marinelli
AN INVITATION TO SIN—Sarah Morgan
A SHADOW OF GUILT—Abby Green
AN INHERITANCE OF SHAME—Kate Hewitt
A WHISPER OF DISGRACE—Sharon Kendrick
A FACADE TO SHATTER—Lynn Raye Harris
A SCANDAL IN THE HEADLINES—Caitlin Crews
A HUNGER FOR THE FORBIDDEN—Maisey Yates

8 volumes to collect—you won't want to miss out!

Maisey Yates

A Hunger for the Forbidden

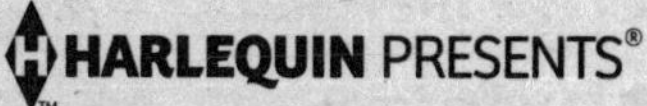

Recycling programs for this product may not exist in your area.

ISBN-13: 978-0-373-13200-3

First North American Publication 2013

Special thanks and acknowledgment are given to Maisey Yates for her contribution to Sicily's Corretti Dynasty series

This edition published by arrangement with Harlequin Books S.A.

For questions and comments about the quality of this book, please contact us at CustomerService@Harlequin.com.

Printed in U.S.A.

CONTENTS

All about the author...
Maisey Yates

MAISEY YATES knew she wanted to be a writer even before she knew what it was she wanted to write.

At her very first job she was fortunate enough to meet her very own tall, dark and handsome hero, who happened to be her boss, and promptly married him and started a family. It wasn't until she was pregnant with her second child that she found her very first Harlequin Presents® book in a local thrift store—by the time she'd reached the happily-ever-after, she had fallen in love. She devoured as many as she could get her hands on after that, and she knew that these were the books she wanted to write!

She started submitting, and nearly two years later, while pregnant with her third child, she received The Call from her editor. At the age of twenty three, she sold her first manuscript to the Harlequin Presents line, and she was very glad that the good news didn't send her into labor!

She still can't quite believe she's blessed enough to see her name on, not just any book, but on her favorite books.

Maisey lives with her supportive, handsome, wonderful, diaper-changing husband and three small children, across the street from her parents and the home she grew up in, in the wilds of southern Oregon. She enjoys the contrast of living in a place where you might wake up to find a bear on your back porch, then walk into the home office to write stories that take place in exotic, urban locales.

Other titles by Maisey Yates available in ebook:

HIS RING IS NOT ENOUGH
THE COUPLE WHO FOOLED THE WORLD
HEIR TO A DARK INHERITENCE *(Secret Heirs of Powerful Men)*
HEIR TO A DESERT LEGACY *(Secret Heirs of Powerful Men)*

A Hunger for the Forbidden

To the fabulous editors at the M&B office.
You push me to be better and to take risks.
And you make my job fun. Thank you.

CHAPTER ONE

ALESSIA BATTAGLIA ADJUSTED her veil, the whisper-thin fabric skimming over the delicate skin of her neck. Like a lover's kiss. Soft. Gentle.

She closed her eyes, and she could feel it.

Hot, warm lips on her bare flesh. A firm, masculine hand at her waist.

She opened her eyes again and bent down, adjusting the delicate buckles on her white satin heels.

Her lover's hands on her ankle, removing her high heels. Leaving her naked in front of him, naked before a man for the first time. But there was no time for nerves. There was nothing more than the heat between them. Years of fantasy, years of longing.

Alessia swallowed and took the bouquet of bloodred roses from the chair they were resting on. She looked down at the blossoms, some of them bruised by the way she'd laid them down.

Brushing her fingertips over the crushed velvet petals brought another wave of memory. A wave of sensation.

Her lover's mouth at her breast, her fingers woven through his thick dark hair.

"Alessia?"

Her head snapped up and she saw her wedding coordinator standing in the doorway, one hand covering her headset.

"Yes?"

"It's time."

Alessia nodded, and headed toward the doorway, her shoes loud on the marble floor of the basilica. She exited the room that had been set aside for her to get ready in, and entered the vast foyer. It was empty now, all of the guests in the sanctuary, waiting for the ceremony.

She let out a long breath, the sound loud in the empty, high-ceilinged room. Then she started her walk toward the sanctuary, past pillars inlaid with gold and stones. She stopped for a moment, hoping to find some comfort, some peace, in the biblical scenes depicted on the walls.

Her eyes fell to a detailed painting of a garden. Of Eve handing Adam the apple.

"Please. Just one night."

"Only one, cara mia*?"*

"That's all I have to give."

A searing kiss, like nothing she'd ever experienced before. Better than any fantasy.

Her breath caught and she turned away from the painting, continuing on, continuing to the small antechamber outside of the sanctuary.

Her father was there, his suit crisp and pressed. Antonioni Battaglia looked every inch the respectable citizen everyone knew he was not. And the wedding, so formal, so traditional, was another statement of his power. Power that he longed to increase, with the Corretti fortune and status.

That desire was the reason she was here.

"You are very much like your mother."

She wondered if there was any truth to the words,

or if it was just the right thing to say. Tenderness was something her father had never seemed capable of.

"Thank you," she said, looking down at her bouquet. "This is what's right for the family."

She knew it was. Knew that it was the key to ensuring that her brothers and sisters were cared for. And that was, after all, what she'd done since her mother died in childbirth. Pietro, Giana, Marco and Eva were the brightest lights in her existence, and she would do, had done, whatever she could to ensure they had the best life possible.

And still, regret settled on her like a cloak, and memory clouded the present. Memories of her lover. His hands, his body, his passion.

If only her lover, and the man waiting behind the doors to the sanctuary, waiting to marry her, were the same.

"I know," she said, fighting against the desolation inside of her. The emptiness.

The double doors parted, revealing an impossibly long aisle. The music changed, everyone turned to look at her—all twelve hundred guests, who had come to watch the union of the Battaglia family and their much-hated rivals, the Correttis.

She held her head up, trying to breathe. The bodice of her dress threatened to choke her. The lace, which formed a high collar, and sleeves that ended in a point over her hands, was heavy and scratched against her skin. The yards of fabric clung to her, heat making her feel light-headed.

It was a beautiful dress, but it was too fussy for her. Too heavy. But the dress wasn't about her. The wedding wasn't about her.

Her father followed her into the sanctuary but didn't

take her arm. He had given her away when he'd signed his agreement with the late Salvatore Corretti. He didn't need to do it again. He didn't move to take a seat, either, rather he prowled around the back of the pews, up the side of the church, his steps parallel to hers. That was Antonioni Battaglia all over. Watching proceedings, ensuring all went well. Watching her. Making sure she did as she was told.

A drop of sweat rolled down her back and another flash of memory hit her hard.

His sweat-slicked skin beneath her fingertips. Her nails digging into his shoulders. Her thighs wrapped around lean, masculine hips...

She blinked and looked up at Alessandro. Her groom. The man to whom she was about to make her vows.

God forgive me.

Had she not been holding the roses, she would have crossed herself.

And then she felt him. As though he had reached out and put his hands on her.

She looked at the Corretti side, and her heart stopped for a moment. Matteo.

Her lover. Her groom's enemy.

Matteo was arresting as ever, with the power to draw the breath from her lungs. Tall and broad, his physique outlined to perfection by his custom-made suit. Olive skin and square jaw. Lips that delivered pleasure in beautiful and torturous ways.

But this man standing in the pews was not the man who'd shared her bed that night a month ago. He was different. Rage, dark and bottomless, burned from his eyes, his jaw tight. She had thought, had almost hoped, that he wouldn't care about her being promised to Alessandro. That a night of passion with her would be like a night with any other woman.

Yes, that thought had hurt, but it had been better than this. Better than him looking at her like he hated her.

She could remember those dark eyes meeting hers with a different kind of fire. Lust. Need. A bleak desperation that had echoed inside of her. And she could remember them clouded by desire, his expression pained as she'd touched him, tasted him.

She looked to Alessandro but she could still feel Matteo watching her. And she had to look back. She always had to look at Matteo Corretti. For as long as she could remember, she'd been drawn to him.

And for one night, she'd had him.

Now…now she would never have him again.

Her steps faltered, her high heel turning sideways beneath her. She stumbled, caught herself, her eyes locking with Matteo's again.

Dio, it was hot. Her dress was suffocating her now. The veil too heavy on her head, the lace at her throat threatening to choke her.

She stopped walking, the war within her threatening to tear her to pieces.

Matteo Corretti thought he would gag on his anger. Watching her walk toward Alessandro, his cousin, his rival in business and now, because of this, his enemy.

Watching Alessia Battaglia make her way to Alessandro, to bind herself to him.

She was Matteo's. His lover. His woman. The most beautiful woman he had ever seen in his life. It wasn't simply the smooth perfection of her golden skin, not just the exquisite cheekbones and full, rose-colored lips. It was something that existed beneath her skin, a vitality and passion that had, by turns, fascinated and confused him.

Her every laugh, every smile, every mundane action, was filled with more life, more joy, than his most memorable moments. It was why, from the first time he'd sneaked a look at her as a boy, he had been transfixed.

Far from the monster he'd been made to believe the Battaglias were, she had been an angel in his eyes.

But he had never touched her. Never breached the unspoken command issued by his father and grandfather. Because she was a Battaglia and he a Corretti, the bad blood between them going back more than fifty years. He had been forbidden from even speaking to her and as a boy he had only violated that order once.

And now, when Salvatore had thought it might benefit him, now she was being traded to Alessandro like cattle. He tightened his hands into fists, anger, anger like he hadn't felt in more than thirteen years, curling in his gut. The kind of rage he normally kept packed in ice was roaring through him. He feared it might explode, and he knew what happened when it did.

He could not be held responsible for what he might do if he had to watch Alessandro touch Alessia. Kiss her.

And then Alessia froze in place, her big, dark eyes darting from Alessandro, and back to him. Those eyes. Those eyes were always in his dreams.

Her hand dropped to her side, and then she released her hold on her bouquet of roses, the sound of them hitting the stone floor loud in the sudden silence of the room.

Then she turned, gripping the front of her heavy lace skirt, and ran back down the aisle. The white fabric billowed around her as she ran. She only looked behind her once. Wide, frightened eyes meeting his.

"Alessia!" He couldn't stop himself. Her name burst from his lips, and his body burst from its position in the pews. And he was running, too. "Alessia!"

The roar of the congregation drowned out his words. But still he ran. People were standing now, filing into the aisle, blocking his path. The faces of the crowd were a blur, he wasn't aware of who he touched, who he moved out of his way, in his pursuit of the bride.

When he finally burst through the exterior doors of the basilica, Alessia was getting into the backseat of the limo that was waiting to carry her and her groom away after the ceremony, trying to get her massive skirt and train into the vehicle with her. When she saw him, everything in her face changed. A hope in her eyes that grabbed him deep in his chest and twisted his heart. Hard.

"Matteo."

"What are you doing, Alessia?"

"I have to go," she said, her eyes focused behind him now, fearful. Fearful of her father, he knew. He was gripped then by a sudden need to erase her fears. To keep her from ever needing to be afraid again.

"Where?" he asked, his voice rough.

"The airport. Meet me."

"Alessia…"

"Matteo, please. I'll wait." She shut the door to the limo and the car pulled out of the parking lot, just as her father exited the church.

"You!" Antonioni turned on him. "What have you done?"

And Alessandro appeared behind him, his eyes blazing with fury. "Yes, cousin, what have you done?"

* * *

Alessia's hands shook as she handed the cash to the woman at the clothing shop. She'd never been permitted to go into a store like this. Her father thought this sort of place, with mass-produced garments, was common. Not for a Battaglia. But the jeans, T-shirt and trainers she'd found suited her purpose because they were common. Because any woman would wear them. Because a Battaglia would not. As if the Battaglias had the money to put on the show they did. Her father borrowed what he had to in order to maintain the fiction that their power was as infinite as it ever was. His position as Minister for the Trade and Housing department might net him a certain amount of power, power that was easily and happily manipulated, but it didn't keep the same flow of money that had come from her grandfather's rather more seedy organization.

The shopgirl looked at her curiously, and Alessia knew why. A shivering bride, sans groom, in a small tourist shop still wearing her gown and veil was a strange sight indeed.

"May I use the changing room?" she asked once her items were paid for.

She felt slightly sick using her father's money to escape, sicker still over the way she'd gotten it. She must have been quite the sight in the bank, in her wedding gown, demanding a cash advance against a card with her father's name on it.

"I'm a Battaglia," she'd said, employing all the self-importance she'd ever heard come from Antonioni. "Of course it's all right for me to access my family money."

Cash was essential, because she knew better than to leave a paper trail. Having a family who had, rather famously, been on the wrong side of the law was helpful in that regard at least. As had her lifelong observation of how utter confidence could get you things you shouldn't be allowed to have. The money in her purse being a prime example.

"Of course," the cashier said.

Alessia scurried into the changing room and started tugging off the gown, the hideous, suffocating gown. The one chosen by her father because it was so traditional. The virgin bride in white.

If he only knew.

She contorted her arm behind her and tugged at the tab of the zip, stepping out of the dress, punching the crinoline down and stepping out of the pile of fabric. She slipped the jeans on and tugged the stretchy black top over her head.

She emerged from the room a moment later, using the rubber bands she'd purchased to restrain her long, thick hair. Then she slipped on the trainers, ruing her lack of socks for a moment, then straightened.

And she breathed. Feeling more like herself again. Like Alessia. "Thank you," she said to the cashier. "Keep the dress. Sell it if you like."

She dashed out of the store and onto the busy streets, finally able to breathe. Finally.

She'd ditched the limo at the bank, offering the driver a generous tip for his part in the getaway. It only took her a moment to flag down a cab.

She slid in the back, clutching her bag to her chest. "Aeroporto di Catania, *per favore*."

"Naturalmente."

Matteo hadn't lingered at the basilica. Instead, he'd sidestepped his cousin's furious questions and gotten into his sports car, roaring out of the parking lot and heading in the direction of the airport without giving it any thought.

His heart was pounding hard, adrenaline pouring through him.

He felt beyond himself today. Out of control in a way he never allowed.

In a way he rarely allowed, at least. There had been a few breaks in his infamous control, and all of them were tied to Alessia. And they provided a window into just what he could become if the hideous cold that lived in him met with passionate flame.

She was his weakness. A weakness he should never have allowed and one he should certainly never allow again.

Dark eyes clashing with his in a mirror hanging behind the bar. Eyes he would recognize anywhere.

He turned sharply and saw her, the breath pulled from his lungs.

He set his drink down on the bar and walked across the crowded room, away from his colleagues.

"Alessia." He addressed her directly for the first time in thirteen years.

"Matteo." His name sounded so sweet on her lips.

It had been a month since their night together in New York City, a chance encounter, he'd imagined. He wondered now.

A whole month and he could still taste her skin on his tongue, could still feel the soft curves of her breasts resting in his palms. Could still hear her broken sighs of need as they took each other to the height of pleasure.

And he had not wanted another woman since.

They barely made it into his hotel room, they were far too desperate for each other. He slammed the door, locking it with shaking fingers, pressing her body against the wall. Her dress was long, with a generous slit up the side, revealing her toned, tan legs.

He wrapped his fingers around her thigh and tugged her leg up around his hip, settling the hardness of his erection against her softness.

It wasn't enough. It would never be enough.

Matteo stopped at a red light, impatience tearing at him. Need, need like he had only known once before, was like a beast inside him, devouring, roaring.

Finally, she was naked, her bare breasts pressing hard against his chest. He had to have her. His entire body trembling with lust.

"Ready for me, cara mia*?"*

"Always for you."

He slid inside of her body, so tight, much more so than he'd expected, than he'd ever experienced. She cried out softly, the bite of her nails in his flesh not due to pleasure now.

A virgin.

His. Only his.

Except she had not been his. It had been a lie. The next morning, Alessia was gone. And when he'd returned to Sicily, she'd been there.

He'd been invited to a family party but he had not realized that all branches of the Corretti family would be present. Had not realized it was an engagement party. For Alessandro and Alessia. A party to celebrate the end of a feud, the beginning of a partnership between the Battaglias and the Correttis, a chance to revitalize the docklands in Palermo and strengthen their family corporation.

"How long have you and Alessia been engaged?" he asked, his eyes trained on her even as he posed the question to Alessandro.

"For a while now. But we wanted to wait to make the big announcement until all the details were finalized."

"I see," he said. "And when is the blessed event?"

"One month. No point in waiting."

Some of the old rage burned through the desire that had settled inside of him. She had been engaged to Alessandro when he'd taken her into his bed. She'd intended, from the beginning, to marry another man the night she'd given herself to him.

And he, he had been forced to watch her hang on his cousin's arm for the past month while his blood boiled in agony as he watched his biggest rival hold on to the one thing he wanted more than his next breath. The one thing he had always wanted, but never allowed himself to have.

He had craved violence watching the two of them together. Had longed to rip Alessandro's hands off her and show him what happened when a man touched what belonged to him.

Even now, the thought sent a rising tide of nausea through him.

What was it Alessia did to him? This wave of possessiveness, this current of passion that threatened to drown him, it was not something that was a part of him. He was a man who lived in his mind, a man who embraced logic and fact, duty and honor.

When he did not, when he gave in to emotion, the danger was far too great. He was a Corretti, cut from the same cloth as his father and grandfather, a fabric woven together with greed, violence and a passion for acquiring more money, more power, than any one man could ever need.

Even with logic, with reason, he could and had justified actions that would horrify most men. He hated to think what might happen if he were unleashed without any hold on his control.

So he shunned passion, in all areas of life.

Except one.

He pulled his car off the road and slammed on his breaks, killing the engine, his knuckles burning from the hard grip he had on the steering wheel, his breath coming in short, harsh bursts.

This was not him. He didn't know himself with Alessia, and he never had.

And nothing good could come from it. He had spent his life trying to change the man he seemed destined to be. Trying to keep control, to move his life in a different direction than the one his father would have pushed him into.

Alessia compromised that. She tested it.

He ran his fingers through his hair, trying to catch his breath.

Then he turned the key over, the engine roaring to life again. And he turned the car around, heading away from the airport, away from the city.

He punched a button on his dashboard and connected himself to his PA.

"Lucia?"

"Sì?"

"Hold my calls until further notice."

It had been three hours. No doubt the only reason her father and his men hadn't come tearing through the airport was that they would never have imagined she would do something so audacious as to run away completely.

Alessia shifted in the plastic chair and wiped her cheek again, even though her tears had dried. She had no more tears left to cry. It was all she'd done since she'd arrived.

And she'd done more since it had become clear Matteo wasn't coming.

And then she'd done more when she'd suddenly had to go into the bathroom and throw up in a public stall.

Then she'd stopped, just long enough to go into one of the airport shops and pick up the one thing she'd avoided buying for the past week.

She'd started crying again when the pregnancy test had resulted in two little pink, positive, yes-you're-having-a-baby lines.

Now she was wrung out. Sick. And completely alone.

Well, not completely alone. Not really. She was having a baby, after all.

The thought didn't comfort her so much as magnify the feeling of utter loneliness.

One thing was certain. There was no going back to Alessandro. No going back to her family. She was having the wrong man's baby. A man who clearly didn't want her.

But he did once.

That thought made her furious, defiant. Yes, he had. More than once, which was likely how the pregnancy had happened. Because there had been protection during their times in bed, but they'd also showered together in the early hours of the morning and then…then neither of them had been able to think, or spare the time.

A voice came over the loudspeaker, the last call for her flight out to New York.

She stood up, picked up her purse, the only thing she

had with her, the only thing she had to her name, and handed her ticket to the man at the counter.

"Going to New York?" he asked, verifying.

She took a deep breath. "Yes."

CHAPTER TWO

HE'D NEVER EVEN opened the emails she'd been sending him. She knew, because she'd set them up so that they would send her a receipt when the addressee opened her message, but she'd never gotten one.

He didn't answer her calls, either. Not the calls to his office, not the calls to his mobile phone, not the calls to the Palazzolo Corretti, or to his personal estate outside Palermo.

Matteo Corretti was doing an exceptional job of ignoring her, and he had been for weeks now while she'd been holed up in her friend Carolina's apartment. Carolina, the friend who had talked her into a New York bachelorette party in the first place. Which, all things considered, meant she sort of owed Alessia since that bachelorette party was the source of both her problems, and her pregnancy.

No, that wasn't fair. It was her fault. Well, a lot of it was. The rest was Matteo Corretti's. Master of disguise and phone-call-avoider extraordinaire.

She wished she didn't need him but she didn't know what else to do. She was so tired. So sad, all the time. Her father wouldn't take her calls, either, her siblings, the most precious people in her life were forbidden from speaking to her. That, more than anything, was threatening to burn a hole in her soul. She felt adrift without them around her. They'd kept her going for most of her life, given her a sense of purpose, of strength and responsibility. Without them she just felt like she was floundering.

She'd had one option, of course. To terminate the pregnancy and return home. Beg her father and Alessandro for forgiveness. But she hadn't been able to face that. She'd lost so much in her life already and as confused as she was about the baby, about what it would mean for her, as terrified as she was, she couldn't face losing the tiny life inside of her.

But she would run out of money soon. Then she would be alone and penniless while Matteo Corretti spent more of his fortune on sports cars and high-rise hotels.

She wasn't going to allow it anymore. Not when she'd already decided that if he didn't want to be a part of their baby's life he would have to come tell her to her face. He would have to stand before her and denounce their child, verbally, not simply by ignoring emails and messages. He would have to make that denouncement a physical action.

Yes, she'd made the wrong decision to sleep with him without telling him about Alessandro. But it didn't give him the right to deny their child. Their child had nothing to do with her stupidity. He or she was the only innocent party in the situation.

She looked down at the screen on her phone. She had her Twitter account all set up and ready to help her contact every news outlet in the area.

She took a breath and started typing.

@theobserver @NYTnews @HBpress I'm about to make an important announcement re Matteo Corretti & the wedding scandal. Luxe Hotel on 3rd.

Then she stepped out of the back of the cab and walked up to the front steps of Matteo's world-renowned hotel, where he was rumored to be in residence, though no one would confirm it, and waited.

The sidewalks were crowded, people pushing past other people, walking with their heads down, no one sparing her a glance. Until the news crews started showing up.

First there was one, then another, and another. Some from outlets she hadn't personally included in her tweet. The small crowd drew stares, and some passersby started lingering to see what was happening.

There was no denying that she was big news. The assumption had been that she'd run off with Matteo but nothing could be further from the truth. And she was about to give the media a big dose of truth.

It didn't take long for them to catch the attention of the people inside the hotel, which had been a key part of her plan.

A sharply dressed man walked out of the front of the hotel, his expression wary. "Is there something I can help you with?"

She turned to him. "I'm just making a quick announcement. If you want to go get Matteo, that might help."

"Mr. Corretti is not in residence."

"That's like saying someone isn't At Home in a Regency novel, isn't it? He's here, but he doesn't want anyone to know it."

The reporters were watching the exchange with rapt attention, and the flash on one of the cameras started going, followed by the others.

"Mr. Corretti is not—"

She whirled around to face him again. "Fine, then

if Mr. Corretti is truly not in residence you can stand out here and listen to what I have to say and relay it to your boss when you deliver dinner to the room he is not in residence in."

She turned back to the reporters, and suddenly, the official press release she'd spent hours memorizing last night seemed to shatter in her brain, making it impossible to piece back together, impossible to make sense of it.

She swallowed hard, looking at the skyline, her vision filled with concrete, glass and steel. The noise from the cars was deafening, the motion of the traffic in front of her making her head swim. "I know that the wedding has been much talked about. And that Matteo chasing me out of the church has been the headline. Well, there's more to the story."

Flashes blinded her, tape recorders shoved into her face, questions started to drown out her voice. She felt weak, shaky, and she wondered, not for the first time, if she was completely insane.

Her life in Sicily had been quiet, domestic, one surrounded by her family, one so insular that she'd been dependent upon imagination to make it bearable, a belief of something bigger looming in her future. And as a result, she had a tendency to romanticize the grand gesture in her mind. To think that somehow, no matter how bleak the situation seemed, she could fix it. That, in the end, she would make it perfect and manage to find her happy ending.

She'd done it on the night of her bachelorette party. New York was so different than the tiny village she'd been raised in. So much bigger, faster. Just being there had seemed like a dream and so when she'd been confronted with Matteo it had seemed an easy, logical thing to approach him, to follow the path their mutual attraction had led them down. It was a prime example of her putting more stock in fantasy, in the belief in happy endings, over her common sense.

This was another.

But no matter how well planned this was, she hadn't realized how she would feel, standing there with everyone watching her. She wasn't the kind of woman who was used to having all eyes on her, her aborted wedding being the exception.

"I'm pregnant, and Matteo Corretti is the father of my baby." It slipped out, bald and true, and not at all what she'd been planning to say. At least she didn't think it was.

"Mr. Corretti—" the employee was speaking into his phone now, his complexion pallid "—you need to come out here."

She released a breath she hadn't realized she'd been holding.

"When is the baby due?"

"Are you certain he's the father?"

"When did you discover you were pregnant?"

The questions were coming rapid-fire now, but she didn't need to answer them because this was never about the press. This was about getting his attention. This was about forcing a confrontation that he seemed content to avoid.

"I'll answer more questions when Matteo comes to make his statement."

"Did the two of you leave the wedding together, or are you estranged? Has he denied paternity?" one of the reporters asked.

"I…"

"What the hell is going on?"

Alessia turned and her heart caught in her throat, making it impossible to breathe. Matteo. It felt like an eternity since she'd seen him, since he'd kissed her, put his hands on her skin. An eternity.

She ached with the need to run to him, to hold on to him, use him as an anchor. In her fantasies, he had long been her knight in shining armor, a simplistic vision of a man who had saved her from a hideous fate.

But in the years since, things had changed. Become more complex, more real. He was her lover now. The father of her child. The man she had lied to. The man who had left her sitting alone in an airport, crying and clutching a positive pregnancy test.

For a moment, the longing for those simple, sun-drenched days in Sicily, when he had been nothing more than an idealized savior, was so sharp and sweet she ached.

"Mr. Corretti, is this why you broke up the wedding?"

"I didn't break up anyone's wedding," he said, his tone dark.

"No, I ran out of the wedding," she said.

"And is what why I broke up the wedding?" he asked, addressing the reporter, stormy eyes never once looking at her.

"The baby," the reporter said.

Matteo froze, his face turning to stone. "The baby." Color drained from his face, but he remained stoic, only the change in his complexion a clue as to the shock that he felt.

He didn't know. She felt the impact of that reality like a physical blow. He hadn't even listened to a single message. Hadn't opened any emails, even before she'd started tagging them to let her know when he opened them.

"Is there more than one?" This from another reporter.

"Of course not," Matteo said, his words smooth, his eyes cold like granite. "Only this one."

He came to stand beside her, his gaze still avoiding hers. He put his arm around her waist, the sudden contact like touching an open flame, heat streaking through her veins. How did he manage to affect her this way still? After all he'd done to her? After the way he'd treated her?

"Do you have a statement?"

"Not at this point," he bit out. "But when the details for the wedding are finalized, we will be in touch."

He tightened his hold on her waist and turned them both around, away from the reporters, leading her up the steps and into the hotel. She felt very much like she was being led into the lion's den.

"What are you doing?" she asked, wishing he would move away from her, wishing he would stop touching her.

"Taking you away from the circus you created. I have no desire to discuss this with an audience."

If he wasn't so angry with her, she might think it was a good idea. But Matteo Corretti's rage was like ice-cold water in a black sea. Fathomless, with the great threat of pulling her beneath the waves.

His hold tightened with each step they took toward the hotel, and her stomach started to feel more and more unsettled until, when they passed through the revolving door and into the hotel lobby, she was afraid she might vomit on the high-gloss marble floors.

A charming photo to go with the headlines.

He released her the moment they were fully inside. "What the hell is the meaning of this?" he asked, rounding on her as his staff milled around very carefully not watching.

"Should we go somewhere more private?" she asked. Suddenly she felt like she'd rather brave his rage than put on a show. She was too tired for that. Too vulnerable. Bringing the press in was never about drawing attention to herself, it was about getting information to Matteo that he couldn't ignore. Giving the man no excuse to say he didn't know.

"Says the woman who called a bloody press conference?"

"You didn't answer my calls. Or return my messages. And I'm pretty sure now that you didn't even listen to any of them."

"I have been away," he said.

"Well, that's hardly my fault that you chose this moment to go on sabbatical. And I had no way of knowing."

He was looking at her like she'd grown an extra head. "Take me to your suite," she said.

"I'm not in the mood, Alessia."

"Neither am I!" she shot back. "I want to talk."

"It's just that last time we were in this hotel, talking was very much not on the agenda."

Her face heated, searing prickles dotting her skin. "No. That's very true. Which is how we find ourselves in this current situation."

"Communication seems to be something we don't do well with," he said. "Our lack of talking last time we were here together certainly caused some issues."

"But I want to talk now," she said, crossing her arms beneath her breasts.

He cocked his head to the side, dark eyes trained on her now with a focus he'd withheld until that moment. "You aren't afraid of me."

"No."

"A mistake, some might say, *cara mia*."

"Is that so?"

"You won't like me when I'm angry."

"You turn green and split your pants?"

"Perhaps taking this somewhere private is the best idea," he said, wrapping his fingers around her arm, just above her elbow, and directing her toward the elevator.

He pushed the up button and they both waited. She felt like she was hovering in a dream, but she dug her fingernails into her palms, and her surroundings didn't melt away. It was real. All of this.

The elevator doors slid open and they both stepped inside. And as soon as they were closed into the lift, he rounded on her.

"You're pregnant?" His words were flat in the quiet of the elevator.

"Yes. I tried to tell you in a less public way, but it's been two months and you've been very hard to get ahold of."

"Not an accident."

"Oh, no, I know. It was far too purposeful to be accidental. You never even opened my emails."

"I blocked your address after you sent the first few."

"Uh," she said, unable to make a more eloquent sound.

"I see it offends you."

"Yes. It does offend me. Didn't it occur to you that I might have something important to tell you?"

"I didn't care," he said.

The elevator stopped at the top floor and the doors slid open. "Is there a point in me going any further, then? Or should I just go back to my friend Carolina's apartment and start a baby registry?"

"You are not leaving."

"But you just said you didn't care."

"I didn't care until I found out you were carrying my child."

She was both struck, and pleased, by his certainty that the child was his. She wouldn't have really blamed him if he'd questioned her at least once. She'd lied about her engagement to Alessandro. By omission, but still. She knew she wasn't blameless in the whole fiasco.

"What did you think I was trying to contact you for? To beg you to take me back? To beg you for more sex? Because that's what we shared that night, that's all we shared." The lie was an acid burn on her tongue. "I would hardly have burned my pride to the ground for the sake of another orgasm."

"Is that true? You would hardly be the first person to do it."

"If you mean you, I'm sure it cost you to take a Battaglia to your bed. Must have been some epic dry spell."

"And not worth the price in the end, I think."

His words were designed to peel skin from bone, and they did their job. "I would say the same."

"I can see now why you ran from the wedding."

A wave of confusion hit her, and it took her a moment to realize that she hadn't told him the order in which the events had occurred. Wedding abandonment, then pregnancy test, but before she could correct him he pressed on.

"And how conveniently you've played it, too. Alessandro would, of course, know it wasn't his child as you never slept with him. I hope you're pleased with the way all of this unfolded because you have managed to ensure that you are still able to marry a Corretti, in spite of our little mistake. Good insurance for your family since, thanks to your abandonment, the deal between our family and yours has gone to hell."

"You think I planned this? You aren't even serious about marrying me, are you?"

"There is no other choice. You announced your pregnancy to the whole world."

"I had to tell you."

"And if I had chosen not to be a part of the baby's life?"

"I was going to make you tell me that to my face."

He regarded her closely. "Strange to think I ever imagined you to be soft, Alessia."

"I'm a Battaglia. I've never had the luxury of being soft."

"Clearly not." He looked at her, long and hard. "This makes sense, Alessia." His tone was all business now. Maddeningly sure and decisive. "It will put to rest rumors of bad blood, unite the families."

"You didn't seem to care about that before."

"That was before the baby. The baby changes everything."

Because he wanted to make a family? The idea, so silly and hopeful, bloomed inside of her. It was her blessing and curse that she always found the kernel of hope in any situation. It was the thing that got her through. The thing that had helped her survive the loss of her mother, the cold detachment from her father, the time spent caring for her siblings when other girls her age were out dating, having lives, fulfilling dreams.

She'd created her own. Locked them inside of her. Nurtured them.

"I… It does?" she asked, the words a whisper.

"Of course," he said, dark eyes blazing. "My child will be a Corretti. On that, there can be no compromise."

CHAPTER THREE

MATTEO'S OWN WORDS echoed in his head.

My child will be a Corretti. On that there can be no compromise.

It was true. No child of his would be raised a Battaglia. Their family feud was not simply a business matter. The Battaglias had set out to destroy his grandfather, and had they succeeded they would have wiped out the line entirely.

It was the hurt on her face that surprised him, and more than that, his response to it.

Damn Alessia Battaglia and those dark, soulful eyes. Eyes that had led him to ruin on more than one occasion.

"Because you won't allow your child to carry my name?" she asked.

"That's right."

"And what of my role in raising my child?"

"You will, of course, be present."

"And what else? Because more than mere presence is required to raise a child."

"Nannies are also required, in my experience."

"In your experience raising children, or being raised?"

"Being raised. I'm supremely responsible in my sexual encounters so I've never been in this situation before."

"Supremely responsible?" she asked, cheeks flushing a gorgeous shade of rose that reminded him of the blooms in his Sicilian palazzo. "Is that what you call having sex with your cousin's fiancée with no condom?"

Her words, so stark and angry, shocked him. Alessia had always seemed fragile to him. Sweet. But tangling with her today was forcing him to recognize that she was also a woman capable of supreme ruthlessness if the situation required it.

Something he had to reluctantly respect.

"I didn't know you were engaged to be married, as you withheld the information from me. As to the other issue, that has never happened to me before."

"So you say."

"It has not," he said.

"Well, it's not like you were overly conscious of it at the time."

Shame cracked over his insides like a whip. He had thought himself immune to shame at this point. He was wrong. "I knew. After."

"You remembered and you still didn't think to contact me?"

"I did not think it possible." The thought hadn't occurred to him because he'd been too wrapped up in simply trying to avoid her. Alessia was bad for him, a conclusion he'd come to years ago and reaffirmed the day he'd decided not to go after her.

And now he was bound to her. Bound to a woman who dug down far too deep inside of him. Who disturbed his grasp on his control. He could not afford the interruption. Could not afford to take the chance that he might lose his grip.

"Why, because only other people have the kind of sex that makes babies?"

"Do you always say what comes to your mind?"

"No. I never do. I never speak or act impulsively, I only think about it. It's just you that seems to bring it out."

"Aren't I lucky?" Her admission gripped him, held him. That there was something about him that brought about a change in her…that the thing between them didn't only shatter his well-ordered existence but hers, too, was not a comfort. Not in the least.

"Clearly, neither of us are in possession of much luck, Alessia."

"Clearly," she said.

"There is no way I will let my child be a bastard. I've seen what happens to bastards. You can ask my cousin Angelo about that." A cousin who was becoming quite the problem. It was part of why Matteo had come to New York, why he was making his way back into circulation. In his absence, Angelo had gone and bought himself a hefty amount of shares for Corretti Enterprises and at this very moment he was sitting in Matteo's office, the new head of Corretti Hotels. He'd been about to go back and make the other man pay. Wrench the power right back from him.

Now, it seemed there was a more pressing matter.

"So, you're doing this to save face?"

"For what other reason? Do you want our child to be sneered at? Disgraced? The product of an illicit affair between two of Sicily's great warring families?"

"No."

Matteo tried not to read the emotion in her dark eyes, tried not to let them pull him in. Always, from the moment he'd seen her, he'd been fascinated. A young girl with flowers tangled in her dark hair, running around the garden of her father's home, a smile on her lips. He could remember her dancing in the grass in her bare feet, while her siblings played around her.

And he had been transfixed. Amazed by this girl who, from all he had been told, should have been visibly evil in some way. But she was a light. She held a brightness and joy like he had never seen. Watching it, being close enough to touch it, helped him pretend it was something he could feel, too.

She made him not so afraid of feeling.

She'd had a hold on him from day one. She was a sorceress. There was no other explanation. Her grip on him defied logic, defied every defense he'd built inside of himself.

And no matter how hard he tried, he could read her. Easily. She was hurt. He had hurt her.

"What is it?" he asked.

She looked away. "What do you mean?"

"Why are you hurt?"

"You've just told me how unlucky we both are that I'm pregnant—was I supposed to look happy?"

"Don't tell me you're pleased about this. Unless it was your plan."

"How could I have…planned this? That doesn't make any sense."

He pushed his fingers through his hair and turned away from her. "I know. *Che cavolo*, Alessia, I know that." He turned back to her.

"I just wanted to tell you about the baby."

He felt like he was drowning, like every breath was suffocating him. A baby. She was having his baby. And he was just about the last man on earth who should ever be a father. He should walk away. But he couldn't.

"And this was the only way?"

Her eyes glittered with rage. "You know damn well it was!"

He did. He'd avoided her every attempt at contacting him. Had let his anger fuel the need for distance between them. Had let the very existence of the emotion serve as a reminder. And he had come back frozen again. So he'd thought. Because now Alessia was here again, pushing against that control.

"Why didn't you meet me at the airport?" she asked, her words a whisper.

"Why didn't I meet you?" he asked, his teeth gritted. "You expected me to chase after you like a dog? If you think you can bring me to heel that easily, Alessia, you are a fool."

"And if you think I'm trying to you're an idiot, Matteo Corretti. I don't want you on a leash."

"Well, you damn well have me on one!" he said, shouting for the first time, his tenuous grip on his control slipping. "What am I to do after your public display? Deny my child? Send you off to raise it on your own? Highly unlikely."

"How can we marry each other? We don't love each other. We barely like each other right now!"

"Is that so bad? You were prepared to marry Alessandro, after all. Better the devil you know. And we both know you know me much better than you knew him."

"Stop it," she said, the catch in her voice sending a hot slash of guilt through his chest. Why he was compelled to lash out at her, he wasn't sure.

Except that nothing with Alessia was ever simple. Nothing was ever straightforward. Nothing was ever neat or controlled.

It has to be.

"It's true, though, isn't it, Alessia?" he asked, his entire body tense now. He knew for a fact he was the first man to be with her, and something in him burned to know that he had been the only man. That Alessandro had never touched her as he had. "You were never with him. Not like you were with me."

The idea of his cousin's hands on her… A wave of red hazed his vision, the need for violence gripping his throat, shaking him.

He swallowed hard, battled back the rage, fought against images that were always so close to the surface when Alessia was around. A memory he had to hold on to, no matter how much he might wish for it to disappear.

Blood. Streaked up to his elbows, the skin on his knuckles broken. A beast inside of him unleashed. And Alessia's attackers on the ground, unmoving.

He blinked and banished the memory. It shouldn't linger as it did. It was but one moment of violence in a lifetime of it. And yet, it had been different. It had been an act born of passion, outside of his control, outside of rational thought.

"Tell me," he ground out.

"Do you honestly think I would sleep with Alessandro after what happened?"

"You were going to. You were prepared to marry him. To share his bed."

She nodded wordlessly. "Yes. I was."

"And then you found out about the baby."

"No," she said, her voice a whisper.

"What, then?"

"Then I saw you."

"Guilt?"

"We were in a church."

"Understandable."

"Why didn't you meet me?" she asked again, her words holding a wealth of pain.

"Because," he said, visions of blood washing through his brain again, a reminder of what happened when he let his passions have control, "I got everything I wanted from you that night. Sex. That was all I ever wanted from you, darling."

She drew back as though he'd struck her. "Is that why you've always watched me?"

"I'll admit, I had a bit of an obsession with your body, but you know you had one with mine."

"I liked you," she said, her words hard, shaky. "But you never came near me after—"

"There is no need to dredge up the past," he said, not wanting to hear her speak of that day. He didn't want to hear her side of it. How horrifying it must have been for a fourteen-year-old girl to see such violence. To see what he was capable of.

Yet, she had never looked at him with the shock, the horror, he'd deserved. There was a way she looked at him, as though she saw something in him no one else did. Something good. And he craved that feeling. It was one reason he'd taken her up on her invitation that night at the hotel bar.

Too late, he realized that he was not in control of their encounter that time, either. No, Alessia stole the control. Always.

No more, he told himself again.

Alessia swallowed back tears. This wasn't going how she'd thought it would. Now she wasn't sure what she thought. No, she knew. Part of her, this stupid, girlish, optimistic part of her, had imagined Matteo's eyes would soften, that he would smile. Touch her stomach. Take joy in the fact that they had created a life together.

And then they would live happily ever after.

She was such a fool. But Matteo had long been the knight in shining armor of her fantasies. And so in her mind he could do no wrong.

She'd always felt like she'd known him. Like she'd understood the serious, dark-eyed young man she'd caught watching her when she was in Palermo. Who had crept up to the wall around her house when he was visiting his grandmother and stood there while she'd played in the garden. Always looking like he wanted to join in, like he wanted to play, but wouldn't allow himself to.

And then…and then when she'd needed him most, he'd been there. Saved her from…she hardly even knew what horror he'd saved her from. Thank God she hadn't had to find out exactly what those two men had intended to use her for. Matteo had been there. As always. And he had protected her, shielded her.

That was why, when she'd seen him in New York, it had been easy, natural, to kiss him. To ask him to make love to her.

But after that he hadn't come to save her.

She looked at him now, at those dark eyes, hollow, his face like stone. And he seemed like a stranger. She wondered how she could have been so wrong all this time.

"I don't want to dredge up the past. But I want to know that the future won't be miserable."

"If you preferred Alessandro, you should have married him while you had him at the altar with a priest standing by. Now you belong to me, the choice has been taken. So you should make the best of it."

"Stop being such an ass!"

Now he looked shocked, which, she felt, was a bit of an accomplishment. "You want me to tell you how happy I am? You want me to lie?"

"No," she said, her stomach tightening painfully. "But stop…stop trying to hurt me."

He swore, an ugly, crude word. "I am sorry, Alessia, it is not my intent."

The apology was about the most shocking event of the afternoon. "I…I know this is unexpected. Trust me, I know."

"When did you find out?" he asked.

"At the airport. So…if you had met me, you would have found out when I did."

"And what did you do after that?"

"I waited for you," she said. "And then I got on a plane and came to New York. I have a friend here, the friend that hosted my little bachelorette party."

"Why did you come to New York?"

"Why not?" She made it sound casual, like it was almost accidental. But it wasn't. It had made her feel close to him, no matter where he might have been in the world, because it was the place she'd finally been with him the way she'd always dreamed of. "Why did you come to New York?"

"Possibly for the same reason you did," he said, his voice rough. It made her stomach twist, but she didn't want to ask him for clarification. Didn't want to hope that it had something to do with her.

She was too raw to take more of Matteo's insults. And she was even more afraid of his tenderness. That would make her crumble completely. She couldn't afford it, not now. Now she had to figure out what she was doing. What she wanted.

Could she really marry Matteo?

It was so close to her dearest fantasy. The one that had kept her awake long nights since she was a teenager. Matteo. Hers. Only hers. Such an innocent fantasy at first, and as she'd gotten older, one that had become filled with heat and passion, a longing for things she'd never experienced outside of her dreams.

"And if…" she said, hardly trusting herself to speak "…if we marry, my family will still benefit from the merger?"

"Your father will get his money. His piece of the Corretti empire, as agreed upon."

"You give it away so easily."

"Because my family still needs the docklands revitalization. And your father holds the key to that."

"And it will benefit Alessandro, too."

"Just as it would have benefitted me had he married you."

Those words, hearing that it would have benefitted him for her to marry someone else, made her feel ill. "So a win all around for the Correttis, then?"

"I suppose it is," he said.

There was a ruthless glint in his eyes now. One she had never seen directed at her before. One she'd only seen on one other occasion.

"What if I say no?" she asked, because she had to know. She wasn't sure why she was exploring her options now. Maybe because she'd already blown everything up. Her father likely hated her…. Her siblings… they must be worried sick. And she wondered if anyone was caring for them properly.

Yes, the youngest, Eva, was fourteen now and the rest of them in their late teens, but still, she was the only person who nurtured them. The only person who ever had.

The life she'd always known, the life she'd clung to for the past twenty-seven years, was changed forever. And now she felt compelled in some ways to see how far she could push it.

"You won't say no," he said.

"I won't?"

"No. Because if you do, the Battaglias are as good as bankrupt. You will be cared for, of course our child will be, too. I'm not the kind of man who would abandon his responsibility in that way. But what of your siblings? Their care will not be my problem."

"And if I marry you?"

"They'll be family. And I take care of family."

A rush of joy and terror filled her in equal parts. Because in some ways, she was getting just what she wanted. Matteo. Forever.

But this wasn't the Matteo she'd woven fantasies around. This was the real Matteo. Dark. Bitter. Emotionless in a way she'd somehow never realized before.

He'd given her passion on their night together, but for the most part, the lights had been off. She wondered now if, while his hands had moved over her body with such skill and heat, his eyes had been blank and cold. Like they were now.

She knew that what she was about to agree to wasn't the fantasy. But it was the best choice for her baby, the best choice for her family.

And more fool her, she wanted him. Still. All of those factors combined meant there was only ever one answer for her to give.

"Yes, Matteo. I'll marry you."

CHAPTER FOUR

THE HUSH IN the lobby of Matteo's plush Palermo hotel was thick, the lack of sound more pronounced and obvious than any scream could have been.

It was early in the day and employees were milling around, setting up for a wedding and mobilizing to sort out rooms and guests. As Matteo walked through, a wave of them parted, making room for him, making space. Good. He was in no mood to be confronted today. No mood for questions.

Bleached sunlight filtered through the windows, reflecting off a jewel-bright sea. A view most would find relaxing. For him, it did nothing but increase the knot of tension in his stomach. Homecoming, for him, would never be filled with a sense of comfort and belonging. For him, this setting had been the stage for violence, pain and shame that cut so deep it was a miracle he hadn't bled to death with it.

He gritted his teeth and pulled together every last ounce of control he could scrape up, cooling the anger that seemed to be on a low simmer in his blood constantly now.

He had a feeling, though, that the shock was due only in part to his presence, with a much larger part due to the woman who was trailing behind him.

He punched the up button for the elevator and the doors slid open. He looked at Alessia, who simply stood there, her hands clasped in front of her, dark eyes looking at everything but him.

"After you, *cara mia*," he said, putting his hand between the doors, keeping them from closing.

"You don't demand that a wife walk three paces behind you at all times?" she asked, her words soft, defiant.

"A woman is of very little use to me when she's behind me. Bent over in front of me is another matter, as you well know."

Her cheeks turned dark with color, and not all of it was from embarrassment. He'd made her angry, as he'd intended to do. He didn't know what it was about her that pushed him so. That made him say things like that.

That made him show anything beyond the unreadable mask he preferred to present to the world.

She was angry, but she didn't say another word. She simply stepped into the elevator, her eyes fixed to the digital readout on the wall. The doors slid closed behind them, and still she didn't look at him.

"If you brought me here to abuse me perhaps I should simply go back to my father's house and take my chances with him."

"That's what you call abuse? You didn't seem to find it so abhorrent the night you let me do it."

"But you weren't being a bastard that night. Had you approached me at the bar and used it as a pickup line I would have told you to go to hell."

"Would you have, Alessia?" he asked, anger, heat, firing in his blood. "Somehow I don't think that's true."

"No?"

"No." He turned to her, put his hand, palm flat, on

the glossy marble wall behind her, drawing closer, drawing in the scent of her. *Dio.* Like lilac and sun. She was Spring standing before him, new life, new hope.

He pushed away from her, shut down the feeling.

"Shows what you know."

"I know a great deal about you."

"Stop with the you-know-me stuff. Just because we slept together—"

"You have a dimple on your right cheek. It doesn't show every time you smile, only when you're really, really smiling. You dance by yourself in the sun, you don't like to wear shoes. You've bandaged every scraped knee your brothers and sisters ever had. And whenever you see me, you can't help yourself, you have to stare. I know you, Alessia Battaglia, don't tell me otherwise."

"You knew me, Matteo. You knew a child. I'm not the same person now."

"Then how is it you ended up in my bed the night of your bachelorette party?"

Her eyes met his for the first time all morning, for the first time since his private plane had touched down in Sicily. "Because I wanted to make a choice, Matteo. Every other choice was being made for me. I wanted to…I wanted to at least make the choice about who my first lover should be."

"Haven't you had a lot of time to make that choice?"

"When? With all of my free time? I've spent my life making sure my brothers and sisters were cared for, really cared for, not just given the bare necessities by staff. I spent my life making sure they never bore the full brunt of my father's rage. I've spent my life being the perfect daughter, the hostess for his functions, standing and smiling next to him when he got reelected for a position that he abuses."

"Why?" he asked.

"Because of my siblings. Because no matter that my father is a tyrant, he is our father. We're Battaglias. I hoped…I've always hoped I could make that mean something good. That I could make sure my brothers and sisters learned to do the right things, learned to want the right things. If I didn't make sure, they would only have my father as a guiding influence and I think we both know Antonioni Battaglia shouldn't be anyone's guiding influence."

"And what about you?"

"What about me?"

The elevator doors slid open and they stepped out into the empty hall on the top floor.

"You live your whole life for other people?"

She shook her head. "No. I live my life in the way that lets me sleep at night. Abandoning my brothers and sisters to our father would have hurt me. So it's not like I'm a martyr. I do it because I love them."

"But you ran out on the wedding."

She didn't say anything, she simply started walking down the hall, her heels clicking on the marble floor. He stood and watched her, his eyes drifting over her curves, over that gorgeous, heart-shaped backside, outlined so perfectly by her pencil skirt.

It looked like something from the Corretti clothing line. One thing he might have to thank his damn brother Luca for. But it was the only thing.

Especially since the rumor was that in his absence the other man was attempting to take Matteo's share in the Corretti family hotels. A complete mess since that bastard Angelo had his hands in it, as well.

A total mess. And one he should have anticipated.

He'd dropped out of the dealings with Corretti Enterprises completely since the day of Alessia and Alessandro's aborted wedding. And the vultures had moved in. He should try to stop them, he knew that. And he could, frankly. He had his own fortune, his own power, independent of the Corretti machine, but at the moment, the most pressing issue was tied to the tall, willowy brunette who was currently sauntering in the wrong direction.

"The suite is this way," he said.

She stopped, turned sharply on her heel and started walking back toward him, past him and down the hall.

He nearly laughed at the haughty look on her face. In fact, he found he wanted to, but wasn't capable of it. It stuck in his throat, his control too tight to let it out.

He walked past her, to the door of the suite, and took a key card out of his wallet, tapping it against the reader. "My key opens all of them."

"Careful, *caro*, that sounds like a bad euphemism." She shot him a deadly look before entering the suite.

"So prickly, Alessia."

"I told you you didn't know me."

"Then help me get to know you."

"You first, Matteo."

He straightened. "I'm Matteo Corretti, oldest son of Benito Corretti. I'm sure you know all about him. My criminal father who died in a fire, locked in an endless rivalry with his brother, Carlo. You ought to know about him, too, as you were going to marry Carlo's son. I run the hotel arm of my family corporation, and I deal with my own privately owned line of boutique hotels, one of which you're standing in."

She crossed her arms and cocked her hip out to the

side. "I think I read that in your online bio. And it's nothing I don't already know."

"That's all there is to know."

She didn't believe that. Not for a moment. She knew there was more to him than that. Knew it because she'd seen it. Seen his blind rage as he'd done everything in his power to protect her from a fate she didn't even like to imagine.

But he didn't speak of it. So neither did she.

"Tell me about you," he said.

"Alessia Battaglia, Pisces, oldest daughter of Antonioni. My father is a politician who does under-the-table dealings with organized-crime families. It's the thing that keeps him in power. But it doesn't make him rich. It's why he needs the Correttis." She returned his style of disclosure neatly, tartly.

"The Correttis are no longer in the organized-crime business. In that regard, my cousins, my brothers and I have done well, no matter our personal feelings for each other."

"You might not be criminals but you are rich. That's why you're so attractive. In my father's estimation at least."

"Attractive enough to trade us his daughter."

She nodded. She looked tired suddenly. Defeated. He didn't like that. He would rather have her spitting venom at him.

"You could walk away, Alessia," he said. "Even now you could. I cannot keep you here. Your father cannot hold you. You're twenty-seven. You have the freedom to do whatever you like. Hell, you could do it on my dime since I'll be supporting my child regardless of what you do."

He didn't know why he was saying it, why he was giving her the out. But part of him wished she would take it. Wished she would leave him alone, take her beauty, the temptation, the ache that seemed to lodge in his chest whenever she was around, with her. The danger she presented to the walls of protection he'd built around his life.

She didn't say anything. She didn't move. She was frozen to the spot, her lips parted slightly, her breath shallow, fast.

"Alessia, you have the freedom to walk out that door if you want. Right now."

He took a step toward her, compelled, driven by something he didn't understand. Didn't want to understand. The beast in him was roaring now and he wanted it to shut up. Wanted his control back.

He'd had a handle on it again. Had moved forward from the events of his past. Until Alessia had come back into his life, and at the moment all he wanted was for her to be gone, and for his life to go back to the way it had been.

He cupped her chin, tilted her face up so that her eyes met his. "I am not holding you here. I am not your father and I am not your jailer."

Dark eyes met his, the steel in them shocking. "No, you aren't. But you are the father of my baby. Our baby. I'm not going to walk away, Matteo. If you want an out, you'll have to take it yourself. Don't think that I will. I'm strong enough to face this. To try to make this work."

"It would be better if you would."

"Do you really think that?"

"You think I will be a hands-on father? That I will

somehow…be an influence in our child's life?" The very thought made him sick. What could he offer a child but a legacy of violence and abuse? But he couldn't walk away, either. Couldn't leave Alessia on her own. But he feared his touch would only poison a child. His baby would be born innocent, unspoiled by the world, and Matteo was supposed to hold him? With his hands? Hands that were stained with blood.

"You think you won't be?"

"How can you give what you never had?"

"I hardly remember my mother, Matteo, but I did a good job with my brothers and sisters."

"Perhaps I find that an absence of a good parent is not the same as having bad ones. What lessons shall I teach our child, *cara*? The kind my father taught me? How to find a man who owes you money? How to break his kneecaps with efficiency when he doesn't pay up? I think not."

He had thought she would look shocked by that, but she hardly flinched, her eyes never wavering from his. "Again you underestimate me, Matteo. You forget the family I come from."

"You are so soft," he said, speaking his mind, speaking his heart. "Breakable. Like a flower. You and I are not the same."

She nodded slowly. "It's easy to crush a flower. But if it's the right kind of flower, it comes back, every year, after every winter. No matter how many times you destroy the surface, it keeps on living underneath."

Her words sent a shot of pain straight to his chest, her quiet strength twisting something deep inside of him. "Don't pretend you were forced into this," he said softly. "You were given your choice."

"And you were given yours."

He nodded once and turned away from her, walked out of the room ignoring the pounding in his blood, ignoring the tightness in his chest. Trying to banish the image of his hand closing around a blossom and crushing the petals, leaving it completely destroyed.

Alessia looked around the lavish, now empty, suite that she was staying in until…until she didn't know when. Weeks of not being able to get ahold of Matteo, not knowing what she would do if she didn't, and now he was suddenly in her life like a hurricane, uprooting everything, taking control of everything.

She really shouldn't be too surprised about it. That was one thing she did know about Matteo Corretti, beyond that stupid ream of noninformation he'd given her. He was controlled. Totally. Completely.

Twice she'd seen him lose that control. Once, on a sunny day in Sicily while he was staying at his grandparents' rural estate. The day that had cemented him in her mind as her potential salvation.

And their night in New York. There had been no control then, not for either of them.

She pictured him as he'd been then. The way he'd looked at her in the low light of the bar. She closed her eyes and she was back there. The memory still so strong, so painfully sweet.

"What brings you to New York, Alessia?"

"Bachelorette party." It was easy enough to leave out that it was for her. If he didn't know about Alessandro, then she wouldn't tell him.

"Did you order any strippers?"

Her cheeks heated. "No, gosh, why? Are you offering to fill the position?"

"How much have you had to drink?" he asked, a smile on his face. It was so rare for her to see him smile. She couldn't remember if she ever had.

"Not enough."

"I could fix that, but I think I'd like a dance and if you're too drunk you won't be able to keep up."

"Why are you talking to me?" she asked. She'd known there was a chance he could be here. He owned the hotel, after all. Part of her had hoped she'd catch a glimpse of him. A little bit of torture, but torture that would be well worth it.

"What do you mean?"

"You haven't spoken to me since—" something flashed in his eyes, a strange unease, and she redirected her words "—in a long time."

"Too long," he said, his voice rough.

Her heart fluttered, a surge of hope moving through her. She tried to crush it, tried to stop the jittery feelings moving through her now.

"So, do you have a dance for me?" he asked. "For an old friend?"

"Yes." She couldn't deny him, couldn't deny herself.

She left her friends in the corner of the bar, at their table with all of their fruity drinks, and let Matteo lead her away from them, lead her to the darkened dance floor. A jazz quartet was playing, the music slow and sensual.

He wrapped his arms around her waist and pulled her against his body. Heat shot through her, heat and desire and lust.

His eyes locked with hers as they swayed in time to the music, and she was powerless to resist the desire to lean in and press her lips to his. His tongue touched the tip of hers, a shot of need so sharp, so strong, assaulting her she thought it would buckle her knees then and there.

She parted her lips for him, wrapping her arms around his neck, tangling her fingers in his hair. Years of fantasies added fuel to the moment.

Matteo Corretti was her ultimate fantasy. The man whose name she called out in her sleep. The man she wanted, more than anything. And this was her last chance.

Panic drove her, made her desperate. She deepened the kiss, her movements clumsy. She didn't know how to make out. She'd never really done it before. Another thing that added fuel to the fire.

She'd never lived. She'd spent all of her life at the Battaglia *castello*, taking care of her siblings, making sure her family didn't crumble. Her life existed for the comfort of others, and she needed a moment, a night, to have something different.

To have something for her.

Matteo pulled away from her, his chest rising and falling heavily with each indrawn breath. "We cannot do that here."

She shook her head. "Apparently not." The fire between them was burning too hot, too fast, threatening to rage out of control.

"I have a suite." A smile curved his lips. "I own the hotel."

She laughed, nervous, breathless. She flexed her fingers, where her engagement ring should be. The engagement ring she hadn't put on tonight as she'd gotten ready for the party.

"Please. Just one night," she said.

"Only one, *cara mia*?"

"That's all I have to give."

"I might be able to change your mind," he said, his voice rough. He leaned in and kissed her neck, his teeth scraping her delicate skin, his tongue soothing away the sting.

Yes. She wanted to shout it. *Yes, forever. Matteo, ti amo.*

Instead, she kissed him again, long and deep, pouring everything out, every emotion, every longing that had gone unanswered for so long. Every dream she knew would never be fulfilled. Because Matteo might be hers tonight, but in just a month, she would belong to another man forever.

"Take me to your room."

Alessia shook her head, brought herself back to the present. Everything had been so perfect that night. It was the morning that had broken her heart. The cold light of day spilling over her, illuminating the truth, not allowing her to hide behind fantasy any longer.

She could remember just how he'd looked, the sheets tangled around his masculine body, bright white against his dark skin. Leaving him had broken her.

She'd wanted so badly to kiss him again, but she hadn't wanted to chance waking him.

Somehow that night she'd let her fantasies become real, had let them carry her away from reality, not just in her imagination but for real. And she couldn't regret it, not then, not now.

At least, she hadn't until recently. The way Matteo looked at her now…she hated it. Hated that he saw her as a leash.

But it was too late to turn back now. The dutiful daughter had had her rebellion, and it had destroyed everything in its path.

"You don't go halfway, do you, Alessia?" she asked the empty room.

Unsurprisingly, she got no answer.

CHAPTER FIVE

"YOU CANNOT SIMPLY take what is mine without paying for it, Corretti."

Matteo looked at Antonioni Battaglia and fought a wave of rage. The man had no idea who he was dealing with. Matteo was a Corretti, the capability to commit hideous acts was a part of his DNA. More than that, Matteo had actually done it before. Had embraced the violence. Both with cold precision, and in the heat of rage.

The temptation to do it again was strong. Instead, he leaned forward and adjusted a glass figurine that his grandmother had had commissioned for him. A perfect model of his first hotel. Not one of the Corretti Hotels, the first hotel he'd bought with his own personal fortune.

"And what exactly is that?" Matteo asked, leaning back in his office chair.

"My daughter. You defiled her. She's much less valuable to me now, which means you'd better damn well marry her and make good on the deal I cut with your grandfather, or the Correttis won't be doing any trading out of Sicily."

"My mistake, I thought Alessia's body belonged to her, not you."

"I'm an old-fashioned man."

"Be that as it may, the law prevents you from owning anyone, which means Alessia does not belong to you." He gritted his teeth, thought of Alessia's siblings, of all she'd given up to ensure they would be cared for. "However, at my fiancée's request, I have decided to honor the agreement." He paused for a moment. "What are your other children doing at the moment?"

"I've arranged for the boys to get a job in the family business."

Matteo gritted his teeth. "Is that what they want?"

"You have to take opportunity where it exists."

"And if I created a different opportunity?" He turned the figurine again, keeping his hands busy, keeping himself from violence.

"Why should I do any more business with a Corretti than necessary?"

"Because I hold your potential fortune in the palm of my hands. Not only that, I'll be the father of your first grandchild. Mainly, though, because you'll take what I give you, and no more. So it's by my good grace that you will have anything."

Antonioni's cheeks turned red. It was clear the old man didn't like being told what to do. "Corretti, I don't have to give your family rights to—"

"And I don't have to give you a damn thing. I know you're making deals with Angelo. And you know how I feel about Angelo, which puts you in my bad book right off. I may, however, be willing to overlook it all if you do as I ask. So I suggest you take steps to make me happy. Send your children to college. I'm paying for it."

"That's hardly necessary."

He thought of Alessia, of all she'd sacrificed for them. "Listen to me now, Battaglia, and remember what

I say. Memorize it. Make a nice little plaque and hang it above your fireplace if need be: If I say it is necessary, then it is. So long as you do what I say, you'll be kept well in the lifestyle you would like to become accustomed to."

The other man nodded. "It's your dime, Corretti."

"Yes, and your life is now on my dime. Get used to that concept."

Had Alessia's father not said what he had, had he not acted as though her virginity, her body, was his bargaining tool, Matteo might not have taken such joy in letting the other man know his neck was, in effect, under his heel.

But he had. So Matteo did.

"I paid for one wedding," Battaglia said. "I'm not paying for another."

"I think I can handle that, too." Matteo picked up the tiny glass hotel, turning it in front of the light. "You're dismissed."

Battaglia liked that last order least of all, but he complied, leaving Matteo's office without another word.

Matteo tightened his hold on the small, breakable representation of his empire, curling his fingers around it, not stopping until it cracked, driving a shard deep into his palm.

He looked down, watched the blood drip down his wrist. Then he set the figurine back on his desk, examined the broken pieces. Marveled at how easy it was to destroy it with his anger.

He pulled the silk handkerchief out of the pocket of his jacket and wrapped the white fabric around his hand, pressing it hard, until a spot of crimson stained the fabric.

It was so easy to let emotion ruin things. So frighteningly easy.

He gritted his teeth, pushed the wall up around himself again. Control. He would have it, in all things. Alessia Battaglia was not allowed to steal it from him. Not anymore.

Never again.

"I've secured the marriage license, and we will have the wedding at my palazzo." His inheritance after the death of his father. A piece of his childhood he wasn't certain he wanted. But one he possessed nonetheless.

"Not at your family home?"

"I have no use for that place," he said, his tone hard. "Anyway, it has all been arranged."

Alessia stood up from the plush bed, crossing her arms beneath her breasts. "Really? And what shall I wear? How shall I fix my hair? Have you written my vows for me?"

"I don't care. Who gives a damn? And didn't someone already take care of writing vows for weddings hundreds of years ago?"

She blinked, trying to process his rapid-fire response. "I… Don't you have… I mean, don't I need to conform to some sort of image you're projecting or… something?"

"This will be a small affair. We may provide the press with a picture for proof. Or perhaps I'll just send them a photocopy of the marriage license. Anyway, you can wear what you like. I've never seen you not looking beautiful."

The compliment, careless, offhanded, sent a strange sensation through her. "Oh. Well. Thank you."

"It's the truth."

"Well, thank you again."

She wasn't sure what to do, both with him being nice and with him giving her a choice on what to wear to the wedding. Such a simple thing, but it was more than her father had given her when it came to Alessandro.

"As long as it doesn't have lace," she said.

"What?"

"The wedding dress."

"The dress for your last wedding was covered in it."

"Exactly. Hellish, awful contraption. And I didn't choose it. I didn't choose any of that."

"What would you have chosen?"

She shook her head and looked down. "Does it matter?"

"Why not? You can't walk down the aisle naked and we have to get married somewhere, so you might as well make the choice."

"I would wear something simple. Beautiful. And I would be barefoot. And it would be outside."

He lifted his hand and brushed it over his short hair. "Of course. Then we'll have it outside at the palazzo and you may forego shoes." He lowered his hand and she saw a slash of red on his palm.

She frowned and stepped forward. "What did you do?"

"What?" He turned his hand over. "Nothing. Just a cut."

"You look like you got in a fight."

His whole body tensed. "I don't get in fights."

"No, I know. I wasn't being serious." Tension held between them as they both had the same memory. She knew that was what was happening. Knew that he was thinking of the day she'd been attacked.

But she wanted to know what he remembered, how

he remembered it, because it was obvious it was something he preferred to ignore. Not that she loved thinking about it except…except as horrible as it had been to have those men touching her, pawing at her, as awful as those memories were, the moment when they'd been wrenched from her, when she'd seen Matteo…the rush of relief, the feeling of absolute peace and certainty that everything would be okay, had been so real, so acute, she could still feel it.

She'd clung to him after. Clung to him and cried. And he'd stroked her cheek with his hand, wiping away her tears. Later she'd realized he'd left a streak of blood on her face, from the blood on his hands. Blood he'd shed, spilled, for her.

He'd been her hero that day, and every day since. She'd spent her whole life saving everyone else, being the stopgap for her siblings, taking her father's wrath if they'd been too noisy. Always the one to receive a slap across the face, rather than allow him near the younger children.

Matteo was the only person who'd ever stood up for her. The only one who'd ever saved her. And so, when life got hard, when it got painful, or scary, she would imagine that he would come again. That he would pull her into impossibly strong arms and fight her demons for her.

He never did. Never again. After that day, he even stopped watching her. But having the hope of it, the fantasy, was part of what had pulled her through the bleakness of her life. Imagination had always been her escape, and he'd added a richer texture to it, given a face to her dreams for the future.

He'd asked if she always spoke her mind, and she'd told him the truth, she didn't. She kept her head down and tried to get through her life, tried to simply do the best she could. But in her mind…her imagination was her escape, and always had been. When she ran barefoot through the garden, she was somewhere else entirely.

When she went to bed at night, she read until sleep found her, so that she could have new thoughts in her head, rather than simply memories of the day.

So that she could have better dreams.

It was probably a good thing Matteo didn't know the place he occupied in her dreams. It would give him too much power. More than he already had.

"I'm not like my father," he said. "I will never strike my wife."

She looked at him and she realized that never, for one moment, had she believed he would. Her father had kept her mother "in line" with the back of his hand, and he'd done the same with her. But even having grown up with that as a normal occurrence, she'd never once imagined Matteo would do it.

"I know," she said.

"You know?"

"Yes."

"And how is it you know?"

"Because you aren't that kind of person, Matteo."

"Such confidence in me. Especially when you're one of the very few people who has actually seen what I'm capable of."

She had. She'd seen his brute strength applied to those who had dared try to harm her. It had been the most welcome sight in all of her life. "You protected me."

"I went too far."

"They would have gone further," she said.

He took a step away from her, the darkness in his

eyes suddenly so deep, so pronounced, it threatened to pull her in. "I have work to do. I'll be at my downtown office. I've arranged to have a credit card issued to you." He reached into his pocket and pulled out a black card, extending his hand to her.

She took it, not ready to fight with him about it.

"If you need anything, whatever you need, it's yours." He turned away and walked out of the room, closing the door behind him.

She'd done the wrong thing again. With Matteo it seemed she could do nothing right. And she so desperately wanted to do right by him.

But it seemed impossible.

She growled, the sound releasing some of her tension. But not enough. "Matteo, why are you always so far out of my reach?"

This was Alessia's second wedding day. Weird, because she'd never technically had a boyfriend. One hot night of sex didn't really make Matteo her boyfriend. *Boyfriend* sounded too tame for a man like Matteo, anyway. Alessia finished zipping up the back of her gown. It was light, with flutter sleeves and a chiffon skirt that swirled around her ankles. It was lavender instead of white. She was a pregnant bride, after all.

There weren't many people in attendance, but she liked that better. Her father, her brothers and sisters, Matteo's grandmother, Teresa, and his mother, Simona.

She took the bouquet of lilacs she'd picked from the garden out of their vase and looked in the mirror. Nothing like what the makeup artist had managed on The Other Wedding Day, but today she at least looked like her.

She opened the guest bedroom door and tried to get a handle on her heart rate.

She was marrying Matteo Corretti today. In a sun-drenched garden. She was having his baby. She repeated that, over and over, trying to make it feel real, trying to hold on to the surge of good feelings it gave her. Because no matter how terrifying it was sometimes, it was also wonderful. A chance at something new. A chance to have a child, give that child the life that had been denied her. The life that had been denied Matteo.

The stone floor was cool beneath her bare feet, the palazzo empty, everyone outside waiting. She'd opted to forego shoes since that was how he said he knew her.

Barefoot in the garden. So, she would meet him as he remembered her. Barefoot in the garden, with her hair down. Maybe then they could start over. They were getting married today, after all, and in her mind that meant they would have to start trying to work things out. They would at least have to be civil.

She put her hands on the rail of the curved, marble staircase, still repeating her mantra. She walked through the grand foyer, decorated in traditional, ornate furniture that didn't remind her one bit of Matteo, and she opened the door, stepping out into the sun.

The music was already playing. A string quartet. She'd forgotten to say what she wanted for music but this was perfect, simple.

And in spite of what Matteo had said, there was a photographer.

But those details faded into the background when she saw Matteo, standing near the priest, his body rigid, his physique displayed to perfection by a custom-made gray suit.

There was no aisle. No loud click of marble beneath her heels, just grass beneath her feet. And the guests were standing, no chairs. Her father looked like he was ready to grab her if she decided to run. Eva, Giana, Pietro and Marco looked worried, and she didn't blame them. She had been their stability for most of their lives, their surrogate mother. And she hadn't told them she was marrying Alessandro for convenience, which meant her disappearance, subsequent reappearance with a different groom and a publicly announced pregnancy must seem a few steps beyond bizarre to them.

She gave them her best, most confident smile. This was her role. To show them it was all okay, to hold everything together.

But her eyes were drawn back to Matteo. He made her throat dry, made her heart pound.

But when she reached him, he didn't take her hand. He hardly looked at her. Instead, he looked at the priest. The words to the ceremony were traditional, words she knew by heart from attending hundreds of society weddings in her life.

There was nothing personal about them, nothing unique. And Matteo never once met her eyes.

She was afraid she was alone in her resolve to make things work. To make things happy. She swallowed hard. It was always her job to make it okay. To smooth it over. Why wasn't it working?

"You may kiss the bride."

They were the words she'd been anticipating and dreading. She let her eyes drift shut and she waited. She could feel his heat draw near to her, and then, the brush of his lips on hers, so soft, so brief, she thought she might have imagined it.

And then nothing more.

Her breath caught, her heart stopped. She opened her eyes, and Matteo was already turning to face their small audience. Then he drew her near to him, his arm tight around her waist. But there was no intimacy in the gesture. No warmth.

"Thank you for bearing witness," Matteo said, both to her father and his grandmother.

"You've done a good thing for the family, Matteo," his grandmother said, putting a hand over his. And Alessia wondered just how much trouble Matteo had been in with his family for the wedding fiasco.

She knew the media had made assumptions they'd run off together. Too bad nothing could be further from the truth.

Still, her father, his family, must think that was the truth. Because now they were back in Sicily, she was pregnant and they were married.

"Perhaps we should go inside for a drink?" her father suggested.

"A good plan, Battaglia, but we don't talk business at weddings."

Simona begged off, giving Matteo a double kiss on the cheeks and saying she had a party to get to in the city. Matteo didn't seem the least bit fazed by his mother's abandonment. He simply followed her father into the house.

She watched him walk inside, her heart feeling heavy.

Teresa offered her a smile. "I'll see that Matteo's staff finds some refreshments to serve for us. I'll only be a moment." The older woman turned and went into the house, too, leaving Alessia with her siblings.

It was Eva, fourteen and emotional, who flung herself into Alessia's arms. "Where did you go?"

"New York," Alessia said, stroking her sister's hair.

"Why?"

"I had to get away…I couldn't marry Alessandro."

"Then why did you agree to the engagement?" This from Marco, the second oldest at nineteen.

"It's complicated, Marco, as things often are with Father. You know that."

"But you wanted to marry Corretti? This Corretti, I mean," asked sixteen-year-old Pietro.

She nodded, her throat tight. "Of course." She didn't want them to be upset. Didn't want them to worry. She maybe should have thought of that before running off to New York, but she really hadn't been able to consider anyone else. For the first time, she'd been burned out on it and she'd had to take care of herself.

"They're having a baby," Giana said drily. "I assume that means she liked him at least a little bit." Then she turned back to Alessia. "I'm excited about being an aunt."

"I'm glad," she said, tugging on her sister's braid.

They spent the rest of the afternoon out in the garden, having antipasti, wine for the older children and Teresa, and lemonade for her and younger kids. Her siblings told her stories of their most recent adventures, which ended up with everyone laughing. And for the first time in months, Alessia felt at ease. This was her family, her happiness. The reason she'd agreed to marry Alessandro. And one of the driving reasons behind her decision to marry Matteo.

Although she couldn't deny her own desire where he was concerned. Still, *happy* wasn't exactly the word that she would use to describe herself at the moment. Anxiety-ridden? Check. Sick to her stomach? That a little bit, too.

The sun was starting to sink behind the hills, gray twilight settling on the garden, the solar lights that were strung across the expanse of the grass illuminating the growing darkness.

Their father appeared on the balcony, his arms folded across his chest, his eyes settled on her siblings.

"I guess we have to go," Marco said.

"I know. Come back and stay with us anytime," she said, not even thinking to ask Matteo if it was okay. As soon as she had the thought, she banished it. If she was going to be married to the man, then she wasn't going to ask his permission to breathe in their shared home. It wasn't only his now and he would have to get used to it.

Her father was the unquestionable head of their household, but she was the heart of it. She'd kept it running, made sure the kids got their favorite meals cooked, remembered birthdays and helped with homework. Her role in their lives didn't end with her marriage, and she wasn't equipped to take on a passive role in a household, anyway.

So, on that, Matteo would just have to learn to deal.

She stopped and kissed her brothers and sisters on the head before watching them go up to where their father stood. All of them but Marco. She held him a bit longer in her embrace. "Take care of everyone," she said, a tear escaping and sliding down her cheek.

"Just like you always did," he said softly.

"And I'm still here."

"I know."

He squeezed her hand before walking up to join the rest of the family.

"And I should leave you, as well," Teresa said, standing. "It was lovely to see you again, my dear."

Teresa hadn't batted an eye at the sudden change of groom, had never seemed at all ruffled by the events.

"You care for him," she said, as if she could read Alessia's internal musings.

Alessia nodded. "I do."

"That's what these men need, Alessia. A strong woman to love them. They may fight it, but it is what they need." Teresa spoke with pain in her eyes, a pain that Alessia felt echo inside of her.

Alessia couldn't speak past the lump in her throat. She tried to avoid the *L* word. The one that was stronger than *like*. There was only so much a woman could deal with at once. So instead, she just nodded and watched Teresa walk back up toward the house.

Alessia stayed in the garden and waited. The darkness thickened, the lights burning brighter. And Matteo didn't come.

She moved into the house, walked up the stairs. The palazzo was completely quiet, the lights off. She wrapped her arms around herself, and made her way back to the bedroom Matteo had put her in to get ready.

She went in and sat on the edge of the bed and waited for her husband to come and claim his wedding night.

CHAPTER SIX

MATTEO DIDN'T GET DRUNK as a rule. Unfortunately, he had a tendency to break rules when Alessia Battaglia—or was she Alessia Corretti now?—was involved.

Damn that woman.

Even after his father's death he hadn't gotten drunk. He'd wanted to. Had wanted to incinerate the memories, destroy them as the fire had destroyed the warehouses, destroyed the man who had held so much sway over his life.

But he hadn't. Because he hadn't deserved that kind of comfort. That kind of oblivion. He'd forced himself to face it.

This…this he couldn't face.

He took another shot of whiskey and let it burn all the way down. It didn't burn as much at this point in the evening, which was something of a disappointment. He looked down at the shot glass and frowned. Then he picked it up and threw it against the wall, watching the glass burst.

Now that was satisfying.

He chuckled and lifted the bottle to his lips. *Dio*, in his current state he almost felt happy. Why the hell didn't he drink more?

"Matteo?"

He turned and saw Alessia standing in the doorway. Alessia. He wanted her. More than his next breath. He wanted those long legs wrapped around his waist, wanted to hear her husky voice whispering dirty things in his ear.

He didn't think she'd ever done that, whispered dirty things in his ear, but he could imagine it, and he wanted it. *Dio*, did he want it.

"Come here, wife," he said, pushing away from the bar, his movements unsteady.

"Are you drunk?"

"I should be. If I'm not…if I'm not there's something very wrong with this whiskey."

Her dark eyes were filled with some kind of emotion. Something strong and deep. He couldn't decipher it. He didn't want to.

"Why are you drunk?"

"Because I've been drinking. Alcohol. A lot of it."

"But why?"

"I don't know, could be because today I acquired a wife and I can't say I ever particularly wanted one."

"Thank you. I'm so glad to hear that, after the ceremony."

"You would have changed your mind? You can't. It's all over the papers, in the news all over the world. You're carrying a Corretti. You, a Battaglia. It's news, *cara*. Not since Romeo and Juliet has there been such a scandal."

"I'm not going to stab myself for you just because you've poisoned your damn self, so you can stop making those parallels anytime."

"Come to me, Alessia."

She took a step toward him, her movements unsteady, her lips turned down into a sulky frown. He wanted to kiss the expression off her face.

"You left your hair down," he said, reaching out and taking a dark lock between his thumb and forefinger, rubbing the glossy strands. "You're so beautiful. An angel. That was the first thing I thought when I saw you."

She blinked rapidly. "When?"

"When we were children. I had always been told you Battaglias were monsters. Demons. And I couldn't resist the chance to peek. And there you were, running around your father's garden. You were maybe eleven. You were dirty and your hair was tangled, but I thought you looked like heaven. You were smiling. You always smile." He frowned, looking at her face again. "You don't smile as much now."

"I haven't had a lot of reasons to smile."

"Have you ever?"

"No. But I've made them. Because someone had to smile. Someone had to teach the children how to smile."

"And it had to be you?"

"There was no one else."

"So you carry the weight of the world, little one?"

"You should know something about that, Matteo."

He chuckled. "Perhaps a little something." He didn't feel so much like he was carrying it now.

He took her arm and tugged her forward, her dark eyes wide. "I want you," he said.

Not waiting for a response, he leaned in and kissed her. Hard. She remained immobile beneath his mouth, her lips stiff, her entire body stiff. He pulled her more firmly against him, let her feel the evidence of his arousal, let her feel all of the frustration and need that had been building inside of him for the past three months.

"Did he kiss you like this?" he asked, pressing a heated kiss to her neck, her collarbone.

She shook her head. "N-no."

"Good. I would have had to kill him."

"Stop saying things like that."

"Why?" he asked. "You and I both know that I could, Alessia. On your behalf, I could. I might not even be able to stop myself." He kissed her again, his heart pounding hard, blood pouring hot and fast through his veins.

"Matteo, stop," she said, pulling away from him.

"Why? Are you afraid of me, too, Alessia?"

She shook her head. "No, but you aren't yourself. I don't like it."

"Maybe I am myself, and in that case, you're wise not to like it."

He released his hold on her. And he realized how tight his grip had been. Regret, the kind he usually kept dammed up inside of himself, released, flooding through him. "Did I hurt you?"

She shook her head. "No."

"Don't lie."

"I wouldn't."

Suddenly, he was hit with a shot of self-realization so strong it nearly buckled his knees. He had done it again. He had let his defenses down with Alessia. Let them? He didn't allow anything, with her it was just total destruction, a sudden, real demolition that he didn't seem to be able to control at all.

"Get out," he said.

"Matteo…"

"Out!" he roared, images flashing before his eyes.

Images of violence. Of bones crushing beneath his fists, of not being able to stop. Not being able to stop until he was certain they could never hurt her again.

And it melded with images of his father. His father beating men until they were unconscious. Until they didn't get back up again.

"What did they do?"

"They didn't pay."

"Is that all?"

"Is that all? Matteo, you can't let anyone disrespect you, ever. Otherwise, it gets around. You have to make them an example. Whatever you have to do to protect your power, you do it. And if people have to die to secure it, so be it. Casualties of war, figlio mio."

No. He wasn't like that.

But you were, Matteo. You are.

Then in his mind, it wasn't his father doing the beating. It was him.

"Out!"

Alessia's dark eyes widened and she backed out of the room, a tear tracking down her cheek.

He sank down into a chair, his fingers curled tightly around a bottle of whiskey as the edges of his vision turned fuzzy, darkened.

Che cavolo, what was she doing to him?

Alessia slammed the bedroom door behind her and tore at the back of her wedding dress, such as it was, sobbing as she released the zipper and let it fall to the floor. She'd wanted Matteo to be the one to take it off her. She hadn't realized how much until now.

Instead, her groom was off getting drunk rather than dealing with her.

"It's more than that," she said out loud. And she knew

that it was. He was getting drunk instead of dealing with a whole lot of things.

Well, it was unfair because she couldn't get drunk. She was pregnant with the man's baby, and while he numbed the pain of it all, she just had to stand around and endure it.

There was nothing new to that. She had to smile. Had to keep it all moving.

She sat down on the edge of the bed, then scooted into the middle of it, lying down, curling her knees into her chest. Tonight, there was no fantasy to save her, no way to avoid reality.

Matteo had long been her rescue from the harsh reality and pain of life. And now he was her harsh reality. And he wasn't who she'd believed he was. She'd simplified him, painted him as a savior.

She'd never realized how much he needed to be saved. The question was, was she up to the challenge? No, the real question was, did she have a choice?

There wasn't a word foul enough to help release the pain that was currently pounding through Matteo's head. So he said them all.

Matteo sat upright in the chair. He looked down at the floor, there was a mostly empty whiskey bottle lying on its side by the armchair. And there was a dark star-shaped whiskey stain on the wall, glass shards gathered beneath.

He remembered…not very much. The wedding. He was married now. He looked down at the ring on his left hand. Yes, he was married now.

He closed his eyes again, trying to lessen the pain in his head, and had a flash of lilac memory. A cloud of purple, long dark hair. He'd held her arm and pulled her against him, his lips hard on hers.

Dio, what had he done? Where had it stopped? He searched his brain desperately for an answer, tried to figure out what he'd done. What she'd done.

He stood quickly, ignoring the dizziness, the ferocious hammering in his temples. He swore again as he took his first step, he legs unsteady beneath him.

What was his problem? Where was his control? He knew better than to drink like that, knew better than to allow any lowered inhibitions.

The first time he'd gotten that drunk had been the night following Alessia's rescue. He hadn't been able to get clean. Hadn't been able to get the images out of his head. Images of what he was capable of.

The stark truth was, it hadn't been the attack that had driven him to drink. It had been what his father had said afterward.

"You are my son."

When Benito Corretti had seen his son, blood-streaked, after the confrontation with Alessia's attackers, he'd assumed that it meant Matteo was finally following in his footsteps. Had taken it as confirmation.

But Matteo hadn't. It had been six years after that night when Benito had said it to him again. And that night, Matteo had embraced the words, and proven the old man right.

He pushed the memories away, his heart pounding too hard to go there.

He knew full well that he was capable of unthinkable things, even without the loss of control. But when control was gone…when it was gone, he truly became a monster. And last night, he'd lost control around Alessia.

He had to find her.

He walked down the hall, his heart pounding a sick tempo in his skull, his entire body filled with lead.

He went down the stairs, the natural light filtering through the windows delivering a just punishment for his hideous actions.

Coffee. He would find coffee first, and then Alessia.

He stopped when he got to the dining room. It turned out he had found both at the same time.

"Good morning," Alessia said, her hands folded in front of her, her voice soft and still too loud.

"Morning," he said, refusing to call it good.

"I assume you need coffee?" she asked, indicating a French press, ready for brewing, and a cup sitting next to it.

"Yes."

"You know how that works, right?" she asked.

"Yes."

"Good."

She didn't make a move to do it for him, she simply sat in her seat, drinking a cup of tea.

He went to his spot at the expansive table, a few seats away from hers, and sat, pushing the plunger down slowly on the French press.

He poured himself a cup, left it black. He took a drink and waited a moment, letting the strong brew do its magic.

"Alessia," he said, his voice rusty, the whiskey burn seeming to linger, "last night…did I hurt you?"

"In what way?" she asked, leaning back in her chair, her dark eyes unflinching.

"Physically."

"No."

The wave of relief that washed over him was profound, strong. "I'm pleased to hear it."

"Emotionally, on the other hand, I'm not sure I faired so well."

"Why is that?"

"Well, let's see, my husband got drunk on our wedding night instead of coming to bed with me. What do you think?"

"I'm sorry if I wounded your pride," he said, "that wasn't my intention." What he'd been after was oblivion, which he should have known wasn't a safe pursuit.

"Wouldn't your pride have been wounded if I'd done the same?"

"I would have ripped the bottle out of your hand. You're pregnant."

There hadn't been a lot of time for him to really pause and think through the implications of that. It had all been about securing the marriage. Staying a step ahead of the press at all times. Making sure Alessia was legally bound to him.

"Hence the herbal tea," she said, raising her cup to him. "And the pregnancy wasn't really my point."

"Alessia…this can't be a normal marriage."

"Why not?" she asked, sitting up straighter.

"Because it simply can't be. I'm a busy man, I travel a lot. I was never going to marry…I never would have married."

"I don't see why we can't have a normal marriage anyway. A lot of men and women travel for business, it doesn't mean they don't get married."

"I don't love you."

Alessia felt like he'd slapped her. His words were so bald, so true and unflinching. And they cut a swath of devastation through her. "I didn't ask you to," she said, because it was the only truth she could bring herself to speak.

"Perhaps not, but a wife expects it from her husband."

"I doubt my father loved my mother, and if he did, it wasn't the kind of love I would like to submit to. What about yours?"

"*Obsession,* perhaps, was a better word. My father loved Lia's mother, I'm sure of that. I'm not certain he loved mine. At least, not enough to stay away from other women. And my mother was—is, for that matter—very good at escaping unpleasant truths by way of drugs and alcohol." His headache mocked him, a reminder that he'd used alcohol for the very same reason last night.

"Perhaps it was their marriages that weren't normal. Perhaps—"

"Alessia, don't. I think you saw last night that I'm not exactly a brilliant candidate for husband or father of the year."

"So try to be. Don't just tell me you can't, Matteo, or that you don't want to. Be better. That's what I'm trying to do. I'm trying to be stronger, to do the right thing."

"Yes, because that's what you do," he said, his tone dry. "You make things better, because it makes you feel better, and as long as you feel good you assume all is right with your world. You trust your moral compass."

"Well, yes, I suppose that's true."

"I don't trust mine. I want things I shouldn't want. I have already taken what I didn't have the right to take."

"If you mean my virginity, I will throw this herbal tea in your face," she said, pregnancy hormones coming to the rescue, bringing an intense surge of anger.

"I'm not so crass, but yes. Your body, you, you aren't for me."

"For Alessandro? That's who I was for?"

"That isn't what I meant."

"The hell it's not, Matteo!" she shouted, not caring if she hurt his head. Him and his head could go to hell. "You're just like him. You think I can't make my own decisions? That I don't know my own mind? My body belongs to me, not to you, not to my father, not to Alessandro. I didn't give myself to you, I took you. I made you tremble beneath my hands, and I could do it again. Don't treat me like some fragile thing. Don't treat me like you have to protect me from myself."

He stayed calm, maddeningly so, his focus on his cup of coffee. "It's not you I'm protecting you from."

"It's you?"

A smile, void of humor, curved his lips. "I don't trust me, Alessia, why should you?"

"Well, let me put you at ease, Matteo. I don't trust anyone. Just because I jumped into bed with you doesn't mean you're the exception. I just think you're hot." She was minimizing it. Minimizing what she felt. And she hated that. But she was powerless to do anything to stop the words from coming out. She wanted to protect herself, to push him back from her vulnerable places. To keep him from hurting her.

Because the loss of Matteo in her fantasies…it was almost too much to bear. As he became her reality, she was losing her escape, and she was angry at him for taking it. For not being the ideal she had made him out to be.

"I'm flattered," he said, taking another drink of his coffee.

"How do you see this marriage going, then?"

"I don't want to hurt you."

"Assume it's too late. Where do we go from here?"

He leaned forward, his dark eyes shuttered. "When exactly are you due?"

"November 22. It was easy for them to figure out since I knew the exact date I conceived."

"I will make sure you get the best care, whatever you need. And we'll make a room for the baby."

"Well, all things considered, I suppose our child should have a room in his own house."

"I'm trying," he bit out. "I'm not made for this. I don't know how to handle it."

"Well, I do. I know exactly how much work babies are. I know exactly what it's like to raise children. I was thirteen when my mother died. Thirteen when my baby sister and the rest of my siblings became my responsibility. Babies are hard work. But you love them, so much. And at the same time, they take everything from you. I know that, I know it so well. And I'm terrified," she said, the last word breaking. It was a horrible confession, but it was true.

She'd essentially raised four children, one of them from infancy, and as much as she adored them, with every piece of herself, she also knew the cost of it. Knew just how much you poured into children. How much you gave, how much they took.

And she was doing it again. Without ever finding a place for herself in the world. Without having the fantasies she'd craved. True love. A man who would take care of her.

You've had some of the fantasies.

Oh, yes, she had. But one night of passion wasn't the sum total of her life's desires.

"All of this," he said. "And still you want this child?"

"Yes, Matteo. I do. Because babies are a lot of work. But the love you feel for them…it's stronger than anything, than any fear. It doesn't mean I'm not afraid, only that I know in the end the love will win."

"Well, we can be terrified together," he said.

"You're terrified?"

"Babies are tiny. They look very easily broken."

"I'll teach you how to hold one."

Their eyes met, heat arching between them, and this time her pregnancy hormones were making her feel something other than anger.

She looked back down at her breakfast. "How's your head?"

"I feel like someone put a woodpecker in my skull."

"It's no less than you deserve."

"I will treat you better than I did last night. That I promise you. I'm not sure what other promises I can make, but that one…that one I will keep."

She thought of him last night. Broken. Passionate. Needy. She wondered how much of that was the real Matteo. How much he kept hidden beneath a facade.

How much he kept from escaping. And she knew just how he felt in some ways. Knew what it was like to hide everything behind a mask. It was just that her mask was smiling, and his hardly made an expression at all.

"Will you be faithful to me?" she asked, the words catching in her throat.

Matteo looked down into his coffee for a moment, then stood, his cup in his hand. "I have some work to see to this morning, and my head is killing me. We can talk more later."

Alessia's heart squeezed tight, nausea rolling through her. "Later?"

"My head, Alessia."

My heart, you jackass. "Great. Well, perhaps we can have a meeting tonight, or something."

"We're busy tonight."

"Oh. Doing what?"

"Celebrating our marriage, quite publicly, at a charity event."

"What?" She felt far too raw to be in public.

"After what happened with Alessandro, we have to present a united front. Your not-quite wedding to him was very public, as was your announcement of your pregnancy. The entire world is very likely scratching their heads over the spectacle we've created, and now it's time to show a little bit of normal."

"But we don't have a normal marriage—I mean, so I've been told."

"As far as the media is concerned we do."

"Why? Afraid of a little scandal? You're a Corretti."

"What do you want our child to grow up and read? Because thanks to the internet, this stuff doesn't die. It's going to linger, scandal following him wherever he goes. You and I both know what that's like. To have all the other kids whisper about your parents. For our part, we aren't criminals, but we've hardly given our child a clean start."

"So we go out and look pretty and sparkly and together, and what? The press just forgets about what happened?"

"No, but perhaps they will continue on in the vein that they've started in."

"What's that?" She'd, frankly, spent a lot of energy avoiding the stories that the media had written about the wedding.

"That we were forbidden lovers, who risked it all to be together."

It wasn't far from the truth, although Matteo hadn't truly known the risk they'd been taking their night together. But she had. And she'd risked it all for the chance to be with him.

Looking at him now, dealing with all the bruises he'd inflicted on her heart, she knew she would make the same choice now. Because at least it had been her choice. Her mistake. Her very first big one. It was like a rite of passage in a way.

"Well, then, I suppose we had better get ready to put on a show. I'm not sure I have the appropriate costume, though."

"I'm sure I can come up with something."

CHAPTER SEVEN

"SOMETHING" TURNED OUT to be an evening gown from the Corretti fashion line. It was gorgeous, and it was very slinky, with silky gold fabric that molded to her curves and showed the emerging baby bump that she almost hadn't noticed until she'd put on the formfitting garment.

Of course, there was no point in hiding her pregnancy. She'd announced it on television, for heaven's sake. But even so, since she hadn't really dealt with it yet, she felt nervous about sharing it with the public like this.

She put her hand on her stomach, smoothing her palm over the small bump. She was going to be a mother. Such a frightening, amazing thing to realize. She'd been tangled up in finding Matteo, and then in the days since—had it really only been days?—she'd been dealing with having him back in her life. With marrying him. She hadn't had a chance to really think of the baby in concrete terms.

Alessia looked at herself in the mirror one more time, at her stomach, and then back at her face. Her looks had never mattered very much to her. She was comfortable with them, more or less. She was taller than almost every other woman she knew, and a good portion of the men, at an Amazonian six feet, but Matteo was taller.

He managed to make her feel small. Feminine. Beautiful.

That night they were together he'd made her feel especially beautiful. And then last night he'd made her feel especially undesirable. Funny how that worked.

She turned away from the mirror and walked out of the bedroom. Matteo was standing in the hall waiting for her, looking so handsome in his black suit she went a little weak-kneed. He was a man who had a strong effect, that was for sure.

"Don't you clean up nice," she said. "You almost look civilized."

"Appearances can be deceiving," he said.

"The devil wore Armani?"

"Something like that." He held his hand out and she hesitated for a moment before taking it and allowing him to lead her down the curved staircase and into the foyer. He opened the door for her, his actions that of a perfectly solicitous husband.

Matteo's sports car was waiting for them, the keys in the ignition.

Alessia waited until they were on the road before speaking again. "So, what's the charity?"

He shifted gears, his shoulders bunched up, muscles tense. "It's one of mine."

"You have charities?"

"Yes."

"I didn't realize."

"I thought you knew me."

"We're filled with surprises for each other, aren't we? It's a good thing we have a whole lifetime together to look forward to," she said drily.

"Yes," he said, his voice rough, unconvincing.

And she was reminded of their earlier conversation in the dining room. She'd asked him point-blank if he would be faithful, and he'd sidestepped her. She had a feeling he was doing it again.

She gritted her teeth to keep from saying anything more. To keep from asking him anything, or pressing the issue. She had some pride. She did. She was sure she did, and she was going to do everything she could to hold on to her last little bit of it.

"Well, what is your charity for, then?"

"This is an education fund. For the schools here."

"That's…great," she said. "I didn't get to do any higher education."

"Did you want to?"

"I don't know. I don't think so. I mean…I didn't really have anything I wanted to be when I grew up."

"Nothing?"

"There weren't a lot of options on the table. Though I did always think I would like to be a mother." A wife and a mother. That she would like to have someone who loved her, cherished her like the men in her much-loved books cherished their heroines. It was a small dream, one that should have been somewhat manageable.

Instead, she'd gone off and traded it in for a night of wild sex.

And darn it, she still didn't regret it. Mainly.

"Mission accomplished."

"Why, yes, Matteo, I am, as they say, living the dream."

"There's no need to be—"

"There is every need to be," she said. "Don't act like I should thank you for any of this."

"I wasn't going to," he said, his tone biting.

"You were headed there. This is not my dream." But

it was close. So close that it hurt worse in some ways than not getting anywhere near it at all. Because this was proving that her dream didn't exist. That it wasn't possible.

"My apologies, *cara*, for not being your dream." His voice was rough, angry, and she wanted to know where he got off being mad after the way he'd been treating her.

"And my apologies for not being yours. I imagine if I had a room number stapled to my forehead and a bag of money in my hand I'd come a little closer."

"Now you're being absurd."

"I don't think so."

Matteo maneuvered his car through the narrow city streets, not bothering with nice things like braking before turning, and pulled up to the front of his hotel.

"It's at your hotel," she said.

"Naturally." He threw the car into Park, then got out, rounding to the passenger side and opening the door for her. "Come, my darling wife, we have a public to impress."

He extended his hand to her and she slowly reached her hand out to accept it. Lighting streaked through her, from her fingertips, spreading to every other part of her, the shock and electricity curling her toes in her pumps.

She stood, her eyes level with his thanks to her shoes. "Thank you."

A member of the hotel staff came to where they were and had a brief exchange with Matteo before getting into the car and driving it off to the parking lot. Alessia wandered to the steps of the hotel, taking two of them before pausing to wait for her husband.

Matteo turned back to her, his dark eyes glittering in the streetlamps. He moved to the stairs, and she advanced up one more, just to keep her height advantage.

But Matteo wasn't having it. He got onto her stair, meeting her eyes straight on.

"There are rules tonight, Alessia, and you will play by them."

"Will I?" she asked. She wasn't sure why she was goading him. Maybe because it was the only way in all the world she could feel like she had some power. Or maybe it was because if she wasn't trying to goad him, she was longing for him. And the longing was just unacceptable.

A smile curved his lips and she couldn't help but wonder if he needed this, too. This edge of hostility, the bite of anger between them.

Although why Matteo would need anything to hold her at a distance when he'd already made his feelings quite clear was a mystery to her.

"Yes, my darling wife, you will." He put his hand on her chin, drawing close to her, his heat making her shiver deep inside. It brought her right back to that night.

To the aching, heart-rending desperation she'd felt when his lips had finally touched hers. To the moment they'd closed his hotel room door and he'd pressed her against the wall, devouring, taking, giving.

He drew his thumb across her lower lip and she snapped back to the present. "You must stop looking at me like that," he said.

"Like what?"

"Like you're frightened of me." There was an underlying note to his voice that she couldn't guess at, a frayed edge to his control that made his words gritty.

"I'm not."

"You look at me like I'm the very devil sometimes."

"You act like the very devil sometimes."

"True enough. But there are other times…"

"What other times?"

"You didn't used to look at me that way."

"How did I look at you?" she asked, her chest tightening, her stomach pulling in on itself.

"When you were a girl? With curiosity. At the hotel? Like you were hungry."

"You looked at me the same way."

"And how do you think I look at you now?"

"You don't," she whispered. "When you can help it, you don't look at me at all."

He moved his other hand up to cup her cheek, his thumb still stroking her lower lip. "I'm looking at you now."

And there was heat in his eyes. Heat like there had been their night together, the night that had started all of this. The night that had changed the course of her life.

"Because you have to," she said. "For the guests."

"Oh, yes, the guests," he said.

Suddenly, a flash pierced the dim light, interrupting their moment. They both looked in the direction of the photographer, who was still snapping pictures in spite of the fact that the moment was completely broken.

"Shall we go in?" he asked. Any evidence of frayed control was gone now, the rawness, the intensity, covered by a mask. And now her husband was replaced with a smooth, cool stranger.

She'd love to say it wasn't the man she'd married, but this was exactly the man she'd married. This guarded man with more layers of artifice than anyone she'd ever met. She had been so convinced she'd seen the man behind the fiction, that the night in the hotel she'd seen the real Matteo. That in those stolen glances they'd shared when they were young, she'd seen the truth.

That in the moment of unrestrained violence, when he'd put himself in harm's way to keep her from getting hurt, she'd seen the real man.

Now she realized what small moments those were in the entirety of Matteo's life. And for the first time, she wondered if she was simply wrong about him.

A feeling that settled sickly in her stomach, a leaden weight, as they continued up the stairs and into the entrance to the hotel's main ballroom.

There were more photographers inside, capturing photographs of the well-dressed crème de la crème of Sicilian society. And Alessia did her best to keep a smile on her face. This was her strength, being happy no matter what was going on. Keeping a smile glued to her face at whatever event she was at on behalf of her father, making sure she showed her brothers and sisters she was okay even if she'd just taken a slap to the face from their father.

But this wasn't so simple. She was having a harder time finding a place to go to inside of herself. Having a harder time finding that false feeling of hope that she'd become so good at creating for herself to help preserve her sanity.

No one could live in total hopelessness, so she'd spent her life creating hope inside of herself. She'd managed to do it through so many difficult scenarios. Why was it so hard now? So hard with Matteo?

She knew she'd already answered that question. It was too hard to retreat to a much-loved fantasy when that much-loved fantasy was standing beside you, the source of most of your angst.

Though she couldn't blame it all on Matteo. The night of her bachelorette party was the first night she'd stopped trying to find solace in herself, had stopped just trying to be happy no matter what, and had gone for what she wanted, in spite of possible consequences.

She spent the night with Matteo's arm wrapped around her waist, his touch keeping her entire body strung tight, on a slow burn. She also turned down champagne more times than she could count. Was she normally offered alcohol so much at a party? She'd never been conscious of it when she was allowed to drink it. Right now it just seemed a cruelty, since she could use the haze, but couldn't take the chance with her baby's health.

Anyway, for some reason it all smelled sour and spoiled to her now. The pregnancy was making her nose do weird things.

Although Matteo smelled just as good as he ever had. The thought made her draw a little closer to him, breathe in the scent of him, some sort of spicy cologne mingling with the scent of his skin. She was especially tuned into the scent of his skin now, the scent of his sweat.

Dio, even his sweat turned her on. Because it reminded her of his bare skin, slick from exertion, her hands roaming over his back as he thrust hard into her, his dark eyes intent on hers. And there were no walls. Not then.

She blinked and came back to the present. She really had to stop with the sexual fantasies, they did her no good.

A photographer approached them. "Smile for me?" he asked.

Matteo drew her in close to his body, and she put her hand on his chest. She knew her smile looked perfect. She had perfected her picture smile for events such as these, to put on a good front for the Battaglia family. She was an expert.

Matteo should have been, as well, but he looked like

he was trying to smile around a rock in his mouth, his expression strained and unnatural.

"A dance for the new bride and groom?" the photographer asked while taking their picture, and she was sure that in that moment her smile faltered a bit.

"Of course," Matteo said, his grin widening. Was she the only one who could see the totally feral light in his eyes, who could see that none of this was real?

The photographer was smiling back, as were some of the guests standing in their immediate area, so they must not be able to tell. Must not be able to see how completely disingenuous the expression of warmth was.

"Come. Dance with me."

And so she followed him out onto the glossy marble dance floor, where other couples were holding each other close, slow dancing to a piece of piano music.

It was different from when they'd danced in New York. The ballroom was bright, crystal chandeliers hanging overhead, casting shimmering light onto caramel-colored walls and floors. The music was as bright as the lighting, nothing darkly sensual or seductive.

And yet when Matteo drew her into his hold, his arms tight, strong around her, they might as well have been the only two people in the room. Back again, shrouded in darkness in the corner of a club, stealing whatever moments together they could have before fate would force them to part forever.

Except fate had had other ideas.

She'd spent a lot of her life believing in fate, believing that the right thing would happen in the end. She questioned that now. Now she just wondered if she'd let her body lead her into an impossible situation all for the sake of assuaging rioting hormones.

"This will make a nice headline, don't you think?"

he asked, swirling her around before drawing her back in tight against him.

"I imagine it will. You're a great dancer, by the way. I don't know if I mentioned that…last time."

"You didn't, but your mouth was otherwise occupied."

Her cheeks heated. "Yes, I suppose it was."

"My mother made sure I had dance lessons starting at an early age. All a part of grooming me to take my place at the helm of Benito's empire."

"But you haven't really. Taken the helm of your father's empire, I mean."

"Not as such. We've all taken a piece of it, but in the meantime we've been working to root out the shadier elements of the business. It's one thing my brothers and I do not suffer. We're not criminals."

"A fact I appreciate. And for the record, neither is Alessandro. I would never have agreed to marry him otherwise."

"Is that so?"

"I've had enough shady dealings to last me a lifetime. My father, for all that he puts on the front of being an honorable citizen, is not. At least your father and your grandfather had the decency to be somewhat open about the fact that they weren't playing by the rules."

"Gentleman thugs," he said, his voice hard. "But I'll let you in on a little secret—no matter how good you are at dancing, no matter how nicely tailored your suit is, it doesn't change the fact that when you hit a man in the legs with a metal cane, his knees shatter. And he doesn't care what you're wearing. Neither do the widows of the men you kill."

Alessia was stunned by his words, not by the content of them, not as shocked as she wished she were. People often assumed that she was some naive, cosseted flower. Her smile had that effect. They assumed she must not know how organized crime worked. But she did. She knew the reality of it. She knew her father was bound up so tightly in all of it he could hardly escape it even if he wanted to.

He was addicted to the power, and being friendly with the mob bosses was what kept him in power. He couldn't walk away easily. Not with his power, possibly not even with his life.

And yet, the Correttis had disentangled themselves from it. The Corretti men and women had walked away from it.

No, it wasn't the content of his words that had surprised her. It was the fact that he'd said them at all. Because Matteo played his cards close to his chest. Because Matteo preferred not to address the subject of his family, of that part of his past.

"You aren't like that, though."

"No?" he asked. "I'm in a suit."

"And you wouldn't do that to someone."

"Darling Alessia, you are an eternal optimist," he said, and there was something in his words she didn't like. A hard edge that made her stomach tighten. "I don't know how you manage it."

"Survival. I have to protect myself."

"I thought that was where cynics came from?"

"Perhaps a good number of them. But no matter how I feel about a situation, I've never had any control over the outcome. My mother died in childbirth, and no amount of feeling good or bad about it would have changed that. My father is a criminal, no matter the public mask he wears, who has no qualms about slapping my face to keep me in line." They swirled in a fast circle, Matteo's hold tightening on her, something dangerous flickering in his eyes. "No matter how I feel about the situation, that is the situation. If I didn't choose to be happy no matter what, I'm not sure I would have ever stopped crying, and I didn't want to live like that, either."

"And why didn't you leave?" he asked.

"Without Marco, Giana, Eva and Pietro? Never. I couldn't do it."

"With them, then."

"With no money? With my father and his men bearing down on us? If it were only myself, then I would have left. But it was never only me. I think we were why my mother stayed, too." She swallowed hard. "And if she could do it for us, how could I do any less?"

"Your mother was good to you?"

"So good," Alessia said, remembering her beautiful, dark-haired mother, the gentle smile that had always put her at ease when her father was in the other room shouting. The sweet, soothing touch, a hand on her forehead to help her fall asleep. "I wanted to give them all what she gave to me. I was the oldest, the only one who remembered her very well. It seemed important I try to help them remember. That I give them the love I received, because I knew they would never get it from my father."

"And in New York? With me?"

"What do you mean?"

"You toed the line all of your life, Alessia. You were prepared to marry to keep your brothers and sisters safe and cared for. Why did you even chance ruining it by sleeping with me?" His hold tightened on her, his voice getting back that rough edge. That genuine quality it had been missing since they'd stepped inside the hotel.

It was a good question. It was *the* question, really.

"Tell me, *cara*," he said, and she glimpsed something in his eyes as he spoke. A desperation.

And she couldn't goad him. Couldn't lie to him. Not now.

"Did you ever want something, Matteo, with all of yourself? So much that it seemed like it was in your blood? I did. For so many years. When we were children, I wanted to cross that wall between our families' estates and take your hand, make you run with me in the grass, make you smile. And when I got older…well, I wanted something different from you, starting about the time you rescued me, and I don't want to hear about how much you regret that. It mattered to me. I dreamed of what it would be like to kiss you, and then, I dreamed of what it would be like to make love with you. So much so that by the time I saw you in New York, when you finally did kiss me, I felt like I knew the steps to the dance. And following your lead seemed the easiest thing. How could I not follow?"

"I am a man, Alessia, so I fear there is very little romance to my version of your story. From the time you started to become a woman, I dreamed of your skin against mine. Of kissing you. Of being inside you. I could not have stopped myself that night any more than you could have."

"That's good to know," she said, heat rushing through her, settling over her skin. It made her dress, so lovely and formfitting a few moments ago, feel tight. Far too tight.

"I don't understand what it is you do to me."

"I thought… I was certain that I must not be so different from all your other women."

"There weren't that many," he said. "And you are different."

It was a balm to her soul that he felt that way. That

she truly hadn't been simply one in a lineup. It was easy for her, she realized, to minimize the experience on his end. It had been easy for her to justify being with him, not being honest with him, giving him a one-night stand, because she'd assumed he'd had them before. It had been easy to believe she was the only one who'd stood to be hurt or affected, because she was the virgin.

That had been unfair. And she could see now, looking into his eyes, that it wasn't true, either.

"Kiss me," he said, all of the civility gone now.

She complied, closing the short distance between them, kissing him, really kissing him, for the first time in three months. Their wedding kiss had been nothing. A pale shadow of the passion they'd shared before. A mockery of the desire that was like a living beast inside of them both.

She parted her lips for him, sucked his tongue deep inside of her mouth, not caring that it would be obvious to the people around them. Matteo was hers now, her husband. She wouldn't hide it, not from anyone. Wouldn't hide her desire.

He growled low in his throat, the sound vibrating through his body. "Careful, Alessia, or I will not be responsible for what happens."

"I don't want you to be responsible," she said, kissing his neck. Biting him lightly. There was something happening to her, something that had happened once before. A total loss of control. At the hands of Matteo Corretti.

It was like she was possessed, possessed by the desire to have him, to take him, make him hers. Make him understand what she felt. Make herself understand what she felt.

"We can't do this here," he said.

"This sounds familiar."

"It does," he said. He shifted, pulled her away from his body, twining his fingers with hers. "Come with me."

"Where?"

"Somewhere," he said.

He led her out of the ballroom, ignoring everyone who tried to talk to them. A photographer followed them and Matteo cursed, leading them a different way, down a corridor and to the elevators.

He pushed the up button and they both waited. It only took a moment for the elevator doors to slide open, and the moment they did, she was being tugged inside, tugged up against the hard wall of his chest and kissed so hard, so deep, she was afraid she would drown in it.

She heard the doors slide closed behind them, was dimly aware of the elevator starting to move. Matteo shifted their positions, put her back up against the wall, his lips hungry on hers.

"I need you," he said, his voice shaking.

"I need *you*," she said.

Her entire body had gone liquid with desire, her need for him overshadowing everything. Common sense, self-protection, everything. There was no time for thought. This was Matteo. The man she wanted with everything she had in her, the man who haunted her dreams. This was her white knight, but he was different than she'd imagined.

There was a darkness to him. An edge she'd never been able to imagine. And she found she liked it. Found she wanted a taste of it. She didn't know what that said about her, didn't know what it meant, but at the moment, she didn't care, either.

"This is a beautiful dress," he said, tracing the deep V of the neckline with his fingertip, skimming silk and skin with the movement. Her breath hitched, her entire body on edge, waiting for what he would do next. Needing it more than she needed air. "But it is not as beautiful as you. And right now, I need to see you."

He reached around, tugging on the zipper, jerking it down.

"Careful," she said, choking on the word. "You'll snag the fabric."

"I'll tear it if I have to," he said.

The top fell around her waist, revealing her breasts, covered only by a whisper-thin bra that showed the outline of her nipples beneath the insubstantial fabric.

He lifted his hand and cupped her, slid his thumb over the tightened bud. "Hot for me?" he asked.

"Yes."

"Wet for me?" He put his other hand on her hip, flexed his fingers.

She couldn't speak, she just nodded. And he closed his eyes, his expression one of pained relief like she'd never seen before.

She put her hand between her breasts, flicked the front clasp on her bra, letting it fall to the elevator floor. He looked at her, lowering his head, sucking her deep into his mouth. An arrow of pleasure shot from there down to her core. She tightened her fingers in his hair, then suddenly became conscious of the continued movement of the elevator.

"Hit the stop button," she said, her voice breathless.

"What?" he asked, lifting his head, his cheeks flushed, his hair in disarray. Her heart nearly stopped. Matteo Corretti undone was the most amazing thing she'd ever seen.

"The elevator," she said.

He cursed and turned around, hitting the red button on the wall, the elevator coming to a halt. He cursed again and reached into his pocket, taking out his cell phone. "Just a second."

"You better not be texting," she said.

He pushed a few buttons, his eyes not straying to her. "Not exactly." He turned the screen toward her and she saw him. And her. And her breasts.

"Oh."

He pushed a few more buttons. "I have disabled the security camera now. Unless you like the idea of being on film."

She had to admit, she had a certain amount of curiosity as to what it looked like when Matteo Corretti made love to her. It was a video she wouldn't mind owning, in all honesty. But she didn't want it on security footage, either.

"Not in the mood to provide security with any early-evening jollies."

"No worries, I have now deleted that little stretch of footage. There are advantages to being a control freak. Having an app on your phone that lets you see all the security at your hotels, and do as you please with the cameras, is one of them."

He discarded his suit jacket and tie then, throwing them onto the floor of the elevator, tossing his phone down on top of them.

"Have you used that trick before?" she asked, before he lowered his head to kiss her again.

"With a woman?"

"Yes."

"Jealous?"

"Hell, yes," she said, not worried if he knew it. She wanted this moment, this desperation that was beyond anything she'd known, to be as foreign to him as it was to her.

"No, I haven't." He kissed her again, his tongue sliding against hers, and she forgot her lingering concerns.

Forgot about everything but what it felt like to have Matteo kissing her. Caressing her.

"Later—" he kissed the hollow of her throat "—I will do this right—" lowered his head and traced the line of her collarbone with his tongue. "I'll taste every inch of you. Take time to savor you. Take your clothes off slowly. Look at those gorgeous curves." He kissed her neck, bit her lightly like she'd done to him earlier. "Now, though…now I just need to be inside you."

He started to gather her skirt up in his hands, the slippery fabric sliding up her legs easily. "Take your panties off," he said.

She complied, her hands trembling as she worked her underwear down, kicking them to the side with her heels. He pushed her dress up around her hips, his hand hot on her thigh. He tugged her leg up around his, her back pinned against the wall of the elevator.

He tested her with his other hand, teasing her clitoris, sending streaks of white heat through her body with each pass his fingers made through her slick folds. "You didn't lie," he said. "You do want me."

"Yes," she said.

"Tell me," he said.

"I want you."

"My name."

"I want you, Matteo."

He abandoned her body for a moment, working at his belt, shoving his slacks and underwear down, just enough to free his erection so that he could sink into her. It was a shock, all those weeks without him, and she'd forgotten just how big he was. Just how much he filled her. She let her head fall back against the wall of the elevator, pleasure building deep inside her, her internal muscles tightening around his length.

And then there was no more talking. There was nothing but their ragged breathing, Matteo moving hard and fast inside her, blunt fingertips digging into her hips as he held her steady, thrusting into her.

He lowered his head, capturing her nipple in his mouth again. A raw sound of pleasure escaped her lips and she didn't even care. She wasn't embarrassed at all.

Because this was Matteo. The man she'd always wanted. Wanted enough to break out of what was expected of her for the first time in her life. The man who had saved her, the man who made her angry and hurt her, the man who made her feel things she'd never felt before.

Matteo scared her. He confused her. He made her feel more than anyone else ever had.

And right now he was driving her to a point she'd never even imagined, to the edge of a cliff so high she couldn't see the bottom of the chasm below.

She was afraid to fall, afraid to let the pleasure that was building in her break, because she didn't know what would greet her on the other side. Didn't know what would happen. And something *would* happen. Something would change. There was no question. None at all.

And then he looked at her, those dark eyes meeting hers, and she saw him. Not the mask, the man. Raw need, desperation and a fear that mirrored her own.

He lowered his head, his lips pressing against her neck, his thrusts losing their measured rhythm. And something in her broke, released. And she was falling, falling into that endless chasm. But she wasn't afraid anymore.

Release rolled through her in waves, stealing every breath, every thought, everything but the moment.

And when she finally did reach bottom, Matteo was there, his strong arms around her. He was breathing hard, too, sweat on his brow, the back of his shirt damp, his heartbeat raging, so hard that, with his body pressed so tightly against hers, she could feel it against her own chest.

He stepped away from her slowly, running his hand over his hair, erasing the evidence that she'd ever speared her fingers through it. That she'd messed with his well-ordered control.

He adjusted his pants. Bent and collected his jacket, putting his phone back into his pocket. And she just stood there, her back to the wall, her dress still pushed partway up around her hips, the top resting at her waist, her underwear on the floor by her feet.

Matteo put his tie around his neck and started straightening it, too, before he looked at her. "Get dressed," he said.

"What?"

"Get dressed," he said. "We have to go back to the party."

"W-we do?"

"It's my charity," he said. "I have a speech to make." He checked his wristwatch. "And it seems I'm not too late for it so I really should try to manage it."

"I..."

"Turn around," he ordered, his voice harsh.

She did as he asked. He put her straps back into place, zipped the dress back up.

"My bra..."

"You don't need it," he said.

"What should I do with it?"

He opened up his jacket and indicated his inner pocket. She bent and scooped up her bra and panties and handed them to him, and he put both tiny garments into his pocket.

"Solved," he said.

She looked down at her chest, cupped her breasts for a moment. "I'm sagging."

"You are not."

He hit the button on the elevator and it started moving again, the doors sliding open. Then he hit the button for the first floor and they waited for the doors to close again.

Alessia felt…used. No, not even that. She just felt sad. Angry, because he was able to do that with her and then go back to his purely unruffled self.

Maybe she'd been making more out of them, and the sex, than she should have. Maybe she was wrong. Maybe it didn't mean anything to him. Nothing more than just sex, anyway, and a man like Matteo surely had it quite a bit.

They rode in silence, and the doors opened again. The photographer was still out there, wandering the halls. Looking for a photo op, no doubt.

Matteo put his arm around her waist and led her through the hall, that false smile back on his face. They started back toward the ballroom and she had the strangest feeling of déjà vu. Like they were back at the beginning of the night. Like their interlude in the elevator hadn't happened at all. But it had. She knew it had.

The photographer snapped a picture. And Alessia didn't bother to smile.

CHAPTER EIGHT

MATTEO WASN'T SURE how he managed to get up and speak in front of the large crowd of people. Not when he could see Alessia in the audience, her face smooth, serene, her dark eyes the only window to the storm that lurked beneath.

A storm he was certain would boil over and onto him once they were alone.

He found he didn't mind. That he welcomed the chance to take her on because it was better than the overwhelming, biting need to take her back to the elevator and have her again. To let the elevator continue up to his suite where he would have her again. And again. Tasting her this time, truly savoring her.

Yes, fighting was infinitely better than that. He would rather have her yelling at him than sighing his name in his ear.

Because he didn't know what to do with her, what to do about his desire for her.

It wasn't what he was used to. Wasn't normal in any way.

Sex was simply a need to be met, like eating or breathing. Yes, he liked some food better than he liked others, but he wasn't a slave to cravings. He believed in moderation, in exercising control in all areas of life.

Alessia was the one craving he didn't seem to be able to fight, and that meant he had to learn how.

Anything else was inexcusable.

"Thank you all for coming tonight, and for your generous donations. I am happy to announce that I am personally matching all of the donations given tonight. And that thanks to your generosity, it is now possible for the Corretti Education Foundation to branch out into college grants. It is my belief that a good education can overcome any circumstance, and it is my goal that every person be given that chance. Thank you again, enjoy the rest of the evening."

He stepped down from the podium, not paying attention to the applause that was offered up for his speech. He could hardly hear anything over the roar of blood in his ears. Could hardly see anything but Alessia. Which was one reason he allowed himself to be pulled to the side by some of the guests, interrupted on his way back to where his wife was standing.

He stopped and talked to everyone who approached him, using it as a tactic to keep himself from having to face Alessia without his guard firmly back in place. Cowardly? Perhaps. But he found he didn't care. Not much, at least.

Alessia didn't make a move to approach him; instead, she made conversation with the people around her. And every so often she flicked him a glare with those beautiful eyes of hers, eyes that glittered beneath the lights of the chandeliers. Eyes that made promises of sensual heaven, the kind of heaven he could hardly risk trying to enter again.

Every time he touched Alessia, she tore down another piece of the wall, that very necessary wall of control he'd built around himself.

People started to disperse, and as they both went along the natural line of people that wanted to converse with them, the space between them started to close. Matteo's blood started to flow hotter, faster, just getting nearer to Alessia.

No matter there were still five hundred people in the room. No matter that he'd had her against a wall an hour earlier. Still she challenged him. Still she made him react like a teenage boy with no control over his baser urges.

Yes, think about that. Remember what that looks like.

Blind rage. Two young men, still and unmoving, blood everywhere. And then a calm. A cold sort of emptiness. If he felt anything at all it was a kind of distant satisfaction.

And then he'd looked at Alessia. At the terror in her eyes.

And he'd done what he'd sworn he would never do.

He'd wrapped his arms around her and pulled her into his chest, brushing away her tears. He'd made her cry. Horrified her, and he couldn't blame her for being horrified. It wasn't the kind of thing a girl of fourteen, or any age, should ever have to see.

When he pulled away, when he looked down at her face, her cheeks were streaked with blood. The blood from his hands. Not the only blood he had on his hands.

He breathed in sharply, taking himself back to the present. Away from blood-soaked memories.

Except it was still so easy to see them when he looked at Alessia's face. A face that had been marred with tears and blood. Because of him.

The gap between them continued to shrink, the crowd thinning, until they met in the middle, in the same group. And there was no excuse now for him not to pull her against his side, his arm wrapped around her waist. So he did.

Alessia's body was stiff at his side, but her expression was still relaxed, her smile easy. A lie. Why had he never noticed before that Alessia's smile wasn't always genuine?

He'd assumed that it was. That Alessia displayed and felt emotion with ease and honesty. Now he wondered.

The last of the guests started to file out, leaving Alessia and Matteo standing in the empty ballroom.

He looked around, at the expansive room. This was his hotel, separate from his family dynasty, and often, looking at it, at the architecture, the expanse of it, filled him with a sense of pride. He had hotels all over the world, but this one, back in Sicily, a hotel that belonged to him and not to his family in any part, had always filled him with a particular amount of satisfaction.

Now it just seemed like a big empty room.

He picked up his phone and punched in a number. "Delay cleaning until further notice, I require the ballroom for personal use for a while."

Alessia looked at him, her dark eyes wide. "What do you need the ballroom for?"

He shrugged. "Anything I want." He walked over to the edge of the stage and sat, gripping the edge. "It is my hotel, after all."

"Yes, and you're a man who takes great pride in the ownership of whatever he can possess," she said.

"And why not?" he asked, loosening his tie, trying not to think of Alessia's fingers on the knot, trying not to imagine her fingers at the buttons of his dress shirt as he undid the collar. "That's what it's always been about in my family. I go out of town—" and off the grid "—and my bastard cousin has taken over my office. My younger brother has managed to charm his way into the top seat of the fashion houses for Corretti. So you see? In my family, ownership is everything. And if you have to stab someone to get it, all the better."

"Metaphorical stabbing?" she asked, wrapping her arms around her waist, as if holding herself together. He hated that. Hated that he might cause her pain in any way.

"Or literal stabbing. I told you, my family has a colorful history."

"You said you and your brothers weren't criminals."

"We're not. Not convicted, anyway," he added, not sure why. Maybe because, in his heart, he knew he was one.

Knew he could be convicted for assault several times over if evidence was brought before a court.

"Why are you saying this?"

"What do you mean, why am I saying this? I'm telling you the truth. Was what I did that day near your father's gardens legal? Answer me," he said, his words echoing in the empty room.

"You saved me."

"Maybe."

"They would have raped me," she said.

He remembered it so clearly. And yet so differently.

Because he remembered coming upon Alessia, backed up against a tree, a stone wall behind her, two men in front of her, pressing her back to the tree, touching her, jeering at her. They had her shirt torn. They were pushing her skirt up. And he'd known what they intended to do. The evil they meant for his angel.

And then he remembered seeing red.

He pushed off from the stage, standing and pacing,

trying to relieve the restless energy moving through him. Trying to ease the tightness in his chest.

He hadn't simply stopped when he'd gotten those men away from Alessia. Hadn't stopped when they quit fighting back. He hadn't stopped until Alessia had touched his back. And then he'd turned, a rock held tightly in his hand, ready to finish what he'd started. Ready to make sure they never got up again, ready to make sure they could never hurt another woman again. Any other woman, but most especially Alessia.

But then he'd looked into her eyes. Seen the fear. Seen the tears.

And he'd dropped his hand back to his side, letting the rock fall to the ground. Letting the rage drain from his body.

That was when he'd realized what he had done. What he had been about to do. And what it had done to Alessia to see it. More than that, it confirmed what he'd always known. That if he ever let himself go, if he ever allowed himself more than his emotionless existence, he would become a man he hated.

"I did more than save you," he said. "A lot more."

"You did what you had to."

"You say it as if I gave it some thought. I didn't. What I did was a reaction. Blind rage. As I was, if you were not there, I wouldn't have ended it until they were dead."

"You don't know that."

"That's the thing, Alessia, I do know that. I know exactly what my next move was going to be, and trust me, it's not something people get back up from."

"I wish you could see what I saw."

"And I wish like hell you hadn't seen any of it," he said, his voice rough.

"You were… I thought…I thought they were going

to get away with it. That no one would hear me scream. No one would stop them. I thought that they would do it. And then you came and you didn't let them. Do you have any idea what that meant to me? Do you know what you stopped?"

"I know what I stopped."

"Then why do you regret it so much?"

"I don't regret it, not like you mean." He could remember his father's face still, as he'd administered punishment to men in his debt. The calm. The absolute calm. But worse, he could remember his father's face when someone had enraged him. Could remember how volatile, how beyond reason, he became in those situations.

And always, the old man had a smug sense that he had done what must be done. Full and complete justification for every action.

Just as Matteo had felt after Alessia's attack. How he had felt after the fire.

"To me you were just a hero," she said, her words soft.

They hit him hard, like a bullet, twisted inside of him, blooming outward and touching him everywhere, scraping his heart, his lungs. For a moment, he couldn't breathe.

"It's so much more complicated than that," he said.

"Not to me. Not to the girl you rescued. You were like… You were every unfulfilled dream from my entire life, showing up when I needed you most. How can you not understand that?"

"Maybe that," he said, "is our problem now. You know a dream, a fantasy, and I am not that man. I'm not the hero of the story."

She shook her head. "You were the hero of my story that day. And nothing will change that."

Coldness invaded him. "Is that what led you to my bed that night?"

She didn't look away. "Yes."

He swore, the word loud in the empty expanse of the ballroom. "So that was my thank-you?"

"No!" she said, the exclamation reverberating around them. "It's not like that at all. Don't make it into something like that it's… No."

"Then what, Alessia? Your fantasy of a knight?" Her cheeks turned pink and then she did look away. "*Dio*, is that what it is? You expected me to be your chivalrous knight in shining armor? What a disappointment this must be for you. You would have likely been better off with Alessandro."

"I didn't want Alessandro."

"Only because you lied to yourself about who I am."

"Who are you, then?" she asked. "You're my husband. I think you should tell me."

"I thought we went over this already."

"Yeah, you gave me that internet bio of a rundown on who you are. We told each other things we already knew."

"Why do we have to know each other?"

"Because it seems like we should. We're…married."

"Not really."

"You took me into an elevator and had me against the wall—what would make it more real for you?" she asked, the words exploding from her, crude and true, and nothing he could deny.

"That's sex, Alessia, and what we have is great, explosive sex. But that kind of thing isn't sustainable. It's not meant to be. It's not good for it to be."

"And you know this because you're constantly having spontaneous, explosive sex with strangers?"

"No."

"Then how do you know?"

"There's no control in it. No sense. We nearly let it get filmed, nearly let the elevator go to the next floor. Neither of us think when sex is involved."

"Maybe you think too much."

"And maybe you don't think enough. You feel, and look where all of that feeling has gotten you."

Her lip curled into a sneer. "Don't you dare blame this on me! Don't you dare act like it was me and my girlish feelings that led us here. That's far too innocent of a take on it, first of all. Yes, I might have built you up as a hero in my head, but what I wanted that night in New York had nothing to do with you being some kind of paragon and everything to do with me wanting you as a woman wants a man. I didn't want hearts and flowers, I wanted sex. And that was what I got. That wasn't led by my feelings," she said, her words cold, "that was led by my body and I was quite happy with the results."

"Too bad the price was so steep."

"Wasn't it?"

Alessia looked at Matteo and, for a moment, she almost hated him. Because he was fighting so hard, against her, against everything. Or maybe she was the one fighting. And she was just mad at him for not being who she'd thought he was.

And that wasn't fair, not really. He couldn't help it if he didn't line up with the fantasy she'd created about him in her head. It wasn't even fair to expect him to come close.

But no one in her life had ever been there for her,

not since her mother. It had all been about her giving. And then he'd been there, and he'd put it all on the line for her, he'd given her all of himself in that moment. And yes, what he'd done had been violent, and terrifying in a way, but it was hard for her to feel any sadness for the men who would have stolen her last bit of innocence from her.

She'd grown up in a house with a criminal father who lied and stole on a regular basis. She knew about the ugliness of life. She'd lost her mother, spent her days walking on eggshells to try to avoid incurring any of her father's wrath.

But in all that time, at least, no one had forced themselves on her sexually, and considering the kind of company her father kept, it had always seemed kind of an amazing thing.

And then someone had tried to take that from her, too. But Matteo had stopped it.

"Do you understand how much of my life has been decided for me?" she asked.

"Yes," he said slowly, obviously unwilling to admit to not understanding something.

"I don't think you do. I spent my days mothering my siblings, and I don't regret it, because it had to be done, but that meant I didn't go away to school. It meant I stayed at home when a lot of girls my age would have been moving out, going to university. I went to events my father wanted me to go to, hosted parties in dresses he deemed appropriate. That day…that day on the road, those two men tried to take another choice from me. They tried to choose how I would learn about sex, how I would be introduced to it. With violence and pain and force. They tried to take something from me, and I don't just mean virginity, I mean the way I saw myself. The way I saw men. The way I saw people. And you stopped them. So I'm sorry if you don't want to have been my hero, but you were. You let me hold on to some of my innocence. You let me keep some parts of life a fantasy. I know about how harsh life can be. I know about reality, but I don't need to have every horrible thing happen to me. And it was going to." Her voice was rough, raw with tears she needed to shed.

She turned away from him, trying to catch her breath.

"And then my father told me that I was going to marry Alessandro. And I could see more choices being taken from me but this time I didn't see a way out. Then my friend Carolina said she would host a bachelorette party for me. And for once my father didn't deny me. I didn't know you would be there. And Carolina suggested we go to your hotel and I…well, then I hoped you'd be there. And you were. And I saw another chance to make a choice. So don't ask me to regret it."

His eyes were black, endless, unreadable. "I won't ask you to regret it, because then I would have to regret it, and I don't. When I found out I was your first…I can't tell you how that satisfied me, and I don't care if that's not the done thing, if I shouldn't care, because I did. I still care. I'm still glad it was me."

"I am, too," she said, her voice a whisper. The honesty cost them both, she knew.

His eyes met hers, so bleak, so filled with need. And she hoped she could fill it. Hoped she could begin to understand the man that he was and not just the man she'd created a fiction about in her head.

She nearly went to him then. Nearly touched him. Asked him to lie her down on the cold marble of the ballroom floor and make love to her again. But then she remembered. Remembered the question he hadn't answered. The one she'd been determined to get the answer to before she ever let him touch her again.

She'd messed up earlier. She hadn't been able to think clearly enough to have a conversation with him. But now, she would ask now. Again. And she would get her answer.

"Will you be faithful to me?" she asked.

He pushed his fingers through his hair. "Why do you keep asking me this?"

"Because it's a simple question and one I deserve the answer to. I'm not sleeping with you if you won't promise I'm the only woman in your life."

"I can't love you," he said, the words pulled from him. Not *I don't love you*, like he'd said earlier, but *I can't.*

"I'm not asking you to love me, I'm asking you to not have sex with other women."

His jaw tightened, his hands clenching into fists at his sides. "To answer that question, I would have to know how I planned on conducting our relationship, and I do not know the answer to that yet."

"Were you planning on asking me?"

He shook his head. "I already told you we won't have a normal marriage."

"Why?" She knew she shouldn't ask, not in such a plaintive, needy tone, but she couldn't help herself, couldn't hide the hurt that was tearing through her. How was it she'd managed to get her dream, only to have it turn to ash the moment her fingers touched it?

"Because I cannot be a husband to you. I can't. I won't love you. I won't… I can't give what a husband is supposed to give. I don't know where to begin. I have an empire to run, my hotels, plus I have my bastard cousin installed in my offices at the family corporation, with his ass in my chair, sitting at my desk like he's the one who worked so hard for any of it. I don't have time to deal with you. If you took me on as a husband you would have me in your bed and nowhere else. And I'm not sure I want to put either of us through that."

"But you are my husband. Whether or not you want to be doesn't come into it at this point. You are my husband. You're the father of my baby."

"And our baby has the protection of my name, the validity of having married parents. I'm able to strike the deal for the docklands with your father thanks to this marriage and your siblings will be cared for. I'm sending them all to school, I don't think I told you."

Her throat closed, her body trembling. "I… No, you didn't."

"My point is, regardless of what happens behind closed doors, our marriage was a necessity, but what we choose to do in our own home rests squarely on us. And there are decisions to be made."

Decisions. She'd imagined that if she married Matteo her time for decision making would be over before it ever started. But he was telling her there was still a chance to make choices. That them legally being husband and wife didn't mean it was settled.

In some ways, the opportunity to make decisions was a heady rush of power she'd only experienced on a few occasions. In other ways…well, she wanted him to want to be married to her, if she was honest.

You're still chasing the fantasy when you have reality to contend with.

She had to stop that. She had to put it away now, the haze of fantasy. Had to stop trying to create a happy place where there wasn't one and simply stand up and face reality.

"So…if I say I don't want to be in a normal marriage, and if you can't commit to being faithful to me, does that mean that I have my choice of other lovers, too?"

Red streaked his cheekbones, his fists tightening further, a muscle in his jaw jerking. "Of course," he said, tight. Bitter.

"As long as there are no double standards," she said, keeping her words smooth and calm.

"If I release my hold on you, then I release it. We'll have to be discreet in public, naturally, but what happens behind closed doors is no one's business but our own."

"Ours and the elevator security cameras," she said.

"That will not happen again."

"It won't?"

"An unforgivable loss of control on my part."

"You've had a few of those recently."

She'd meant to spark an angry reply, to keep the fight going, because as long as they were fighting, she didn't ache for him. Wasn't so conscious of the tender emotions he made her feel. And she wasn't so overwhelmed by the need to be skin to skin to him when they were fighting. But she didn't get anger. Instead, she got a bleak kind of pain that echoed in her soul, a hopelessness in his dark eyes that shocked her.

"Yes," he said. "I have. Always with you."

"I don't know how you are in other areas of your life. I only know how you are with me," she said.

His eyes grew darker. "A pity for you. I'm much more pleasant than this, usually."

"I make you misbehave."

He chuckled, no humor in the sound. "You could say that. We should go home."

She nodded. "Yes, we should."

They were in an empty ballroom, and she really would have loved a romantic moment with him here. The chance to dance as the only two people in the room. To go up to his suite and make love. To share a moment with each other that was out of time, apart from reality.

But they'd had their fantasy. Reality was here now, well and truly.

She still didn't want to leave.

Matteo picked up his phone and dialed. "Yes, you can send in the crew now."

She swallowed hard, feeling like they'd missed a key moment. Feeling like she'd missed one.

"Let's go," he said. There was no press now, no one watching to see if he would put his arm around her. So he didn't. He turned and walked ahead, and she followed behind him, her heart sinking.

Matteo didn't know what he wanted. And she didn't, either.

No, that was a lie, she knew what she wanted. But it would require her to start dealing with Matteo as he was, and at some point, it would require him to meet her in the middle, it would require him to drop his guard.

She wasn't sure if either of them could do what needed to be done. Wasn't sure if they ever had a hope of fixing the tangled mess that they'd created.

She wasn't even sure if Matteo wanted to.

CHAPTER NINE

MATTEO WAS TEMPTED to drink again. He hated the temptation. He hated the feeling of temptation full stop. Before Alessia there had been no temptation.

No, that was a lie. The first temptation had been to break the rules and see what the Battaglias were really like. And so he had looked.

And from there, every temptation, every failing, had been tied to Alessia. She was his own personal road to ruin and there were some days he wondered why he bothered to stay off it.

At least he might go up in flames in her arms. At least then heat and fire might be connected with her, instead of that night his father had died.

Yes, he should just embrace it. He should just follow to road to hell and be done with it.

And bring her with you. Bring the baby with you.

Porca miseria. The baby.

He could scarcely think of the baby. He'd hardly had a moment. He felt a little like he was going crazy sometimes, in all honesty. There was everything that was happening with Corretti Enterprises, and he had to handle it. He should go in and try to wrench the reins back from Angelo, should kick Luca out of his position and expose whatever lie he'd told to get there because he was sure the feckless playboy hadn't gotten there on merit alone.

Instead, Matteo was tied up in knots over his wife. Bewitched by a dark-haired vixen who seemed to have him in a death grip.

She was the reason he'd left, the reason he'd gone up to a remote house he owned in Germany that no one knew about. The reason he hadn't answered calls or returned emails. The reason he hadn't known or cared he was being usurped in his position as head of his branch of the family business.

He had to get a handle on it, and he had no idea how. Not when he felt like he was breaking apart from the inside out.

The business stuff, the Corretti stuff, he could handle that. But he found he didn't care to, and that was the thing that got to him.

He didn't even want to think about the baby. But he had to. Didn't want to try to figure out what to do with Alessia, who was still sleeping in the guest bedroom in the palazzo, for heaven's sake.

Something had to be done. Action had to be taken, and for the first time in his life, he felt frozen.

He set his shot glass down on the counter and tilted it to the side before pushing the bottom back down onto the tile, the sound of glass on ceramic loud and decisive. He stalked out of the bar and into the corridor, taking a breath, trying to clear his head.

Alcohol was not the answer. A loss of control was not the answer.

He had to get a grip. On his thoughts. On his actions. He had a business to try to fix, deals to cement. And all he could think about was Alessia.

He turned and faced the window that looked out on

the courtyard. Moonlight was spilling over the grass, a pale shade of gray in the darkness of night.

And then he saw a shadow step into the light. The brightness of the moon illuminated the figure's hair, wild and curling in the breeze. A diaphanous gown, so sheer the light penetrated it, showed the body beneath, swirled around her legs as she turned in a slow circle.

An angel.

And then he was walking, without even thinking, he was heading outside, out to the courtyard, out to the woman who woke something deep in his soul. Something he hadn't known existed before she'd come into his life.

Something he wished he'd never discovered.

But it was too late now.

He opened the back door and stepped out onto the terrace, walking to the balustrade and grasping the stone with his hands, leaning forward, his attention fixed on the beauty before him.

On Alessia.

She was in his system, beneath his skin. So deep he wondered if he could ever be free of her. It would be harder now, all things considered. She was his wife, the mother of his child.

He could send her to live in the *palazzolo* with his mother. Perhaps his mother would enjoy a grandchild.

He sighed and dismissed that idea almost the moment it hit. A grandchild would only make his mother feel old. And would quite possibly give her worry lines thanks to all the crying.

And you would send your child to live somewhere else?

Yes. He was considering it, in all honesty.

What did he know about children? What did he know

about love? Giving it. Receiving it. The kind of nurturing, the father-son bond fostered by his father was one he would just as soon forget.

A bond forged, and ended, by fire.

He threw off the memories and started down the steps that led to the grass. His feet were bare and in that moment he realized he never went outside without his shoes. A strange realization, but he became conscious of the fact when he felt the grass beneath his feet.

Alessia turned sharply, her dark hair cascading over her shoulder in waves. "Matteo."

"What are you doing out here?"

"I needed some air."

"You like being outdoors."

She nodded. "I always have. I hated being cooped up inside my father's house. I liked to take long walks in the sun, away from the…staleness of the estate."

"You used to walk by yourself a lot."

"I still do."

"Even after the attack?" The words escaped without his permission, but he found he couldn't be sorry he'd spoken them.

"Even then."

"How?" he asked, his voice rough. "How did you keep doing that? How did you go on as if nothing had changed?"

"Life is hard, Matteo. People you love die, I know you know about that. People who should love you don't treat you any better than they'd treat a piece of property they were trying to sell for a profit. I've just always tried to see the good parts of life, because what else could I do? I could sit and feel sorry for myself, but it wouldn't change anything. And I've made the choice to stay, so that would be silly. I made the choice to stay and be there for my brothers and sisters, and I can't regret it. That means I have to find happiness in it. And that means I can't cut out my walks just because a couple of horrible men tried to steal them from me."

"And it's that simple?"

"It's not simple at all, but I do it. Because I have to find a way to live my life. My life. It's the only one I have. And I've just learned to try to love it as it is."

"And do you?" he asked. "Do you love it?"

She shook her head. "No." Her voice was a whisper. "But I'm not unhappy all the time. And I think that's something. I mean, it has to count for something."

"What about now? With this?"

"Are you happy?"

"Happiness has never been one of my primary goals. I don't know that I've ever thought about it too closely."

"Everybody wants to be happy," she said.

Matteo put his hands into his pockets and looked over the big stone wall that partitioned his estate from the rest of the world, looked up at the moon. "I want to make something different out of my family. I want to do something more than threaten and terrorize the people in Palermo. Beyond that…does it matter?"

"It does matter. Your happiness matters."

"I haven't been unhappy," he said, and then he wondered if he was lying. "What about you, Alessia?"

"I made a decision, Matteo, and it landed me in a situation that hasn't been entirely comfortable. It was my first big mistake. My first big fallout. And no, not all of it has been happy. But I can't really regret it, either."

"I'm glad you don't regret me."

"Do you regret me?"

"I should. I should regret my loss of control more

than I do—" a theme in his life, it seemed "—but I find I cannot."

"What about tonight? In the elevator? Why did you just walk away?"

"I don't know what to do with us," he said, telling the truth, the honest, raw truth.

"Why do we have to know what we're doing?"

"Because this isn't some casual affair, and it never can be." Because of how she made him feel, how she challenged him. But he wouldn't say that. His honesty had limits, and that was a truth he disliked admitting even to himself. "You're my wife. We're going to have a child."

"And if we don't try, then we're going to spend years sniping at each other and growing more and more bitter, is that better?"

"Better than hurting you? I think so."

"You've hurt me already."

"I did?"

"You won't promise to be faithful to me, you clearly hate admitting that you want me, even though as soon as we touch…Matteo, we catch fire, and you can't deny that. You know I don't have a lot of experience with men, but I know this isn't just normal. I know people don't just feel this way."

"And that's exactly why we have to be careful."

"So we'll be careful. But we're husband and wife, and I think we should try…try for the sake of our child, for our families, to make this marriage work. And I think we owe it to each other to not be unhappy."

"Alessia…"

"Let's keep taking walks, Matteo," she said, her voice husky. She took a step toward him, her hair shimmering in the dim light.

He caught her arm and pulled her in close, his heart pounding hard and fast. "I can't love you."

"You keep saying."

"You need to understand. There is a limit to what we can share. I'll have you in my bed, but that's as far as it goes. This wasn't my choice."

"I wasn't your choice?"

Her words hit him hard, and they hurt. Because no, he hadn't chosen to marry her without being forced into it. But it wasn't for lack of wanting her. If there was no family history. If he had not been the son of one of Sicily's most notorious crime bosses, if there was nothing but him and Alessia and every other woman on earth, he would choose her every time.

But he couldn't discount those things. He couldn't erase what was. He couldn't make his heart anything but cold, not just toward her, but toward anyone. And he couldn't afford to allow a change.

Alessia had no idea. Not of the real reasons why. Not the depth he was truly capable of sinking to. The man underneath the iron control was the very devil, as she had once accused him of being. There was no hero beneath his armor. Only ugliness and death. Only anger, rage, and the ability and willingness to mete out destruction and pain to those who got in his way.

If he had to choose between a life without feeling or embracing the darkness, he would take the blessed numbness every time.

"You know it wasn't."

She thrust her chin into the air. "And that's how you want to start? By reminding me you didn't choose me?"

"It isn't to hurt you, or even to say that I don't want you. But I would never have tied you to me if it wasn't a necessity, and that is not a commentary on you, but on me, and what I'm able to give. There are reasons I never intended to take a wife. I know who I am, but you don't."

"Show me," she said. And he could tell she meant it, with utter conviction. But she didn't know what she was asking. She had no way of knowing. He had given her a window into his soul, a glimpse of the monster that lurked beneath his skin, but she didn't know the half of it.

Didn't know what he was truly capable of. What his father had trained him for.

And what it had all led to seven years ago during the fire that had taken Benito's and Carlo's lives.

That was when he discovered that he truly was the man his father had set out to make him. That was when he'd discovered just how deep the chill went.

He was cold all the way down. And it was only control that held it all in check.

There was only one place he had heat. Only one way he could get warm. But it was a fine line, because he needed the cold. Needed his control, even with it… even with it he was capable of things most men would never entertain thoughts of. But without it he knew the monster would truly be unleashed. That it would consume him.

"I know what I'd like to show you," he said, taking a step toward her, putting his hand on her cheek. She warmed his palm. The heat, the life, that came from her, pouring into him. She shivered beneath his hand, as though his touch had frozen her, and he found it oddly appropriate.

If he kissed her, if he moved nearer to her now, he was making the choice to drag her into the darkness with him. To take what he wanted and use her to his own selfish ends.

He could walk away from her now and he could do the right thing. Protect her, protect their child. Give them both his name and a home, his money. Everything they would need.

She didn't need him in his bed, taking his pleasure in her body, using her to feel warm.

To court the fire and passion that could burn down every last shred of his control. It would be a tightrope walk. Trying to keep the lusts of his body from turning into a desire that overwhelmed his heart.

If he wanted Alessia, there was no other choice.

It was easy with her, to focus on his body. What he wanted from her. Because she called to him, reached him, made him burn in a way no other woman ever had.

With her, though, there was always something else. Something more.

He shut it down. Severed the link. Focused on his body. The burn in his chest, his gut. Everywhere. He was so hard it hurt. Hard with the need for her. To be in her. To taste her.

He could embrace that, and that only. And consign her to a life with a man who would never give her what she deserved.

In this case, he would embrace the coldness in him. Only an utter bastard would do this to her. So it was a good thing that was what he was.

He bent his head and pressed his lips to hers. It wasn't a deep kiss, it was a test. A test for him. To see if he could touch her without losing his mind.

She was soft. So soft. So alive. A taste of pure beauty in a world so filled with ugliness and filth. She reached into him and shone a light on him. On the darkest places in him.

No. He could not allow that. This was only about sex. Only about lust.

"Only me," she said when they parted.

"What?"

"You either have only me, or every other woman you might want, but before you kiss me again, Matteo, you have to make that decision."

His lips still tasted of her skin. "You." It was an easy answer, he found.

She put her hands on his face and drew up on her tiptoes. Her kiss was deep. Filled with the need and passion that echoed inside of his body. He wrapped his arm around her waist and relished every lush detail of holding her. Her soft curves, those generous breasts pressed against his chest. He slipped his hand over her bottom, squeezed her tightly. She was everything a woman should be. Total perfection.

She kissed his jaw, her lips light on his skin, hot and so very tempting. She made him want more, stripped him of his patience. He had always been a patient lover, the kind of lover who worked to ensure his partner's pleasure before taking his own. Because he could. Because even if he took pleasure with his body, his actions were dictated by his mind.

But she challenged that. Made him want so badly to lose himself. To think of nothing but her. Alessia. He was hungry for her in a way he had never hungered for anyone or anything.

He slid his hands over the bodice of her nightgown, cupped her breasts through the thin fabric and found she had nothing on underneath. He could feel her nipples, hard and scarcely veiled by the gauzy material.

He lowered his head and circled one of the tightened buds with his tongue, drew it deep into his mouth. It wasn't enough. He needed to taste her.

Her name pounded through his head in time with the beat of his heart. His need a living, breathing thing.

He gripped the straps of her gown and tugged hard, the top giving way. It fell around her waist, exposing her to him. He smoothed his hand over her bare skin, then lowered his head again, tasting her, filling himself with her.

He dropped to his knees and took the fabric in his hands, tugging it down the rest of the way, ignoring the sound of tearing fabric.

"I liked that nightgown," she said.

"It was beautiful." He kissed her stomach. "But it was not as beautiful as you are."

"You could have asked me to take it off."

"No time," he said, tracing a line from her belly button down to the edge of her panties. "I needed to taste you."

Her response was a strangled "Oh."

"Everywhere." He tugged at the sides of her underwear and drew them down her legs, tossing them to the side. He kissed her hip bone and she shuddered. "I think you should lay down for me, *cara*."

"Why is that?"

"All the better to taste you, *cara mia*."

"Can't you do it from where you are?"

"Not the way I want to."

She complied, her movements slow, shaky. It was a sharp reminder of how innocent she still was.

You let me hold on to some of my innocence.

Her words echoed in his mind as she sank to the

ground in front of him, lying back, resting on her elbows, her legs bent at the knees.

No, he would not allow himself to be painted as some kind of hero. He might have saved her innocence then, but he had spent the past months ensuring that what remained was stripped from her. And tonight, he would continue it.

Keeping her bound to him would continue it.

It was too late to turn back now. Too late to stop. He put his hand on her thigh and parted her legs gently, sliding his fingers over the slickness at the entrance of her body. "Yes," he said, unable to hold the word back, a tremor of need racking his body.

He lowered his head to take in her sweetness, to try to satiate the need he felt for her. A need that seemed to flow through his veins along with his blood, until he couldn't tell which one was sustaining him. Until he was sure he needed both to continue breathing.

He was lost in Alessia. Her flavor, her scent.

He pushed one finger deep inside her while he continued to lavish attention on her with his lips and tongue. She arched up against him, a raw cry escaping her lips. And he took it as her approval, making his strokes with mouth and hands firmer, more insistent.

She drove her fingers deep into his hair, tugging hard, the pain giving him the slight distraction he needed to continue. Helping him hold back his own need.

He slipped a second finger inside of her and her muscles pulsed around him, her body getting stiff beneath him, her sound of completion loud, desperate. Satisfying to him on a level so deep he didn't want to examine it too closely.

He didn't have time to examine it because now he

needed her. Needed his own release, a ferocity that had him shaking. He rose up, pausing to kiss her breasts again, before taking possession of her mouth.

He sat up and tugged his shirt over his head, shrugging his slacks down as quickly as possible, freeing his aching erection.

"Are you ready?" he asked. He needed the answer to be yes.

"Yes."

He looked at her face, at Alessia, and as he did, he pushed inside the tight heat of her body. He nearly lost it then, a cold sweat breaking out over his skin, his muscles tense, pain coursing through him, everything in him trying to hold back. To make this last.

"Matteo."

It was her voice that broke him. Her name on his lips. He started to thrust hard into her, and no matter how he told himself to take it slow, take it gentle, he couldn't. He was a slave to her, to his need.

Finesse was lost. Control was lost.

She arched against him every time he slid home, a small sigh of pleasure on her lips. He lowered his head, buried his face in her neck, breathing her in. Lilacs and skin. And the one woman he would always know. The one woman who mattered.

Sharp nails dug into the flesh on his shoulder, but this time, the pain didn't bring him back. He lost himself, let his orgasm take him over, a rush of completion that took him under completely. He was lost in a wave, and burning. Burning hot and bright, nothing coming to put him out. To give him any relief. All he could do was hang on and weather it. Try to survive a pleasure so intense it bordered on destructive.

And when it was over, she was there, soft arms wrapped around him, her scent surrounding him.

"Will it always be like this?" Alessia's voice was broken with sharp, hard breaths.

He didn't have an answer for her. He couldn't speak. Couldn't think. And he hoped to God it wouldn't always be like this because there was no way his control could withstand it. And at the same time he knew he couldn't live with her and deny himself her body.

He would keep it under control. He would keep his heart separate from his body. He'd done it with women all his life. He'd done it when his father had asked him to learn the family business. The night his father had forced him to dole out punishment to a man in debt to the Corretti family.

He had locked his heart in ice and kept himself from feeling. His actions unconnected to anything but his mind.

He could do it again. He would.

"We should go inside," he said, sitting up, his breathing still ragged.

"Yeah. I'm pretty sure I have grass stains in…places."

He turned to her, a shocked laugh bursting from him. A real laugh. He couldn't remember the last time he'd laughed and meant it. "Well, you should be glad I made quick work of your gown, then."

"You tore it," she said, moving into a standing position and picking up her shredded garment.

"You liked it."

He could see her smile, even in the dim light. "A little."

There was a strange lightness in his chest now, a feeling that was completely foreign to him. As though a rock had been taken off his shoulders.

"I'm hungry," she said.

She started walking back toward the house, and he kept his eyes trained on her bare backside, on the twin dimples low on her back. She was so sexy he was hard again already.

He bent and picked his underwear up from the ground, tugging the black boxer briefs on quickly and following her inside. "Do you want to eat?" he asked.

"Yes, I do." She wandered through the maze of rooms, still naked, and he followed.

"And what would you like?"

"Pasta. Have you got an apron?"

"Have I got an apron?"

"You have a cook, yes?"

"Yes."

"Does he have an apron?"

"She." He opened the pantry door and pulled a short red apron off a hook.

Alessia smiled and slipped the apron over her head, tying it tight. She was a lot taller than the little round woman he'd hired to cook his meals. The apron came down just to the tops of her thighs and it tied in the back, exposing her body to him from that angle.

"Dinner and a show," he said.

She tossed him a playful glare, then started riffling through the cabinets. "What kind of pasta have you got?"

"Fresh in the fridge," he said.

She opened up the stainless-steel fridge and bent down, searching for a few moments before popping up with a container that held pappardelle pasta and another that had marinara sauce.

She put a pan of water on the stove, then put the

sauce in another pan to reheat, and leaned back against the counter, her arms crossed beneath her breasts.

"Didn't you ever hear that a watched pot never boils?"

"No. Who says that?"

"People do," he said.

"Did your mom say it to you?"

"No. A cook we had, I think."

"Oh. It's the kind of thing my mother probably would have said to me someday. If she had lived."

"You miss her still."

"I always will. But you lost your father."

Guilt, ugly, strangling guilt, tightened in his chest. "Yes."

"So you understand."

He shook his head slowly. "I'm not sure I do."

"You don't miss him?"

"Never."

"I know your father was hard to deal with. I know he was…I know he was shady like my father but surely you must—"

"No," he said.

"Oh."

"Will you miss your father?"

"I think so. He's not a wonderful man, but he's the only father I have."

"I would have been better off without one than the one that I had."

Alessia moved to put the pasta into the pan. "You say that with a lot of certainty."

"Trust me on this, Alessia."

They stood in silence until the pasta was done. Matteo got bowls out of the cupboard and set them on the counter and Alessia dished them both a bowl of noodles and sauce.

"Nothing like a little post…you know, snack," she said, lifting her bowl to her lips, her eyes glued to his chest. "You're barely dressed."

"You should talk," he said.

She looked down. "I'm dressed."

"Turn around." She complied, flashing her bare butt to him. "That's not dressed, my darling wife."

"Are you issuing a formal complaint?"

"Not in the least. I prefer you this way."

"Well, the apron is practical. Don't go tearing it off me if you get all impatient." She took a bit of pasta and smiled, her grin slightly impish. It made it hard to breathe.

There was something so normal about this. But it wasn't a kind of normal he knew. Not the kind he'd ever known. He wasn't the sort of man who walked barefoot in the grass and then ate pasta at midnight in his underwear.

He'd never had a chance to be that man. He wondered again at what it would be like if all the things of the world could simply fall away.

"Matteo?"

"Yes?"

"I lost you for a second. Where were you?"

"Just thinking."

"Mmm." She nodded. "I'm tempted to ask you what about but I sort of doubt you'd want to tell me."

"About my father," he said, before he could stop himself.

"You really don't miss him?"

"No." A wall of flame filled his mind. An image of the warehouse, burning. "Never."

"My father has mainly ignored my existence. The only time he's ever really acknowledged me is if he needs something, or if he's angry."

Rage churned in Matteo's stomach. "Did he hit you?"

"Yes. Not beatings or anything, but if I said something that displeased him, he would slap my face."

"He should feel very fortunate he never did so in front of me."

Alessia was surprised at the sudden change in Matteo's demeanor. At the ice in his tone. For a moment, they'd actually been getting along. For a moment, they'd been connecting with clothes on, and that was a rarity for the two of them.

He was willing to try. He'd told her that. And he would be faithful. Those were the only two promises she required from him. Beyond that, she was willing to take her chances.

Willing to try to know the man she'd married. Past her fantasy of him as a hero, as her white knight, and as the man he truly was. No matter what that might mean.

"I handled it," she said.

"It was wrong of him."

She nodded. "I know. But I was able to keep him from ever hitting one of the other kids and that just reinforced why I was there. Yes, I bore the brunt of a lot of it. I had to plan parties and play hostess, I had to take the wrath. But I've been given praise, too."

"I was given praise by my father sometimes, too," Matteo said. There was a flatness to his tone, a darkness in his words that made her feel cold. "He spent some time, when I was a bit older, teaching me how to do business like a Corretti. Not the business we presented to the world. The clean, smooth front. Hotels, fashion houses. All of that was a cover then. A successful cover in its own right, but it wasn't the main source of industry for our family."

"I think…I mean, I think everyone knows that."

"Yes, I'm sure they do. But do you have any idea how far-reaching it was? How much power my father possessed? How he chose to exercise it?"

She shook her head, a sick weight settling in her stomach. "What did he do, Matteo? What did he do to you?"

"To me? Nothing. In the sense that he never physically harmed me."

"There are other kinds of harm."

"Remember I told you I wasn't a criminal? That's on a technicality. It's only because I was never convicted of my crimes."

"What did he do to you, Matteo?" Her stomach felt sick now, and she pushed her bowl of food across the counter, making her way to where Matteo was standing.

"When I was fifteen he started showing me the ropes. The way things worked. He took me on collection calls. We went to visit people who owed him money. Now, my father was only ever involved on the calls where people owed him a lot of money. People who were in serious trouble with him. Otherwise, his men, his hired thugs, paid the visits."

"And he took you on these…visits?"

Matteo nodded, his arms crossed over his bare chest. There was a blankness in his eyes that hurt, a total detachment that froze her inside.

"For the first few weeks I just got to watch. One quick hit to the legs. A warning. A bone-breaking warning, but much better than the kind of thing he and his thugs were willing to do."

"*Dio.* You should never have… He should never have

let you see…" She stopped talking then, because she knew there was more. And that it was worse. She could feel the anxiety coming off him in waves.

She took a step toward him, put her hand on his forearm. It was damp with sweat, his muscles shaking beneath her touch.

"One night he asked me to do it," he said.

His words were heavy in the room, heavy on her. They settled over her skin, coating her, making her feel what he felt. Dirty. Ashamed. She didn't know how she was so certain that was what he felt, but she was.

"What happened?" She tried to keep her voice steady, tried to sound ready to hear it. Tried to be ready to hear it. Because he needed to say it without fear of recrimination from her. Without fear of being told there was something wrong with him.

She knew that as deeply, as innately, as she knew his other feelings.

"I did it," he said. "My father asked me to break a man's legs because he owed the family money. And I did."

CHAPTER TEN

MATTEO WAITED FOR the horror of his admission to sink in. Waited for Alessia to turn from him, to run away in utter terror and disgust. She should. He wouldn't blame her.

He also desperately wanted her to stay.

"Matteo..."

"These hands," he said, holding them out, palms up, "that have touched you, have been used in ways that a man should never use his hands."

"But you aren't like that."

He shook his head. "Clearly I am."

"But you didn't enjoy it."

"No. I didn't enjoy it." He could remember very vividly how it had felt, how the sweat had broken out on his skin. How he had vomited after. His father's men had found that terribly amusing. "But I did it."

"What would your father have done to you if you hadn't?"

He shook his head. "It doesn't matter."

"Yes, it does, Matteo, you were a boy."

"I was a boy, but I was old enough to know that what my father did, what he was, was wrong."

"And you were trapped in it."

"Maybe. And maybe that would be an acceptable excuse for some people, but it's not for me."

"Why not? You were a boy and he abused you. Tell me, and be honest, what did he say he would do to you if you didn't do it?"

Matteo was afraid for one moment that his stomach might rebel against him. "He told me if I couldn't do it to a grown man, there were some children in the village I might practice on."

Alessia's face contorted with utter horror. "Would he have done that?"

"I don't know. But I wasn't going to find out, either."

"He made you do it."

"He manipulated me into doing it, but I did it."

"How?" she asked, her voice a whisper.

"It's easy to do things, anything, when you can shut the emotion down inside yourself. I learned to do that. I learned that there was a place inside of myself as cold as any part of my father's soul. If I went there, it wasn't so hard to do." It was only after that he had broken. In the end, it was both the brokenness, and the cold, that had saved him.

His father had decided he wasn't ready. Didn't want his oldest son, the one poised to take over his empire, undermining his position by showing such weakness.

And after, the way he'd dealt with the knowledge that he'd lived with a monster, the way he'd dealt with knowing that he was capable of the very same atrocities, was to freeze out every emotion. He would not allow himself to want, to crave power or money in the way his father did. Passion, need, greed, were the enemy.

Then he'd seen Alessia. And he had allowed her a place inside him, a place that was warm and bright, one that he could retreat to. He saw happiness through her eyes when he watched her. His attraction to her not physical, but emotional. He let a part of himself live through her.

And that day when he'd seen those men attacking her, the monster inside him had met up against passion that had still existed in the depths of him, and had combined to create a violence that was beyond his control. One that frightened him much more than that moment of controlled violence in his father's presence had.

More even than that final act, the one that had removed his father from his life forever.

Because it had been a choice he'd made. It had been fueled by his emotion, by his rage, and no matter how deserving those men had been…it was what it said about himself that made him even more certain that it must never happen again. That he must never be allowed to feel like that.

"Do you see?" he asked. "Do you see what kind of man I am?"

She nodded slowly. "Yes. You're a good man, with a tragic past. And the things that happened weren't your fault."

"When I went back home the day of your attack, there was still blood all over me. I walked in, and my father was there. He looked at me, saw the evidence of what had happened. Then he smiled, and he laughed," Matteo spat. "And he said to me, 'Looks like you're ready now. I always knew you were my son.'"

That moment was burned into his brain, etched into his chest. Standing there, shell-shocked by what had happened, by what he had done. By what had nearly happened to Alessia. And having his father act as though he'd made some sort of grand passage into manhood. Having him be proud.

"He was wrong, Matteo, you aren't like him. You were protecting me, you weren't trying to extort money out of those men. It's not the same thing."

"But it's the evidence of what I'm capable of. My father had absolute conviction in what he did. He could justify it. He believed he was right, Alessia, do you understand that? He believed with conviction that he had a right to this money, that he had the right to harm those who didn't pay what he felt he was owed. All it takes is a twist of a man's convictions."

"But yours wouldn't be..."

"They wouldn't be?" He almost told her then, but he couldn't. The words he could never say out loud. The memory he barely allowed himself to have. "You honestly believe that? Everyone is corruptible, *cara.* The only way around it is to use your head, to learn what is right, and to never ever let your desire change wrong to right in your mind. Because that's what desire does. My father's desire for money, your father's desire for power, made them men who will do whatever it takes to have those things. Regardless of who they hurt. And I will never be that man."

"You aren't that man. You acted to save me, and you did it without thought to your own safety. Can't you see how good that is? How important?"

"I don't regret what I did," he said, choosing his words carefully. "I had a good reason to do it. But how many more good reasons could I find? If it suited me, if I was so immersed in my own needs, in my own desires, what else might I consider a good reason? So easily, Alessia, I could be like Benito was."

"No, that isn't true."

"Why do you think that?"

"Because you're...good."

He laughed. "You are so certain?"

"Yes. Yes, Matteo, I'm certain you're good. Do you know what I remember from that day? The way you held me after. Do you know how long it had been since someone had tried to comfort me? Since someone had wiped away my tears? Not since my mother. Before that, I had done all of the comforting, and then when I needed someone? You were there. And you told me it would be okay. More than that, you made it okay. So don't tell me you aren't good. You are."

He didn't believe her, because she didn't know the whole truth. But he wanted to hold her words tightly inside of him, wanted to cling to her vision of him, didn't want her to see him any other way.

"I got blood on your face," he said, his voice rough. "That day when I wiped your tears."

She looked at him with those dark, beautiful eyes. "It was worth it." She took a step toward him, taking his hand in hers. "Come on. Let's go to bed."

And he was powerless to do anything but follow her.

Alessia woke the next morning with a bone-deep feeling of contentment. She noticed because she'd never felt anything like it before. Had never felt like things were simply right in the world. That there wasn't anything big left to accomplish. That she just wanted to stay and live in the moment. A moment made sweeter by the fact that there was nothing pressing or horrible looming in the future.

Then she became conscious of a solid, warm weight at her back, a hand resting on her bare hip. And she was naked, which was unusual because she normally slept in a nightgown.

A nightgown that was torn.

A smile stretched across her face and she rolled over to face Matteo. Her lover. Her husband. He was still sleeping, the lines on his forehead smoothed, his expression much more relaxed than it ever was when he was awake.

She leaned over and kissed his cheek, the edge of his mouth. She wanted him again. It didn't matter how many times he'd turned to her in the middle of the night, she wanted him again. It didn't matter if they had sex, or if he just touched her, but she wanted him. His presence, his kiss, him breathing near her.

This moment was one she'd dreamed of for half of her life. This moment with Matteo Corretti. Not with any other man.

She'd woken up next to him once before, but she hadn't been able to savor it. Her wedding had been looming in the not-too-distant future and guilt and fear had had her running out the door before Matteo had woken up.

But not this morning. This morning, she would stay with him until he woke. And maybe she would share his bed again tonight. And every night after that. He was her husband, after all, and it only seemed right that they sleep together.

They were going to try to make a real marriage out of a legal one.

He'll never love you.

She ignored the chill that spread through her veins when that thought invaded her mind. It didn't matter. She wouldn't dwell on it. Right now, she had a hope at a future she could be happy with. Matteo in her bed. In her life.

And she was having his baby. At some point, that

would sink in and not just be a vague, sort of frightening, sort of wonderful thought.

But right now, she was simply lingering in the moment. Not wondering if Matteo's feelings would ever change, not worrying about changing diapers.

He shifted then, his eyes fluttering open. "Good morning," he said. So much different than his greeting the morning after their wedding.

"Good morning, handsome."

"Handsome?"

"You are. And I've always wanted to say that." *To you.*

"Alessia…you are something."

"I know, right?" Matteo rolled over onto his back and she followed him, resting her breasts on his chest, her chin propped up on her hands. "Last night was wonderful."

He looked slightly uncomfortable. Well, she imagined she wasn't playing the part of blasé sophisticate very well, but in her defense…she wasn't one. She was a woman with very little sexual experience having the time of her life with a man who'd spent years as the star attraction in her fantasies. It was sort of hard to be cool in those circumstances.

He kissed her, cupping her chin with his thumb and forefinger. She closed her eyes and hummed low in her throat. "You're so good at that," she said when they parted. "I feel like I have a post-orgasm buzz. Is that a thing?"

He rolled onto his side again and moved into a sitting position, not bothering to cover himself with the blankets.

"I don't know," he said. "I can't say I've ever experienced it."

"Oh." That hurt more than it should have. Not because she wanted him to have experienced post-orgasm buzz with anyone else, but because she wished he'd experienced it with her.

"What is it, *cara*?"

"Nothing." She put her palm flat on his chest and leaned in, her lips a whisper from his. Then his phone started vibrating on the nightstand.

"I have to take that," he said, moving away from her. He turned away from her and picked it up. "Corretti." Every muscle in his back went rigid. "What the hell do you want, Alessandro?"

Alessia's stomach rolled. Alessandro. She would rather not think about him right at the moment. She felt bad for the way things had ended. He'd been nice enough to her, distant, and there had been no attraction, but he'd been decent. And she'd sort of waited until the last minute to change her mind.

She got out of bed and started hunting for some clothes. There was nothing. Only a discarded red apron that she knew from last night didn't cover a whole lot.

"I'm busy, you can't just call a meeting and expect me to drop everything and come to you like a lapdog. Maybe you're used to your family treating you that way, but you don't get that deference from me."

Alessia picked the apron up and put it on. It was better than nothing.

Matteo stood from the bed, completely naked, pacing the room. She stood for a moment and just watched. The play of his muscles beneath sleek, olive skin was about the sexiest thing she'd ever seen.

"Angelo?" The name came out like a curse. "What are you doing meeting with that bastard?" A pause. "It was a commentary on his character, not his birth. Fine. Noon. Salvatore's."

He pushed the end-call button and tossed the phone down on the bed, continuing to prowl the room. "That was Alessandro."

"I got that."

"He wants me to come to a meeting at our grandfather's. With Angelo, of all people."

"He is your cousin. He's family, and so is Alessandro."

"I have enough family that I don't like. Why would I add any more?"

"You don't even like your brothers?"

"No."

"Why don't you like your brothers?"

"Because if I ever do seem to be in danger of being sucked into the Corretti mind-set it's when we start playing stupid business games."

"But they're your family."

"My family is a joke. We're nothing but criminals and selfish assholes who would sell each other out for the right price. And we've all done it."

"So maybe someone needs to stop," she said, her voice soft.

"I don't know if we can."

"Maybe you should be the first one?"

"Alessia…"

"Look, I know I'm not a business mind, and I know I don't understand the dynamics of your family, but if you hate this part of it so much, then end it."

"I need to get dressed."

"I'll go make breakfast," she said. "I'm dressed for it."

"You might give my staff a shock."

"Oh—" her cheeks heated "—right, on second thought I might go back to my room."

"That's fine. And after that, you can ask Giancarlo if he would have your things moved into the master suite."

"You want me to move in?"

"Yes. You tramping back to your room in an apron is going to get inconvenient quickly, don't you think?"

Alessia felt her little glow of hope grow. "Yeah. Definitely it would be a little bit inconvenient. I would love to move into your room."

"Good." He leaned in and dropped a kiss on her lips. "Now, I have to get ready."

When Salvatore had been alive, Matteo had avoided going to his grandparents' home as often as he could. The old man was a manipulator and Matteo was rarely in the mood for his kind of mind games.

Still, whenever his grandmother had needed him, he had been there. They all had. This had long been neutral ground for that very reason. For Teresa. Which made it a fitting setting for what they were doing today.

Matteo walked over the threshold and was ushered back toward the study. He didn't see his grandmother, or any of the staff. Only a hostile-looking Alessandro, and Angelo sitting in a chair, a drink in hand.

"What was so important that you needed to speak to me?"

"Sorry to interrupt the blissful honeymoon stage with your new bride. I assume she actually went through with your wedding," Alessandro said.

"She did," he said.

Angelo leaned back in one of the high-backed chairs, scanning the room. "So this is what old Corretti money buys. I think I prefer my homes."

"We all prefer not to be here," Matteo said. "Which begs the question again, why are we?"

"You married Alessia, I can only assume that means you've cut a deal with her father?"

"Trade in and out of Sicily is secured for the Correttis and the docklands are ours. The revitalization project is set to move forward."

"Handy," Angelo said, leaning forward, "because I secured a deal with Battaglia, as well." Angelo explained the details of the housing development he was working on, eased by Battaglia's connections.

"And what does that have to do with us?"

"Well," Angelo continued, "it can have a lot to do with you. Assuming you want to take steps to unify the company."

"We need to unify," Alessandro said, his tone uncompromising. "Otherwise, we'll just spend the next forty years tearing everything apart. Like our fathers did."

Matteo laughed, a black, humorless sound. "You are my cousin, Alessandro, but I have no desire to die in a warehouse fire with you."

"That's why this has to end," Alessandro said. "I have a proposal to make. One that will see everyone in the family with an equal share of power. It will put us in the position to make the company, the family, strong again. Without stooping to criminal activity to accomplish it."

Alessandro outlined his plan. It would involve everyone, including their sisters, giving everyone equal share in the company and unifying both sides for the first time.

"This will work as long as this jackass is willing to

put some of the extra shares he's acquired back into the pot," Alessandro said, indicating Angelo.

"I said I would," Angelo responded, his acquiescence surprising. Equally surprising was the lack of venom and anger coming from the other man. Or maybe not. Matteo had to wonder if Angelo had met a woman. He knew just the kind of change a woman could effect on a man.

"There you are," Alessandro said. "Are you with us?"

Matteo thought of the fire. Of the last time he'd seen his father. Of all that greed had cost. This was his chance to put an end to that. To start fresh. The past could never be erased, it would always be there. But the future could be new. For him. For Alessia. For their child.

He had too many other things in his life, good things, to waste any effort holding on to hatred he didn't even have the energy to feel.

He extended his hand and Alessandro took it, shaking it firmly. Then Matteo extended his hand to Angelo and, for the first time, shook his hand. "I guess that means you're one of us now," he said to Angelo. "I don't know if you should be happy about that or not."

"I'll let you know," Angelo said. "But so far, it doesn't seem so bad."

"All right, where do I sign?"

CHAPTER ELEVEN

MATTEO WAS EXHAUSTED by the time he got around to driving back to his palazzo. Dealing with Alessandro, going to his grandfather's house, had been draining in a way he had not anticipated. And yet, in some ways, there was a weight lifted. The promise of a future that held peace instead of violence. The first time his future had ever looked that way.

And he had Alessia to go home to. That thought sent a kick of adrenaline through him, made him feel like there was warmth in his chest. Made him feel like he wasn't so cold.

He left the car parked in front of his house with the keys in the ignition. One of his staff would park it for him later. And if not, he didn't mind it being there in the morning. But he couldn't put off seeing Alessia, not for another moment. He needed to see her for some reason, needed affirmation of who he was. To see her face light up. To have someone look at him like they didn't know who and what he was.

Alessandro and Angelo didn't know about his past, but they knew enough about the family to have an idea. Alessandro certainly hadn't escaped a childhood with Carlo without gaining a few scars of his own.

But Alessia looked at him like none of that mattered. Like she didn't know or believe any of it.

That isn't fair. She should know.

No, he didn't want her to know. He wanted to keep being her knight. To have one person look and see the man he might have been if it weren't for Benito Corretti.

He would change what it meant to be a Corretti for his child. He would never let them see the darkness. Never.

A fierce protectiveness surged through him, for the first time a true understanding of what it meant for Alessia to be pregnant.

A child. His child.

He prowled through the halls of the palazzo and found Alessia in a sitting room, a book in her hands, her knees drawn up to her chest. She was wearing a simple sundress that had slid high up her thighs. He wanted nothing more than to push it up the rest of the way, but he also found he didn't want to disturb her. He simply wanted to look.

She raised her focus then, and her entire countenance changed, her face catching the sunlight filtering through the window. Her dark eyes glittered, her smile bright. Had anyone else ever looked at him like that?

He didn't think they had.

"How did the meeting go?"

"We called each other names. Insulted each other's honor and then shook hands. So about as expected."

She laughed. "Good, I guess."

"Yes. We've come up with a way to divide Corretti Enterprises up evenly. A way for everyone to get their share. It's in everyone's best interests, really. Especially the generation that comes after us. Which I now have a vested interest in."

She smiled, the dimple on her left cheek deepening. "I suppose you do. And…I'm glad you do."

He moved to sit on the couch, at her feet, then he leaned in. "Can you feel the baby move yet?"

She shook her head. "No. The doctor said it will feel like a flutter, though."

"May I?" he asked, stretching his hand out, just over the small, rounded swell of her stomach.

"Of course."

He swallowed hard and placed his palm flat on her belly. It was the smallest little bump, but it was different than it had been. Evidence of the life that was growing inside her. A life they'd created.

She was going to be the mother of his child. She deserved to know. To really understand him. Not to simply look at him and see an illusion. He'd given her a taste of it earlier, but his need for that look, that one she reserved just for him, that look he only got from her, had prevented him from being honest. Had made him hold back the most essential piece of just why he was not the man to be her husband.

The depth to which he was capable of stooping.

Because no matter how bright the future had become, the past was still filled with shadows. And until they were brought into the sunlight, their power would remain.

"There is something else," he said, taking his hand from her stomach, curling it into a fist. His skin burned.

"About the meeting?"

"No," he said. "Not about the meeting."

"What about?"

"About me. About why…about why it might not be the best idea for you to try to make a marriage with me. About the limit of what I can give."

"Matteo, I already told you how I feel about what happened with your father."

"By that you mean when he took me on errands?"

"Well…yes."

"So, you don't mean what happened the night of the warehouse fire that killed him and Carlo."

"No. No one knows what happened that night."

"That isn't true," he said, the words scraping his throat raw. "Someone knows."

"Who?" she asked, but he could tell she already knew.

"I know."

"How?"

"Because, *cara mia*, I was there."

"You were there?"

He nodded slowly. Visions of fire filled his mind. Fire and brimstone, such an appropriate vision. "Yes. I was there to try to convince my father to turn over the holdings of Corretti to me entirely. I wanted to change things. To end the extortion and scams. All of it. But he wouldn't hear it. You see, at the time, he was still running criminal schemes, using the hotels, which I was managing, to help launder money. To help get counterfeit bills into circulation, into the right hands. Or wrong hands as the case may have been. I didn't want any part of it, but as long as my father was involved in the running of the corporation, that was never going to end. I wanted out."

"Oh," Alessia said, the word a whisper, as if she knew what was coming next. He didn't want her to guess at it, because he wanted, perversely, for her to believe it impossible. For her to cling to the white-knight image and turn away from the truth he was about to show her.

"I don't know how the fire started. But the warehouse was filled with counterfeiting plates, and their printing presses. That's one way to make money, right? Print your own."

He looked down at his hands, his heart pounding hard, his stomach so tight he could hardly breathe. "The fire spread quickly. I don't know where Carlo was when it broke out. But I was outside arguing with my father. And he turned and…and he looked at the blaze and he started to walk toward it."

Matteo closed his eyes, the impression of flames burning bright behind his eyelids. "I told him if he went back into that damned warehouse to rescue those plates, I would leave him to it. I told him to let it burn. To let us start over. I told him that if he went back, I would be happy to let him burn with it all, and then let him continue to burn in hell."

"Matteo…no." She shook her head, those dark eyes glistening with tears. She looked horrified. Utterly. Completely. The light was gone. His light.

"Yes," he said, his voice rough. "Can you guess what he did?"

"What?" The word was scarcely a whisper.

"He laughed. And he said, 'Just as I thought, you are my son.' He told me that no matter how I dressed it up, no matter how I pretended I had morals, I was just as bloodthirsty as he was. Just as hungry for vengeance and to have what I thought should be mine, in the fashion I saw fit. And then he walked back into the warehouse."

"What did you do?"

Matteo remembered the moment vividly. Remembered waiting for a minute, watching, letting his father's words sink in. Recognizing the truth of them. And embracing them fully. He was his father's son. And if he, or anyone else, stood a chance of ever breaking free, it had to end.

The front end of the warehouse had collapsed and Matteo had stood back, looking on, his hand curled around his phone. He could have called emergency services. He could have tried to save Benito.

But he hadn't. Instead, he'd turned his back, the heat blistering behind him, a spark falling onto his neck, singeing his flesh. And then he'd walked away. And he hadn't looked back, not once. And in that moment he was the full embodiment of everything his father had trained him to be.

He'd found out about Carlo's and Benito's deaths over the phone the next day. And there had been no more denial, no more hiding. No more believing that somewhere deep down he was good. That he had a hope of redemption.

He had let it burn in the warehouse.

"I let him die," he said. "I watched him go in, watched as the front end of the building collapsed. I could have called someone, and I didn't. I made the choice to be the man he always wanted me to be. The man I always was. I turned and I walked away. I did just as I promised I would do. I let him burn, with all of his damned money. And I can't regret the choice. He made his, I made mine. And everyone is free of him now. Of both of them."

Alessia was waxen, her skin pale, her lips tinged blue. "I don't know what to say."

"Do you see, Alessia? This is what I was trying to tell you. What you need to understand." He leaned forward, extending his hand to her, and she jerked back. Her withdrawal felt like a stab to the chest, but it was no less than he deserved. "I'm not the hero of the story. I am nothing less than the villain."

She understood now, he could see it, along with a dawning horror in her eyes that he wanted to turn away from. She was afraid. Afraid of him. He wasn't her knight anymore.

"I think maybe I should wait a few days to have my things moved into your room," she said after a long moment of silence.

He nodded. "That might be wise." Pain assaulted him and he tried to ignore it, tried to grit his teeth and sit with a neutral expression.

"I'll talk to you later?"

"Of course." He sat back on the couch and watched her leave. Then he closed his eyes and tried to picture her smile again. Tried to recapture the way she'd looked at him just a few moments before. But instead of her light, all he could see was a haunted expression, one he had put there.

Alessia was gasping for breath by the time she got to her bedroom. She closed the door behind her and put her hand on her chest, felt her heart hammering beneath her palm.

Matteo had let Benito and Carlo die.

She sucked in a shuddering breath and started pacing back and forth, fighting the tears that were threatening to spill down her cheeks.

She replayed what he had said again in her mind. He hadn't forced Benito or Carlo back into the burning building. Hadn't caused them harm with his own hands.

He had walked away. He had washed his hands and walked away, accepting in that moment whatever the consequences might be.

Alessia walked over to her bed and sat on the edge of it. And she tried to reconcile the man downstairs with the man she'd always believed him to be.

The man beneath the armor wasn't perfect. He was wounded, damaged beyond reason. Hurting. And for the first time she really understood what that meant. Understood how shut down he was. How much it would take to reach him.

And she wasn't sure if she could do it. Wasn't sure she had the strength to do it.

It had been so much easier when he was simply the fantasy. When he was the man she'd made him be in her mind. When he was an ideal, a man sent to ride to her rescue.

She'd put him in that position. From the moment she'd first seen him. Then after he had rescued her, she'd assigned him that place even more so.

The night of her bachelorette party…

"Damn you, Alessia," she said to herself.

Because she'd done it then, too. She'd used Matteo as part of her fantasy, as part of the little world she'd built up in her mind to keep herself from crumbling. She had taken him on her own terms, used him to fill a void, and never once had she truly looked into his. Never once had she truly tried to fill it.

Being there for Matteo, knowing him, meant knowing this. Meant knowing that he had faced down a terrible decision, and that he had made a terrible choice.

The wrong choice, at least in traditional terms of right and wrong.

Very few people would hold it against him that he hadn't raced into the burning building after his father, but to know that he had also not called for help. That he had meant what he'd said to his father. That he would let him, and all of it, burn. In flame. In greed. And he had.

Her lover, her Matteo, had a core of ice and steel. Getting through it, finding his heart, might be impossible. She faced that, truly faced it, for the first time.

Matteo might never love. The ending might not really be happy. The truth was, she lived her life in denial. The pursuit of contentment at least, at all costs, and if that required denial, then she employed it, and she'd always done it quite effectively.

Walking down the aisle toward Alessandro had been the first time she'd truly realized that if she didn't do something, if she didn't stop it, it wouldn't stop itself.

She wrapped her arms around herself, cold driving through her. She had another choice to make. A choice about Matteo. And she wouldn't make it lightly.

There was no sugarcoating this. No putting on blinders. It was what the wives of these Corretti men, of the Battaglia men, had always done. Looked the other way while their husbands sank into destruction and depravity, but she wouldn't do that.

If she was going to be Matteo's wife, in every sense, then she would face it all head-on.

It was empty to make a commitment to someone if you were pretending they were someone they weren't. It was empty to say you loved someone if you only loved a mirage.

Love. She had been afraid of that word in connection to Matteo for so long, and yet, she knew that was what it was. What it had always been. At least, she'd loved what she'd known about him.

Now she knew more. Now she was going to have to figure out whether she loved the idea, or the man.

* * *

Matteo lay in bed. It was past midnight. Hours since he'd last seen Alessia. Hours since they'd spoken.

His body ached, a bleeding wound in his chest where his heart should be. The absence of the heart was nothing new, but the pain was. He had lived in numbness for so long, and Alessia had come back into his life.

Then things had started to change. He'd started to want again. Started to feel again. And now he felt like he was torn open, like the healed, scarred-over, nerveless pieces of himself had been scrubbed raw again. Like he was starting over, starting back at the boy he'd been. The one who had been taken into his father's hands and molded, hard and cruel, into the image the older man had wanted to see.

He felt weak. Vulnerable in a way he could never recall feeling at any point in his life.

Alessia had walked away from him, and he couldn't blame her. In a way, it comforted him. Because at least she hadn't simply blithely walked on in her illusion of who she wanted him to be. She had heard his words. And she'd believed them.

He should be completely grateful for that. Should be happy that she knew. That she wasn't committed to a man who didn't truly exist.

But he couldn't be happy. Selfishly, he wanted her back. Wanted the light and heat and smiles. Wanted one person to look at him and see hope.

"Matteo?"

He looked up and saw Alessia standing in the doorway, her dark hair loose around her shoulders.

"Yes?" He pushed into a sitting position.

"I felt like I owed it to you to really think about what you said."

"And you owed it to you."

She nodded. "I suppose I did."

"And what conclusion have you come to?"

"You aren't the man I thought you were."

The words hit him with the force of a moving truck. "No. I'm sure in all of your fantasies about me you never once dreamed that I was a killer."

She shook her head. "I didn't. I still don't think you're that. I don't think you're perfect, either, but I don't think it was ever terribly fair of me to try to make you perfect. You had your own life apart from me. Your own experiences. My mistake was believing that everything began and ended during the times our eyes met over the garden wall. In my mind, when you held me after the attack, you went somewhere hazy, somewhere I couldn't picture. I didn't think about what you did after, not really. I didn't think of the reality of you returning home, covered in blood. I didn't think about what your father might have said to you. I knew Benito Corretti was a bad man, but for some reason I never imagined how it might have touched you. I only ever pictured you in the context of my world, my dreams and where you fit into them. It was my mistake, not yours."

"But I wouldn't have blamed you if you never imagined that. No one did. Not even my family, I'm certain of that."

"Still, I wasn't looking at you like you were a real person. And you were right to make me see."

"Alessia, if you want—"

"Let me finish. I see now. I see you, Matteo, not just the fantasy I created. And I don't want to walk away. I want to stay with you. I want to make a family with you."

"You trust me to help raise your child after you found out what I'm capable of?"

"That night of your life can't live in isolation. It's connected to the rest of your life, to all of it. To who your father was, the history of what he'd done to other people, to what he'd done to you."

"He never did anything to me, he just—"

"He forced you to do things you would never have done. He made you violate your conscience, over and over again until it was scarred. He would have turned you into a monster."

"He did, Alessia. That's the point. He did."

She shook her head. "You put a stop to it."

"I had to," he said, his voice rough. "I had to because you don't just walk away from the Correttis. It's not possible. My father would not have released his hold."

"I know. I understand."

"And you absolve me?"

"You don't need my absolution."

"But do I have it?" he asked, desperate for it, craving it more than his next breath.

She nodded. "If I have yours."

"For what?"

"For what I did. For not telling you about Alessandro. For agreeing to marry him in the first place. For trapping you in this marriage."

"You didn't trap me."

"You said—"

"Alessia, I have been manipulated into doing things far worse than marrying you, and I have done it with much greater coercion. A little news piece on what a jerk I am for not making your child legitimate was hardly going to force my hand."

"Then why did you do it?"

"To cement the deal. To give our child my name. All things I could have walked away from."

"Then forgive me, at least, for lying to you. For leaving you in the hotel room."

"I do. I was angry about it, but only because it felt so wrong to watch you walking toward him. To know that he would have you and not me. If I had known that there was a deal on the table that could be secured by marriage to you I would have been the one volunteering for the job."

A ghost of a smile touched her lips. "When my father first told me about the deal with the Correttis, that it would be sealed by marriage, I said yes immediately. I was so sure it would be you. And when it was Alessandro who showed up at the door to talk terms the next day I thought…I thought I would die."

"Waiting for your knight to rescue you?"

"Yes. I was. But I've stopped doing that now. I need to learn to rescue myself. To make my own decisions."

"You've certainly been doing that over the past couple of months."

"I have. And some of them have been bad, ill-timed decisions, but they've been mine. And I want you to know that I've made another decision."

"What is that?"

"You're my husband. And I'll take you as you are. Knowing your past, knowing the kind of man you can be. I want you to understand that I'm not sugarcoating it, or glossing over the truth. I understand what you did. I understand that…that you don't feel emotion the same way that I do. The same way most people do."

"Do you really understand that? I keep it on a leash for a reason, Alessia, a very important reason, and I won't compromise it."

She nodded. "I know."

"And still you want to try? You want to be my wife? To let me have a hand in raising our child?"

"Yes. No matter what, you're the father of my child, Matteo, and there is no revelation that can change that. I don't want to change that."

"How can you say that with such confidence?"

"Because no matter what you might have done, you aren't cruel."

She leaned in and he took a strand of her hair between his thumb and forefinger. Soft like silk. He wanted to feel it brushing over his skin. Wanted to drown out this moment, drown out his pain, with physical pleasure.

"Am I not?" he asked.

"No."

"You're wrong there," he said. "So very wrong. I am selfish, a man who thinks of his own pleasure, his own comfort, above all else. No matter how I pretend otherwise."

"That isn't true."

"Yes, it is. Even now, all I can think about is what your bare skin will feel like beneath my hands. All I want is to lose myself in you."

"Then do it."

His every muscle locked up, so tight it was painful. "Alessia, don't."

"What?"

"Don't sacrifice yourself for me!" he roared. "Don't do this because you feel sorry for me."

"I'm not." She took a step toward him. "I want this because I want to be close to you. To know you. To be your wife in every way." A smile tugged at the corners of her lips. "I'm also not opposed to the orgasms you're so good at giving me. This is by no means unselfish on my part, trust me."

His skin felt like it was burning. Or perhaps that was the blood beneath his skin. Either way, he felt like he would be consumed by his need. His desire. Passion he swore he would never allow himself to feel.

Emotion he swore he would never feel.

But in this moment with Alessia, her eyes so bright and intense, so honest, he could hold back nothing. Deny her nothing. Least of all this.

She knew the truth, and still she wanted him. Not as a perfect figure, a knight in shining armor, but as the man he was. It was a gift he didn't deserve, a gift he should turn away, because he had no right to it.

But he had spoken the truth. He was selfish. Far too selfish to do anything but take what was on offer.

"Show me you want me." His words were rough, forced through his tightened throat. "Show me you still want me." Those words echoed through his soul, tearing through him, leaving him raw and bleeding inside.

Alessia wrapped one arm around his neck, her fingers laced in his hair, and put the other on his cheek. She pressed a kiss to his lips, soft, gentle. Purposeful. "Always."

There was no hope of him being noble, not now, not tonight. But then, that shouldn't be a surprise. He didn't do noble. He didn't do selfless. And it wouldn't start now.

He kissed her, deep and hard, his body throbbing, his heart raging. He wrapped his arms around her and pulled her in close, reveling in the feel of her. Touching Alessia was a thrill that he didn't think would ever become commonplace. He had hungered for her touch, for her closeness, for so many years, and he knew his desire for it would never fade.

If anything, it only grew.

He slid his hands down her waist, over her hips, her thighs, and gripped her hard, tugging her up into his arms, those long, lean legs wrapping around his waist as he walked them both to the bed.

Alessia started working on the knot on his tie, her movements shaky and clumsy and all the sexier for it. He sat on the bed, and Alessia remained on top of him, now resting on her knees. She tugged hard on the tie and managed to get it off, then started working at the buttons on his shirt.

He continued to kiss her, deep and desperate, pushing her dress up, past her hips, her waist, her breasts, and over her head. Her lips were swollen from kissing, her face flushed, her hair disheveled from where he'd run his fingers through it.

She looked wild, free, the most beautiful thing he'd ever seen. But then, Alessia had been, from the moment he'd seen her, the most beautiful sight he'd ever beheld. And then, when his vision of her had been one of innocence, protectiveness, it had been all about that glow that was inside of her.

He could see it, along with the outer beauty that drove him to madness. Now that their lives, their feelings, had no more innocence left, he could still see it. Still feel it deep inside of him, an ache that wouldn't ease.

She pushed his shirt off his shoulders, the buttoned cuffs snagging on his hands. A little growl escaped her lips. He wrapped one hand around her waist to hold her steady and lay back on the bed, leaving her perched over him, then he undid the buttons as quickly as possible and tossed the shirt to the side.

Alessia moved away from him, standing in front of the bed, in front of him. She met his eyes, and put her hands behind her back, her movement quick. Her bra loosened, then fell, baring her breasts to him. His stomach tightened, he could barely breathe.

She smiled, then hooked her fingers into the sides of her panties and tugged them off.

He wanted to say something. To tell her how beautiful she was, how perfect. But he couldn't speak. He could only watch, held completely under her spell.

She approached the bed, her fingers deft on his belt buckle, making quick work of his pants and underwear, and leaving him as naked as she was.

"You're so much more…just so much more than I ever imagined," she said. "I made fantasies about you, but they were a girl's fantasies. I'm not a girl, though, I'm a woman. And I'm glad you're not only that one-dimensional imagining I had of you. I'm glad you're you."

She leaned in, running the tip of her finger along the length of his rock-hard erection. Every thought ran from his head like water, his heart thundering in his ears.

Lush lips curved into a wicked smile and she leaned in, flicking her tongue over the head of his shaft. "I've never done this before. So you have to tell me if I do it wrong."

"You couldn't possibly do it wrong," he said, not sure how he managed to speak at all. It shouldn't be possible when he couldn't breathe.

And she proved him right. Her mouth on him hot, sweet torture that streaked through his veins like flame. But where other flames destroyed, this fire cleansed. He sifted his fingers through her hair, needing an anchor.

Needing to touch her, to be a part of this. Not simply on the receiving end of the pleasure she was giving him.

He needed more. Needed to taste her, too.

"Get on the bed," he growled.

She complied, not abandoning her task as she got up onto the bed, onto her knees. He sat up and she raised her head, her expression confused. Then he grasped her hips and maneuvered her around so that she was over him, so that he could taste her like she was tasting him.

She gasped when his tongue touched her.

"Don't stop," he said, the command rough, firmer than he'd intended it to be, but she didn't seem to mind.

He slipped a finger inside of her while he pleasured her with his tongue, and she gasped again, freezing for a moment before taking him fully into her mouth. His head fell back, a harsh groan on his lips.

"I can't last much longer," he said.

"Neither can I," she panted, moving away from him, returning a moment later, her thighs on either side of his. She bent down and pressed a kiss to his lips. "Ready?" she asked.

"More than."

She positioned her body so that the head of his erection met with her slick entrance, then she lowered herself down onto him, so slowly he thought he would be consumed utterly by the white heat moving through him.

She moved over him, her eyes locked with his. He grasped her hips, meeting each of her thrusts, watching her face, watching her pleasure.

He moved his hand, pressed his palm flat over her stomach, then slid it upward to cup one of her breasts. He liked the view. Liked being able to see all of her as she brought them both to the brink.

She leaned forward, kissing his lips, her breath getting harsher, faster, her movements more erratic. He lowered his hand back to her hip and strengthened his own movements, pushing them farther, faster.

They both reached the edge at the same time, and when he tipped over into the abyss, all he could do was hold on to her as release rushed through him like a wave, leaving no part of him untouched. No part of him hidden.

When the storm passed, Alessia was with him.

She rested her head on his chest, her breath hot on his skin. He wrapped his arms tight around her, held her to him.

He would keep her with him, no matter what.

Yes, he was a selfish bastard.

But in this moment, he couldn't regret it. If it meant keeping Alessia, he never would.

CHAPTER TWELVE

ALESSIA WOKE UP a few hours later, feeling cold. She wasn't sure why. It was a warm evening, and she had blankets, and Matteo, to keep her warm.

Matteo.

He made her heart feel like it was cracking apart. She wanted to reach him. Wanted to touch him. Really touch him, not just with her hands on his skin, but to touch his heart.

This was so close to what she wanted. A baby. The man she loved. *Dio*, she loved him so much. It made her hurt. Not just for her, but for him. For what she knew they could have that he seemed determined to wall himself off from.

A tear slipped down her cheek and she sat up, getting out of bed and crossing to the window. Now she was crying. She wasn't really sure why she was crying, either.

But she was. Really crying. From somewhere deep inside of herself. From a bottomless well that seemed to have opened up in her.

Why did she never get what she wanted? Why was it always out of reach?

Her mother's love had been there, so briefly, long enough for her to have tasted it, to know what it was.

Just so she could feel the ache keenly when it was gone? And then there was Matteo. The man she'd wanted all her life. Her hero. Her heart's desire.

And when her father said she would marry a Corretti, of course it was Matteo who had come to mind. But she'd been given to Alessandro instead. And then, one more chance, Matteo at the hotel. And she'd managed to mess that up.

In the end, she'd gotten Matteo, but in the clumsiest, most dishonest way imaginable. Not telling him she was engaged, announcing to the world she was pregnant, forcing him to marry her, in a sense.

And now there was this…this heat between them that didn't go deeper than skin on his side. This love that was burning a hole through her soul, that he would never, ever be able to return.

"Alessia?" She turned and saw Matteo sitting up, his voice filled with concern. "Are you okay? Did I hurt you?"

"No." She shook her head. And he hadn't. She'd hurt herself. "I was just…thinking." There was no point in hiding the tears. Her voice was wobbly, watery. Too late to bother with the fiction that she was fine.

"About what?"

She bit her lip. Then opted for some form of honesty. "I've been pretending."

"What do you mean?"

"My whole life. I thought if I pretended to be happy, if I made the best of what I had, that I would be okay not having it all. That if I smiled enough I would get past my mother being gone. That my father's most recent slap to my face hadn't hurt me deeper than I wanted to admit. I had to, because someone had to show my brothers and sisters that you made a choice about how you handled life. We only had what we had, and I didn't want them…I didn't want them to be sad, or to see me sad. So I protected them from what I could. I made sure they didn't know how hard it was. How bad it was. I've been carrying around the burden of everyone's happiness and just trying to make what I had work. But I'm not happy." It burst from her, truer than any words she'd ever spoken. "I don't want to smile about my childhood. It was horrible. My father was horrible. And I had to care for my siblings and it was so hard." She wiped at a tear on her cheek, tried to stop her hands from shaking. But she couldn't.

She couldn't stop shaking.

"I love them, so much, so I hate to even admit this but…I was willing to give everything for them. And no one…no one has ever given even the smallest thing for me. And I'm sorry if that makes me a bad person but I want someone to care. I want someone to care about me."

"Alessia…"

"I'm sorry," she said, wiping at more tears. "This is…probably hormones talking."

"Is it?"

She nodded, biting her lip to keep a sob from escaping. "I'm feeling sorry for myself a little too late."

"Tell me what you want, Alessia."

It was a command, and since he was the first person to ever ask, she felt compelled to answer.

"I wish someone loved me."

"Your brothers and sisters do."

She nodded. "I know they do."

Matteo watched Alessia, her body bent in despair, her expression desolate, and felt like someone was stabbing him.

Her admission was so stark, so painful. He realized then that he had put her in a position, as his angel, his light, and he had never once sought out whether or not she needed something.

He was taking from her instead. Draining her light. Using it to illuminate the dark and void places in himself. Using her to warm his soul, and he was costing her. Just another person intent on taking from her for his own selfish needs.

"It's not the same as what you mean, though, is it?" he asked slowly.

"It's just…I can't really be myself around them," she said. "I can't show them my pain. I can't…I can't let my guard drop for a moment because then they might know, and they'll feel like they're a burden, and I just… don't want them to carry that. It's not fair."

"But what about you?"

"What about me?"

Matteo felt like someone had placed a rock in his stomach. Only hours ago, he had been content to hold Alessia tight against him. Content to keep her because she had accepted who he was, hadn't she?

But he saw now. He saw that Alessia accepted far less than she should. That she gave at the expense of herself. That she would keep doing it until the light in her had been used up. And he would be the worst offender. Because he was too closed off, too dark, to offer anything in return.

Sex wouldn't substitute, no matter how much he wanted to pretend it might. That as long as he could keep her sleepy, and naked and satisfied, he was giving.

But they were having a baby, a child. She was his wife. And life, the need for support, for touch, for caring, went well outside the bedroom. He knew that, as keenly as he knew he couldn't give it.

"I have to go," he said, his words leaden.

"What?"

"I have to go down to my offices for a few hours."

"It's four in the morning."

"I know, but this cannot wait."

"Okay," she said.

Damn her for accepting it. Damn him for making her.

He bent down and started collecting his clothes, running his fingers over his silk tie, remembering how she'd undone it only hours before with shaking fingers. How she'd kissed him. How she'd given to him.

He dressed quickly, Alessia still standing by the window, frozen, watching him.

He did the buttons on his shirt cuffs and opened his closet, retrieving his suit jacket. Then he took a breath, and turned his back on Alessia.

"I should be back later today. Feel free to go back to bed."

"In here?"

"Perhaps it would be best if you went back to your room. You haven't had your things moved, after all."

"But I made my decision."

"Perhaps I haven't made mine."

"You said you had earlier."

"Yes, I did, and then you decided you needed more time to think about it. Now I would like an extension, as well. That seems fair, doesn't it?"

He took his phone off the nightstand and curled his fingers around it. A flashback assaulted him. Of how it had been when he'd turned his back on the burning warehouse, leaving the people inside of it to deal with the consequences of their actions without his help.

But this was different. He was walking away for different reasons. It wasn't about freeing himself. This was about freeing her.

And when he returned home later in the day, perhaps he would have the strength to do it. To do what needed to be done.

Alessia didn't go back to sleep. Instead, she wandered around the palazzo like a zombie, trying to figure out why she'd exploded all over Matteo like that. And why he'd responded like he had.

It was this love business. It sucked, in her opinion.

Suddenly she'd felt like she was being torn open, like she was too full to hold everything in. Like she'd glossed over everything with that layer of contentment she'd become so good at cultivating.

She wanted more than that, and she wasn't sure why. Wasn't sure why she couldn't just keep making the best of things. She had Matteo. That should be enough.

But it wasn't.

Because you don't really have him.

She didn't. She had his name. She was married to him. She was having his baby, sharing his bed and his body, but she didn't really have him. Because the core of him remained off-limits to her. Not just her, but to everyone.

She wanted it all. Whether she should or not. Whether it made sense or not. But that was love. Which brought her back around to love sucking. Because if she could just put on a smile and deal with it, if she could just take what he was giving and not ask for any more, she was sure there could be some kind of happiness there.

But there wouldn't be joy. There wouldn't be anything deep and lasting. And she was tired of taking less than what she wanted to keep from making waves. She was so tired of it she thought she might break beneath the strain of it.

"Buongiorno."

Alessia turned and saw Matteo standing in the doorway, his hair a mess, as though he'd run his fingers through it a few too many times, his tie undone, his shirt unbuttoned at the collar. His jacket had been discarded somewhere else.

"Hello, Matteo. Did you have a good day at work?"

"I didn't go to work," he said.

His admission hit her hard. "You didn't?"

"No. I was running again. Like I did the day of your first wedding. That was what I did, you know. You asked me to go to the airport, and I nearly went. But in the end I was too angry at you. For lying. For being ready to marry him. So I went to my house in Germany, mainly because no one knows about it. And I did my best to be impossible to reach, because I didn't want to deal with any accusations. I didn't want to hear from my family. And I didn't want to hear from you, because I knew you would be too much of a temptation for me to resist. That if I read your emails or listened to your messages, I would want you back. That I would come back to you."

"So you hid instead?"

"It was easier. And today I thought I might do the same thing. Because I don't like to see you cry. I don't like seeing you sad, knowing that it's my fault."

"It's not your fault."

"Mainly I just drove," he said, as if she hadn't spoken. "A little too fast, but that's what a Ferrari is for."

"I suppose so."

"I've come to a decision."

"Wait, before you say anything, I want to say something."

"Why is it your turn?"

"Because you left this morning before I could finish. All right, not really, I didn't know what I was going to say then. But I do now."

"And what are you going to say?"

"I love you, Matteo. I think, in some ways, I always have. But more over the past months, more still when you told me your story. I am in love with you, and I want you to love me back. I'm tired of not having everything, and I think you and I could have everything. But you have to let us."

"Alessia…I can't."

"You can, you just have to….you have to…"

"What? I have to forget a lifetime of conditioning? I have to ignore the fact that my losing control, that my embracing emotion, might have horrible, devastating consequences, not just for you, but for our child? I have to ignore what I know to be true about myself, about my blood, and just…let it all go? Do you want me to just forget that I'm the sort of man who walked away and left his father to die in a burning warehouse? To just take that off like old clothes and put on something new? It wouldn't work. Even if it did it would be dangerous. I can't forget. I have to keep control."

"I don't believe you," she said.

"You don't believe me? Did you not listen to what I told you? Did you not understand? All of that, breaking that man's legs, leaving my father, that was what I am capable of when I have the most rigid control of myself. What I did to those men who attacked you? That blind rage? I didn't know what I was doing. I had no control, and if you hadn't stopped me…I would have killed them. I would have killed them and never felt an ounce of guilt for it."

"So you would have killed rapists, am I supposed to believe that makes you a bad, horrible, irredeemable person? That you would have done what you had to do to save a young girl?"

"That isn't the point," he said. "As long as I control it…as long as I don't feel, I won't do something I regret. I won't do something beyond myself. Even with control, do you see what I can do? What I have done? I can never afford to let it go. I can't afford—"

"I don't believe it. That isn't it. You're running scared, Matteo. You aren't afraid of losing control, you're afraid that if you feel you're going to have to face the guilt. The grief. You're hiding from the consequences of your actions. Hiding behind this blessed wall of cold and ice, but you can't live there forever."

"Yes, I can."

"No, you can't. Because at least for the sake of our child, our baby, Matteo, you have to break out of it."

"Has it ever once occurred to you that I don't want to?" he roared. "I don't want to feel, Alessia, I damn well don't. I don't want to face what I've done. To feel the full impact of my life. Of what was done to me. I don't want it. I don't need it. And I don't want you."

She stepped back, her body going numb suddenly. Shock. It must be that. Her body's defense because if it allowed her to feel the pain, she would collapse at his feet.

"You don't want me?" she asked.

"No. I never did. Not outside the bedroom. I told you that if you didn't expect love we would be fine. It was the one thing I told you could never be. I said no love.

I promised faithfulness, a place in my home, my bed, what more did you want? I offered everything!"

"You offered me nothing," she said, her voice quivering, a slow ache starting to break through the numbness, shards of pain pushing through. "None of that means anything if you're withholding the only thing I really want."

"My love is so important? When has love ever given you anything but pain, Alessia?"

"I don't know because I've never had it for long enough to see."

"Then why make it so important?"

"Because I deserve it!" She broke then, tears spilling down her cheeks. "Don't I deserve it, Matteo?"

Matteo's face paled, and he took a step back. "Yes."

She didn't take it as a sign that she had gotten what she wanted. No, Matteo looked like someone had died.

She didn't say anything. She just waited.

"You deserve that," he said finally. "And you won't get it from me."

"Can't you just try?"

He shook his head. "I can't."

"Stop being so bloody noble. Stop being so repressed. Fight for us. Fight for this."

"No. I won't hold you to me. I won't hold you to this. That is one thing I will do for you, one thing I'll do right."

"You really think removing yourself is the only way to fix something? Keeping yourself distant?" It broke her heart. More than his rejection, it was his view of himself that left her crippled with pain.

"It's a kindness, Alessia. The best thing I've ever done. Trust me."

He turned and walked out of the room, left her standing there in the massive sitting area by herself. She couldn't cry. Couldn't bring herself to make the sound of pain that was building inside her. Endless. Bereft.

She wanted to collapse. But she couldn't. Because she had to stand strong for her child. Matteo might have walked away, but it didn't change the fact that they were having a baby. Didn't change the fact that she would be a mother in under six months.

It didn't change the fact that, no matter what, she loved Matteo Corretti with everything she had in her.

But she would never go back and demand less. Would never undo what she'd said to him. Because she had a right to ask for more. Had a right to expect more. She was willing to give to Matteo. To love him no matter who he was. No matter what he had done.

But she needed his love in return. Because she wasn't playing at love, it was real. And she refused to play at happiness, to feign joy.

She sank into one of the plush love seats, the pain from her chest spreading to the rest of her body.

She had a feeling there would be no happiness, fake or genuine, for a very long time.

CHAPTER THIRTEEN

MATTEO DIDN'T BOTHER with alcohol this time. He didn't deserve to have any of the reality of the past few hours blunted for his own comfort. He deserved for it to cut him open.

He shifted into Fifth and pushed harder on the gas pedal. Driving always helped him sort through things. And it helped him get farther away from his problems while he did it. But Alessia didn't feel any farther away.

She was with him. In him. Beneath his skin and, he feared, past his defenses.

Those defenses he had just given all to protect.

You aren't afraid of losing control, you're afraid that if you feel you're going to have to face the guilt.

That was just what he was. Afraid. To his very core.

He was scared that if he reached a hand out and asked for redemption it would truly be beyond his reach. He was afraid that if he let the door open on his emotions there would be nothing but pain, and grief, and the unending lash of guilt for all he had done, both under his father's influence, and the night of the fire.

He was afraid that he would expose himself, let himself feel it all, and he would still fall short for Alessia. That he wouldn't know how to be a real husband, or a real father.

He was afraid to want it. Afraid to try it.

She wanted him to fight for them. Nothing good came from him fighting.

Except the time you saved her.

Yes, there was that. He had always held that moment up as a banner displaying what happened when he lost control. A reminder that, as dangerous as he was in general, it was when he felt passion that he truly became a monster.

He pulled his car over to the side of the road, heart pounding, and he closed his eyes, let himself picture that day fully.

The fear in Alessia's eyes. The way those men had touched her. The rage that had poured through him.

And he knew one thing for certain in that moment. That no matter how blinded he was by anger, he would never hurt Alessia. He would never hurt his child. No, his emotions, not his mind, told him emphatically that he would die before he let any harm come to them.

That he would give everything to keep them safe.

He had been so certain, all this time, that his mind would protect him, but it had been his heart that had demanded he do whatever it took to save Alessia Battaglia from harm. It had been his heart that had demanded he spend that night in New York with her.

And it was his heart that was crumbling into pieces now. There was no protecting his defenses, because Alessia had slipped in beneath them years ago, before they had fully formed, and she was destroying them now from the inside out.

Matteo put his head on the steering wheel, his body shaking as pain worked its way through him, spreading through his veins like poison.

Something in him cracked open, every feeling, every

desire, every deep need, suddenly acute and sharp. It was too much. Because it was everything all at once. Grief for the boy he'd been, for the man his father had become and what the end had done to both of them. Justification because he'd done what he had for his whole family. To free everyone. To free himself. Guilt, anguish, because in some ways he would always regret it.

And a desperate longing for redemption. A desperate wish he could go back to the beginning, to the start of it all, and take the path that would form him into Alessia's white knight. So that he could truly be the man she'd seen.

Alessia. He thought of her face. Her bright smile. Her tears.

Of meeting her eyes in the mirror at a bar, and feeling a sense of certainty, so deep, so true, he hadn't even tried to fight it.

And he felt something else. A light, flooding through his soul, touching everything. Only this time, it wasn't brief. Wasn't temporary. It stayed. It shone on everything, the ugly, the unfinished and the good. It showed him for what he was, what he could be.

Love. He loved Alessia. He had loved her all of his life.

And he wasn't the man that she should have. He wasn't the man he could have been if things had gone differently.

But with love came hope. A hope that he could try. A hope for redemption. A hope for the future.

For every dirty, broken feeling that he'd unleashed inside of him, he had let loose the good to combat it.

He had never imagined that. Had never believed that there was so much lightness in him.

It was Alessia. His love for her. His hope for their future.

He might not be the man she'd once imagined. He might not be the man he might have been in different circumstances. But that man was the one that Alessia deserved and no less.

So he would become that man. Because he loved Alessia too much to offer her less.

Matteo picked up his phone, and dialed a number he rarely used if he could help it. But this was the start. The start of changing. He was too tired to keep fighting, anyway. Too tired to continue a rivalry he simply didn't want to be involved in. A rivalry created by his father, by Alessandro's father. They both hated those bastards so what was the point of honoring a hatred created and fostered by them?

No more. It had to end.

"Corretti."

"It's Matteo."

"Ah, Matteo." Alessandro didn't sound totally thrilled to hear from him.

"How is everything going? In terms of unifying the business?"

"Fine."

"Great. That's not exactly why I called."

"Why did you call, then? I'm a little busy."

"I called because I want to make sure that as we unify the company, we unify the family, as well. I…I don't want to keep any of this rivalry alive. I've been holding on to some things for far too long that I need to let go. This is one of them."

"Accepting my superiority?"

"If that's what it takes."

Alessandro paused for a moment. "You aren't dying, are you?"

"It feels like it. But I think it will pass." It had to. "I don't want to carry things on like Carlo and Benito did, and I don't just mean the criminal activity. If we have a problem, I say we just punch each other in the face and get it over with, rather than creating a multigenerational feud."

"That works for me."

"Good. See you at the next meeting." He hung up. It wasn't like he needed to hug it out with his cousin or anything, but he was ready to start putting things behind him. To stop shielding himself from the past and embrace the future.

A future that would include Alessia.

Alessia looked up when the Ferrari roared back onto the grounds. She was standing in the garden, doing her best to at least enjoy the waning sunlight. It was better than the whole dissolving-into-never-ending-tears bit.

Matteo left the car in the middle of the drive and strode into the yard, his eyes fixed on hers. When he reached her, he pulled her into his arms, his expression fierce. Then he lowered his head and kissed her. Long. Deep. Intense.

She wrapped her arms around his neck and kissed him back, her face wet, tasting salt from tears. She didn't know whose. She didn't care.

She didn't want to ask questions now, she just wanted to live in this moment. When they parted, Matteo buried his face in her neck and held her tight. And she held him, too. Neither of them moved, neither of them spoke.

Emotion swelled in her chest, so big she wasn't sure she could stand it. Wasn't sure she could breathe around it.

"I love you," he said. "I have never said it before,

Alessia. Not to anyone. Not to a woman, not to family. So when I say it, I mean it. With everything I have, such as it is. I love you."

A sob broke through her lips and she tightened her hold on him. "I love you, too."

"Still?"

"Always."

"You were right. I was afraid. I'm still afraid. But I can't hide anymore. You made it impossible. I want to be the man worthy of that look you used to give me. I want to be everything for you, I don't just want to take from you. I was content to just take that light you carry around in you, Alessia. To let it warm me. But you deserve more than that. So I'll be more than that. I'm not everything I should be. I'm broken. I've done things that were wrong. I've seen things no man should have to see. But I will give you everything that I have to give, and then I'll reach deep and find more, because you're right, you deserve it all. And I want you, so that means I have to figure out a way to be it all."

"Matteo, no, you don't. You just have to meet me in the middle. And love will cover our shortcomings."

"Just meet you in the middle?"

"Mainly, I just need you to love me."

"That I can do, Alessia Corretti. I've been doing it for most of my life."

"You might not believe this, Matteo, but as you are, you're my knight in shining armor. You are flawed. You've been through unimaginable things, and you love anyway. You're so strong, so brave, so utterly perfect. Well, not perfect, but perfect for me. You're the only man I've ever wanted, the only man I've ever loved. And that will never change."

"How is it that you see me, all of me, and love me, anyway?"

"That's what love is. And you know what? It's not hard to love you. You're brave, honorable. You were willing to cut off any chance at having your own happiness to try to protect the people around you. To try to do right. You're the most incredible man I've ever known."

"Quite the compliment coming from the most amazing woman. Your bravery, your willingness to love, in spite of all you've been through, that's what pulled me out of the darkness. Your light won. Your love won."

"I'm so glad it did."

He put his hand on Alessia's stomach. "This is what I want. You, me, our baby. I was too afraid before to admit how much I wanted it. Too afraid I didn't deserve it, that I would lose it. I'm still afraid I don't deserve it, but I want it so much." He leaned in and kissed her lips. "I'm not cold anymore."

"Never again," she said.

He wrapped his arms tight around her and spun them both in a circle. She laughed, and so did he. Genuine. Happy. Joy bloomed inside of her. Joy like she'd never felt before. Real, true. And for her. Not to keep those around her smiling.

"We agreed on one night. This is turning into a lot longer than one night," he said when they stopped spinning.

"It is," she said. "All things considered, I was thinking we might want to make it forever."

"Forever sounds about right."

EPILOGUE

THE CORRETTIS WERE all together. But unlike at the funerals that had been the most common reason for them to come together in the past, unlike Alessia and Alessandro's wedding-that-wasn't, there was no veiled animosity here at the celebration of Teresa's birthday. And not just Teresa's birthday, but the regeneration of the docklands. The culmination of a joint family effort. Of them coming together.

After the big ceremony down at the docklands, they'd returned to the family estate.

They had all sat down to dinner together. They had all talked, business and personal, and not a single punch had been thrown. And it wasn't only Correttis. Some of the Battaglias, Alessia's siblings, were there, as well.

Matteo considered it a resounding success.

After dinner, they all sat in the garden, lights strung overhead, a warm breeze filtering through. And Matteo felt peace.

"Hey there." Alessia walked away from where she'd been talking to his sister Lia and came to stand beside him, their daughter, Luciana Battaglia-Corretti, on her hip.

"The most beautiful women here have graced me with their presence. I am content," he said, brushing his knuckles over Alessia's cheek and dropping a kiss onto Luciana's soft head.

Matteo looked at his wife and daughter, at his family, all of them, surrounding him. That word meant something new now. The Correttis were no longer at war.

He bent down and extracted Luciana from her mother's arms, pulling his daughter close, the warm weight of her, her absolute trust in him, something he would never take for granted.

Alessia smiled at him, her eyes shining, her face glowing. "The way you look at me," he said. "Like I'm your knight in shining armor."

"You are," she said. "You saved me, after all."

Matteo looked around one more time, at all of the people in his life. People that he loved. "No, Alessia. You saved me."

* * * * *

Read on for an exclusive interview with Maisey Yates!

BEHIND THE SCENES OF SICILY'S CORRETTI DYNASTY

It's such a huge world to create—an entire Sicilian dynasty. Did you discuss parts of it with the other writers?

Yes, we had a loop set up for discussion, and there were a *lot* of details to work out. And every so often messages would come in with the funniest subject lines I've ever seen.

How does being part of a continuity differ from when you are writing your own stories?

I think it takes a little bit to attach to characters you didn't create from scratch, but in the end, for me, I work so hard to find that attachment that I think continuity characters end up being my favorite.

What was the biggest challenge? And what did you most enjoy about it?

I think getting to the heart of my hero. Just because you've been given an outline with characters doesn't mean you've been given all the answers. In Matteo's case he was hiding something very dark and it was up to me to dig it out of him. I love a tortured hero, so this was right up my alley.

As you wrote your hero and heroine was there anything about them that surprised you?

Hee, hee… This goes with the above. Yes, Matteo surprised me with the depth of the darkness in him. I think

Alessia surprised me with her strength. Every time she opened her mouth she had something sassy to say.

What was your favorite part of creating the world of Sicily's most famous dynasty?

I loved the family villas, the idea of old-world history and beauty. I love a country setting.

If you could have given your heroine one piece of advice before the opening pages of the book, what would it be?

It's never too late to try to claim your own independence…but next time maybe do it before you're walking down the aisle.

What was your hero's biggest secret?

Oh, now, see, I can't tell you that. I'd have to kill you. He's a very good dancer, though.

What does your hero love most about your heroine?

Her strength, her ability to love and feel in spite of everything she'd been through. He feels like he's on the outside, looking in at all that light and beauty, unable to touch it.

What does your heroine love most about your hero?

The man beneath the cold exterior. The man who has braved so much pain and come out the other side standing strong. The man who gave so much to free his family from their father.

Which of the Correttis would you most like to meet and why?

Matteo. Because he's a sexy beast. I can't lie.

The Highest Price to Pay

For Jenny, my editor. Your confidence in me is always inspiring. You've pushed me to become a better writer, and you can't know how much that means to me.

And for my husband, Haven.
There's a little bit of you in all my heroes.

CHAPTER ONE

"THIS IS IT?" The man, tall dark and handsome as sin, who had just walked into Ella's small boutique gave his surroundings a dismissive glance.

She forced a smile. "Yes. All of the clothing here in the boutique is a part of the Ella Stanton line, and at the moment everything is quite scaled back as we're working on a..." *budget.* "Local level."

The fashion industry wasn't a cheap one to operate in, and Ella was most definitely still working her way up. But she was able to have her line produced, and sell it in her own boutique, and that certainly wasn't a small feat.

"I was merely curious," he said, taking a step toward her, "about my most recently acquired assets."

Ella blinked. "And by that you mean?"

"The Ella Stanton label, and the boutique, such as it is." His voice was smooth, husky as though he were issuing some kind of practiced pickup line, even though what he was really saying was far too ridiculous to be true. And yet, there was something else there, a hardness that lingered just beneath that suave accent. It was a hardness, an authority, that made all of the words that were swirling in her head get caught in her throat.

He took a step toward her and recognition punched

her in the stomach with brutal force. Blaise Chevalier. Rogue investor, ruthless corporate raider and tabloid superstar. He was famous in Paris or, rather, infamous. Wealthier than Midas, beyond handsome with his deep mocha skin, and striking toffee-colored eyes, perfect bone structure, good enough to be a model, except he didn't possess the androgynous quality many male models did. No, Blaise was utterly masculine, tall and broad shouldered with a physique that was meant to be wrapped in an expensive, custom-made suit.

She should have recognized him immediately. Her only excuse was that mere photographs simply didn't do him justice. Three dimensional, in the flesh, he was something entirely different than he was in the paper. None of the carefree, playboy demeanor was present now. Just a dark intensity that made her insides tremble, a sensual energy that no photograph would ever be able to capture.

He reached into his jacket pocket and took out a thin stack of folded papers. It wasn't cheap, bright white printer paper like she used in her office. This was cream colored, thick and textured. Official looking. A tremor skated down her spine and she shook it off, straightening her shoulders and holding out her hand.

He gave her the documents and stood there looking at her, his expression impossible to read. Ella looked down at the papers in her hand, skimming them frantically. Her stomach sank to her toes and the words blurred slightly.

"Would you mind translating? I'm not fluent in legalese," she said, hoping her voice didn't sound as echoey and distant to him as it did to her.

"Bottom line? I am now the lien holder on your business loan. A sizable amount."

She felt her face get hot, the way it always did when she thought of the screaming amount of debt she'd gotten in to get her business off the ground.

"I'm aware of that. How did this…happen?" If it had been anyone else, she simply wouldn't have believed them. But she knew this man, even if it was only by reputation. And it wasn't a good thing that he was here with bank documents that possessed both the name of her business and the stark truth of just how little actually belonged to her.

"The bank that originally held your loan has been bought out by a larger financial institution. They auctioned off most of the small business loans, including yours. I bought your loan in a bundle with several others that are of much greater interest to me."

"So you own my business…and I'm uninteresting?" Ella pushed her blond hair off her face and sat down in one of the chairs reserved for her boutique customers.

"That's the summation."

It didn't get worse. It couldn't. And at that moment she just wanted to fall to her knees and scream at the sky. Because hadn't she been through enough? How much was she expected to overcome in her lifetime?

Blaise Chevalier had a reputation as a man who was self-indulgent, reckless and ruthless enough to betray his own brother in the coldest way imaginable. He crushed companies, large or small, if they passed into his sphere of power and he deemed them to be unprofitable.

And he was now the owner of her boutique, her workshop, her apartment…everything down to her sewing machines. Everything in her life that meant anything.

"And what's your conclusion?" she asked, standing again. She wasn't going to crumble. Not now. Not when the stakes were so high. Her career, her line, it was her life. It was everything she'd worked so hard to achieve, a dream she wasn't about to let go of now, not while she still had some hope.

"I'm in the business of making money, Ms. Stanton. And your boutique and clothing line are not making enough to cover the expense of running them and earn you a decent living."

"They will. I need a couple of years. By then, with some extra advertising I'll have built a larger client base and I can start doing the bigger runway shows, getting broader exposure."

He raised one dark brow. "And then?"

"And then..." She took a deep breath. She knew this. She had everything planned down to what color her dress would be at Fashion Week. "Then Paris Fashion Week, New York, Milan. More boutiques picking up my collection. I hope to have a retail line. I have it all in a portfolio if you'd like to see it. It's my five-year plan."

He had the gall to look bored, disinterested. "I don't have five years to wait for a venture to pay out. And as a result you don't have five years, either."

A hot shot of anger infused her with much-needed adrenaline. "What do you want me to do, march up and down the boulevard with a sandwich board strapped to my chest to drum up enough business to satisfy you? These things take time. Fashion is a very competitive industry."

"I was thinking something a bit more high-end, something with more...class." The slight curl of his lips suggested he didn't think she possessed any class at all.

She scrunched her curls, curls she knew were a little bit disheveled. That was the idea. She didn't do anything by accident, not even things that looked accidental. Everything, down to her spiky heeled, open-toed boots, was about her image and her business. Was about cultivating interest in her brand.

"Well, you weren't talking class, you were talking urgency."

"I thought you might be after a slightly more upscale clientele as opposed to tourists and backpackers," he said, his rich, slightly accented voice sending a shiver through her. Stupid. She talked to a lot of French men who were looking for clothing for their wives or girlfriends…or themselves, she should be used to the smooth charm of the accent by now.

For some reason it sounded different coming from him, a harder edge to complement the rounded vowels. His English was tinged with French, but also with another flavor she couldn't place, something that made his speech all the more exotic and fascinating.

It didn't change the fact that he had walked into her boutique like he owned the place and then proceeded to tell her that, in effect, he did.

"What's the point of advertising at all if you're just going to demand that I pay you back with money I haven't got?" she asked.

"I didn't say I was going to do that. I said that I expect you to start turning major profits in much less than five years' time."

"Have a magic wand in that briefcase?" She knew how to handle people like him, people who exercised control over others. Never show fear. Never show weakness. A hard-learned lesson, one she carried with her, always.

"I don't need magic," he said, his full lips curving slightly.

No, she imagined he didn't. He wasn't only famous

for being the bad boy of the business world, he was famous for making millions just a few years after leaving his father's investing firm and stepping out on his own.

More than once, when she was struggling to make a loan payment, she'd seen an article about him in the business section of the paper and wondered how in the world he'd done it. Gone off on his own like that and made an almost instant success out of himself.

"Fairy dust?" she asked, crossing her arms beneath her breasts.

"Only the weak need luck and magic," he said. "Success comes to those who act, to those who make things happen."

Things like shutting down businesses and wrecking what *Style* magazine had called the wedding of the century. No secret that Blaise Chevalier made things happen, things that served him well. And that he did it with absolutely no conscience.

"And what exactly do you want to make happen with *my* company?" she asked, feeling her stomach tighten.

She was at a loss. She was going to lose control of her business, at best. At worst she would lose it entirely and if that happened, what was left?

No workshop. No boutiques. No industry parties. None of the friends she'd made thanks to the meager status that she'd achieved. It was like standing on the edge of an endless chasm staring down into nothing. The void was so dark, so empty. She'd crawled her way out of there once, and she couldn't go back. She wouldn't sink back down into oblivion, into nothing. She wouldn't let them be right about her.

"I'll admit, the fashion industry is of very little interest to me. But when I purchased the loan bundle from your financial institution, yours came wrapped up with what I actually wanted. A little research has shown me that it is time for me to pay more attention to the fashion industry, perhaps. It's much more lucrative than I had thought."

"If you play your cards right, yes, there's a lot of money to be made," she said. Although, massive amounts of money had never been what it was about for her. It was the success.

"Yes, if you play your cards right. But you're not exactly a master of the game. I, however, am." He moved closer to her, ran his hand along the carved wooden back of the chair she'd been sitting in earlier. She took a step back, strangely aware of the movements of his fingers over the intricate carving, almost like he was touching her, not the chair. Her heart pounded a little bit faster.

"I'm hardly a novice. I went to school for business and design. I have a business plan and a couple of investors."

"Low-level investors that lack the proper connections or sufficient funding. You need more than that."

"What do I need?"

"Publicity and cash and your five-year plan becomes a six-month plan."

"That's not even..."

"It is, Ella. I can have you at Paris Fashion Week next year, and in that time frame your work will have graced magazine covers, billboards. Selling your own work in your own boutique is one thing, but having worldwide distribution and recognition is another. I can give you that."

She could feel the reins slipping out of her fingers, feel herself losing control. She gritted her teeth. "In return for what? My eternal soul?"

A short chuckle escaped his lips. "While it has been

reported that I may be missing my own soul, I have no interest in yours. This is about money."

It was about more than that for her. Money was money. She could make money doing a lot of different things. But this, this was about being something. Being someone. She didn't want to have this man, anyone, so involved in her business, so involved in her achievements.

She didn't want it, but she wasn't stupid.

The amount of money she owed, money that was now owed to him, was staggering. More than she could hope to pay back with the way things stood. She was in debt to him up to her Petrova diamond earrings and if she ever hoped to get out of that debt, her business had to succeed. More than succeed, it had to reach the kinds of heights that, at the moment, were firmly in the realm of fantasy.

"You think you can just dictate to me?"

"I know I can. As the lien holder I have to be satisfied that you're doing everything in your power to ensure the success of your business. I'm not overly convinced at the moment," he said, his eyes sweeping the small boutique in a dismissive manner.

As if it were nothing. As if she were nothing. Her stomach burned with emotion, anger, helplessness. Fear. She hated the fear most of all. In theory she'd gotten over being afraid of bullies a long time ago.

"What if I don't want you running *my* business for me?" she asked, despising the slight quiver in her voice. She wasn't some scared little mouse and she wouldn't behave like one. She'd endured worse than this, and she'd triumphed. She would do it now, too.

"Then I pull the plug. I don't have the time to waste

on a venture that isn't going anywhere, and it's not in my nature to simply sit back."

"But you'll be collecting interest on your investment, won't you?"

"Twenty-five percent," he said.

"Highway robbery," she responded, her voice finding some of its strength.

"Not in the least. I will be working for that money, and I will expect you to do the same."

"And you expect me to do as you say?"

He gripped the back of the chair, his large hands drawing her attention again. His appearance was so together, so perfectly polished that it would be easy to assume he was a civilized man. But beneath all of that, beneath the well-fitted suit and hand-crafted Italian shoes that were so gorgeous they gave her heart palpitations, was a hardness that betrayed him. A hardness that spoke of the ruthlessness that he was so famous for. That let her know he wouldn't hesitate to pull everything out from under her if it was in his best interest.

"Consider yourself lucky, Ella. Normally I would charge a hefty hourly fee to give out business advice. In this scenario, unless you make money, you don't give me any money. This is fair, more than fair."

She blinked rapidly. "Are you expecting me to thank you for this hostile takeover?"

"It's not hostile at all. It's business. I invest where it is advantageous to do so, I do not waste time when it's not. There is a place for charity, and this is not it."

Ella looked around her carefully organized boutique, at the racks of clothing, each one her own design. She'd painted the crisp black and white walls herself, had installed the glossy marble floor with the help of a couple of male models who'd done runway shows for her.

It was personal to her, there was no way she could reduce all of her hard work to numbers and projections. But he'd done it.

And he would do more than that. Even without his reputation she wouldn't doubt him. The glint of fire in his golden eyes and the firm set of his angular jaw told her that he was not a man to be taken lightly.

"You're quite into the party scene, aren't you?"

Blaise watched as Ella stiffened, her bubblegum-pink lips tightening into a firm line. She didn't like his assessment of her. She didn't like his presence full stop, that much was clear.

But she could hardly deny that when her picture made it into the paper, it was because she was at some high profile soiree. It seemed she went to any and every event in Paris, at least those she could gain admittance to. And, from what he'd discovered, there were spare few she couldn't. A gorgeous American heiress with a sensational, tragic backstory was always in demand. And she took advantage of that.

"It's called promo, weren't we discussing that earlier?" she asked, arching one finely groomed brow.

Yes, she was beautiful, fine bone structure, bright blue eyes overly enhanced now by a thick line of blue pencil drawn all the way around them, making them look wider, more cat-shaped. It was obvious that she had no problem drawing attention to herself. She was wearing a short black dress that displayed her long, shapely legs to perfection, and ornate ankle boots with buckles and a cutout at the toe that showed off shockingly pink toenails.

A sharp shot of lust stabbed at his stomach. He dismissed it. This wasn't about lust; this was about business. He'd learned long ago to separate the two. Learned never to let desire lead him around like a dog on a leash.

"It's ineffective," he said sharply. "Yes, it gets your name in the paper to go to every night club opening in Paris, but it's not elevating you to the level this boutique suggests you want to be at."

"At this point, I just need to get my name in the paper. I do what I can to drum up interest in the Ella Stanton label."

"You don't do enough."

"Thank you," she said, her tone flat.

"It cheapens you."

Her blue eyes widened. "It isn't as though I'm out engaging in questionable activities, you make it sound like I'm dancing on tables while shouting the name of my label. I always behave in a professional manner."

"You have to surround yourself with potential clients. Tell me, are any of those hard-partying patrons of the events you frequent going to come and spend money on your clothes?"

"Some of them…"

"Not enough of them. You need to build connections in the industry. You need to build real connections with the sort of clientele you want."

"I'm working up to that point but it isn't as though invitations to exclusive events land in my mailbox every day." She shifted her weight and put her hand on one shapely hip.

He noticed them then. Patches of pink, shiny skin marring the creamy perfection of her fingers. This was what had made her instantly newsworthy when she'd come to Paris. The scarred, American heiress who wore her pain like a trophy and used her personal tragedy to her best advantage. Her sob story, the house fire that had left her burned, was half of her appeal to the media, and she made the most of it.

A quality he admired. Although, his first thought upon seeing that Ella Stanton's business loan was rolled in with the others he'd wanted to purchase had been to unload it as quickly as possible. He didn't have time to waste on a spoiled little rich girl playing at a career that suited her idea of over-the-top glamour.

After looking at her sales figures, he'd been forced to put that idea away, and talking to a couple of industry professionals and gaining insight on their opinion of Ella's talent had further altered his first impression. She wasn't playing; she was good at what she did.

She was working hard to advance her line, harder than he'd imagined she might be. But he knew he could take it further. Take her further.

The bottom line was profit; it was all that mattered. And he would wring every ounce of profit possible out of the Ella Stanton label.

"They do land in mine. And I know what to do when such opportunities for networking present themselves. I already have connections you can only dream of. I know you've read about my ability to crush companies if the need arises, but I can build them, too. In fact, I excel at it. The only question is which of my famed skills would you like to see employed here?"

There was a determined glint in her eyes, one that only served to add weight to the desire already settled in his gut.

"What exactly do you require of me?" she asked, speaking through her tightly gritted teeth.

"It's simple. When it comes to matters of business, you do as I say. To the letter."

"So all you want is total control then? Not too much

to ask." Her tone was even, her expression placid, but he could sense the barely controlled emotion that was all but radiating from her.

"What I want is to take your brand and make it a household name. To have every fashionista wanting the next big thing out of the Ella Stanton line. To have your clothing everywhere, from high-end boutiques to department stores. If I have to take control to see that happen, I will."

"What if I can buy out the loan?"

"You would rather try to keep going on your own than take this opportunity?"

"This is my business, not your moneymaking venture," she said, breathing hard, full breasts rising. He couldn't help but let his eyes linger there, to go further and admire the small indent of her waist, the round curve of her hip. A shame he didn't mix business with the pleasures of the flesh. It was too complicated, and when it came to women, he didn't do complicated.

"Do you think anyone would loan you money at this point, Ella? Your debt to income ratio is not the sort of thing a bank would want to see."

Color flooded her pale cheeks. "I know it's not what it could be but my plan is good and..."

"There are a lot of variables in your plan, from what I hear. And while it may be good in a general sense, it is not going to be guarantee enough for most banks as things stand. You've accumulated a lot more debt in the time since you took out this loan."

"Fashion shows are expensive. The last one I did cost me five figures, and I only earned a percentage back." Her voice cracked.

Ella felt like she was watching everything slide through her fingers. All the years of working toward something no one had believed she could achieve. She'd pushed herself so hard to make it this far. She'd done it on her own, without support from her family. The boutiques, the fashion line, they were hers. They were everything.

But now they were his. And unless she wanted to lose them altogether, she had to play his game. She'd known it would come down to that, from the second he'd shown her the paperwork, she'd known. She just hadn't wanted to accept it. But she had to now. There wasn't another choice.

Giving up her control, inviting someone else into her life, her business, was as close to a living nightmare as she could imagine. But losing everything went so far beyond a nightmare that she couldn't even think about it.

She sucked in a sharp breath and schooled her face into what she hoped was an expression of calm serenity. "I'm willing to work with you in whatever way I can to ensure our success."

A wry smile curved his wicked mouth. He wasn't fooled by her display of calm, and that made her angry. He could see through her, was amused by her. She curled her hands into fists and dug her fingernails into her palms.

"This isn't personal, Ella. This is about the bottom line, and I intend to see a substantial profit. If at any point it becomes clear that isn't going to happen, I will abandon the project."

Ella extended her hand and he grasped it. Lightning shot through her, unexpected, instant, as if she'd touched a naked wire. It mingled with the anger, the adrenaline that was already pounding through her and made her feel shaky, like her knees might give out at any moment.

She looked up and met his eyes, and saw heat.

Attraction. He looked down at where their hands were joined, his large and dark, hers small and pale and marred. He ran his thumb over one of the scars that blazed a jagged path over the back of her hand.

The heat fled her, leaving in its place an icy shiver that made her feel cold inside. She pulled her hand from his grasp.

His gaze lingered on her. "It will be a pleasure doing business with you."

CHAPTER TWO

"HERE IT IS." Ella pushed open the door to her workshop and led the way in and Blaise followed. It had been a couple of days since their meeting in her boutique.

It had given him time to assess some of the other companies he now held loans for, and it had also given him the chance to decide that Ella's was the one he wanted to focus on. The more research he'd done, the more he'd become convinced that the moneymaking potential was there.

When he'd called this morning about seeing her studio she'd been irritated. Even now she was barely looking at him, blue eyes slanted the other way when she spoke to him. He found it highly amusing.

The workshop was spacious, with a flair that matched its owner. Each steel beam that ran the length of the ceiling was painted a different bright color, and the ceiling itself was done in black. It reminded him of how she dressed.

Today she was wearing black leggings and a long shirt that was belted at the waist. The top clung to her curves and he was hard-pressed to keep his eyes off her tight, rounded bottom as she walked ahead of him and to the back of the room.

"I keep all of my samples and patterns here." She

gestured to the back wall that was lined with rows of full racks, filled with brightly colored clothing.

"You have a large body of work."

She put her hands on her waist and blew out a breath. "I do. It's expensive work, though. I have a couple of investors, but the start-up alone was huge and shows are…well, they're more than I have at my disposal."

His eyes were drawn to her lips again, still painted that same bubblegum-pink. He couldn't help but wonder if she tasted like bubblegum. Or if she just tasted like a woman, sweet and earthy at the same time.

His body responded to the idea of that and he had to grit his teeth hard to fight the rising tide of attraction that was building inside of him.

"I'd like to take a closer look at some of the sales records for your boutique," he said, moving to stand in front of one of the racks, pretending to look at the clothing there.

He could hear her teeth click together. "All right." She definitely wasn't happy.

He turned to her and she looked away again. He cupped her chin gently and her blue eyes flew to his, wide and utterly shocked. It was the first time he'd seen her mask come down completely. It was fleeting.

"Did you need something?" she asked.

He ignored his body's emphatic *hell yes.* "Just those sales records. It's business, Ella. I need to know what I'm working with here."

"Sorry," she said curtly, stepping away from his touch. "I'm not accustomed to people rooting around in my things." She pulled a laptop out of the oversize bag she was carrying with her and set it on one of the worktables. She hit the power button then leaned forward, idly twisting the large, flower-shaped ring on her finger.

"I promise, it will be quick and painless."

She raised an eyebrow and gave him a sideways glance. "Is that what you say to your dates?"

The minute the words came out of her mouth, Ella knew she'd overdone it. There was a small, nearly imperceptible change in Blaise's expression, a curve to his full lips, a golden glint in his eyes. He moved to where she was standing at the table and leaned in, his eyes never leaving hers.

"My dates never need the reassurance," he said, his voice surprisingly soft, his face so close to hers that she could feel his breath fanning over the bare skin of her neck. She shivered slightly, hoped he didn't notice. "They know what they want, and they know I will give it to them."

Another biting retort clung to the tip of her tongue, but she held it back. Blaise had a well-established reputation, and he wasn't the only one.

She was known in the industry for being bold, even a little bit brash at times, but that was an act, a wall she put up to separate herself from the world. It was to keep the woman she was inside safe, protected by her facade. And in the context of small parties and backstage at shows, it worked well, helped her establish dominance.

But here and now, with Blaise, she was in over her head.

They were alone, and he was close enough that if she moved, just a little bit, her lips would touch his cheek. That thought made her throat go dry, made her stomach tighten almost painfully.

She turned her focus back to the computer and cleared her throat. She clicked on the folder that had all of her business stuff in it and turned the laptop so that it was facing Blaise.

He scrolled through a couple of spreadsheets, his expression never changing. He was like a solid piece of mahogany. Hard and unforgiving. Beautiful, too, but it didn't change the fact that a collision with him would be absolutely devastating.

"You do pretty well," he said, closing the laptop screen.

She let out a breath, one she didn't realize she'd been holding. But with Blaise, it always felt like she was waiting for the guillotine to drop. Waiting for him to decide none of this was worth it, to have him decide to call the loan in. Like it or not, their unwanted alliance was her best hope for a future for her clothing line, and that meant she needed to keep working with him, no matter how much it made her want to scream.

"Yes," she said. "I do. It's a small boutique, but it's in a prime location."

"And yet you have very little profit."

"I have almost no profit," she said dryly. "It's an expensive business. And now that the boutique has gotten busier, I've had to get employees."

No matter how successful she got in the industry, it required more of her. More time, more money, more manpower, and with every increase in income, there was an increase in cost. It made it nearly impossible for her to get ahead, and certainly impossible to make the kind of jump in status that Blaise seemed to want her to make.

"I like what I've seen here. I'd like to invest more." He named a sum that made her feel slightly ill.

He said it so casually, as though it meant nothing. Although, to a man with a billion dollars, or whatever it was he had these days, it likely was nothing. To a woman who ate instant noodle soup for dinner most nights, it definitely wasn't nothing.

She dealt in large amounts of money, but almost the moment they hit her bank account they were gone again, going to the next big thing. And this was more money than she'd ever thought to see in a lifetime.

"That's…a lot of money," she said.

"Yes, it is. But I don't believe in going halfway. I want this to be a success, and that means putting in the necessary investment to ensure that it is."

It was a slippery slope. It wasn't a loan: it was an investment, but this put her over her head in debt as far as she was concerned. It gave him more power. It pushed her out further.

But what choice was there? If she didn't take it she would keep on with her tortoise pace and Blaise would grow impatient. And that would be the end of everything.

None of this had mattered three days ago when Blaise Chevalier was just a name in the tabloids. But now he was the driving force behind the Ella Stanton label. Ironic that he even owned her name. It felt like he owned her. Allowing him to invest that much money would only tighten the chains that she felt closing around her wrists.

But it was all she could do, accept the fact that she was indebted to him until she could buy her freedom. At least at some point she would have the hope of paying him back, of buying him out. If she didn't go along with him she wouldn't have anything.

The bottom line, the amount earned, had never mattered as much to her as the level of success. She'd happily keep eating instant soup for the next ten years if it meant making herself a success at what she loved. But that wasn't an option anymore, and what had only ever been a concern for her out of practicality had now become the primary focus.

"Then we both want the same thing," she said, even though it was a lie. He wanted money, and while she did want to make money, it was about more than that to her. It was about being something, accomplishing her goals. Becoming more than anyone around her had ever believed she would be.

A slow smile spread over his face and her heart thundered in response. She didn't know why. Except that when he smiled, it didn't look like an expression of happiness. It was more like watching a predator, satisfied in the knowledge that he was closing in on his prey.

She had a feeling that, in this scenario, she was very much the gazelle to his panther. She also knew that he was more than comfortable going in for the kill. A little blood on his hands wouldn't cause him to lose a moment of sleep. He was a man who accomplished his goals no matter who got in his way. Not a comforting thought.

"More or less," he said, slowly, his accent pronounced as he drew out the syllables, his voice enticing, despite the underlying danger. He didn't need to pounce on his prey, he could talk his prey into coming to him, and that made him even more deadly.

"Somehow I think as far as the method goes we might be more on the 'less' side than the 'more' side."

"Certainly possible." The deep, husky quality to his voice was shiver inducing. It made her stomach clench tight, made her entire body feel jittery, like she'd over-indulged in espresso at one of the local cafés.

"Where are you from originally?" she asked, feeling stupid the minute the words left her mouth. Because it was his accent, and the strange curling sensation created in her stomach, that had prompted her to ask. And she really didn't want him to know that.

Didn't want him to think that anything about him interested her at all. Who knows what he might do with that bit of information.

"France, originally. My father is a very wealthy businessman, a native of France. But I spent a portion of my childhood in Malawi, with my mother."

"Why wasn't she in Paris?"

He shrugged. "My parents divorced. She wished to return to her homeland." He said it with as little interest, as little emotion, as he said everything. She couldn't help but wonder if it had really been so casual as he made it sound. To go from Paris to Malawi as a child couldn't possibly be a nonevent; neither could being separated from his father.

Although, she knew as well as anyone that sometimes cutting ties with family wasn't the worst thing in the world.

Still, it made her wonder about him. Made her feel a small sliver of sympathy for the boy he'd been. Why? He clearly didn't feel anything for her, and she wasn't asking for it.

They might have a tentative truce, but it was tenuous. She had his word, and his word alone that they would work on her business, rather than him simply wiping it out of existence by demanding money she didn't have.

Not a comforting thought considering his reputation. And that meant her mind had to stay on matters of business, and not the exotic flavor of his accent. Not on the boy he'd been, but the man he'd become.

"So, being that you're the mastermind," she said, breaking the silence, hoping to do something about the odd, thick tension that had settled between them, to get rid of that strange, tight feeling in her chest, "what are your plans?"

"I was thinking a Times Square billboard and a cover for *Look* magazine."

She coughed. "What?"

"I know the editor for the magazine. She said if I could get a look from you that would go well with a spring editorial that she would use it for an ad and the cover."

"But that's…that's huge exposure."

"*Oui.* I told you I was good."

"Very good." She felt like she'd been hit in the head, dazed and a little bit woozy. "It doesn't seem possible. She would do that, just because she knows you?"

"I had her look up your work online. She was impressed by you. It's hardly charity."

"But it's…"

"I told you I could turn your five-year plan into a six-month plan," he said, his tone laced with arrogance. "She might like to interview you, too. Do a designer profile."

It was the kind of exposure she both dreamed of and dreaded. The kind that would give her the success she knew she was capable of. The kind that would give her a lot of exposure, both personal and private.

She'd already dealt with it on a small scale. It was easy to just put up the wall, smile and laugh, turn for the picture to expose the scar on her neck. Give the people what they wanted. She didn't bother to hide the past, the marks it had left on her skin.

She also kept some of it to herself. She didn't want to flaunt the worst of it. She gave just enough, just enough that no one pressed for more. Not that there was anything left to be said that could hurt her. She'd heard every insult, every cutting remark. Some of it from the mouth of her own mother. She'd survived. She hadn't crumbled then, she wouldn't crumble now.

She was going to grasp the opportunity with both hands. Make the most of her unasked for association with Blaise. If the man could get her a billboard ad, a cover and an interview, she might grow to resent him less.

"That would be great, more than that, it would be amazing."

"I know you love publicity," he said, one side of his mouth curved up.

"I like the sales that come with it," she said, her voice flat.

Publicity, in a certain sense, she could take or leave.

"What would you pick for the shoot?"

Ella crossed the room, grateful for the distance between them. She didn't know what it was about him that made her feel tight and jittery inside.

His looks, his reputation, it all combined to make him a pretty potent mix. One she was afraid she didn't know how to handle. She worked with male models all the time, and their boyish quality didn't bother her at all. Sure, sometimes when she measured their finely toned physiques she got a mild thrill, but she was a woman after all, and they were men.

But it was nothing like the intense jumble of feeling she got when she just looked at Blaise. One part attraction mingled with a lot of nerves and anger.

And he was no boyish model. He was a man, a man who, if the tabloids were to be believed, knew exactly how to handle a woman in the bedroom.

She felt her cheeks getting hot and she turned her

face away from him, pretending to study some clothes on another rack. She bit her cheek again, harder this time. She had to focus, and not on how good Blaise's physique looked in his suit.

She had noticed of course. Everyone had a thing that attracted their attention and hers happened to be a well dressed man. But he wasn't her type; his suit was her type. That was the beginning and end of it.

She didn't have the time or the inclination to encourage some weird attraction to the man who had just performed a hostile takeover of her life. She didn't have the time or inclination to indulge in an attraction to anyone, but him most of all.

She could just imagine the look of abject horror on his face if she were to make a move on him. If he were to see the parts of her body that she kept carefully concealed. A man who dated a different, gorgeous woman every week wouldn't want to handle any damaged merchandise.

And she was that and then some.

"Blue, I think," she said, turning her focus back to the clothes. Back to her job. "This one." She pulled out a short blue dress with long ruched sleeves. "With the right boots this will be stunning."

She looked at him, waited for a flicker of…something. His expression remained neutral. "If you think it will work."

"Don't you want to weigh in?" she asked, both perturbed and relieved that he didn't seem to have an opinion on the matter.

"Why?"

"Because. Aren't we…isn't that why you're here?"

He came over to stand beside her, his eyes on the dress. When he reached out and took the thin fabric between his thumb and forefinger, rubbing it idly, it was like he was touching her hand again, running his finger over her scar. No one did that. Ever. Another reason she had no problem showing off the more superficial scars: it kept people from getting too close.

Not Blaise, apparently.

She touched the back of her hand, rubbed at it, trying to make the tingling sensation ease.

"I am not overly concerned with fashion. I leave these sorts of decisions to you."

"I have decision-making power?"

He turned to face her, the impact of his golden eyes hitting her like a physical force. "If I sat down at one of these sewing machines you would get nothing. I leave you to your expertise, you leave me to mine."

That was more than she'd expected from him. Far more. And yet, it didn't exactly inspire warm fuzzy feelings. He was right. If she walked, he had nothing. Nothing but sewing machines he didn't know how to use. An interesting realization. She'd underestimated her own power in the situation. And she would use it. She had to.

"So you're not expecting to dress my models for me?" she asked, keeping her voice stilted, cool.

"I never said I was."

"Your reputation goes before you," she said archly. "I thought I was dealing with a pirate. Someone who makes his living by preying on the bounty of others."

He chuckled, a rusty sound, as though he were unaccustomed to it. "All those stories you've read about me."

"They aren't true?" she asked, hoping, for some reason, that they might be lies. That he wasn't the callous, unfeeling man the media made him out to be.

"Every last one of them is true," he said, his eyes

never leaving hers. "*All* of them. My decisions are made for my own benefit. It is not charity that I allow you this measure of control, it is what's best for the company, and what's best for my wallet. That's the beginning and end of it."

It wasn't spoken like a threat. His voice was smooth, even as ever. Controlled. He was simply stating what was. But just like that, the glimmer of hope was replaced with a heavy weight that settled in her stomach, made her feel slightly sick.

"Right, well, I guess I'll take what I can." She hated that he made her feel so nervous, so unsure. She usually did better than this. She was accustomed to taking command of whatever room she was in, accustomed to having the control over conversation and interaction.

She didn't seem to have it in his presence. She couldn't even control her body's response to him. She wasn't even sure what to call the response. He scared her, which made her angry. He was attractive and when he looked at her the appraisal of his compelling gaze made her stomach twist. It was confusing. A mass of jumbled feelings she just didn't have time to sort through.

She breathed in deep, hoping to find the numbness that helped her get through life. That helped her get through uncomfortable moments. That helped her deal with people who wanted to hurt her.

She couldn't find it, couldn't shield herself from the things he was making her feel. He looked at her, looked at her as though he could see right through all the walls she'd spent the past eleven years building to partition herself off from the world. And she felt naked. Like he could see the worst of her scars, into her, past the damage on her skin.

"Do you have pictures of this dress?" he asked, pulling her out of her thoughts, his focus on the business at hand helping rebuild some of her crumbling defenses.

"I take pictures of every piece. I have them in my portfolio."

"Excellent. Email it to me and I'll send it to Karen at *Look*."

"Yeah, I'll do that."

He turned to go then. Without even saying goodbye. It was like his mere move to exit should be sufficient. Standing in her own studio, he managed to make her feel like she was the one who had been dismissed.

She gritted her teeth against rising annoyance. Annoyance and something else that made her feel hot all over, made her face prickle.

She opened her laptop again and got ready to send the email to Blaise, using the address he'd so helpfully provided on the loan paperwork, those documents that gave him so much power.

So much power over her. She hated that. Hated him a little bit, too. This was meant to be her success, not his. The evidence of how far she'd come. Of all that she was capable of.

She attached the picture and left the body of the email blank. She didn't have anything to say to the man. She would work with him, do what she had to do to hold on to her business. And as soon as she could, she was paying him back and getting things back on track. Back on her terms.

She looked at the clock on her computer's task bar and swore mildly. She'd been invited to a Parisian socialite's birthday party and she needed to make an appearance. Blaise might not think it was effective marketing, but she thought differently.

He might own her business, but despite what she'd thought in her most dramatic moments, he didn't own her.

And she had a party to go to.

CHAPTER THREE

SHE WAS A PRO at working a room, that was certain. Blaise tipped his drink to his lips but didn't take in any of the bubbly liquid. Alcohol and the buzz that came with it held little appeal to him. Losing control wasn't his idea of fun.

He watched as Ella talked to the small group of women that stood around her. She laughed, lifting up her foot slightly so they could get a better look at the electric-pink stilettos she was wearing.

The dress was sleeveless, showing off rough discolored patches of skin, the flesh on the upper portion of her left arm obscured completely by the marks. She seemed unconcerned, making grand, sweeping gestures as she talked.

He noticed that while no one looked at her with disdain, they did stand at a distance. He wondered if the scars were to blame. Ella didn't seem to care either way.

She was bubbly, confident. She was smiling, something he didn't know if he'd ever seen her do, not in a genuine way. But then, she didn't like him very much. Something he should be used to by now.

He set his drink on the bar and wove through the crowded club. Ella looked up from her friends and he saw her blue eyes widen, watched as her smile became forced.

"Mr. Chevalier, I wasn't expecting to see you here," she said, her manner smooth, but he could feel the strain it was taking for her to remain composed.

"I was invited, but wasn't sure if I could make it." This wasn't his usual scene. If he wanted to find quick and easy female company then he might bother with party attendance, otherwise, he had no reason to go to events like this.

Lately he hadn't even felt compelled to find a temporary lover. He found the games tiresome. Sex had been a catharsis after Marie had left, a way to try to wash away the memory, but now the endless stream of one-night stands had become boring. More than that, it filled him with a vague sense of disgust. Not anything new, but he found no reason to add to his sins.

Even now, one of the women in Ella's group was giving him a look that let him know all he had to do was ask and she would be his for the night. Knowing that a few months ago he wouldn't have hesitated to take her up on it made him feel a tinge of discomfort.

It shocked him. He couldn't remember the last time he'd cared whether or not his actions were moral. That ship had sailed a long time ago. Every last shred of honor he'd possessed had been stripped from him and he had simply embraced the man the world thought him to be. Because it was easier to be that man, easier to simply follow the path he'd started down than to retrace his steps back to the point where he'd gone wrong.

"But you did make it. Yay." She said it with about as much enthusiasm as a woman who'd just discovered she needed a root canal.

"Somehow, I knew you'd be happy to see me."

Her lip curled slightly, her smile morphing into a near sneer. She crossed her arms beneath her breasts, thrusting them into greater prominence, and a stab of lust assaulted him. It was unexpected in its intensity, especially after the clear invitation of the other woman had failed to arouse anything in him other than distaste.

"Well, I thought you felt these sorts of events were beneath you?"

"Not at all." The small group of women was quiet now, watching their interplay with avid curiosity. "Come with me."

"I'm fine here, thanks," she said archly.

"We need to talk."

The women looked from him to her, their eyes round with interest. One of them actually pulled out her cell phone and fired off a quick text, either to spread information or to try to garner some.

"Talk then," Ella said.

"Privately." He leaned in and took her hand in his. The action drew the attention of several more people in the crowded room, including guests that he guessed to be reporters.

He had noticed the last time he'd touched her hand, how shockingly smooth it had been, and the scar was even smoother, robbed of its texture by flames.

Her full pink lips parted slightly, her eyes round. She looked frozen, shocked by the touch. Didn't her lovers touch her like that? Or did they avoid the parts of her body that were less than perfect?

The women he'd been with had always been examples of universal beauty, the occasional botched plastic surgery aside. It was impossible to know what he would do if presented with her naked body. His liaisons didn't require that much thought. That was the plus side to one-night stands.

Of course, at the moment, the thought of Ella naked ruined his thought process anyway. It erased logic, left only that strong, elemental desire, desire that roared through his body with the force of a fire.

He tightened his hold on her and led her away from the group. Ella made sure he knew she was allowing it grudgingly, her body stiff as she walked behind him.

He drew her into an alcove away from the dance floor, the bass still throbbed, loud enough to make the walls vibrate. He leaned in, bracing his arm on the wall and Ella took a step away from him, her eyes widening a bit when her back came into contact with the wall.

She made him feel like an evil villain about to lure her onto the tracks. But then her mask came back down, her face serene, bight blue eyes glittering in challenge.

"So, what was it you needed?"

"A chance to talk. And we were drawing attention so I thought we might make the most of it."

"Okay, talk then."

"I must admit, I did not give you enough credit when we first met," he said.

Her expression registered surprise that she wasn't able to conceal. "What?"

"I didn't realize how much money there was to be made in fashion if everything is executed properly."

"Not an industry insider, huh?" she asked, dryly.

"Only if dating models counts."

She huffed out a laugh. "Unless your pillow talk consists of discussing the going rate for hand spun wool, no, it doesn't count."

"Then no, I'm not an industry insider."

She pressed her shoulders back against the wall, as

if she were trying to melt into the surface, her eyes focused somewhere past his shoulder. She tilted her head slightly and he could see that the pink scarring extended to the curve of her neck. It looked painful. Unhealed. And yet, from what he knew, it had to be.

It wasn't beautiful. It drew attention away from the creamy beauty of the skin around it. Uneven and discolored, it drew him, drew his focus. All of her did. He raised his hand and brushed his index finger lightly over the damaged skin. Surprisingly soft. Like the rest of her.

She pulled away from him, stepping back from the wall, mouth tight, the confidence she had displayed earlier, gone.

"Don't," she said, her voice sharp. She started to walk away.

"Don't?" He caught her hand and drew her back to him. She complied, but he imagined she only did so because every eye in the room was trained on them. His sex life was a constant fascination to the public, and any woman he was seen with was assumed to be a lover. He couldn't remember the last time it hadn't been true.

His muscles tightened at the thought of a night with Ella, his blood flowing hotter, faster. He responded to her on an elemental level, one that didn't seem concerned with the scars that marred her otherwise perfect flesh.

She leaned in so that he could hear her over the pulse of the music. "Don't touch me like you have the right to. You bought my business loan, you didn't buy me," she said finally, her voice low, trembling.

"I had not forgotten."

"So what was it then, morbid curiosity? It's called a burn scar, I got in a house fire. I would have thought you'd have read that somewhere by now. The *Courier* did a particularly nice article on the subject, if you're interested."

Ella's heart thundered heavily, her stomach churning. She hated that. Hated that the simple touch had done that to her. Every insecurity, every shortcoming felt like it had been thrown in her face, had been brought to glaring light.

She hated that the scars still made her feel that way. No matter how much she pretended to be fine with them, she still hated what she saw when she looked in the mirror. Hated the feel of them beneath her fingertips when she scrubbed herself in the shower.

No one ever…no one had ever touched them like that. The way he moved his thumb over the marks on her hand, the way he'd stroked her neck.

Only one man had ever put his hands on her scars, and that had only been with the intent of humiliating her, which he very thoroughly had.

Her mother and father had stopped touching her altogether after the fire. No loving embraces, no casual brushes of their hands. Nothing but cold distance as they wrapped themselves in their guilt. Even her pain became about them.

The soft, hot graze of Blaise's fingers had hit her with the force of an electric shock, shaken her out of her thoughts, tiny sparks of sensation continuing along her veins well after the initial contact. And then she had looked at him. At the smooth, mahogany perfection of his skin. She had been reminded then, of why she shouldn't let him touch her.

The stark realization had made her feel like she was drowning in shame and she didn't want him to see it. She didn't even want to acknowledge it to herself. Even now she wanted to break free of his arms and run out of the club. But she felt paralyzed, trapped. They were the focus of every guest in attendance and she knew there were reporters. She didn't want a reputation as the woman who ran out of a party like Cinderella fleeing the ball.

She was strong. She wasn't running.

"I suppose since you're in the habit of taking what doesn't belong to you, it didn't occur to you I might not be willing," she said, compelled to make him feel as exposed as she was. "Businesses. Women."

The change in his face wasn't drastic, but his eyes turned to golden ice, a muscle ticking in his jaw. "I only take what is not well guarded. Your business for example—if you weren't in so much debt, my power would be minimal."

"I see. So you're blaming me for this. Does that mean your brother is to blame for you stealing his fiancée? It was right before the wedding, right? You slept with her in their bed and then went public with her, touching and kissing her at every hot spot in town." The ice in his eyes melted, leaving a blazing fire, and every part of her body burned. She tilted her chin up. "You said every story written about you in the tabloids was true. Unarguably, that is what you're best known for."

He didn't flinch, the barb glancing off his granite defenses.

"Clearly you've done your research, but none of this is new information to me."

She had. She'd looked him up on the internet. And she'd allowed all manner of righteous indignation flood over her as she'd read about the betrayal of his brother because it allowed her to be angry at him. And being angry at him was so much safer than feeling anything else.

"I know my part in that incident very well," he said, his voice toneless. "I was very much involved, after all."

"A pirate in all manner of things," she said.

"I had never thought of it that way. But it's a nice way to romanticize it," he said, his voice a near whisper, his face so near hers now that it made her lips tingle.

"I'm not romanticizing. I find nothing appealing about a man with no honor."

He released his hold on her, strong, square hands curling into fists, the tendons becoming more prominent, showing the weight of the gesture and the intensity of the emotion behind it, even though his face remained smooth, unreadable.

"Honor. An interesting concept, one I've yet to bear witness to."

Join the club. She wasn't sure how much honor she'd ever seen in her life. As a teenager, stuck in a hospital room, it had made a nice fantasy. A knight in shining armor riding in on his steed. But she'd given up on that by the time she'd reached the end of high school.

And instead of a knight on his steed she got a buccaneer on his galleon intent on plundering twenty-five percent of her gold. Brilliant.

She looked up and his eyes locked with hers, she felt the heat again, inside this time, making her blood feel like warm honey in her veins, the ensuing languor making her reserve, her anger, begin to evaporate.

How did he do that? How did he make her melt inside with just a look?

Her lips suddenly felt dry and she darted her tongue out quickly, dampening them. She watched as his eyes followed the motion and she felt a yawning, aching sensation open up inside of her. She knew what it was. It was arousal, and she wasn't a stranger to it. She'd just never been in a man's arms while experiencing it. Had never had the object of her desire so close that she could place her hand on the hard wall of his chest if she chose to.

This wasn't a safe fantasy in the privacy of her bedroom. Not a dim, gauzy dream that sent vague sensations of pleasure rolling through her. This was a real, live, man. And he was looking at her lips with much more than just a passing interest.

No wonder his brother's fiancée hadn't said no. No wonder she had broken her commitment to be with him. He was temptation incarnate. His eyes, his chiseled physique, promised a woman pleasure beyond fantasy.

Oh, yes, what a fantasy. She flashed back to his finger skimming her scar. It wouldn't be a fantasy for him; it would be a waking nightmare. And she couldn't even fathom the thought of him seeing her, all of her. The idea was too horrifying to even contemplate.

And why was she thinking of it at all? It was like there was a war going on in her. Common sense versus basic instincts. It was a good thing she'd gained control over that basic part of herself a long time ago.

It suddenly felt unbearably hot, even though she was certain the temperature couldn't have actually changed. Or maybe it had. Maybe more people had filed into the small club and that was it. It couldn't really be him, his gaze, making her feel dizzy with heat.

He leaned in slightly and she didn't move, she stayed, rooted to the spot, keeping her eyes on his as he drew nearer to her. Her eyes tried to flutter closed and she caught them, wouldn't allow it.

She still didn't move away.

He stopped suddenly, his lips so near hers she could feel the heat of them. "Don't worry. I don't need to possess honor to help make you a very rich woman. In fact, it helps that I don't."

The gauzy curtain of arousal that had been shrouding them lifted suddenly and broke her trance as effectively as a gust of icy wind.

"I'm ready to leave," she said, stepping away from him, finally.

"I'll stay," he said, golden gaze already wandering. He would probably stay and find some slim, sexy socialite to hook up with.

It made her feel ill, and it shouldn't make her feel anything at all.

"Good. Great. Have fun."

She turned and walked out of the club, embracing the chill of the night air as it hit her face. She needed it, needed a good dose of reality. What had happened in there wasn't real. It wasn't possible for a woman like her. And even if it were, she couldn't think of a single man she should want less.

It didn't change the fact that her heart was still pounding wildly and her body felt empty and unsatisfied. Didn't change the fact that when she closed her eyes it was his face that she saw.

CHAPTER FOUR

"IT'S HEADLINE NEWS in the society pages," she said, still feeling numb with the shock of her discovery.

"The press has an unhealthy fascination with my sex life," Blaise responded, his voice still rich and enticing, even over the phone.

Ella stared down at the picture of the two of them, shrouded in near darkness in a secluded corner of the club, their lips nearly touching. Her stomach contracted and heat flooded her face. His body, so near to hers, so hot and dangerously tempting.

She shook her head and tried to banish the rogue thoughts. "I thought you said the press always printed the truth about you."

"Usually, if I'm with a woman, she's my lover. Or she will be by the time the night has ended."

That thought made her scalp prickle, made her breasts feel heavy. "Well, I'm not."

"No, but we were together. And they know I recently purchased your loan, a move that they presume was a bailout, a way for me to help out the current woman in my life."

"Shoddy reporting," she said tightly. "Someone needs to write a letter to the editor."

She sat down in front of her laptop and pulled up

the statistics for her website. It was something she did out of habit every day. She liked to know what brought people to her website, to get a window into the kind of people that viewed her work and to help get an idea of where she needed to buy advertising.

Her eyes widened when she saw the number of visitors she'd had, and they widened even more when she saw the keywords that had brought them to the site. Blaise Chevalier and Ella Stanton lovers. Blaise Chevalier Ella Stanton girlfriend. Blaise Chevalier Ella Stanton engaged. The last one made her inhale the sip of tea she'd been taking. She coughed into the phone.

"Are you all right?" he asked.

"I…I have about four times the normal amount of traffic to my website and…almost everyone was searching for information about the two of us." She looked back down at the article in the paper. "I…wow."

"That is the kind of press you need."

"And I got it at the kind of event you said was beneath me," she said, feeling the need to point it out because his superior tone grated.

"It helped that you were keeping the proper company."

That rendered her speechless for a full three seconds. "Your ego really is staggering," she managed to say.

"I fail to see how acknowledging my appeal to the media is evidence of my ego."

"Hmm."

"You disagree?"

She couldn't deny that she never would have gotten such a prominent feature in the society pages if it weren't for him. She couldn't deny that Blaise's aristocratic heritage, his reputation for being completely ruthless and his status as a first rate womanizer, and the fact that she was with him, were probably the key elements to the fact that there was any interest in her attendance at the party. But she didn't have to like it. And she could still think he had a big ego. Because he did. Any man who could callously walk off with his brother's intended bride and then, after the damage had been done, abandon her as well, was hardly a man of humility.

Or integrity.

But darn if he didn't get things done. His mere presence had created a mini media whirlwind. One that could only be good for her. And it hadn't even taken valuable advertising dollars to make it happen.

"I'll concede the point," she said, idly tracing the image of the two of them in the paper. Her eyes went straight to the biggest scar on her arm. Of course they'd taken the photo from her left side, her arm exposed by the sleeveless dress she'd been wearing last night. It was easy enough to feign confidence when she wasn't forced to look at the reality of her body.

She tossed the paper down on her table. "Without you, I never would have ended up in such a prominent paper, with such a large photo. The exposure was obviously worth it."

"Careful, my ego is growing."

"Ha-ha," she said, standing from her place at the table and walking over to the fridge, rooting around for a moment before closing the door, empty-handed. "I don't want to waste your time so I'll talk to you… when I talk to you."

She felt awkward suddenly. She'd called his mobile number, which he'd given to her. But for some reason it seemed personal. It seemed…it was awkward, which was why she *felt* awkward. That much she was sure of.

Of course, it wouldn't feel that way if she only felt hostility for him, but try as she might, that spiraling, stomach tightening, heart pounding attraction just kept squishing down the resentment.

"This is business. I hardly consider it a waste of my time."

"Wow. That was almost a compliment."

"I've told you, Ella. None of this has been personal. I am not out to get you. I'm out to make a profit, and frankly, it only benefits you that I am."

"Yeah," she said, padding across the kitchen and moving to her living room window. She had a great view of the neighboring building's brick wall. "I get that. Because you make money, I make money, everyone's happy. But this is more than that to me."

"What more is there to business?"

Ella blinked. "Passion. A dream. The thrill of success, the feeling of accomplishment. There's a lot more to it." There was for her at least. Sometimes she felt like she was her fashion career. Like if it crashed and burned there would be nothing left of her. She'd poured everything into it. Time, money, hope.

If she failed…she just couldn't fail. It was everything.

"Ah, but unlike you, Ella, I *am* in it for the money. If something isn't profitable, I cut it loose. I do not waste my time."

"And I'm not wasting your time, so I suppose I'm meant to feel flattered?"

"Why would you?"

Oh, right. It wasn't personal. "Good question."

"I've had an email from Karen Carson, the editor of *Look*."

"Oh." She was excited to hear that, but a little bit annoyed since she wanted clients to work with her, not her all-powerful, unwanted benefactor. “And?”

“She liked the photographs.”

“Great, does she want the look for the ad?” Her heart was pounding a little bit harder, and this time at least it was over something concerning work and not Blaise’s butter-smooth voice.

“Non.”

“Oh…I…that’s okay, it was a good try.” And now all she could do was obsess about what she’d done wrong, worry about why her look hadn’t been good enough. Why she hadn’t been good enough.

Melodramatic much, Ella?

But that was the hazard of being so wrapped up in something. It felt personal when it shouldn’t. It made her feel like she’d just been dumped. Which had never happened to her before, but she was guessing that was what it would feel like.

“She wants you to create something else.”

“What?”

“The blue dress wasn’t right, but she said she liked your…how did she put it?” He paused for a moment and she assumed he was skimming the email. “Aesthetic.”

“Well, great. What does she want? I can do anything she needs me to do.” She felt a little bit like an overexcited puppy and she had a feeling she might sound like one, too, but she didn’t care right then.

“I’ll forward you the message. She wants something more formal, something in that same color scheme. Something only for *Look*.”

The resentment she felt for Blaise was pushed down a little bit further. There were some definite advantages to this enforced, uneven partnership. Exposure like the article in the paper, and like this ad campaign, didn't just drop into a person's lap. At least they hadn't dropped into hers before.

Under normal circumstances she would have had to build a web of connections and climb the threads to get to the top, dealing with all the sticky hazards along the way. But she'd just skipped all of that, the boost from Blaise's connections propelling her much further ahead of where she should be.

"Thank you," she said, her throat suddenly, horrifyingly tight. She didn't want to do something stupid like crying. She didn't want to show him so much vulnerability.

"You have a strange habit of acting like a prickly little…hedgehog and then thanking me for something."

"A hedgehog?"

"Yes, that," he said, his voice matter-of-fact and full of certainty.

"Well, you have a strange habit of being a jackass and then turning around and making something pretty amazing happen, so I think it's a cause-and-effect kind of thing."

"A jackass?"

"Yes," she returned, "that."

"I've been called worse."

She knew he had. She'd seen it in black and white, in the tabloids, on the online gossip sites.

"So have I," she said, looking down at her hands, grateful he was just a disembodied voice on the phone and not actually here to fix those all-too-knowing golden eyes on her.

"I've forwarded Karen's email to you. You have about a week to get the dress made. They'll handle the styling."

"Great." Thank God they were off the personal topics and back onto business.

"I'll be by later in the week to check in on your progress."

"Great," she said again. Her body didn't get the memo that she was decidedly unenthusiastic about meeting up with him again and it immediately dosed her with a nice shot of adrenaline.

"Good luck, Ella."

"Only the weak need luck and magic," she said, repeating to him what he'd told her that first day. Reminding herself what sort of man he was so that her body would calm down a little bit and stop getting so darn excited every time he said something with that knee-weakening, stomach-tightening voice of his. "I don't need luck. I make fabulous clothes."

"Make sure that you do. Because if not, the ad could backfire on you in a major way, and I won't continue to support a dying business."

Her stomach tightened for an entirely different reason now. Annoyance and a prickle of unease spread through her. He was right—this was huge, and blowing it would cause far-reaching damage.

But doing it well would be the key to her success.

"I will," she said as she hung up the phone.

She would. She would make the best dress she was capable of, because everything was riding on this right now. And failing simply wasn't an option.

He was giving Ella special attention, or rather, he was giving her business special attention. He recognized it, and yet, he didn't feel compelled to change anything.

Blaise watched as Ella knelt down in front of the

mannequin. She was fitting a pale blue gown to it, adding and removing pins, tugging fabric and humming absently.

He was struck again by how different her studio was than her neat, slick looking boutique. It wasn't a paired down black and white scheme with the occasional punch of color. It looked like there had been a color explosion in the converted warehouse. There were boards covered in swatches of fabric hung on the walls, bolts of fabric stacked into piles on the floor, on tables. A rack of bright threads, buttons and ribbons was at the center of the room. It was neat but chaotic in its choice of color and style.

A study in organized eccentricity. Like Ella.

She stood, tugging on the straps of the gown. Even now she matched the space she worked in. Tight dark jeans with bright pink stitching, the fabric clinging tightly to the perfect curve of her lush little backside, a black clinging top, a shocking magenta flower loosely pinning her wild blond hair into a low bun. Her look seemed casual, thrown together, and yet he had a feeling she worked for that effect.

There was no question that, as much as Ella might come across as some carefree, party-prone socialite, she wasn't that at all. Everything, even the chaos, was controlled and purposeful. That was something he understood. Control. Because without it, there was no limit to the depths a man might sink when he threw it all away.

Control was everything.

"That looks nice," he said, the compliment flowing from him with surprising ease. He didn't usually feel the need to give people that sort of assurance. But with her, he did. Perhaps it was the same, indefinable thing that had made him come here when a phone call would have sufficed as a means of assessing her progress.

Her shoulders bunched tight and she turned around to face him, blue eyes wide, finely arched eyebrows moved halfway up her forehead.

"Couldn't you, like…knock?" she asked, hand on her chest, bright pink fingernails glowing against the black background of her top. "You scared me."

"Perhaps you could try locking the door?"

"Is that your apology?" she asked, one hand on her hip now, her weight thrown onto one foot, causing her curves to become more exaggerated. Full breasts, small waist, absolute perfection. Perhaps her appeal was not indefinable. Perhaps it simply boiled down to her luscious figure, her enticing pink lips, and the fact that when he closed his eyes at night it was her image that left him hard and aching.

"How are things going?"

She narrowed her eyes. "Good. I thought you were just going to call or something."

"I decided to stop by and see how things were going. I like to have a personal hand in some of my larger investments." And the fact that her killer curves had played into the visit was something he was intent on ignoring. This was business. He kept his life compartmentalized, everything in its place. All the better to make sure he had a firm grasp on things.

Ella stepped slightly behind the dress form, her heart still thundering from Blaise's unannounced entry. He'd just startled her, that was all. But her body seemed to be having an awfully prolonged reaction to it. And it only got worse as he began to walk toward her, all fluid grace and hard, masculine lines. A compelling combination.

The deep charcoal suit he was wearing conformed

to his physique like a dream, the color the perfect foil for his rich skin tone. His shoulders and chest seemed impossibly broad. She had to add shoulder pads to suits for most of the male models she worked with and didn't get an effect half as dynamic.

It was easy for her to acknowledge interest and appreciation for his suit. That was her comfort zone. It was quite another to confess, even to herself, that she was more interested in what was beneath the suit.

"So, what do you think?" she asked, not because she really wanted to know, but because she was desperate to distract herself from the heavy tension that had settled in her stomach.

"It is…different."

"It's not made out of Lycra or covered in sequins, so I understand it might seem a bit out of the ordinary for you."

"A commentary on the women I date?"

"Um…yeah."

"Thank you for that, but I think the press has the commentary covered."

And he didn't care. She could hear it in his dismissive tone. Why did she care so much? Not about what the press said about him, but what they said about her. About the way her arms looked in a picture in the paper.

She just cared. She wished she didn't.

She cleared her throat. "Anyway, it's a mix of flow and structure, a little bit of Grecian inspired draping and the pleating on the bodice is to help give the model a good silhouette, and to add a more complex design element."

"If you say so."

He moved closer and she receded behind the dress form a little bit more. She didn't know where her bold confidence went. She was pretty certain she'd left it in the club a few nights ago. Darn him for being able to shake her like that.

It was one thing to play at a little bit of flirtation when she was certain a man would do nothing about it. Although when they saw the marks on her skin, they didn't want to go there. She was confident in the ability to use those physical imperfections as a shield.

But Blaise had touched them. He had looked right at them, not in horror. And he hadn't looked away and pretended not to see what was so very obvious.

He put his hands out, gripped the hips of the form and turned it slightly, his hands masculine and dark against the frothy, feminine fabric.

"I don't see any of that, I confess," he said softly, his eyes locked with hers. "But I can easily imagine a woman wearing it. The way these lines would conform to the curve of her waist." He ran his index finger lightly over the pleating she'd hand stitched into the bodice. "And these lines here—" he let his finger drift over the gown, up to where the pleating was done more loosely, with wider strips of fabric "—to make the woman's curves look even more dramatic."

She sucked in a breath as his finger skated over where the breast would be. She felt her own breasts grow heavy in response, felt her nipples get tight, as though he were touching her.

And all the while one large hand was resting on the hip of the form. She could almost feel the weight of his hand on her body, anchoring her to the ground so she didn't float away.

He moved his hand down, grazing every fabricated curve on the dress form before gripping the filmy fabric of the skirt.

She could feel it. What it would be like to be in that gown. To have his touch firm and sure, over every swell and hollow of her body, to have him take a handful of the skirt of her dress. Maybe he would push it up next. The fabric would glide over her body with ease, cool and light, while his touch would be hot and heavy in the absolute best way.

The air suddenly seemed thick and it was a struggle to draw breath. A struggle to stop her knees from buckling.

He dropped the handful of fabric he'd been holding, his eyes still locked with hers. The faint whisper of the chiffon, mingled with her strangled breathing and her heart pounding in her ears was the only sound in the room.

Her lips tingled, her body ached. He hadn't put his hands on her, and yet she felt branded. She felt as though something major, something completely altering, had happened, when all he had done was touch fabric draped over a dress form.

"I certainly wouldn't mind if my date showed up wearing this," he said, stepping back, appraising the gown casually as though…as though all he'd ever been doing was looking at the dress.

Because of course, that was what he'd been doing. That was all he'd been doing in his own mind. It was her mind, her sex-starved body that had made it into more than it was. She'd had too many fantasies. Fantasies where men looked past the imperfections of her body and desired *her,* the woman beneath the scars.

Although, even in those fantasies, she never saw herself as damaged. When she thought of being in a man's bed, his hands moving over her back, her mind saw smooth, flawless skin. Her mind made her beautiful, a match for her dream lover. It was a lie.

And so was the moment she had just conjured up in her mind.

"Great. I think Karen will like it, don't you?"

"As I said, fashion is not my thing. As a man I can say I would be drawn to the ad."

"Well," she said, her throat still tight, "hopefully women like it, too, since they're the majority of *Look*'s readership."

"I'm sure they will."

"Thanks." Now she just wanted him to leave, so she could forget what she'd just felt. So she could think of him as the pirate and not as the man who had set her body on fire with just a look, not as another thing she wanted that was forever out of reach.

There was no reason for her to want him. In this instance, the scars were offering protection. She shouldn't want any part of the man he was. Of a man who thought so little of betraying those he was supposed to love.

Focus on that. Not his muscles.

"I did have one other thing I wanted to speak to you about," he said.

Great. "What?"

"I want to take you to the sort of event that will actually be of practical use to you. I'd like for you to go to the Heart's Ball with me tonight. Perhaps we can give the media something more to talk about."

CHAPTER FIVE

THE HEART'S BALL was one of the biggest charity events in France, if not the world. Tickets were amazingly expensive, and that was only for entry. After that, there was dinner, which would cost around three hundred Euros a plate.

All of it went to fund the Heart association, aiding people with heart problems, helping them pay for medications and surgeries. It also helped the rich and famous rub elbows with each other and give some good PR.

And there was no way Ella could ever afford the cost of the event.

"Are you footing the bill?"

"Naturally. I always pay for my dates."

"I want to buy my own dinner," she said, wincing as she thought of giving up that amount of money. "It's a good cause, and I'd like to support it myself, too."

She realized, a little too late, that she'd just agreed to go with him. But how could she not? He was right, and the web traffic didn't lie. If being seen in a club at a minor celebrity's birthday bash was enough to make the news, then this would do even more for her.

She would love to refuse, would love to say "I don't need you or your publicity." But the simple fact was, she did. She needed it badly. Spending time with him was, ironically, the key to getting rid of him faster. The key to getting the money she needed, to getting her control back.

If that meant spending a few hours in his company, she would do it.

Her body prickled with heat, a treacherous physical excitement building in her as she thought of him holding her close to him, like a man would a date. It was highly charged, adult version of the guilt she used to feel as a child when she was about to do something she knew she shouldn't do.

But she wasn't going to do anything. She wasn't. But she couldn't stop the little pulses of adrenaline from spiking in her, couldn't hold back the slow arousal that was building along with it.

"I will buy your dinner. You can make a donation in the amount you see fit," he said, that voice hard and uncompromising. As much as she wanted to argue with him, her bank balance made it seem like a very stupid idea.

"All right, that sounds…no, it doesn't sound fair, it still sounds lopsided."

"A man should always pay for his date. What manner of idiot do you usually associate with?"

"Oh my gosh, did you really just give me a lesson in chivalry?" she asked, bristling because no one had taken her on a date since high school. And that had ended…badly. Badly enough that she still didn't like to think about it.

"You seemed to need it."

"Not from a man like you." And she regretted that the moment it left her mouth. Because while Blaise could be hard to deal with, he'd never insulted her. And she'd lashed out at him deliberately more than once now, using his past against him. If he'd done the same to her, she would have been devastated. Although, she doubted it was possible to devastate Blaise.

He didn't react to the barb, not hugely. Nothing beyond the slight tightening of his jaw. "Not from a pirate like me?"

"I didn't..." She sucked in a breath, regret and oxygen filling her. "Forget it."

"No, you did, and you're right. I'm not exactly the sort of person who should give advice on how to live in civilized society, and I don't claim to be. But one thing I do is take care of the woman I'm with, whether I'm with her for a night or for a long-term relationship."

She could well imagine that he did take care of them, in a physical way at least. His smooth voice spoke of all kinds of pleasures, pleasures she couldn't begin to imagine with her nonexistent experience. But physical was about all he would be good for. Nurturing didn't really seem to be his thing. His track record was poor to say the least when it came to caring for those he supposedly loved.

She looked at him, at his chiseled face, so hard it seemed to be carved from stone, and she felt an instant stab of guilt for the thought. And why, she didn't know. Only that she, of all people, should know better than to take people at face value.

Blaise seemed almost too comfortable with his role of villain at times. So much so that it made her wonder now what was beneath it.

Nothing. Don't go there.

She wasn't going to allow herself to pretend that he wasn't exactly who he appeared to be, just because she wanted him to be. It was something she'd done with her parents for years until the stark realization had hit her that they would never, ever love her more than they loved themselves. Would never be able to look beyond their own grief to see hers.

People didn't change just because she wished they would.

"What time is the ball?"

"Eight," he said, brushing his fingers lightly over the front of the gown that was still pinned to the dress form, making another little zip of sensation shoot through her.

She clenched her teeth. "Then you'd better go so that I have time to get ready."

"It's meant to be a costume party, by the way."

The excitement was back, building, growing, along with a little bit of anger, anger that he so easily called a response from her body. And desire to get revenge. To make him burn with the same physical discomfort that she burned with every time she looked at him.

To make him ache for her, as she did for him.

"Now, a costume, I can do."

Everything at the old châteaux where the Heart's Ball was held was draped in glittering lights and gemstones. Swathes of fabric hung from the ceiling, and ornate, hand folded paper hearts had been placed on every surface.

All of it spoke of an excess that had long ago stopped impressing Blaise. Although it certainly had at first. All of it, the wealth, the grandeur had been a source of fascination to him when he'd returned to Paris at the age of sixteen. When he'd left, he'd been a boy, but after eight years away he had been ushered into a whole different world. His family, his father and brother, had wealth and influence he could scarcely remember, and they had welcomed him into it.

But in the fourteen years since, he had begun to see the grime on the highly polished facades of the elite that frequented these events. He had been tarnished with it himself, had gone on to spread it to others.

No, the setting held no appeal to him. But Ella, her body wrapped in crimson lace that barely covered her long, shapely legs, lace that gave hints of the pale skin beneath without revealing too much of her lovely curves, she had the power to turn his head. Interesting since it had been at least three years since a woman had possessed the ability to do anything but arouse him in a generic, physical sense.

Passing sexual interest was common enough, but the burning ache of desire that Ella had ignited in his gut was another.

"What are you supposed to be?" he asked, taking her hand, a hand that was covered by fingerless, lace gloves, and leading her down into the ballroom.

Her lips, cherry-red tonight, curved into a smile. A gold mask covered part of her face, making her eyes look even brighter, more mysterious. "I'm temptation."

Yes, she was. And three years ago, he would have set out to give into that temptation with single-minded focus. He would have allowed his desire for her, for the satisfaction of his flesh, to overrule his mind.

But he wasn't that man now. He had seen where that led. He believed in control now, in the denial of that part of himself when it was appropriate to deny it.

"What are you supposed to be?" she asked, giving his black suit a critical once-over.

He leaned in, the scent of her, light, feminine, teasing him, making his stomach tighten with arousal. "I'm a man who does not like to wear costumes."

He was rewarded with a laugh, a genuine laugh that

seemed to bubble up from somewhere deep inside of her. “Well, I sincerely doubt anyone will challenge you over it.”

“I would imagine not.”

His reputation was too cemented, too ingrained in the minds of everyone here for them to give him so much as a wrong look. But he knew they all thought unflattering things. He was the boy who was all but raised by wolves in the wilds of Africa, as far as they were concerned. The man whose father had welcomed him back, sent him to the best college, attempted to make a success of him. The man who had taken his father’s efforts and made a mockery of them by betraying his brother, the older man’s much beloved heir.

Fine, he used the public’s perception to his advantage. It left him free to do what he liked, it gave him very little competition, mostly because the general public imagined there was no low he would not stoop to.

And he thought they might be right. Was there any lower for him to go? He seriously doubted it.

“That isn’t fair, you know,” Ella said, giving him a smile, a genuine one. A strange thing for him to be on the receiving end of.

“Why is that?”

“I dressed up.”

“Yes, you did.” The lace looked so delicate, it would be easy to tear from her body, exposing her to him, one gossamer strip at a time. He could kiss the color off of those cherry lips. He would maybe leave the mask, though. It made for a very naughty image. Ella, naked except for the golden mask.

He would know it was her, though. There was no question. Even in his fantasy of her, the marks on her arms were there, the discolored skin on her neck. The scars that signified her as Ella, and not just some faceless woman.

Ella felt as though Blaise was looking straight through her gown, which was, admittedly, a little on the daring side. It was thin, but with enough fabric to obscure the bits of her body that needed obscuring, either for public decency or for her own vanity.

At the moment, she was very grateful for the mask. It felt like a little something extra to hide behind.

"When do we get to sit down to this extravagant dinner?" she asked, eager to get a table between them, something to help divide his focus, because at the moment it was very much on her mind and it made her feel totally edgy.

It had been empowering, putting on the short, shocking dress in her bedroom, imagining getting back at him for the episode in her studio. She'd wanted to put him off his footing a little bit, like he'd been doing to her.

But no, he was still making her feel uncomfortable when she should be feeling confident. Clothes usually did that for her. That was just one reason fashion had become such a passion for her. By taking control over her looks, by playing to her own strengths, she could completely change people's perception of her. And that appealed to her immensely.

It was failing her now, though. She felt like she'd overplayed her hand a little bit. Because when he'd come to pick her up and his golden eyes had slid over her, appraising her, he'd looked like he might devour her.

And what would she do with a man like him if he did decide to do that? What would he do with her?

Probably run screaming from the room once he got the dress off, horrified that he had nearly sullied himself by making love to someone who was so disfigured.

Maybe her scars weren't that bad, but they were all she saw when she looked at her body. And she hadn't been tempted to try to find out what someone else might think, not since her disastrous prom date with the boy whose aim had been to get her top off so he could see just how ugly she was.

Not since the only comfort her mother had been able to offer was a softly murmured, "you used to be so beautiful."

No, she hadn't felt like trying since then. And if she ever did…it would have to be with someone she really knew. Someone who really cared for her. Not someone who was just lusting after the facade she managed to show the world.

"Later. I think they want to give everyone a chance to schmooze first."

"Is that the technical term?"

"I believe so, but I have never been one for it."

She could believe that. Blaise didn't seem to care what anyone thought about him. In fact, he seemed to go out of his way to be aloof half the time.

It was opposite to the way she handled social situations. If she feigned confidence, if she was the one to instigate conversation, then she had the control. It was the same idea as the daring lace dress. Show confidence no one can question, and they'll be too afraid to issue a challenge. Combine that with her scars, something that seemed to set most people on edge, unsure of whether to look or look away, and she usually had the upper hand in social situations.

Unfortunately it didn't seem to work that way with Blaise. Of course, she expected there was very little in the world that could possibly intimidate him. He seemed outside of laws and, therefore, exempt from the usual reactions she got from those around her.

In fact, he met her challenges head-on. Even touching her. She could feel it still, if she thought back to that night at the club. His fingers drifting over her skin, skin that had been untouched by anyone other than herself. Who else would want to touch it?

She still didn't know why *he* had.

"Well, maybe we can schmooze with each other," she said, regretting it as soon as it left her lips. "What I mean is…we can talk business."

"Right," he said, snagging two glasses of champagne from a passing waiter's tray. He handed one to her and she took it, grateful to have something to hold on to. Grateful to have something to distract her.

The way he was looking at her, the way he had been looking at her, from the moment he'd seen her tonight, set her teeth on edge and made her body feel restless, aching. Needing. Wanting.

But there were just too many reasons why not to give in to all the demands of her body. And even if she did try to give in, there were two people involved. Facing the rejection, the look of disgust on his face, should he decide he didn't want her once he unwrapped the entire package…she didn't want that. She could survive it, but there were a lot of things she could survive that she didn't necessarily want to experience.

"Right," she said lightly, taking a sip of her champagne. She didn't want it going to her head. She didn't really have a legendary alcohol tolerance and Blaise already made her feel dizzy without adding anything else into the mix.

"How is the gown for *Look* coming along?" he asked, those wicked golden eyes appraising her, making her insides feel like warm liquid honey. He was reminding her of just what had happened earlier in the day, that gown acting as the centerpiece to her mini downfall.

She had wanted, so badly, to lean in and touch him. To press her lips to his. To make him feel what she was feeling.

She blinked. “Great. About the same as it was when you left this afternoon. Karen had already seen a sketch and was pleased with it, so I’m feeling confident. As confident as I can feel over something so huge.”

He shrugged and she noticed he hadn’t taken a drink of his champagne. “Every step you take is another step. I treat every business deal with equal importance. That way, I never let anything slip.”

“Hmm.” She tapped on the side of the glass. “And it keeps you from getting too nervous over something big, I guess.”

“I don’t get nervous.”

“Never?”

“No. I make a decision and I act on it. I don’t do nerves. I don’t do regret.”

The tone of the conversation shifted, Blaise’s voice getting darker, his tone hard. She wondered if that was true. If he moved through life with no regrets. If he had truly stolen the love of his brother’s life, then discarded her, with no regret at all.

Part of her, the physical part, that was looking into his eyes, that could see the uncompromising set of his jaw, the tightly clenched fist at his side, that part could believe it. But something inside her didn’t. Couldn’t. She didn’t know why because she was pretty sure that in this case, she should believe her eyes and not her silly, fantasy-prone heart.

“That must be…freeing.”

She could see how it would be. She regretted a lot of things. Things she'd never had the ability to control. Things she'd never made a decision on, but that simply were. Things that twined around her, ensnared her like a rabbit in a trap.

"Interesting choice of words," he said, managing to sound coolly disinterested even now.

"Not really. It must be nice to have so much confidence in everything you do."

"You never seem short on confidence, Ella," he said, his tongue all but caressing her name, his accent making it sound exotic in a way she'd never noticed before.

He leaned in slightly and she lowered her eyes, desperate to avoid his gaze. But she just ended up fixated on his fingers as they stroked the stem of the champagne flute, the motion making her think of his hands on her skin, stroking, caressing.

"Although," he said, "sometimes your cheeks get a little bit pink. Like now."

She took a step back. "It's hot in here."

"Would you like to step outside for a moment?"

She nodded, heading for the balcony, away from him. Except that he was coming with her, which totally defeated the purpose.

"I'm fine," she said, welcoming the cool night air, waiting for it to penetrate her heated flesh, to knock a little bit of common sense into her, and some of the clouding arousal out of her.

"It is bad form for a man to leave his date."

"Again with the chivalry?"

"I am just ever conscious of my glowing reputation." His voice was tinged with sarcasm, and a hint of bitterness that made her think that, although he really wanted her to believe he lived with no regrets, it probably wasn't completely true.

"Or at least of what the caption might read beneath our names in tomorrow's news," she said, hoping to lighten the mood a little bit.

She leaned back against the balcony's railing and looked at the glowing white lights, woven between the overhanging lattice that was also draped with grapevines. If she could only focus on that instead of the man standing near her, she might be okay.

"It will be interesting to see, that's for certain."

"Especially since we've now disappeared onto the very private balcony for what can only be described as a tête-à-tête."

He laughed, the sound shocking in the quiet night, shocking because it had been so silent, and because it had come from Blaise. "You should work for the media."

"I don't have the stomach for it," she said.

Strains of music from the ballroom filtered through the open doors and Ella closed her eyes, enjoying the soft, subtle sounds.

"You like it?" he asked.

"Yes. Club music isn't really my thing, to be honest."

"But promotional opportunities are?"

"I've met a lot of people, a lot of clients, by spending time at the right nightclubs. But I very much consider it business and not pleasure."

He reached out and took the glass of champagne from her hand, setting it, along with his, on the stone railing behind her. He touched her hand, a soft touch that sent heat feathering through her, gentle and pleasant.

Then he took her hand in his and drew her to him,

slowly. And her feet moved to him, her body leaning in, far before her brain had a chance to catch up.

He looped his arm around her waist, pulled her to him.

She knew the expression on her face was quite possibly one of dumb shock, but actually having him touch her, being in full contact with his body, was a shock to her senses. Her breasts were pressed against his very hard chest, the delicious pressure working to ease some of the ache that had been building in her.

"I thought you deserved a chance to dance, as you enjoy the music so much," he said, his breath hot against her ear as he whispered the words. She shivered, goose bumps breaking out over her arms.

"Oh," she said, heart hammering so hard she was certain he must be able to feel it against his chest.

She didn't know why she didn't pull away. Why she didn't say no.

No, she did know. It was because it felt good. And she had felt so much pain in her life it just felt…it felt so foreign and amazing to just let herself feel good.

To revel in the warm weight of his hand on her lower back, the feeling of his other large hand enveloping her much smaller one. Swaying with him, moving in one accord with him instead of just fighting him. Instead of fighting herself.

"Temptation," he whispered, his cheek against the curve if her neck, his words a whispered enticement. "Such a fitting choice of costume."

He released her hand then, placing his on the curve of her hip, moving it to the indent of her waist, stopping just beneath the swell of her breast. She had imagined his touch earlier, felt the slide of his fingers as he'd moved it over the gown she was making.

But that had been fantasy, just like it always was for her. But this was real. His hands on her body, the thin red lace the only barrier between his flesh and hers.

The rhythm of the music seemed to fade and they made their own, his movements so slow and sensual, seductive on a level she could have never imagined. And when he moved nearer to her, she felt that he was as aroused as she was, the hard length of him pressed against her a proof that couldn't be denied.

He moved his head, hot breath tracing a line from just beneath her ear, over her scar and to her shoulder. His lips never touched her skin, only hovered there, making her body tighten with need, making her want to pull him to her so she could feel the press of his mouth on her.

She wanted it. So much. So much that it scared her, made her feel hollow and nervous and like she might fold in on herself if she couldn't have more of him, more of his touch. His hands on her skin, without the dress in the way, his lips, not just the impression of them.

She swayed slightly in his arms, her breasts brushing against his chest, sensation pouring through her, drowning her senses in desire. Being in his arms, just held by him, so close, was beyond anything she'd ever experienced, anything she'd ever imagined.

She tilted her head to the side, exposing more of her neck to him. Warm breath continued to tease her, the tip of his nose skating lightly over the delicate skin.

He pulled away, looked at her, then gently tilted her head the other way, repeating the action with the other side of her neck. She stiffened when she could no longer feel his heat, when she lost the sense of the slow glide of his touch. She put her hand to the back of his head, felt that he was still there, touching her. But she couldn't feel it.

There could be pain or pleasure, heat or chill, and she wouldn't know. The scar that distorted her skin was an outward sign of the damage that lay beneath. Nerves lost that would never be recovered, feeling she could never regain.

She released her hold on him, jerked back, stumbling slightly. "I'm sorry," she said, helpless to say anything else. It wasn't really an apology, not to him. She was just sorry. More of those regrets. "We should see about that dinner, maybe?"

His was an unreadable mask, his body stiff. "Are you hungry?"

She was sick. Her stomach felt as though it had been filled with leaden weight, her entire body shaking. "It's late. And anyway, it really should be spectacular, gold dusted chocolate cake or something." He still didn't move, didn't speak. "Thanks for the dance," she said, because there really was no way to ignore it. All she could do was try to make light of it. Try to pretend her whole world hadn't just been shaken. It seemed like she'd been trying to pretend that ever since Blaise had stormed into her life.

He nodded and offered her his hand. She clenched her teeth, tight, trying to hold back frustrated tears. She couldn't touch him now. If she did, she might crumble.

But she wasn't weak. She never let anyone see her cry, and she wasn't going to start now.

"I think I can manage to find my way back into the ballroom," she said stiffly, keeping her hands at her sides.

A small smile curved one side of his mouth. "Of course."

At least now there would be a physical barrier between them, a table, and maybe some wealthy society people to create a buffer.

Although, now it all just felt like too little too late.

CHAPTER SIX

CHEVALIER ROMANCE HEATS UP!

The press had done their job admirably. They hadn't missed the chance to snap photos of a very rare event: Blaise Chevalier with the same woman twice.

Not for the first time, he felt a small stab of disgust over the interest the media had with the salacious details of his life. Over the fact that there were so many salacious details. He was not a saint, not by any stretch of the imagination, and the press didn't have to tweak too many truths in order to write stories about him.

But he used his reputation to his advantage, no reason not to. He made money. It was what he knew how to do. It allowed him to set up foundations in Malawi in his mother's memory. Support causes that had meant so much to her.

The money that he made, the success he had achieved in business, was the one thing that kept his father from writing him off entirely. Not that he truly sought out redemption, not from him. Their relationship was strained at the best of times, his father still harboring anger at Blaise's eight-year-old self for choosing to leave with the woman who had betrayed him.

Then there was Luc. That Luc had offered forgiveness so freely for what had happened with Marie was still something that didn't settle well with Blaise.

It would have been better, in so many ways, if his brother had demanded a pound of flesh for the betrayal, if he had worked to extract pain and revenge. But he had not. And there were times when Blaise felt there was still penance to be paid.

Although, that implied that he was seeking absolution. He was not. Such a thing was beyond men like him. He accepted it. Owned it. Used it, as he did all things.

Just as he knew he and Ella could use the press to their advantage in the building of her business.

Ella. Temptation.

She was, much more than he had envisioned. Women, in his mind, were women. Sex was sex. Looking at it any other way had drastic consequences. But Ella, her smell, the feel of her skin, the temptation of those full, brightly painted lips of hers, turned him on faster than any woman in his memory.

Even Marie. And the control he had allowed Marie to exert over him had been nothing short of shameful.

He knew the man he was when he allowed emotion to lead. Knew what he was capable of when he let his desires take charge, when he abandoned decency in the pursuit of his own satisfaction. He had no intention of ever being that man again. Which was why his control was his own now, why he never allowed it to be shaken.

He put the paper down on his desk, allowing his gaze to linger on the photograph of Ella and himself out on the balcony. His face was tilted down, close to the curve of her neck.

Her head was tilted back, her face in profile. Red lips parted, eyes closed, long lashes fanning over her high cheekbones. She was a beautiful woman, no question about it. But there were many beautiful women. Women who didn't come with so many strings attached. Women who didn't test the edges of his tightly leashed control.

His mobile phone rang, the name *Karen Carson* flashing on the screen. "Chevalier."

"Hello, Blaise," she said, her voice tinged with a little bit of flirtation. Invitation.

He'd met Karen on a few occasions, but their meetings had been strictly platonic. From the sound of things, she wouldn't mind a change.

He entertained the thought for a full second, toying with the idea of using her to take his mind off Ella. He'd done it before. There had been countless women after Marie, each one used to try to wash away the impression the only woman he'd ever cared for had left on his body.

The thought of doing that now filled him with disgust, and he wasn't sure why.

"Is there something wrong with the sketches Ella sent you?"

"No, I quite liked them," she said, taking a cue from him, her voice hardening into a more businesslike tone, the flirtatiousness evaporating.

"Then all will go ahead as planned? The cover and the ad?"

"A cover now, too," she said, not sounding terribly surprised.

"Ella is very talented. I want to see that talent rewarded."

Karen cleared her throat. "Ah, yes, well as I've seen in the news recently there is speculation that you know a great deal about her talents."

The note of jealousy in her voice made him tighten his jaw out of annoyance. Ella had talent; he believed that now with a decent level of conviction. He wasn't about to have this opportunity dangled before her, only to have her lose it because of a woman mourning the loss of a night of sex that he'd never had any intention of having with her.

"I am only a man," he said, "but I am also a businessman. If I didn't think this would be a good move, for your magazine and for her, I wouldn't suggest it."

Karen cleared her throat. "Actually I was so impressed with the sketches I was thinking of including some more Ella Stanton pieces in a spread we're doing. There will be several designers represented. It will be very good exposure for her. We're thinking a beach shoot in formalwear. Very dramatic."

"Dramatic indeed. Have you scouted locations?"

"We were thinking Hawaii."

"Boring," he said. "Overdone."

"And you have a better idea?"

"Naturally."

"Do you have enough staff to cover a week away?"

Ella jumped slightly, gripping the edge of the counter to keep from losing balance on her three inch heels. "You really like the whole unannounced entrance thing, don't you?"

"I couldn't reach you by phone."

"The boutique has a phone," Ella said, jabbing the old-fashioned rotary phone with her finger.

"Charming. Does it work?"

She narrowed her eyes, hoping to capitalize on the annoyance that was currently flooding her. It was easier than dealing with the wild galloping of her heart.

"Of course it works. But you wouldn't know, because you decided just walking in here would be better."

"It's a public place, isn't that what most people do?" he asked.

She clenched her teeth. "Yeah. Anyway, why didn't you call my cell?"

"I did. It went straight to your voice mail."

"Oh." She crouched down behind the counter and fished around in her magenta leather bag, finding her phone buried at the bottom. Either she'd switched it off or the battery had died. Great. Very professional. "Sorry," she said, putting it on the counter.

She flashed back to what he'd said when he'd first walked in, registering the words for the first time rather than just that voice that sent her heart rate into overdrive.

"You asked if I could go away for a week?"

"Karen would like you to consult on the photo shoot. She wants your gown for the cover and the billboard ad."

Excitement tugged at her stomach, excitement that had nothing to do with Blaise for once, and everything to do with the achievement. This was so big. It was a key, to bigger and better. To worldwide exposure. To runway shows she couldn't even afford to buy tickets to now.

"She wants me to consult? She wants my opinion?"

"She'd also like for you to bring some additional looks, for a spread they're doing in the same issue that has your cover. She wants formal gowns. On the beach. I've been told this is very high fashion."

"It is," she said. "I think…I think I'm going to hyperventilate."

"*Non, belle,* don't do that," he said, brushing his knuckles lightly over her cheek.

She pulled back, decided not to acknowledge the

touch, or the lightning fast pulse of pleasure it sent streaking through her. "Yeah, um…so when do we leave?"

"Tomorrow. Can you have everything covered here?"

"I should be able to work that out. Yes, I will work it out." She started mentally rebuilding the boutique schedule in her mind. Because she was going to grab this opportunity with both hands, no question.

"Good."

"Are you…I mean, how am I getting there?"

A slow, sexy smile curved his lips. "We will be taking my private jet."

Her eyebrows shot up. "That's extravagant."

"Not really, it's a small jet."

"And you're coming, too?"

"Of course." He said it as though it should have been a foregone conclusion, and it really should have been. Still, a slug of surprise hit her stomach, followed by a tight curling of pleasure, similar to the kind that had assaulted her the night she'd gotten to be his date for the ball.

"We're doing the shoot in Malawi," he said. "It's a very tropical setting, the lake has water so clear you can see all of the fish swimming beneath the surface. It is the most beautiful place in the world."

There was a distance to his voice, a strange detachment. He said it was beautiful, and she believed him, but she also thought there was sadness there. Sad memories maybe. She thought again of him as a boy, leaving Paris, leaving everything he knew, his father, to go to a new country. A very different country. What had it been like? Had he been scared?

She couldn't imagine it now. Even in his well-cut suit he looked like a battle-hardened warrior. He didn't look like a man who had any concept of fear, or failure or any of the things that mere mortals seemed to struggle with.

He was a man apart. She envied him for it. She also wished she could come into his world, just a little bit. And it was so not the right thing to wish for.

"I'm…I'm looking forward to seeing it." She almost said she was looking forward to sharing it with him. But that was the wrong thing to say, the wrong way to look at it. Blaise wasn't going to share with her.

Those words, those thoughts, didn't even have a place in her mind. Neither did the ache that was spreading from physical body parts and beginning to lodge itself in her heart. She didn't know what to do with it. There was nothing to do with it, and yet she couldn't seem to shake it off.

But then, she was currently enduring steady doses of Blaise exposure, so that wasn't helping.

"Bring clothing suited to very warm weather," he said, the heat in those honey-gold eyes only reinforcing the demand.

"Okay," she said.

If only there was a way to cool down the warmth that Blaise brought with him whenever he was within ten feet of her. If only there was a way to forget how he'd touched her the night of the Heart's Ball.

But she couldn't. She was marked by him. And she knew that some marks didn't fade easily. And some of them lasted forever.

"So, I'll see you tomorrow then?" she asked, anxious to get him out and away from her so she could have a little time to herself before she embarked on a week filled with his presence.

"Where would you like to be picked up?"

"My studio…it's below my apartment so that will

be easiest." And then he wouldn't have to come up to her apartment and be in her space. Because if that happened, the impression of him would officially be embedded in every aspect of her life, and she just didn't want that. Not even a little bit.

"Then I will see you tomorrow morning."

"Yeah, see you then."

Sleep wasn't going to come easy tonight.

Ella could definitely get used to luxury travel. None of the nonexistent legroom or intimate acquaintance with the shoulder of the person next to you. Not to mention the fabulous perk of being able to bypass airport security.

Blaise's "small jet" had turned out to be a heavenly travel experience. Complete with silken leather seats that reclined all the way and champagne with strawberries.

The only drawback had been the fact that, even though he sat on the opposite side of the cabin, it was a lot of Blaise in an enclosed space. It gave her ample chance to really get tuned into his smell, his movements, short noises he made in his throat when he was thinking. And all of it made her stomach twist just a little more each time.

It was an effort to keep from squirming in her seat after an hour of travel. Being alone with him. Being so near him. The futility of the desire, that was the worst part. She was burning with need for him, and she knew that she could never arouse the same kind of desire in him. He was masculine perfection, the kind of man who could entice women to trade in their favorite pair of shoes in exchange for a night of pleasure in his arms. There was no way he would ever want her.

When they landed on the island of Likoma, she practically kissed the ground, so thankful to be out in the open, to detox from her Blaise overload. To try to regain some of her sanity.

A sleek black car, heavy and old-fashioned, but in pristine condition, met them at the tiny airport and she was whisked from the burning heat back into an air-conditioned environment.

Ella settled in the backseat, her relief at exiting the plane dipping sharply when the door to the car closed and she found herself getting cozy with Blaise again.

"It is beautiful here," she said, looking at the shoreline of the vibrant lake as they passed, the green trees and the shocking blue of the lake blending together.

It wasn't what Ella thought of when she pictured a lake. Waves crashed against the sandy shore, children splashing in the vibrant, crystal-clear water.

She smiled, watching them laugh as the cold water washed over them. She wondered if she'd ever been so happy as a child. Maybe she had been before the fire, but she couldn't remember. Her family had had everything. Money, status in the community. It hadn't protected them. And it hadn't offered her any comfort when she'd needed it most.

"In my opinion, the natural beauty you find here is unmatched. But there is much to be done as far as helping the people with the quality of life. It is better now," he said. "I've been working to improve the infrastructure, the roadways, trying to make things more accessible, that's been another challenge. Health care facilities, hospitals, clean water systems. And yet, there is always more." He sounded tired. She didn't think she'd ever heard him sound tired.

"You…you've done all of that?"

He shrugged, clearly uncomfortable with the subject. "I have done small things. It is what anyone would do."

Except it wasn't. It wasn't something anyone would do, and it wasn't small. And the media had never once said anything about Blaise's charitable efforts. The only time his heritage was mentioned was in a derogatory fashion.

In Paris, he seemed rootless, a rogue. A man who didn't care what others thought. He took action swiftly, decisively, without care for how it affected others so long as the bottom line was well-served.

Not here. Here were his roots. Here was his responsibility. Something he cared for more than money. People that meant more to him than a bottom line. He'd said that business was not the place for charity, but apparently he believed it had a place.

He'd also said he didn't believe in honor. But his honor was here, too.

"We'll be doing the shoot here," he said, gesturing to the shoreline.

"It will be dramatic. I love the idea of formalwear in this environment." She was happy to be back to the safety of business. She tried to keep her mind there by imagining what hairstyle she would have the stylist do with each gown, what sort of makeup.

The distraction was short-lived. Because Blaise was still right next to her, close and so very male and tempting.

She shivered slightly, even though it was hotter than blazes outside and the air conditioner only served to take the edge off. She wasn't cold. She was hot inside. Burning up. Consumed with an internal fire that she had never allowed herself to confront before.

It wasn't that she had spent eleven years void of

sexual desires. She had simply channeled them into fantasies about movie stars, heroes in books. Men she would never meet, or, better still, weren't real. Men who couldn't reject her.

It was more than a fear of rejection, though. It was the bone-deep fear that her mother was right. That things would be easier if she had died in the fire instead of living with the damage, confronting her mother with the damage, left behind.

But things wouldn't be better. She could do anything she wanted, fulfill her dreams. She was in the most beautiful place she'd ever seen, with the most beautiful man she'd ever seen, on the edge of the biggest break of her career.

And even though she would never truly have the man, it wouldn't stop her from enjoying the fantasy.

She looked at Blaise again, watched him as he stared out the window at the passing landscape, square jaw enhanced by the angle of his head, rich mocha skin begging for the touch of her lips, a taste from her tongue.

Somehow, being so near to him, the memory of his fingertips gliding over her skin, made all of those fantasies that had always been sufficient seem pale.

"Where will we be staying?" she asked.

"Another thing I have been working toward, bringing more tourism into the area. There is no shortage of attractions, but accommodations for wealthier guests have been limited."

"And you've taken care of that, too?"

"Yes," he said simply, turning his focus to his smartphone.

She had a feeling that she was getting close to seeing the man that Blaise truly was. And she could tell that he didn't want her to see it.

CHAPTER SEVEN

ELLA HADN'T ANTICIPATED the absolute decadence of the resort. She should have. It was Blaise's, and he didn't do anything in half measures.

It was hidden from the harsh sun beneath a thick canopy of trees. Built from stone and covered in vines, it looked as though it had grown up from the impossibly beautiful landscape. It was cool, calm and completely inviting.

"We will be staying in my personal villa," he said.

"We?" she said, her face starting to burn, and not from the heat.

"I have given it some thought. The Heart's Ball created a huge media stir. The press loved the more…intimate photos they were able to capture of us."

"And?"

"And I would like to give them some more fodder."

"The press won't be here, will they?"

"Ella, there will be models, stylists, writers, photographers and a photo shoot director. I think someone might mention something. Especially as I'm certain there were photos taken of us boarding the plane in Paris this morning."

"Oh…you think there were?"

"If the press wasn't taking a day off. I made no effort to be discreet. The press are weaving a romantic fantasy around our association and it is attracting a lot of attention to your clothing line. And this time, whoever wrote the article about the two of us mentioned you were wearing one of your own designs. He also named you best dressed of the night."

"I…I saw that." Seeing the pictures that had been taken of the two of them, some when they had been on the balcony, so close, desire so clear in her eyes it had horrified her. But the article had been wonderful, and the next day she'd had two women into the boutique asking about the red lace dress.

So he was right. The media was paying attention, and as a result, so was the public. But the idea of shacking up with him for a week was a little bit disconcerting.

"I'll have my own room, right?"

"It's a big villa. You won't have to see me if you don't want to."

That wasn't what concerned her. It was that she did want to see him. It was that being near him made her long for things that she had no business longing for. Not now, not with him.

The Town car bypassed the main building and drove them down toward the shore. The villa was situated at the very edge of the covering of trees, the front door nearly resting on the white sand beach, the crystalline water lapping at the shore a mere fifty yards away.

It was made of stone, just like the main building, the roof fashioned out of woven grass. It was like a private island fantasy. Like the two of them had been shipwrecked. Shipwrecked with the pirate—there was a nice one to save for later when she was in her bed. Alone. Aching. Longing.

She turned her thoughts off that particularly depressing track and back onto the scenery.

The slight rusticity of the environment dissolved the moment they walked into the villa. High ceilings, that were plastered, proved the woven grass was for show. White stone floors and French Provincial style furnishings gave it a look of timeless, expensive elegance. The curved, sweeping staircase that led to the second floor made it feel palatial. And Ella felt like a princess for a second. A feeling that was so foreign she thought she might be dreaming.

And then there was Blaise, and the feelings he created in her. Now that was complicated. There was the desire, desire that had been there since day one, and then there was the growing tenderness. A well had opened up behind the walls surrounding her heart and seemed to be expanding.

Coming here with him had changed the way she saw him. It had opened up another side of the enigma to her. This wasn't simply a moneymaking venture for him. She knew that. Sensed it. This brought in tourism, and with it, tourism dollars. It created jobs.

It forced her to look at him in a new light, though she didn't want to. Even when she thought he was nothing more than a cold, ruthless man who would stop at nothing to get what was his, a man who would think nothing of betraying his brother, even then it had been hard enough to stop herself from weaving fantasies around him.

Add this unexpected glimpse into his humanity and she felt like she might be in serious trouble.

"I will ask that dinner is served soon," he said.

"I can find something in the kitchen." The idea of spending a quiet, intimate evening filled her with excitement, which gave way to mild panic. She should feel that way about him, about spending time with him.

"Ella, must you always bc so stubborn?"

"I think so."

"For once, don't. Tonight, just enjoy yourself."

"Okay," she said.

Her heart thundered hard in her chest. Because nothing scared her more at the moment than the thought of giving in to what she really wanted and truly enjoying herself. Because, if she did, she not only faced the possibility of rejection, but of Blaise seeing how weak she truly was.

The scene was set for seduction, and never had there been a woman who looked more ready to be seduced. Blaise could only stare at Ella when she came down the stairs and met him in the open living area of the villa.

Ella, with her loosely contained blond curls accented by a shockingly pink flower. Ella, with lipstick and a daring dress to match. The neckline was too high for his taste, denying him the sight of her luscious breasts. But the fabric was fitted, clinging lovingly to every dip and curve of her body. And the hemline was brief, showing more of her mile long legs than should be legal.

It was the first time he'd seen her in simple, flat sandals, and he imagined the only reason she'd abandoned her daring high heels was out of deference to the sand.

He hadn't realized quite how petite she was. She seemed softer, more delicate this way. And it made his stomach tighten with urgency. He wanted to shield her, from what he didn't know. And to make her his.

And that he understood very well. He knew just what sort of possession he sought. The most basic, elemental sort. Her soft body beneath his as he found satisfaction within her, as he gave her pleasure, took his own pleasure.

The strength, the immediacy of it, was beyond anything he had felt in so long. He couldn't remember if he'd ever felt that way. He had shut down so much of himself after Marie because he had seen what happened when he gave his emotion free rein. It was an ugly thing.

"Dinner was set out for us on the terrace."

"Oh, nice," she said, but she didn't really sound like she thought it was nice.

"Were you expecting different?"

"I just thought…maybe a restaurant."

"Are you afraid to be alone with me?"

She blinked rapidly, pale gold lashes sweeping up and down with the motion. "I…why would I be?"

He took her hand in his, and she let him, curling soft slender fingers around his. "I don't know," he said, tracing the back of her hand with his thumb.

"Well, I'm not. I just thought we would go out. I'm overdressed."

"You look perfect. As always."

He watched as her pretty pink lips wobbled, only for a moment, before she set them into a firm line again. Her blue eyes looked brighter than usual, suspiciously so. "I will accept the compliment," she said, her voice thick.

How could such a simple compliment touch her so? Careless words, words he meant, but not words he had spent time thinking over. Nothing he hadn't said to another woman, only to be treated to a petulant pout until he expanded on the sentiment.

Not Ella. The simple, pure reaction was totally honest. He wasn't sure what to do with it. It made him want to say more. It made him want to offer to take her out, somewhere where he wouldn't be tempted to seduce the woman with the steel exterior, but possibly fragile interior.

But no, Ella wasn't fragile. She was tough. She was confident. He had simply caught her in an emotional moment, and heaven knew women had plenty of those.

He continued holding her hand, and she continued to hold his, as he led her up the stairs and through double French doors out to the sweeping terrace. White lanterns hung from the sheltering roof, introducing a soft glow to the warm, purple evening.

The view of the lake was stunning, the table setting was stunning. But neither thing touched the beauty of his companion.

Ella sat down before Blaise could do something else sweet. Like pulling her chair back for her or something. She already felt like a wreck.

You look perfect. As always.

She had never been perfect. Not before the fire. Certainly not after. And he had stripped her bare of every last piece of armor with the compliment. Because it was a tease of the one thing she'd always dreamed of. The longing she would never even say out loud, not even in an empty room.

To have someone accept her as she was. Love her as she was.

It was such an impossible fantasy. She didn't love *herself* as she was, how could anyone else? Least of all a man like Blaise. A man of such physical perfection, who dated women possessing the same physical perfection. It was impossible.

But her mind had taken that little thread and immediately begun weaving a web with it. One of pretty words and happy endings. Lies.

She picked up the wineglass that was, thankfully, already full and touched it to her lips, taking a small sip. Anything to distract herself.

"This looks great," she said, placing her glass back on the table. It was inane conversation, but the grilled fish and bright, fresh vegetables did look great and at least it was a safe topic.

"Naturally."

"Because you only hire the best in the world?" she asked, arching one eyebrow.

"I had the best in the world come here and train some of the local people. Everyone that works here is from Malawi."

More of that tenderness spread through her. She could almost feel her heart melting.

"How old were you when you came here?" she asked. She shouldn't ask. She didn't need to know. And yet she wanted to know.

"I was eight. But I didn't live on the island. I lived on the mainland, just outside Mzuza. My mother worked at a bank there. We were not impoverished, as so many others here are."

"But why did your mother bring you here?" She'd wondered. She knew his brother had been raised in France with their father.

"It was part of the deal," he said, his voice rough. "If she left Europe, she could have me. Otherwise, she would never see either of us."

"Why…why would your father do that?"

He slid his fingers up and down the stem of his wineglass, a muscle in his jaw ticking. "I think he was hurt and he wanted to hurt her back. I also don't think he believed she would truly go. It is my understanding that she had an affair, although, I have never been angry at her for it. I think when they fell in love they were perhaps a bit idealistic. They were able to see past cultural differences, skin color difference, and then many others were not. And there was tension."

Blaise leaned back, releasing his hold on the glass. "They imagined that love would be enough. It was not. Of course, things have changed now. I don't believe there would be the same issues. I've certainly never had them, and I have dated all types of women. But at the time..."

"And you came with your mother," she said softly.

"I wanted to," he said, "I never regretted it."

"When you came back...did you hate your father for what he'd done? For...banishing you?"

He shrugged. "My father is a hard man. He demands perfection. Control in all areas of life. I don't regret that I wasn't raised with him. But I don't hate him, either. All of us act poorly at times when passion is involved," he said, his voice taking on a bitter tinge.

She wondered if he was thinking of himself now, if he regretted the affair with his brother's fiancée. She wouldn't ask, though. Not now. She didn't want to engage in an exchange of information.

"True," she said. Not that she would know.

Her life had been so void of passion. She had channeled it all into her work. Everything had gone into her work. But it hadn't felt as all-consuming lately, hadn't felt quite as essential. Which she imagined was good. Feeling so much about anything was dangerous, as Blaise had just pointed out.

It was strange, though, feeling like her focus was splintered. Since her senior year of high school she'd moved toward her goal of having a successful fashion career, and she'd done it single-mindedly. Nothing had distracted her. She'd gone to Paris, she'd studied business and fashion in college, she'd gotten low-level jobs, gotten loans, started her own boutique and clothing line.

Nothing had ever turned her head away from that. Until now.

Now she saw the beauty of the setting she was in, the food tasted more intense, flavors bursting on her tongue. Her skin felt sensitive, her entire body on edge. It was as though a part of herself that had been dormant had just woken up.

Her focus had broadened. Her desires had broadened.

Blaise was looking at her, the same glittering heat in his honey eyes that she'd seen at the Heart's Ball. Her heart started pounding harder, her palms growing damp, her stomach so tight it made it hard to draw breath.

She stood from her chair and walked over to the edge of the terrace, looking at the lake glittering in the pale moonlight. It was beautiful, a natural wonder. It made her feel empty. Because she suddenly realized she'd never truly enjoyed the beauty of her surroundings. She'd always lived with such manic desperation, to be better, to be more successful.

Then Blaise was standing beside her, his large masculine hand gripping the wrought-iron rail. Before meeting Blaise she'd never really stopped to admire the differences between a man's hand and a woman's hand. She had never stopped to appreciate the effect that difference had on her.

He lifted the hand she'd been so focused on, cupped her cheek.

She lifted her eyes, met his gaze. It was easier in the dim light. He slid his hand down her neck, the undamaged side, and she shivered at the sensation. He leaned in, pressing his cheek against hers, his skin hot, roughened by stubble.

He pressed his lips to the hollow beneath her ear and a sharp groan escaped her lips. It was shocking. It was pleasure beyond anything she'd known before, that brief brush of his mouth on her tender flesh.

He kissed her again, this time on curve of her neck, the tip of his tongue teased the skin there. He raised his head, golden eyes searching hers.

She wanted to beg for him to kiss her lips, and yet she didn't want to alter his plan. She wanted to see what he would do next. Her heart was thundering in her ears, drowning out thought and reason, drowning out everything but the kind of desire she'd only ever dreamed about.

He kissed her again, his lips brushing the corner of her mouth this time. His hand cupped the back of her head, his fingers worked into her hair, gripping her, clinging to her as though he had to hold her to him. It thrilled her that she could affect a man like him. That he wanted her.

She felt her lips part of their own volition, her tongue sliding out to moisten them. He took it as an invitation, and she was glad, because she'd certainly meant it as one.

He didn't crash down on her like a wave. He dipped his head slowly, his lips hovering over hers, sending sparks of need raining through her. Her entire body begged for his touch, but her lips ached.

He rubbed his nose against hers, slowly, lightly, before closing the distance between them. He teased the seam of her lips with his tongue, but she was suddenly afraid to move. Afraid that if she did, she might wake herself up, that she might discover it was nothing more than a dream, and that she was alone in her apartment in Paris.

One hand still buried in her hair, he snaked the other arm around her waist, hand spread over her back, the heat breaking her from her fog. This wasn't a dream. Blaise was real. And he was kissing her.

She parted her lips for him then, gladly, enthusiastically. She shivered when his hot tongue slid against hers, exploring her mouth, tasting her, savoring her as though she were a delicacy.

She felt her hands unclench, lifted them so she could cling to his shoulders. If she didn't, she would simply melt into a puddle at his feet.

The boys she had kissed hadn't prepared her for a man like Blaise, couldn't possibly have prepared her for the tidal wave of desire that a simple kiss had sent crashing through her entire body.

He untangled his fingers from her hair, one hand anchored on her hip now, the other roaming over her curves, cupping her breast, his thumb sliding over her nipple until it ached, until she felt hollow and needy, ready and desiring to be filled by Blaise.

"I have to touch you," he whispered, abandoning her mouth, lowering his head to press a kiss to her cloth-covered breast.

His hand reached around to her zipper. "Ella," he said, his voice husky, thick with desire.

She shock of air that hit her skin, the slide of the zipper and the cold reality of her own name, brought her back to her senses, and with it, brought a rush of panic.

This had been a fantasy. She had been floating, allowing herself to pretend. But her name, whispered on his lips, was like getting doused with a bucket of cold water.

She wasn't the sort of woman who made love with gorgeous men beneath a blanket of stars. She wasn't the sort of woman to inspire that sort of desire in a man, any man, but especially one like Blaise. She was just Ella. She was the woman with disfiguring scars. The virgin whose lack of experience proved just what an insecure, damaged person she was. If she were to sleep with Blaise, he would know that. He would see her worst, he would see her fears, her pain. How could she show him that? How could she ever show anyone? It was less about her skin, more about her. About the scars beneath her skin, the weakness.

"No," she said, releasing his shoulders, her hands flying behind her back to stop him from lowering the zipper further.

"No?" he asked.

"I can't. I can't. Oh, I'm so sorry, but I can't." Words came out in a jumbled rush, and she felt tears pooling in her eyes, ready to spill.

She was devastated. She was angry. She was scared. And she still wanted him more than she wanted her next breath. But she couldn't.

When he touched her, he was in charge, he commanded her body, he orchestrated the movements. And she had nothing to cling to. No facade of confidence, of being at ease with herself. She didn't want him to know, didn't want him to see into her, to see all her insecurity. All her fear.

She turned and went back into the house. And she cursed. She had run away. She was the worst kind of coward. And she was too afraid to be anything else.

CHAPTER EIGHT

"THE ART DIRECTOR wants the blue boots." One of the gofers for the photo shoot was standing in front of Ella, the sand colored boots she'd selected for the china-blue gown dangling from her fingertips.

Ella gritted her teeth. It had been like this for most of the day. They had Ella give her opinion on accessories, makeup and hair. And then the director sent the model, or the shoes, or the belt back to be changed.

Ella reached behind her to the bag full of shoes and rifled for a pair of sky-blue velvet ankle boots. She handed them back to the gofer. "Here. I'm sure these will translate better in pictures."

Grudgingly she had to admit they probably would. They would make a brilliant foil for the white sand beach. She was just touchy because of Blaise. More specifically, because the imprint of Blaise's lips was branded on her skin, and her own cowardice, her own fear, was laughing quietly over its victory.

Fortunately Blaise had been absent for the entirety of the shoot so far. Ella moved from beneath the tents that had been set up on the shore to provide the crew with relief from the sun and went to stand near the photographer.

The wafer-thin model with pale blond hair and dark

eye makeup was most certainly working her look, contorting her body in a way that made her look like a sad, beautiful, broken doll.

A little shiver of excitement wound through Ella, momentarily chasing away her annoyance and regret. The model was Carolina, a very highly sought after editorial model, and to see the woman in her designs was like seeing her dreams truly come into fruition.

"She looks good." Blaise's voice penetrated her reverie and brought reality back in on her.

Ella didn't turn toward the sound of his voice. If she did…the flashbacks would ensure she ended up melted into a puddle. "She does."

"Going well?"

"Yes, we're almost done for the day. Tomorrow we're going to move to an inland location, have her pose in a waterfall."

"You are sure this magazine is meant to sell to women?"

Ella turned sharply this time. "It's not going to be a wet T-shirt contest. It's high fashion."

"My apologies." He sounded amused. She cursed him mentally twenty different ways.

"This isn't a men's magazine," she added, for good measure, knowing she sounded like a prude.

"Point taken."

The director called it a wrap and Ella started to wander back to the tents. Blaise followed.

"Haven't you got…somewhere to be?" she asked.

"No. I'm through with my business for the day."

"And what did that business include?" she asked, in spite of the fact that she should be trying to get rid of him, not continuing a conversation with him.

"Discussing the drilling of more wells in some of the

outlying villages. And getting more ambulances, mobile care units, something to help the people who live far out of the cities in a medical crisis."

Ella stared at him. "You carry a lot of weight on your shoulders." She heard herself say it, and realized how true it was at the same time.

Piercing eyes appraised her. "So do you, I think."

A crushing amount. "Not really." She shrugged, trying to remove the heavy feeling. It was impossible. "I wanted to thank you," she said, clinging to her water bottle like it was her life support, keeping her focus on the bright blue label, and away from Blaise.

"For?"

"Not for—" she felt her cheeks get hot "—I just wanted to thank you for this. All of this. I know that our working relationship has been…rocky. But I'm grateful for it now. This has helped." She still planned on paying him back as quickly as possible, but what he had done for her in such a short space of time simply wasn't something she could have accomplished on her own.

"It is business, Ella. Nothing more."

"But there's more to you than that," she said. She didn't know why she said it, why she wanted him to admit it.

"Not really."

"What you do here, in Malawi, that's not just business."

"Don't be fooled by a few charitable acts, Ella. A tax write-off is a tax write-off."

Her heart tightened. She didn't believe him for a moment, but watching his face get hard, seeing his walls come up around him, that hurt.

Her defenses seemed permanently crippled, and his remained as high as ever. Blaise was perfectly happy playing the bastard, even as it became abundantly clear there was more to him.

The way he had treated her last night was an example of that. He didn't plunder, or take. He had given to her. His lips had been both gentle and firm, demanding and generous. And when she had withdrawn, he had respected her.

It wasn't only his response that offered her the window into him. It was the fact that he was using the same methods she had used for the past eleven years. Don't let anyone in. Don't betray any emotion.

He was better at it than she was, though. Something she'd envied at first. Something she wasn't sure she envied anymore. She felt like she had one foot behind her own emotional walls, one foot testing out the other side.

She was afraid. Last night she'd been too afraid, and today she'd tried to resurrect her defenses to no avail.

She looked at Blaise, at his profile, his body held so strong and masculine, his posture so straight a military officer would be envious. He was a sinner, it was widely known. But he also built hospitals and dug wells.

And he had shown her things about herself, unlocked things in her she hadn't imagined were in there.

She had stepped into the fashion industry, a woman with scars, a woman who had been tormented by the fashionable girls in high school. And she had done it without fear, without hesitation, because it was her dream.

Last night, she'd wanted a man. She'd wanted Blaise, so much she trembled with it. And she had let her fear have dominion over her. She had seized control in her professional life, had set out to achieve her goals with single-minded focus. Why should any other area of her life be different?

It was time for her to stop being afraid.

* * *

He had been up half the night, his body aching, unfulfilled. He wanted Ella. His mind had been plagued by images of her, naked, her nipples, pink and tight, begging for his touch, her lips, soft and moist on his body.

All day he had pictured her blue eyes filled with desire for him, with none of the abject terror he'd seen flash in their depths when she'd pulled away from him on the terrace.

He would kiss her neck again. The curve of it, where it was smooth and creamy, the other side, where it was not. Not for the first time he thought it strange that his fantasies did not make her body unblemished. In his mind, he pictured every scar that he'd seen before. Because that was her. It was Ella. And his body, for whatever reason, desired only Ella.

And every mark that signified who she was.

His body tightened, hardened as he thought of her. She was so soft. He could imagine, very easily, the feeling of every soft inch of her pressed against his body.

He had left the photo shoot before Ella today, but he knew she would have returned by now. He closed his laptop and leaned back in the office chair. He'd thought to check on some of his investments to distract himself, but stocks weren't doing anything for him. Not tonight. Not when he knew Ella was somewhere in the house, downstairs probably.

This desire, this need, had a strength that bothered him.

Obsession. He remembered it well. Had vowed never to allow himself to give in to it again. That driving need to have something, someone, regardless of the cost. It was a weakness. A lack of control. That he was weak at his core was something he preferred to forget.

But Ella reminded him. Because Ella stirred up a kind of specific longing in him he hadn't felt since Marie. Then he had called it love. Had imagined that it made a sufficient excuse to act purely for himself.

"Love conquers all," he said bitterly. Love was a lie. An excuse.

He knew better now. What he felt for Ella was lust, nothing more. Strong lust, the sort of lust that promised untold pleasures, but only lust. Human desire at its most basic.

He had enough experience with that to recognize it. But with Ella, it was so much stronger. She made everything feel stronger. He needed to find his cool passivity again, his detachment.

The temptation she presented seemed too great to combat. All the more reason for him to do so. He had to maintain control. He had seen what happened when he didn't.

He would not indulge himself, would not give in to the need that was pounding through him, making his hands shake with the effort it took to keep from going downstairs and finding her, kissing her, making love to her. He had to prove he could stay distant. He couldn't afford anything else, anything more.

He needed to find another woman when he got back to France. That thought cooled his ardor faster than any cold shower ever could.

The breeze blowing in from the lake was cool; it blew across Ella's heated skin and made goose bumps raise up on her arms. She had not seen Blaise for most of the day.

She wasn't avoiding him now because she was scared

of him, she was avoiding him because she hadn't decided what she wanted yet, and she had a feeling that any time spent alone with him would see her decision made quickly.

It was the speed that scared her. It made her feel like she was in a car with no brakes, careening down a mountain. No control, no way to stop. If she was going to be with him she needed control.

Her moment of tranquility was interrupted by the sound of the French doors opening behind her.

"Did you have dinner?" Blaise asked, his footsteps heavy on the stone terrace.

"Yes. I got something from the restaurant in the hotel lobby." Another avoidance tactic she'd used, to great effect.

"Did you enjoy it?"

She looked at him and immediately regretted the action. Her heart slammed into her breast, thundering rapidly, as though it were trying to escape. She couldn't look away, though, because then he would know.

"Of course I enjoyed it. Everyone here does a fabulous job."

"I am glad to hear it."

She found her eyes riveted to his throat, to the up and down motion of his Adam's apple. Even there, he was so different than she was. Fuzzy images drifted through her mind, silken sheets, dark and pale limbs entwined, her lips on that strong throat.

She shook her head, tried to shake off the drugging arousal that was creeping in on her.

She felt like running. To him. Away from him. She felt like jumping out of her skin, as though her body couldn't contain everything that was swirling around inside of her.

This was what she'd been running from. From what Blaise made her feel.

She was still running. Even after she'd decided not to let fear control her. And now she really *did* want to jump out of her skin. To be someone else. Someone else here with this man who made her feel all of this amazing, burning passion.

But she couldn't. She turned away from Blaise, looked back out at the water, her heart hammering, but for a different reason now.

She couldn't be someone else, and in all probability, her scars looked now as they would look in forty years. They were healed, as much as they would ever be. She'd never accepted that, and she hadn't realized it until now.

Relationships, sex, all of that had seemed like something that would happen later. But she was twenty-five, and it hadn't happened. Because in her mind she had always imagined herself being with a man and looking beautiful, perfect, and while logically she'd always known that would never be, a part of herself had been clinging to the insane hope.

But she wanted Blaise. And he might reject her. So might any man, a man she might not want half as much.

It was now, or not at all. She had to take the step, to claim her life. The fire had taken so much from her. And she was seeing now that she had given it even more than it had taken; she had fed the flames with her fear for the past eleven years, aided by her mother's thoughtless words, by her classmates tormenting her, and she wouldn't do it anymore.

She turned to Blaise again, and she was certain he would be able to see the pulse fluttering at the base of her neck.

She took a step to him, and another, then put her palms flat against his chest. She stood like that, frozen, feeling his heart pound beneath her hands, letting his warmth spread through her.

She slid one hand up, curved it around his neck. He lowered his head slightly and she tilted hers up, capturing his lips. Her heart rate quickened, her breasts felt heavy, her body empty, in need of him. Of Blaise.

She knew what she wanted. The only thing stopping her was fear. Fear couldn't have this. It would take this from her.

Blaise wrapped his arms around her, pulled her in tight, kissing her urgently, hungrily. She wanted to cry. To be wanted, to be held so tightly, as though he were afraid of losing her, it was like balm, healing unseen wounds inside her.

She could feel his desire for her, hard and heavy against her belly. She moved against him, desperately seeking some kind of satisfaction. He lowered one of his hands, cupping her bottom, kneading her flesh. She wiggled against him with more intent, his touch making every part of her burn with need.

"Inside," she said, her voice reflecting her desperation. And she didn't care.

He moved his hand down her thigh, stopping when his hand moved from the bottom of her dress to bare skin, then he pushed the fabric upward. He kissed her temple, her cheek, nipped her earlobe. "I can work with what we have out here."

Out here, in the open. She would feel too exposed. And she didn't possess the knowledge or experience to engage in any sort of serious sexual acrobatics. She didn't really want him to know that.

"Inside," she repeated, lending her voice a commanding note.

She felt his lips curve against her neck. "Whatever you desire."

CHAPTER NINE

BLAISE CLOSED THE bedroom door behind them. There was no need—there was no one else in the house, but the action made her feel so much more secure. She wondered if he'd known it would.

"I often wondered if your lips tasted like bubblegum," he said, crossing the room and coming to stand in front of her. He curved his hand around her neck, stroking the back of it with his thumb.

"And?" she asked, breathless.

"They don't," he said, leaning in, kissing her lightly. "They are much richer, more decadent. I cannot place the flavor. It is uniquely you."

"If you had walked into my boutique with some lines like that I might not have been so hostile."

"It is not a line," he said. "It is true."

Her heart tightened and she tried hard to ignore it. This wasn't about her heart. It wasn't about finer emotions. It wasn't for Blaise, and it wouldn't be for her. This was risk enough without introducing anything like that.

"I want you," she said. Because she couldn't think of anything else to say. Her desire for him was pouring through her, it was in her blood, a part of her now.

He moved against her, the evidence of his arousal

clear. She had never been this intimate with a man, had never experienced what it might be like to have a man desire her as Blaise did now.

She placed her hand on his chest again. His heart was raging faster now, stronger. For her. She let her hand drift down, and she could feel the muscle beneath his button-up shirt, could feel the hard-cut definition. She sucked in a sharp breath as her fingers drifted below the waistband of his pants, the tips lightly brushing the solid length of his erection.

He sucked in a breath, his eyes intense on hers. She touched him again, more firmly this time, with more intent, cupping him, testing him.

It wouldn't be so easy to pretend to be experienced. She'd thought she could do it, after all, given her age the likelihood of there being any real physical evidence of her virginity was low. But her basic knowledge of male anatomy hadn't prepared her for Blaise.

You want him. Take him.

She squeezed him lightly, then more firmly and she watched his expression change to one of pure pleasure, a harsh groan escaping his lips.

She abandoned him then, letting her hands drift back up to his shirt collar as she slid one button through its hole at a time, slowly baring his chest to her, his torso. She pushed the shirt off his shoulders and let it fall to the floor.

He was the epitome of male physical perfection. Rich brown skin, well-defined muscles with just enough dark hair sprinkled over them to remind her that he was a man.

Tight, defined ab muscles contracted as he drew in a breath and she could only watch the slight movement of his powerful body with awe. She had known he would be perfect. But she hadn't quite understood how intimidating being faced with the perfection would be.

Never before had she been so conscious of just how lopsided this trade was. He was giving himself, his body, his experience. She was giving him her body, her imperfect, untried body and her knowledge of sexual tips and tricks that were limited to what she'd read in women's magazines.

It was too far to turn back, but a part of her wanted to. Wanted to wrap herself up in her fear and run.

"Can we turn the light off?" she asked.

He pulled her to him, and she pressed her hands against his chest, loving the feel of his bare skin beneath her palms. He kissed her slowly, thoroughly.

"I want to see you," he said softly.

They were the most terrifying words she'd ever heard in her life.

"I don't…you don't."

"Ella," he said, brushing her hair from her face. "I do. But if it makes you more comfortable, I can turn off the lights."

"It's just. I'm sorry, you don't know how bad the rest of the…the rest of my body looks."

"Have your other lovers had problems with your scars?" he asked, anger lacing his voice.

It was the question she had feared. The one she didn't want to answer, because it would expose her, would let him know that the Ella she showed the world was a lie.

It was the question she had to answer now, honestly.

"I haven't had other lovers."

Blaise released his hold on her, his heart pounding hard, from arousal, from shock. "Not possible," he said.

"Very possible," she said, her voice tight.

She had no reason to lie. And yet, it was nearly impossible for him to believe. But he did. He had to. The look on her face, defiance mixed with shame, told him she spoke the truth.

He felt as though he'd been punched in the stomach. This moment was not meant for him; he knew that, emphatically and without doubt. This moment was for a man who could promise Ella love. A commitment. Something other than a few nights of careless pleasure.

He had made up his mind to resist her, to take control of the near mind-numbing desire she aroused in him. And yet, he had not done that. Now she was telling him she was a virgin. Of all his many sins, taking a woman's virginity was not on the list.

He should keep it so. Keep that one blot off his record.

He was acutely aware of the imbalance between them. She was an innocent, of all things, and he…he had been with more women than he could readily tally up. He had followed his own flesh selfishly, had used love as an excuse to take his brother's future wife into his bed.

But this was more than virginity. She hadn't been with a man for a reason, and she had now decided that reason was no longer important. This wasn't a no-strings sexual encounter; it never could have been with Ella. But this…this made it more.

And he had nothing to offer her. Not love. Not commitment. Nothing. He had no right to touch her, no right to seek his own pleasure in her, to feed his own desires with her innocence.

He should go. He should walk away now. Confess his mistake and leave Ella untainted by his hands.

Yet he could not turn away from her. From those wide blue eyes, filled with need, and confusion and fear.

He lifted his hand, and cupped her cheek, the tremble in his fingers likely visible to her. She affected him so strongly, her beauty, her vulnerability. The simple sweetness in her smile, the occasional sharpness of her tongue.

He lowered his hand. It felt hard to do. Heavy.

He tightened his hands into fists. Made the decision to go.

"Blaise." She touched him lightly, her hand on his chest, fingertips exploring him, grazing his nipples. "Please."

"Ella…"

She bit her lip, pink and swollen from the kisses they'd shared, her eyes glittering. Her walls were down, her defenses destroyed. He would be a bastard to take her now. A bastard to leave.

His spot in Hell was already secure, this would only stoke the fire. And he welcomed the burn. He was too far gone now. Too far gone in every way. There was no redeeming him, and there was no stopping the flame of need that had ignited inside him.

He pulled her back to him, kissed her, sliding his hands over her cloth-covered curves. She sighed, let her head fall back. He kissed her, kissed the scar that ran from her shoulder, up her neck and disappeared into her hairline.

She looked at him, eyes wide.

"Belle," he said, English deserting him completely for a moment.

"The lights," she whispered, "please."

It took him a moment to translate the meaning of her words, for understanding to penetrate his desire-fogged brain. He pressed a kiss to her forehead before releasing her and walking over to flick the lights off.

Ella let out a breath she hadn't realized she was holding. This would make it easier. He would still feel the damage, but it wouldn't require her to reveal everything to him all at once. Confessing that she was a virgin had been enough. More intimate in some ways than what they were about to do.

She'd thought, for one gut-wrenching moment that he would leave her when she told him she hadn't been with anyone else. But he hadn't.

When Blaise came back to her, he hesitated before putting his arms around her again and a stab of horror lanced her in the chest. "Don't do this because you feel sorry for me," she said.

He took her chin between his thumb and forefinger. The moon, filtering pale light through the open window, gave her hints of his serious expression. "I am doing this because I want you. So much that my entire body aches with it."

"Mine, too," she whispered.

He placed his mouth next to her ear, whispered every illicit thing he wanted to do with her, while his hands roamed over her body, cupped her breasts, teased her nipples into tight points.

"Blaise." She shuddered, gripping his shoulders as her arousal increased, her body aching with a hollow pain, the need to have him inside of her.

"I'm here," he said, moving his hands to the zipper at the back of her dress.

She closed her eyes as he slid the zipper down. Cool air skimmed over her body as her dress fell to the floor, pooling at her feet. She was still wearing her high heels, and nothing but a small bra and panty set.

She could only see the outline of his body in the dim light, and she imagined that was all he could see of her.

She still felt almost overwhelmed, her senses swamped with arousal, need, shame.

She heard the metal sound of his belt buckle being undone, saw him push his pants down his legs and add them to the growing pile of clothes on the floor.

"Stand in front of the window," he said, his voice rough.

The window faced the lake, and she knew no one would see her. She crossed the room and went to stand in front of the glass.

"Beautiful," he whispered. "Take your bra off for me, *cherie*."

Her fingers trembled as she reached around and unclasped the flimsy article of clothing, freeing her breasts. She gasped as the air hit her sensitized nipples, as she became aware of the full weight of her breasts, longing for Blaise's touch, for his lips, his hands.

"You have such a perfect figure," he said.

She knew the moon was making her silhouette more prominent, outlining her body in a glowing, silver halo, revealing her shape while still concealing her scars. She turned to the side, to give him a different view. He sucked in a sharp breath, loud in the silence of the dim room, and a rush of power and desire assaulted her.

"Come here," he said, another command.

In this situation, she found she enjoyed his commands.

He put his arms around her, drew her to him, and she wanted to simply enjoy the feeling of her bare breasts against his chest, his crisp chest hair teasing her nipples.

Instead she went still when he placed his hands on her back. She closed her eyes as he slid his palms over the worst of her scars. The left side bore the worst of the damage, all of the nerves destroyed. She couldn't feel the fine points of his touch, the texture of his skin, the heat from his palm, she could sense only firm pressure, the weight of his touch, but nothing more.

She waited for him to pull away, to move his hands at least. He had to feel the scars, had to be aware of the dips and craters in her flesh.

He didn't stop touching her, didn't pull his hands away. He went on caressing her, kissing her again, his hot shaft pressed against her belly. When he did move his hands it was so he could shape the outline of her curves, grip her hips and slide her panties down her legs.

She stepped out of them, kicking them to the side.

He put his hands on her hips, got down on his knees. Ella put one hand on his shoulder, one on his head, running her hand lightly over his short hair.

Rough, masculine fingers skimmed her ankle as he worked the tiny buckles on her high-heeled shoes. His thumb massaged her instep as he removed the first shoe, and a shiver moved through her body. She'd never thought the act of shoe removal could ever be erotic, but Blaise took it there. By the time her second shoe had been dispatched, she was shaking, quivering beneath his touch.

He caressed the back of her knees with his hands, leaned in and kissed her there and she was shocked when a lightning bolt of need crashed through her. He worked his way upward, kissing a trail up to her inner thigh. Hot lips pressed against the tender skin and she let her head fall back on a sigh.

When he moved his lips to a more intimate place, licking, kissing, sucking, she moved both hands to his shoulders, clinging to him so that she didn't fall over.

Her thighs started shaking, waves of pleasure washing over her. Just before she could reach the peak he pulled back, pulled away and stood. Desire gnawed at her, unfulfilled, unsatisfied.

He led her to the bed and she went gladly. He opened the nightstand drawer and pulled out a condom packet, placing it on the pillow beside her head. He moved his hand between her legs, stroking her, drawing wetness up and slicking his thumb over her clitoris.

She moaned, her muscles tightening, contracting. He continued to stroke her as he penetrated her with one finger, testing her. He added a second, stretching her slightly, making sure she was ready.

Everything in her was strung tight, she could hardly breathe, her body poised on the brink of cracking beneath the building pleasure. Her orgasm crashed over her suddenly, like a wave, swallowing her whole and carrying her, weightless and breathless to the shore.

He kissed her, reaching for the condom packet, opened it quickly and rolled it on deftly. “Ready?” He asked.

She nodded. She was ready. She was replete, and yet she still wanted more. Still wanted him. Inside her.

He entered her slowly, allowing her body time to stretch to accommodate him. It didn’t hurt, she simply felt full. Deliciously so.

She gripped his shoulders again, let her head fall back. He kissed her, deeply, passionately as he began to move inside her.

She was surprised by how quickly the pleasure started to build in her again, how fast he was able to bring her to the edge again, panting, clawing at his back. His movements became uncontrolled, as hers did, as she rocked against him, seeking her own pleasure as she gave all that she knew how to give to him.

"Blaise," she said hoarsely when her second climax hit, deeper this time, the pleasure starting at her center and radiating out.

He thrust into her one last time, freezing above her as he found his own release, his shaft pulsing within her as he gave himself up to it, overtaken as she had been. She held him to her, her hands splayed across his sweat-slicked back, his heart pounding heavily against her chest. She didn't want to move, didn't want to face the reality of what had happened between them.

She just wanted to revel in the moment. Revel in being connected to someone. Connected to Blaise.

He withdrew after a moment, rolling over and climbing out of bed. She stayed as she was, unable to move. He walked into the bathroom and returned a few moments later, climbing back in beside her.

Relief swept over her. He would stay with her.

Tonight, he was hers.

And she wasn't afraid.

Blaise could only stare at Ella's back as the morning light filtered in through the window, casting a harsh ray of sun over the affected skin. She was still asleep, her back to him, the sheet she was covered in riding low on her hips, exposing her entire upper body and the rounded curves of her butt. And the scars. His first instinct was to touch, but he held back. Not for fear of hurting her, just out of respect.

He had touched them last night, had felt the uneven skin beneath his fingertips. He had imagined, fantasized, about running hands over her smooth skin. There was so much of her skin that wasn't smooth.

Uneven coloring, pockets and craters covered the

landscape of her back. It spoke of trauma, it spoke of pain. Pain so deep, so real, it made his chest ache.

But even with the stark difference between Ella and every other woman he'd been with, she had lived up to every expectation. Sex with Ella had been pleasure beyond anything he'd ever known. She had stripped him of his control, of his ability to think straight.

He had lost control, for the second time in his life. He didn't like the man it made him then, he liked the man he was now even less. To take Ella's virginity when he had nothing for her. It was more than that. It was the fact that her facade was a lie. The fact that she truly didn't wear her scars like trophies, as he had once thought she did.

What she showed the world was a shield. To keep people from looking too closely.

She hid the worst of them. The worst of her pain. And when she had revealed the fact that she'd never been with a man last night, she had revealed that her scars went well beneath the surface of her skin.

And he did not possess the power to heal them. All he had ever done for those in his life was cause pain. He had caused his mother pain by reminding her of his father, had caused his brother pain by taking the woman he loved for his own. He had even caused Marie pain in the end.

It would only continue with Ella. Like an infection, he spread the worst of himself to each person who touched his life. He had hurt his father by going with his mother, had hurt his mother in a way, by enabling her to come back to Malawi, where she had died because of their inability to get to a proper medical facility. And his brother…he had destroyed Luc.

It was why he had stopped trying. Why he had cut

off his emotions, embraced his ability to be ruthless and single-minded in his pursuits, mixing it with control to keep himself distant from anyone who cared about him.

Not last night, though. There had been no control then. There wasn't any more control now. He had stopped noticing guilt a long time ago. It was a constant companion and he had grown immune to the gnawing sensation of it.

But this morning, he felt it, so strong it was as if physical weight had been placed on his chest.

Still he didn't move.

He reached out and ran his fingertips over her skin, memorizing the way it felt beneath his hands. The pain and suffering the marks represented were beyond what he could understand in a physical sense.

They were beyond what anyone should be expected to endure. Least of all a woman like Ella.

"Blaise?" She sat up suddenly, her back still to him, her head bent low as she tried to gather up the sheet around her shoulders.

"No, don't." He sat up, reached around her, captured her hands in his, lowering them slowly, and with them, the sheet.

If fell around her waist, and she sat there, her spine held rigid, her muscles trembling beneath his touch. He flattened his palms against her back, slid them down, back up again.

"They don't hurt, do they?"

She shook her head. "No." Her voice sounded strangled.

"Was anyone else injured in the fire?"

"No." Just no. Nothing else. But that single word held a wealth of pain.

"How bad was it?"

"I was in the hospital for a few months. The same walls. Horrible food. And the pain. And then there were the skin grafts. So many surgeries. Recovery from burns is worse than getting the burns in the first place. At least, it was for me."

Her head was still bent down, her shoulders bunched tight. He put his hands on her shoulders, slid them down her arms, repeating the motion until he felt her relax beneath his hands.

"I have extensive nerve damage," she said, her voice soft. "I don't have feeling on the left side of my back. The scar on my neck…it's the same. I have no feeling there."

He bent his head, his forehead resting against her back, between her shoulder blades. Pain lancing his chest.

"Then I will have to kiss you twice as much on the right side, to make up for it," he said.

Ella's heart felt like it would pound out of her chest, tears stinging her eyes as she bit her lip in hopes of keeping them from falling.

Last night with Blaise had gone so far beyond anything she'd ever imagined possible for her. And he was still here. In the full light of day he was still in bed with her, touching her. Saying the most romantic things she'd ever heard in her life.

"I would be a fool to turn down that offer," she said, her voice trembling.

"I would be, too." He paused for a moment, pressing a kiss to her shoulder. "I don't want to hurt you, Ella."

The admission seemed torn from him, as though it pained him to admit something good and decent about himself.

"You didn't hurt me. You won't. You…I never imagined any man would want me." It hurt to admit that. To admit that she'd allowed her tormentors at school, her mother's comments spawned from her own guilt, to poison her so much.

"I…this boy in school asked me on a date. I was eighteen. He took me parking, you know? And he put his hand under my shirt. And he felt my back. That was the end of the parking and he told…he told everyone that I was disfigured. Hideous."

Blaise bit out a foul curse in his native language. "If I ever met the man, I would not be held responsible for what I did to him."

There was more. But she couldn't admit that. Couldn't possibly let him know the extent of it. It was too humiliating. Being made to feel second-rate by classmates was one thing. It happened to so many people. But experiencing it at the hands of her own mother…that was what she carried closest to her heart.

"It doesn't matter now." She took a breath. "I didn't want to be afraid anymore." She turned to face him, not bothering to cover her breasts with the sheet. It had been much more intimate, much more difficult to show him her back. "And I'm not. I feel like I just won something, in fact."

Blaise looked at Ella's radiant smile, at her pink tinged cheeks. Such an odd choice of words she'd used. Like she'd won something. Because he felt like he was losing something. Something he was desperate to hold on to.

CHAPTER TEN

ELLA WASN'T HAPPY about having to get out of bed. She wanted to stay there, wrapped in the sheets, tangled in Blaise.

But it was day two of the photo shoot and duty called.

She thought of Blaise, though, while she watched Carolina posing beneath the waterfall in full formalwear. When she was with Blaise, she felt real confidence. Real happiness. He made her feel beautiful.

A laugh bubbled up in her throat and the photo shoot director turned to give her a hard look. As though he thought she was laughing at him. The man was an *artiste.* He possessed no sense of humor and more than his fair share of narcissism. But the laughter had nothing to do with him.

Beautiful. She hadn't felt beautiful in eleven years. There had been a time when she'd been a part of the in crowd, the golden girl from a golden family. Until the fire had burned it all away. No one had known what to do with the lasting effects of the blaze. No one had known how to react to her.

So they had made her an object of ridicule.

But today, she felt some of that melt away.

The warm breeze kissed her face, and she smiled. She was finally taking control. No, she hadn't asked for the scars, and if she had the choice, she wouldn't pick them, but she'd spent so many years being angry because of the fire. Shaking her fist at the sky because it wasn't fair.

It still wasn't. But it was the way things were. It was her life.

And last night she had taken the first step to making herself a life that had some balance, that wasn't so controlled by an event that had happened so long ago. A step to finding freedom.

Control had been the name of the game for so long. But it was a tightly controlled prison. It didn't allow anyone in, and it only allowed pieces of her out. Only allowed her to feel and experience certain things.

Since meeting Blaise her focus had started to expand, and after last night…it was as though a veil had been ripped from her eyes. It made her face, really face, how much she had held herself back.

It was more than that, though. Being with Blaise had changed something, something inside of her. She felt alive, excited about life. About more than just work. It was like waking up.

As long as it didn't grow into more. It wouldn't. Blaise had been…good to her. But he was a practiced seducer, and that's what he was doing with her: seducing her. She didn't mind it, because that was what she wanted.

But she would have to be an idiot to fall in love with a man who was such a bad bet. And while she'd been called a whole host of very insulting things, that wasn't one of them.

"I'm back," Ella called when she walked into the villa. It was late, the sun was sinking into the lake and she was starving.

Blaise didn't answer.

She wandered around the sitting room, and then sat on the plush velvet couch. There was a folded piece of paper on the side table and she picked it up. It was a note, from Blaise, and written in surprisingly elegant handwriting.

Dinner. On the lake.

Elegant handwriting, but a very masculine missive. No hearts or frills for Blaise Chevalier. She smiled.

She had gotten hot and sweaty during the photo shoot, but she was too hungry to change before eating. It was a desperate matter, in her mind. Some women might be able to skip a meal now and then, but she wasn't one of them.

She had on a nice sundress anyway, the kind that showed her legs. Blaise seemed to like them. She smiled as she headed out the back door of the villa.

Blaise was there, his white shirt untucked and open at the collar, a single rose in his hand. It was a small thing, the rose, but it made her stomach tighten. The last time she'd gotten flowers she'd been in a hospital bed.

There was a large white boat moored on the dock. The place where their dinner awaited. A yacht and a rose.

"I wish I would have dressed up."

"You always look beautiful," he said, walking toward her, his hand outstretched.

She took the rose from him and lifted it to her face, brushing the velvet petals over her cheek lightly as she inhaled the delicate scent. "Thank you," she said.

"Hold on to it, I have plans for that rose later."

"That sounds…like it has the possibility of being a little bit naughty."

A wicked grin parted his lips. "I never claimed to be nice."

No, he hadn't. But he certainly did a good impression of a nice man on occasion. And that was what confused her.

Because she was well acquainted with Blaise the corporate raider, and the media version of Blaise: the rabid womanizer and ruthless thief of his brother's fiancée. And she had just met the man who had deep roots in his mother's homeland, who did so much to make it a better place. Even more recently she'd met Blaise, the lover. The man who touched her scars without flinching, who invited her to dinner on a yacht.

And she had the terrible feeling that it was Blaise, her lover, who was in danger of evaporating one day.

But until then, she would make the most of every possible minute with him.

"How was the shoot?" he asked, his hand on the small of her back, guiding her to the dock.

"Great. Better today. It's…it's funny. I was so concerned about maintaining my control, and I'm now facing the reality that there are so many people involved in the making of a career. Models, directors, stylists, and I'm only a piece. I create the clothes, but it's not all up to me."

"You imagined it would be?"

"Yes, I think I did. I mean, I knew that all of those people would have roles, but I hadn't considered how every person who touches the gown makes it slightly different than it was when I created it, either through the pose they choose or the way they style it."

"And are you okay with that?"

"Yesterday, I didn't think I would be. But today I saw why a collaboration works, and I was happy. I let go, and that's not something I like to do, but it was rewarding." She took a deep breath of the heavy, fragrant air. "That's one reason I was so put off by you."

"But only one reason," he said, lacing his fingers with hers as he led her up the gangplank and onto the yacht.

"Well, there were several reasons," she said absently, her heart expanding as she looked at the surroundings.

There were candles placed near a plush, velvet blanket that was spread out on the deck, surrounded by large, jewel tone throw pillows. There was a classic, woven picnic basket set off to the side, and two wineglasses near an opened bottle of white.

"There were…there were reasons," she said, smiling slightly.

"And what were they?"

"They've slipped my mind," she said. "Because if you had brought this out the first night we met, I think I would have warmed to you more quickly."

"Ah, so you can be bought."

"With a picnic on a private yacht? Yeah." She turned and smiled at him and her heart tightened when she saw him smiling back. A real smile. It was such a rare thing to see on his handsome face. Sometimes it seemed his face was chiseled into that set, impassive expression.

Not right now. Not with her.

"Shameless," he said, drawing her to him, his fingers tangling in her hair.

"Maybe." She felt breathless now, with him so close. She wanted him to kiss her, wanted to lose herself in the sensual mastery of his touch. It had been too long. Way too long.

"I think you need food more than you need a kiss."

Did she? She'd thought so a few minutes earlier, but

now, now that she was with him, she was changing her mind. "I don't know about that."

"I do. You were out in the heat all day, and you probably didn't take an adequate lunch break."

"I got too involved to stop and eat."

"I'm not surprised."

"Don't even accuse me of being a workaholic, Blaise Chevalier, because I would just turn that one right around back to you."

"I wasn't going to deny being a workaholic. Tonight, though, I think I will leave work where it belongs, *oui?*"

"I will, too."

Blaise sat on the blanket and she joined him. It was getting dark now, the streaks of orange from the setting sun fading into a dusky gold, the air turning purple around them. There were no streetlights, nothing to interfere with the emerging moon and stars.

Blaise poured them each a half glass of wine and Ella opened the basket and pulled out a platter of meat, cheese and fruit.

"Lovely," she said, picking up a piece of salami and taking a bite. She noticed Blaise looking at her and she narrowed her eyes. "What? I'm hungry, remember?"

"I'm glad. Eat."

"Don't stare then!" she said, laughing, unable to stop the bubble of joy from escaping her lips. She felt happy. She noticed because it wasn't very often she felt completely content right where she was. She always looked to the future, to goals she had yet to achieve. Not now. Now she was just living in the moment.

He smiled, at her, making her feel like she was the only woman on the planet. "I am only staring because you're so beautiful."

She bit her lip, her stomach tightening a touch, dimming the joy she'd felt a moment earlier. "I don't know how you can say that."

His dark brows locked together. "You don't know how I can think you're beautiful?"

She shook her head, setting the meat down on the plate. "No. I don't."

"Then I will tell you," he said, eyes intent on hers. "You have such beautiful eyes, expressive, deep. And your lips…a man could weave fantasies about your lips. I know I have." He reached his hand out and stroked his thumb over her lower lip, slowly, gently. "What they would feel like against my skin, how they would taste and I am not disappointed."

He slid his hand down, fingers skimming her collarbone and down further, teasing her tightening nipples. "Your breasts fit in my hands so perfectly, your whole body is shaped just as a woman's body should be. As though you were molded in my dreams."

She could feel her face burning, her heart racing. The words, such perfect, sincere words, spoken in that deep seductive voice, resonated through her. It was difficult to believe. Impossible in some ways. And yet, his eyes were on fire with the truth of it.

She blinked, tears assaulting her again. That seemed to happen with Blaise. She'd spent the past eleven years cultivating her defenses, ensuring no one ever knew they affected her, making absolutely certain that no one ever saw the weakness in her.

But Blaise had demolished her defenses, left her open and vulnerable. And for some reason, she didn't feel weaker for it. In some ways she felt stronger.

He took his hand away, picked up his wine and turned his attention to dinner. The silence between them wasn't awkward, it was companionable. Comfortable.

"Thank you," she said softly, satisfied by the food, happy to be with him. His words echoed in her, reverberating through her.

She cleared her throat, still fighting not to cry. "This is so nice."

"You need to relax more, Ella. Come here." He patted the blanket in front of him and she moved so that she was sitting with her back to him, his powerful thighs bracketing her.

He moved his hands to her shoulders, kneaded away some of the tension. She couldn't remember the last time someone had done that for her. She'd never paid anyone to give her a massage because that would require her showing the parts of herself she hadn't come to terms with.

But Blaise had seen the worst now. He knew what was beneath her fashionable dresses and cool demeanor. And he was still here. He could still touch her.

She felt his hand on the zipper of her dress, felt it sliding down, exposing her skin to the warm evening air. Blaise kissed her neck, first her scar, then the other side, twice. "No one can see us here," he whispered.

He pushed the thin straps of her dress down, baring her breasts, her back, entirely. "How much sensation have you lost?" he asked.

"Close to half of my back has nerve damage," she said. "My arms aren't as bad—they have feeling at least, even the left one."

"I see." He leaned sideways, picking up the rose from where she'd set in on the blanket. "Do you feel this?"

The sensation of soft, velvet petals skimmed over her neck, the top of her shoulder.

"Yes," she said, "Blaise, what..."

"I want to know where you can feel my touch. How

I can best pleasure you. I want to know your body." She felt the rose, guided by Blaise's hand, gliding softly over her skin. "Can you feel this?"

"Yes," she whispered.

A breeze blew in off the surface of the water, the sharp cold and her near unbearable arousal tightening her nipples to painful peaks.

He moved the rose lower and her sense of it evaporated. "And here, Ella?"

"No," she said, her throat tight. She wished she could feel him. All of him. Everywhere. The fact that her body denied that filled her with frustration.

Then his touch was there again, cool and featherlight at the base of her spine. "There. I can feel you there," she whispered.

"Here?" She felt the petals skim across her lower back.

"Yes, *oh, yes,*" she sighed, her body aching for more of his touch, for a firmer touch. And yet, she was enjoying the tease, the sensual torture. There was no more frustration, only need. Only the desire to be with Blaise again. To be joined to him.

"And this?" he asked. She felt his lips, hot and firm against her shoulder blade. She felt the sensation down to her core, internal muscles clenching tight as her heart rate increased.

She could only nod, biting her lip to keep a moan of pleasure from escaping. Her entire body shuddered and she didn't even try to hold back her sounds of approval when she felt the tip of his tongue trace the line of her spine.

"I felt all of that," she said, her throat so constricted it was hard to force the words out.

"Here," he said, his fingers drifting to a place she

could no longer feel. "This is where the worst of the damage is." He leaned in again and even though she couldn't see, she knew he'd kissed her there.

A tear spilled down her cheek and she didn't bother to brush it away.

"But here." He kissed her on her shoulder. "Here you feel me?"

"Yes," she whispered, closing her eyes.

"I have a map of you now," he said, his fingers drifting over her.

She wanted to tell him that he now knew her body better than she did, but she couldn't speak for fear she'd dissolve completely into tears.

So she turned and kissed him instead, pouring every ounce of her emotion into it. He kissed her back, his hands moving now to cup her breasts, tease her nipples.

"Oh, I was waiting for that," she sighed and let her head fall back.

"So was I," he said, nipping her lip lightly and soothing the sting away with his tongue.

"You're overdressed," she said, touching his chest.

"I can remedy that."

He made quick work of his clothes, discarding them onto the deck. She ran her hands over his chest, over his perfect, unblemished skin, his tight, muscular form. "You're so perfect," she murmured.

He caught her hand, kissed the tender underside of her wrist. "No more than you."

Tears assaulted her again and she blinked them back, determined not to cry now, not when she craved release so very much. And crying would certainly destroy the mood of sensual intimacy that surrounded them.

She only wished she could give to him, as he had to her. What he had done was more than a sexy exercise, more than simple foreplay. He had touched her, looked at her, brought the part of herself she was most ashamed of into the affair, rather than ignoring it, or tolerating it.

He had taken the time to learn her body. All of it.

She stood for a moment, shimmying out of her dress and underwear, kicking her shoes off and idly hoping she was able to find them in the dim evening light.

She dropped to her knees, kissing his chest, running her tongue over his perfectly sculpted pecs. She craved him, more than food or drink, was suddenly driven by the need to taste him. She traced a line down the center of his torso and she felt his muscles contract sharply beneath her touch.

She gripped the thick, hard length of him in her hand, then dipped her head lower still, hoping she could give him half the pleasure tonight that he'd given her the night before. It was her turn to explore. Her turn to learn.

One of his hands gripped her shoulder, the other, forked through her hair, his masculine groans of pleasure fueling her own desire. That she could make his muscles tremble, bring him to the brink of sexual ecstasy, was a heady rush she'd never anticipated.

"Ella," he rasped, his voice strained. "Enough, *ma belle.* I need all of you now."

She lifted her head, could see his eyes, glittering with desire, the stars reflected in them. "I need all of you," she said, pushing lightly on his chest. He leaned back against the pillows, giving to her slight physical command. "Condom?"

He grinned wickedly, white teeth shining in the moonlight as he reached beneath one of the pillows and produced a packet. She took it from his hand, tearing it open.

"So sure of yourself?" she asked.

"I did provide you with dinner on a yacht," he said, still smiling.

And so much more. "Yes, you did."

She fumbled with the condom for a moment, allowing him to place his hand over hers to help her roll it onto his length.

"I'll figure it out next time," she said.

"I'm not complaining at all." He placed his hand on her cheek, kissed her lightly on the lips as his other hand cupped her buttocks, urged her to come nearer to him, to straddle his body as the kiss intensified.

She positioned herself above him, moving until she could feel the blunt head of his erection pressing against the entrance to her body. She lowered herself onto him slowly, her breath hissing through her teeth as he filled her.

"Good?" she asked.

He tightened his hold on her rear. "Yes."

She started to move over him, finding her rhythm, the one that made her body pulse and made Blaise's eyes close in ecstasy. His hands roamed over her back, traced the path where she was able to feel him expertly.

"Beautiful," he grated. "So beautiful."

His words, the movement of his hands, of his body, pushed her over the edge, her orgasm overtaking her, radiating through her body with all the force of a tremor. Shaking her, rocking her to her core.

He tightened his hold on her, gripped her tightly around the waist and reversed their positions, keeping himself buried deep inside her. He set the pace now, seeking his own release, still adding to her pleasure.

And when he found his release, she was hit with an aftershock, more mild than the first, a slower roll of pleasure that seemed to grow as it fed off his. She looked up at the stars, watched as they seemed to rain down over her.

She gripped his shoulders tight, kissed his collarbone.

He rolled to the side, his arms encircling her. She rested her hand on his chest, sheltered her face in the curve of his neck.

"I didn't need the yacht or the picnic," she whispered. "This was enough."

Blaise's body still ached for Ella, even after the most explosive sex of his life. He wanted more. And even when he'd had it, he was certain his satisfaction would last for only a moment before the need to have her grew to near unbearable levels again.

He stroked his hand over her side, skimming the indent of her waist, the curve of her hip. She was unique, in so many ways. He could never mistake her for another woman. An innocent siren, perfect and yet damaged. She was a study in contradiction, and she fascinated him endlessly.

It was a new feeling. Women were indistinct in his mind, his past sexual encounters blurring together. Especially the ones that had happened just after Marie left him.

Marie was distinct still. But with her it had been a need to possess, to claim her for himself. He'd long since realized that what he'd felt for her hadn't been love. He'd stopped believing in the emotion, or at least in his ability to truly experience it.

What he had with Ella felt different. It wasn't about mere possession. He wanted to give to her. To know her body as intimately as possible so he could give her the pleasure she deserved to get from her lover.

Of course, any gift from him was something of a poison chalice.

And even with that realization, he didn't release her. He continued to hold her, continued to stroke the contours of her body.

"No one except for doctors and nurses have ever touched my scars like that," she said, her voice muted. "After the fire…my mother couldn't even touch me anymore."

He clenched his jaw tight. His own mother had struggled with the same issue, and then his father later. He had been caught in the middle of a bitter divorce, and as good to him as his mother had been, as passionate as she had been about taking him to Malawi with her, there were moments when he reminded her too much of his father. And when he'd returned to France at the age of sixteen, after his mother's death, his father had seen too much of his mother in him, and had seen the son who'd left him.

"A reflection of her own issues," he said tightly, "not yours."

"I understand that. Now. I'm starting to anyway."

"What happened, Ella?"

He felt a hot tear roll from her cheek and drop onto his chest. His stomach tightened. He didn't do well with female tears. But Ella didn't sob, didn't give any indication she was crying other than the moisture she left on his skin.

"My family lived in upstate New York in this huge manor home. It was like a maze. Three stories, thousands of square feet and a lot of rooms. We were all asleep. By the time we woke up…it was so hot." Her voice was distant, as though she were relaying secondhand information, not talking about something that had happened to her personally. "The knob on my bedroom door burned my hand." She held out her left hand, traced the nearly invisible crescent of wrinkled skin on that palm. "I was too scared to jump from a third-floor window so I tried to just…walk out."

He tightened his hold on her, a sick feeling hitting him. Seeing Ella's scars, he knew there had been pain, and he was conscious of that fact every time he saw them. But to hear of it, that was something different.

He was helpless to do anything but listen. He hated the feeling. Hated that he had nothing to give her. Mostly he hated that it had happened to her. He had set the fire in his own life, and his consequences were his own. Ella had done nothing to earn such suffering.

"How did you get out?" he asked.

"The second-story window. I tried to get down the stairs to the front but it was…consumed and I was already burned from trying to make it down the hallway… I couldn't breathe anymore."

"Your family?" he asked, his throat tight.

"Was safe. They were on the lawn, all clinging to each other."

"They had gone into my sister's room and gotten her out first and then…they couldn't come back inside for me." Another tear landed on his chest. "And it is terrible of me to wonder why it went that way. To feel angry that they didn't risk their lives for me."

"But you do."

Silence settled between them and he sensed the struggle in her, the war that raged in her body.

"Yes," she whispered. "I have spent my life trying to prove I was worthy of the sacrifice they wouldn't give to me. But it doesn't matter. It doesn't change anything. They can't…they can hardly look at me because they blame themselves, too, and…and they can't handle their guilt."

"And you're not allowed to be angry."

She shook her head.

"I'm sorry, Ella," he said, the words torn from him. "You are worth more than that." It was the absolute truth. She was worth more than a family that couldn't put away their own guilt to help Ella heal. She was worth more than a man who could offer her nothing more than physical pleasure in the bedroom.

Her family was too selfish to see outside of their own pain and into Ella's. And he was too selfish to let her go.

"What about your family?" she asked. "Do you see them now."

"Yes," he said. "Sometimes."

"Your brother?"

His hands tightened slowly into fists. "Yes."

She paused for a moment as if waiting for him to go on. "That's good," she said.

"We're going back to Paris tomorrow."

"I know," she whispered.

"You sound sad."

"I kind of like the yacht." She laughed, the sound shaky still, her voice thick with the remaining tears.

He let his fingers drift from her arm to her collarbone, down to her breasts, tracing lightly around her taut nipple. "I have yachts in France."

CHAPTER ELEVEN

AS SOON AS they were back on French soil, Ella started seeing evidence of the effects of their time in Malawi. Tabloids had photos of them, standing together on the beach at Lake Nyasu for the photo shoot, Blaise's hand resting on her lower back in a casually intimate manner.

And the morning the story had hit the lifestyle pages, her boutique had been slammed with customers, all looking to see if they could find the white shift dress Ella had been wearing on the beach that day. Fortunately it had been stocked and it had translated to sales. It had also meant that owners of other boutiques had been calling, trying to find out if they could get her clothing in their larger stores.

It was the kind of thing that Ella had only ever imagined happening to her before, but it was happening now. The fact that she got to share it with Blaise only made it better.

Blaise. She couldn't think of him without a smile curving her lips. Her lover. The man who held her in his arms at night, the man who looked at her body with desire in his eyes rather than revulsion or detachment.

Ella finished placing and sizing the last photo in her virtual portfolio and readied it to send on to Statham's department store. The massive retail chain had requested a chance to look at her more commercial pieces.

That was the biggest boon of all. And the ad campaign for *Look,* featuring her designs, hadn't even been released yet. She couldn't even imagine what might happen when it was.

Getting her line in such a prominent chain of stores would be the beginning of her being a household name. It would be the beginning of her feeling valid. Of her proving that she was worth it. That it was worth it for her to be alive. To prove that to her mother.

And yet, she found it just didn't matter in that way anymore.

She was proud of the accomplishment, thrilled that it had come from the work she'd done with Blaise. Pleased that something she was passionate about was being received well. But it wasn't about proving her worth anymore.

Because she felt like she was worth something. She had been validated by industry professionals and consumers.

And then there was Blaise.

They'd been back for two days and she hadn't had a chance to see him. She missed him. Missed his touch, his kiss, his possession. She curled her toes in her boots and hit Send on the email, with her portfolio attached, to Statham's.

She leaned back in her office chair, her heart thundering in her chest. She'd been a virgin for twenty-five years and she'd managed to bear it. Now, after two days without Blaise she felt like she might explode with pent-up sexual energy.

But he was busy. She was busy. She'd had a lot to catch up on with the boutique, and the different portfolio and meeting requests. But she was caught up now, until more came in.

She shouldn't call him. Not until he called her. She really shouldn't.

Snatching her mobile phone from the desk, she hit the speed dial for Blaise's number and chewed her bright pink thumbnail, heart thundering in her temples as it rang.

"Ella."

She shivered when he said her name, his voice as affecting, as sinfully delightful now as it had been the first time she'd heard it. No, more now. Because now she'd heard it whispering all the intimate, delicious things he wanted to do to her body. And better still, she had the experience of him being a man of his words.

"Hi. I was just…I know I've been really busy, but I just sent off the last of my unfinished business."

She waited. Waited for him to take the hint and say he wanted to see her. This was almost more terrifying than the first time he'd seen her scarred skin. Because she was showing him more than just her external imperfections. She was giving him a look into her, into her feelings.

Feelings she wasn't certain had a place in her life, or in his.

He didn't say anything, so she pressed on. "I was wondering if you wanted to see me tonight?"

"I'm attending a social gathering tonight," he said, his voice closed off.

"A party."

"A gathering of people."

"Yeah, a party." She gripped her phone tightly, her palm slick with sweat. "You don't want to take me?" It was a stupid question. Stupid to let her insecurity show like that. Stupid to *be* so insecure.

"I didn't think you would be interested. I'm going to talk business."

"And if I had a business social function to attend would you expect to go with me?"

"Yes," he said, without hesitation.

"Can you say 'double standard'?"

"Double standard," he said wryly. "I didn't say I was right, I simply said I would expect to go with you."

"You implied that you were right," she said acidly, "because you always think you're right."

"True."

She blew out a breath. "Okay, I know that what we're doing here isn't a permanent thing. I know that this is physical. But in my mind, it's a relationship. I was a virgin because of the scars, because I was so afraid to be rejected because of them. But I think, even without them, I would have taken a sexual relationship seriously. And that means I sort of expect to be the date to things." Her stomach tightened. "You aren't taking someone else with you, are you?"

"I see no point in playing two women at once. If I want a woman, I take her. If I do not, I break it off with her," he said, his tone hard, more like the Blaise she'd first met than her fantasy lover of the past week.

But she'd insulted him, she realized that. She'd accused him of cheating, basically, and she had no reason to do so. "Sorry. But you have to admit, not telling me about something like this seems a little shady from my perspective."

"It was not my intent to be—" he seemed to be searching for a word "—shady. But I keep my business life and my personal life separate."

"Except when you're managing my business."

"What has happened between us was unavoidable. Normally I would not sleep with a business associate."

"I feel all warm inside now," she said, her voice flat.

"Are you determined to start a fight?"

"No. I'm sorry."

"How do I make you happy now?" he asked, frustration edging his voice.

She laughed. "It's not…I'm not trying to be petulant and get my way. You go to the party by yourself if you want to. I just felt excluded. If I'm a two-night stand then tell me, but I was assuming that we were going to continue on."

"You're not a two-night stand," he said roughly.

Her thoughts wandered back to the night on the yacht, when he'd drifted the rose over her body, his fingers following, as he learned the map of her body, how to touch her. No, it was more than a simple fling, she was sure of that. She just wasn't sure Blaise wanted it to be more.

"And you're not ashamed of me?"

"*Mon dieu!* Ella, no I am not ashamed of you." He sounded genuinely affronted by that.

"Sorry again. My own family was, though. My parents wouldn't allow me to wear a normal swimsuit when we went to the Country Club. I had to wear one that was styled like the Olympic swimmers wear."

Silence hung between them. Again, she'd said too much. She'd told him things she'd never told another soul before. But she longed to get it out now, longed to purge herself of it and be done with it.

"Ella, I don't know what you want from me," he said slowly.

"Honesty," she said, her throat tight. "I'll take honesty."

"And I'll give it to you."

"Thank you."

"I'll talk to you later."

Ella nodded, even though he couldn't see, and pressed the End Call button on her phone.

Blaise swore loudly into the empty silence of his office. It did nothing to make him feel better. Ella made him feel like the inside of his chest was bleeding sometimes. To realize she thought him ashamed of her, to know why she felt that way, because of her family and the clumsy way they had dealt with the aftermath of the fire.

He wasn't the right man to handle her. He had tried to distance himself since their return to Paris, in an effort to cool things between them, in an effort to stop before she got hurt. Before he hurt her.

But then she'd called, her siren's voice luring him to the rocks again.

He'd been so close to asking her to come with him tonight anyway. But he would not be manipulated. Marie had been a master of manipulating him. And he had allowed it.

He would not allow Ella to do the same.

Most of his relationships in the past three years had been brief one- or two-night encounters, and he didn't want that with Ella. He wasn't through with her yet. Just the thought of her had him hard and aching to be in her again. He was dying for the taste, the touch of her, to be sheathed in her tight, wet body while they were both driven to the peak.

But she was working at his control. He recognized that. He couldn't allow it.

No. He held the cards in their relationship. There was no question. And he wanted Ella. Tonight. He wanted her by his side at the party, and he wanted her in his bed later.

And he would have her.

"It was a mistake, to think I would be better off without you for the evening."

Ella blushed beneath Blaise's rather intimate appraisal. Mostly because she still felt ashamed for acting so transparent earlier, and for essentially begging herself a spot as his date for the night.

But when he'd called back less than twenty minutes after their initial conversation she'd been hard-pressed to say no when he'd asked her to go with him. It would just seem way too contrary and ridiculous to refuse after making such a big deal of it. She only wished she hadn't said anything.

It had been honest, though. She wasn't in this relationship lightly. Even if it was only sexual. It had been huge for her to open up to him, to show him her body, to let him touch her, caress her. Revealing her physical self to him had been the beginning of revealing all of herself.

Blaise wore his scars on the inside, and that afforded a kind of protection she didn't have. Blaise knew more about her than anyone else on the planet, and she couldn't help but feel like she had some claim on him because of that.

He didn't share with her. Nothing but his body.

She'd tried to find out about his family when they'd been on the yacht, but she'd only gotten simple, one word answers that had left her with nothing real to go on. It bothered her more than she wanted to admit, because he had gotten hold of her heart.

"Thank you for the almost-compliment," she said, tight lipped as he led her into the ballroom of the luxury hotel.

He was meeting with a potential client, someone he was interested in investing in. Someone who was hesitant to get Blaise involved thanks to his reputation, so he'd told her on the limo ride over.

He gripped her arm and turned her to face him. "It was a compliment. I made a mistake. What more do you want?"

"Nothing," she said. "Except for you to have thought to ask me in the first place." She winced as soon as the words left her mouth.

"I did think of it," he said, his voice low, eyes intent on hers. "But this is a business meeting as far as I'm concerned and I need to concentrate." His gaze flickered over her and she became acutely conscious of just how short and tight her gown was. And she warmed when she saw the heated approval reflected in the golden depths of his eyes. "I do not need to walk around so turned on I can scarcely see straight."

She felt the corners of her lips turn up.

"You enjoy that?" he asked.

"Crude as compliments come, but yes, I enjoyed it a little bit."

Far better to have him not want her here because she was a distraction than to have him not want her here because he was bored with her already.

"Glad to hear it."

"Somehow, I don't think you are."

"Oh, I am." Blaise took her arm and turned her to

him, seemingly unfazed by the people that were watching them with rapt interest. “What man doesn’t want to hear that he’s satisfied his lover?”

“Am I your lover?” she asked.

Blaise dipped his head, his lips skimming her cheek as he leaned in. “Do you not remember?” he whispered.

A sensual shiver crawled over Ella’s skin, reached into her and made her entire body tighten at the memory of his touch, his kiss. Of course she remembered. She could do nothing else.

“It’s hard to remember since it’s been so long,” she said, trying to keep her voice steady.

“Has it?”

“I thought you might have lost interest.”

His lips flattened, his eyes growing distant. “I don’t do the insecure-female thing, Ella.”

Anger ignited in her, just as hot as the longing it replaced. “This isn’t the ‘insecure-female thing.’ This is me not being appreciative of the lack of contact. I’m not needy, but I do expect some respect.”

“Have I ever given you a reason to believe I disrespect you?”

“Only when you didn’t call after we came back to Paris. Fine if you want to keep things casual, but not if you expect to go incommunicado and only come around for booty calls.”

He raised an eyebrow. “Classy.”

“No, it’s not. And that’s why I don’t want any part of something like that.”

“I thought you might need space.”

From anyone else, it might have seemed like a line, but she could feel the real sincerity in his voice. And she knew he was probably right. She really, probably did need space. Because their intimacy had been so complete in Malawi. He had been in her, and not just in a physical sense. She had shared everything with him. Had given him a piece of her.

And maybe space would keep her feeling from developing into something that was absolutely futile.

"Well, I don't. I mean, it would have been nice to be sure of where we stood when we came back here."

Blaise dropped a soft kiss on her lips and she froze, luxuriating in the feel of his mouth on hers. It really had been too long.

When they parted he stayed close to her, his voice low. "No matter what I intended, I think it's clear what our relationship has to be, as long as we're in close proximity."

Ella shivered. "I suppose so."

He let his fingers drift over her cheek, his eyes intent on hers. "I cannot seem to keep my hands off of you."

The crowd completely receded, the low hum of voices becoming nothing more than white noise. There was only Blaise, only his hand on her cheek, his gaze on her, full of a deep longing that echoed in her body.

She closed the distance between them, sliding her tongue delicately over the seam of his lips, tasting him, savoring him like a craving she'd been aching to partake of.

She placed her hands lightly on his chest, felt his heart raging against her palm. He gripped her wrist and pulled it back, stepped away from her.

"No," he said, his voice rough.

"Why not?"

"Business, remember?"

"Oh, right."

It probably wouldn't look very good for Blaise to be

making out with her in the middle of the oh-so-upscale event. Especially since he had business to discuss.

"I promise to behave myself," she whispered.

He looked at her for a long moment, her skin burning beneath his close scrutiny. "Now, that is a shame."

Ella felt her body get hot everywhere, her breasts heavy. She longed for his hands to cup her there, to alleviate the ache of unsatisfied longing. Not here. Of course not here.

Blaise took Ella's hand and led her to the bar, to the purpose for his attendance. Calder Williams, owner of a very upscale chain of hotels, and the next project Blaise wanted to invest his money in.

Ella shifted next to him, her breast brushing his arm. All of his blood rushed south. His body was on fire with the need to be inside her again, to move his hands over her body, to be in her body. Two days had been more than enough time apart. It had been important to him to prove that he could conquer his need for her by staying away.

But he had proven that point, and he was done waiting. Business first, though, pleasure later.

"Calder," Blaise said, extending his hand, his mind back on business, even if his body was still stubbornly stuck on Ella.

"Blaise—" Calder accepted his hand "—good to see you again." His eyes were firmly fixed on Ella, the interest there obvious.

Blaise gritted his teeth. "Yes, it is."

"And you are?" Calder said to Ella.

"Ella Stanton." Ella extended her hand and Calder lifted it to his lips, brushing his mouth over Ella's creamy-soft skin.

Something ugly and dark kicked Blaise in the gut.

The need to stake his claim, to show that Ella was his, blotted out everything else in his mind. He slid his arm around her waist, cupping her hip possessively, stroking her idly as he brought up his thoughts on Calder's hotel expansion project.

Calder's eyes continued to linger on Ella, his interest clearly on her curves not on business.

His dates had always been an accessory, in his mind, and if men had wanted to admire them, he had never cared. But he didn't want Calder looking at Ella. Didn't want him looking at her flawless face and luscious figure, and finding her desirable. Didn't want him looking at her scars and finding her lacking.

Ella was his.

"I think," Blaise said, his voice icy, "we should continue this discussion in my office another day."

A knowing smile curved Calder's lips. "I'll call your PA."

"Good."

"Nice to meet you, Ella," Calder said.

"You, too." Ella sounded unfazed, as though she had no idea that Calder had been contemplating having her for dessert. The thought made Blaise's blood run hot.

"Do you have a business card?" Calder asked.

Ella reached into her bright pink handbag and produced one. "Yes, this has all the info for the boutique and how to contact me personally for info about the clothing line."

"A fashion designer, I should have known."

"Calder, perhaps you should try preying on one of the single women in attendance and leave my date to me."

Ella stiffened beside him, Calder's grin widened. "Of course," he said, tucking Ella's business card into the interior pocket of his jacket.

"Nice to meet you," Ella said, gripping Blaise's arm. "I think I'm ready to go."

Ella released her hold on him once they got a few feet away from Calder, moving quickly to keep ahead of him, weaving through the crowd and heading toward the door.

Blaise followed her out into the empty corridor. "And what is your problem? I thought you wanted to come?"

"I didn't know you were going to spend the evening acting like a jealous jerk."

"Like you were earlier today?"

She gritted her teeth and let out a mild growl. "I didn't embarrass you in front of anyone."

"He was ready to devour you in front of me."

"But I wouldn't have allowed it, so what was the problem?"

"The problem is that this was meant to be a business meeting of sorts, and that was decidedly unprofessional."

"Don't blame me for your display of possessive male behavior, Blaise Chevalier."

Her blue eyes were on fire, all but spitting sparks at him, her cheeks red with her very indelicate rage. But his eyes went straight to her lips. Full, electric-pink thanks to her expertly applied gloss. Kissable. Edible. *Necessary.*

Ella had been a virgin less than a week ago. Out of deference to that, he shouldn't follow through with the fantasies rioting in his brain. But he couldn't stop himself.

There was a time in his life when he'd considered himself a man of honor. A man in control of his baser instincts.

All pretense of that had been well and truly destroyed

three years ago, and he had destroyed it with his own hands. Tonight he would not be gaining those qualities back. He had to taste Ella. He *had* to. It was a matter far beyond simple attraction. It was elemental, bone deep and as necessary as breathing. To prove that she was his. That he was the man she wanted, not Calder, or any other. To ensure that no matter how many men brought her to pleasure after him, he would be the one she always remembered.

He captured her mouth. His body shuddering as her lips softened, parted for him immediately. He delved in, his tongue sliding over hers, his body instantly hard, instantly aching from the sweet pressure of her lips.

She kissed him back. Roughly. Passionately. Her hands moving up to bracket his face. He stepped forward and she moved with him until her back was against the wall. And he kept kissing her, like he was dying and this was the last moment he would ever have to seize the most essential experience before the end.

The kiss was fueled by desperation, a desperation he couldn't understand or control. It was coursing through him with an intensity that rocked him to the core, driving him on with an urgency he'd never experienced before. Maybe it was his anger, mixing with hers, creating a substance that was deadly and explosive.

This was no civil prelude to an evening of uncomplicated pleasure. This was something more. Something deeper. As it had been from the moment he'd first touched Ella.

"Blaise," she whispered.

"Ella." He met her eyes, kissed her cheek, her neck, right on the place where the fire had marked her skin. Then he moved to kiss the other side of her neck, leaving two kisses there, as he had promised to do.

She arched against him, and he put his hand between them, palmed her breast, his thumb stroking over her hardened nipple.

She was everything he remembered and more. Her flavor richer, more intoxicating, the feeling of her against him more arousing than anything in his memory. The sounds of her pleasure, the movement of her body as she exulted in his touch, it was all so much more, and it all served to fray the edges of his tightly held control.

He moved his hand down, gripped her hips, pulled her hard against his body so she could feel the heavy length of his erection. So she would know exactly what she was doing to him.

A voluptuous sigh escaped her lips and she let her hands move down his back, gripping his butt, drawing his body even tighter into hers.

He was on the brink, in the corridor where anyone could see them, not even a convenient pillar to shield them from prying eyes, he was ready to come. When it came to sex, Blaise preferred a bedroom and privacy, but it didn't seem important now.

Nothing did. Nothing except his need to have Ella.

There was a sharp sound as the main doors to the ballroom opened and came into contact with the metal doorstop.

Ella froze, slowly releasing her hold on him. He moved away from her, but only fractionally, keeping one hand on her waist.

A small group of people wandered out, talking and laughing, visibly intoxicated and not paying any attention to Ella and himself.

Ella dropped her head, her forehead pressing against

his shoulder after the group passed by. "Oh…that was…I don't know what just happened."

"Lust."

"Lust," she repeated. "Maybe that's it." But she didn't sound convinced. She didn't convince him.

Ella's eyes looked huge, her pupils dilated, her breasts rising and falling unevenly, along with her breathing.

"Your place or mine?" he asked, his voice strangled.

"I only have a single bed."

Another stark reminder of how innocent she was. Of what a bastard he was.

"Mine then."

CHAPTER TWELVE

BLAISE'S APARTMENT WAS A brilliant reflection of the man himself. Hard, cool, with smooth lines and nothing that betrayed a clue about his true inner workings.

Not a family photo. Not even artwork that went beyond generic, modern prints that Ella was certain an interior designer had selected for him.

It reflected what he showed the world, but it didn't reflect what she knew about him. Blaise was Malawi. The lake, the sky, the sense of beauty that hadn't been, and never could be, tamed.

But this, this slick, cool environment, was what he wanted the world to believe. Was what he was comfortable with.

"Lovely view," Ella said, gesturing to a wall of windows that revealed the Paris skyline, the brightly lit Eiffel tower glittering prominently.

Blaise shrugged, flickering the windows a disinterested glance. "I hardly notice it."

Ella nearly choked. "Then why…I mean, this didn't come cheap. Why have it if you don't appreciate the location?"

"Oh, I do appreciate the location. This penthouse was a good investment, because of the view, mainly."

She cleared her throat. "That's…well, it's very you."

"You have the soul of an artist, Ella," he said, his tone indulgent. "I have the soul of a financier. You see art, I see monetary value."

"That's your passion then, money?"

He shrugged again, discarding his coat carelessly on the couch and loosening his tie. "Not money itself. Making it. The challenge, the risk."

"So, you're a gambler?"

"Hardly. My risks are all very carefully calculated. I don't take chances."

"You don't consider your association with me taking a chance?"

"*Non.* You have talent, Ella. It has been confirmed by everyone I've spoken to on the subject."

Ella took a deep breath, continuing to survey the vast, empty feeling space. Everything was so unnaturally clean, so strangely organized.

"I'm not home very often," Blaise said, answering some of the questions that were rattling around in her head.

"Ah."

Blaise crossed the room, his eyes intent on her, and the sterile background faded away.

The moment his lips met hers, the fire was reignited in him, and he was consumed by it. Consumed by his need to have her. It had never been like this before. Not with any woman, not in any fantasy.

It managed to reach in past the walls he'd built inside himself, managed to make him feel the full force of his need, the full force of his arousal, without the protective shield that he prized so much.

And he didn't want to stop her. Didn't want to do anything that might dampen any part of what she made him feel.

Her hands went to his chest, fingers working the buttons of his shirt without any finesse. She made a small sound of frustration when she stumbled at one of the buttons, and he laughed, finished the job for her and consigning his shirt to the floor.

"You're perfect," she whispered, her hand skimming his bare chest.

His heart squeezed tight. She meant his body, because if she could see inside him, she would know what a lie that statement was. Would know just how far from perfect he was.

"My bedroom is upstairs," he said, moving it all into safer territory. To bed. He could give her everything there. All of his desire, all of the pleasure that was possible for her to have.

It was the only place he could give her everything she deserved.

She smiled wickedly, parting from him and sauntering up the curved staircase that led to his room. Her backside swayed back and forth in an enticing rhythm and he was powerless to look anywhere else.

His room had the same view as the living area, the Paris skyline, the *Tour Eiffel.* A view that represented nothing to him. Nothing but broken promises. Marie's and his own. It was a view he had purchased at Marie's command.

The view was all that remained the same. After she'd left, gone off with the new love of her life, he'd brought in a decorator to eradicate the feminine frills his ex had brought into the penthouse. He had made a valiant effort to erase every reminder of her. What he hadn't been about to do was sell a valuable piece of real estate at a bad time, not even when he was—or so he'd believed then—heartbroken.

So he'd spent three years ignoring the view. But now, when he looked out his windows, he would see Ella's silhouette in the foreground, the lights glittering behind her, as he did now. She was looking at him with stark longing on her face, none of the coyness some of his other lovers liked to employ.

Ella wanted him, and she did not bother to hide it. Her honesty was stunning, more than he deserved. And yet he wanted it. Wanted her. All of her.

She looked behind her, at the open windows.

"It is privacy glass. Even with the lights on, no one can see in," he said.

Ella nodded, reaching behind her back. "Good. Because tonight—" he heard the rasp of her zipper "—I want the lights on."

He could see she was nervous, could see the slight tremor in her hand as she eased her sheath dress down her body, shimmying to release it over the curve of her hips.

His body hardened to the point of pain at the sight of her, her gorgeous curves on display, barely covered by a nearly sheer bra and panty set. This was the first time, during a sexual encounter, that she had revealed her body to him in full light.

Ella Stanton was the bravest woman he had ever met. A combination of softness and strength, insecurity and confidence. A woman who had endured such pain with no support.

She threw the vapid nature of his life, of the lives of the people he associated with, into sharp relief.

His mind went clear of everything but the sight of her as she unhooked her bra and revealed her breasts. Soft and pale, light pink tips that looked like the sweetest treats. Treats he couldn't resist.

He moved to her, brushing his fingers lightly over her collarbone, down around the outside curve of her breast to her ribs. She whimpered slightly and he repeated the motion, not touching her where he knew she longed for it.

His own body pulsed in protest. He didn't want slow. He wanted now. He wanted immediate satisfaction. He also wanted to savor her. To give her everything he had to give. This was it for him, the beginning and the end of what he had for her.

It wasn't enough.

She wiggled against him, tugging her panties down and kicking them to the side, along with her spiky heels.

He reached between them, rubbing his fingers over the intimate heart of her body, dipping one finger into her, drawing out her moisture and slicking it over her clitoris. He did it again. Again, until she was weak in his arms, desperate sounds of pleasure escaping her lips.

He pushed another finger into her, searching for the point inside of her body that would bring her to the heights faster. He continued moving his thumb over the bundle of nerves at the apex of her thighs.

She clung to his shoulders, and he welcomed the bite of her nails, the pain distracting him from the force of his arousal, helping him hold on when he was so close to slipping over the edge into oblivion without giving her satisfaction.

"Blaise, I can't..." she panted.

"Come for me," he said roughly, driven to feel her climax around his fingers, to experience her pleasure that way.

She bit her lip, pink color flooding over her skin, spreading across her cheeks, down over her breasts. When her orgasm hit, she shuddered against him, her body trembling, growing heavier as she rested her weight on him.

"Ma belle," he whispered, scooping her into his arms and carrying her to the bed. He gently placed her in the middle, working at discarding the rest of his clothes before joining her.

She took his erection in her hand, her eyes locked with his as she squeezed him, pleasured him. This was no practiced move performed for hundreds of others; this was simply for him. He owed her the same.

He pressed his lips to her neck, nibbled the delicate skin there before moving on to her breasts. "You are like a dessert," he said, running the tip of his tongue around the outside of one hardened nipple. "Strawberries and cream. But much better, much richer."

He sucked the tightened bud between his lips and she arched against him, abandoning her attentions on his body, her focus solely on her own satisfaction. As it should be. As he wanted it to be.

"I want you, Blaise," she said, her fingers skimming over his biceps, his shoulders, his back. "Only you."

His body pulsed with the need to be inside her, the need to take her, but he held on to the last shred of his control, moved his attention to her other breast.

"Please," she said. "Now."

His control shattered, all thoughts of drawing things out, of bringing her to peak after peak, dissolved. His mind was blank of everything but his need, his need to be in her, to be sheathed in her tight body.

Ella's body.

With shaking fingers he took a condom from his side table drawer and ripped open the packaging. Ella held out her hand. "Let me."

"No," he ground out. "If you touch me, I'm going to come."

"I don't mind," she said, a wicked smile playing over her lips.

"Not like this, Ella."

"Yes," she said, taking the packet from his hand and setting it on the bed. "Like this."

She leaned forward, running her tongue over the length of him. His stomach seized tight, every muscle in his body locked, frozen, as she explored him with her mouth, her lips, her tongue.

She cupped him, took him deep into her mouth. The feeling of her tongue on him so intense he nearly lost it. He speared his fingers through her hair, planning to protest, to stop her, unable to bring himself to do it.

When she pressed a hot kiss to him he jerked away.

"Ella," he said. "I can't..."

She looked at him, her blue eyes hot. "Come for me, Blaise."

She turned her attention back to his body, back to his pleasure, taking very little effort to bring him past the point of no return and push him over the edge. He was no longer in control. She had taken it from him.

In a graceful movement, she came to rest beside him, her hand on his chest, her cheek on his shoulder.

"I love the contrast of your skin against mine," she said, her voice muffled.

"You do?"

"Yes. It's like art."

"As I said, you have the soul of an artist." And the lips of an enchantress.

She sighed, a soft sound, filled with emotion he couldn't guess at. "I'm sort of exhausted," she said.

"You are?" If anyone should be exhausted, it was him

She smiled at him, a smile that didn't quite reach her eyes. "Very."

He'd never been in tune with the feelings of his lovers, he'd been told that very thing by several of them, but he knew that something was wrong with Ella. Sensed some kind of deep sadness in her. Felt it echo in his chest.

He shouldn't be surprised. It was all he'd ever given to those in his life that meant the most to him.

Ella's eyes fluttered closed, her breathing becoming deep and even. Blaise laid his head back on the pillow, his eyes wide-open. Sleep wouldn't be coming for him tonight.

Ella's entire body ached. In the early hours of the morning, Blaise had finished what they'd started, taking her to heights she hadn't imagined possible. Showing her things about herself she hadn't realized.

Ella rolled over in bed, her hand coming to rest on the cold spot where Blaise had been. She blew out a breath.

She didn't know how it happened, when it had happened, but at some point last night, after she'd lost her patience with his slow, controlled seduction and she'd taken it upon herself to shatter his control, as he'd shattered hers, she realized that she loved him.

She was in love with Blaise Chevalier. Notorious womanizer, the man who had stolen his brother's fiancée, the man who had commandeered her business loan like the pirate that the press said he was.

In her mind, she knew he was all of those things. *Every word they've printed about me is true.* He'd said it. He'd meant it. But she didn't see it in him.

He was the man who traced her scars. The man who

had held her while she'd told him all of her darkest secrets, tears streaming down her face. The man who believed in her talent, her visions. The man who thought she was beautiful.

He hardly seemed like he could be the same man the press wrote about. The man the people of France loved to hate.

The question was, what did it mean for her?

She'd known his darkest secrets from day one. But it hadn't stopped her from falling in love with him. Couldn't stop her. He was a bad bet, no question. Falling in love with him was akin to begging for heartbreak, and yet…she wasn't afraid, or sad, that she loved him.

Because last night, she had felt like a whole woman. A whole person. Someone who could be with the man she loved, do whatever she pleased, with the man she loved. There was nothing holding her back, no voice telling her she wasn't good enough or pretty enough.

Her effect on Blaise was obvious. He wasn't lying about his attraction to her. And that a man like him, a man who epitomized masculine perfection, could find her beautiful was something that made her rethink everything she'd ever thought about herself.

She wasn't in the waiting room of her own life anymore. She was living it. And she was very likely going to get her heart broken. But she wasn't hiding anymore.

Blaise came back into the bedroom, a towel wrapped around his waist, water droplets running down his impressive chest. She just wanted to lick them off. She was seriously starting to wonder if she was insatiable.

"Tell me about Marie," she said, the words slipping out of her mouth before she had a chance to think them through.

He froze for a moment, then undid the towel and let

it drop before moving over to the large, dark armoire in the corner of the bedroom, totally unconcerned with his nudity. "Why?"

"Because. Shouldn't I know?"

She saw his jaw tighten, a fractional movement that someone less in tune with him would have missed. "Look it up on the internet."

Her stomach tightened. "I have."

"Was that not enough?"

"No. It's not even close to being enough."

"It doesn't matter, Ella."

"Yes, Blaise, it matters."

"Why do you say that?" he asked, rolling his powerful shoulders as if trying to ease off stress. As if she was causing him stress.

"Because if it wasn't a big deal you would tell me about her."

He opened the top drawer to the armoire and took out a pair of black boxer briefs. He put them on, his body backlit by the sun filtering through the window.

"She was engaged to Luc. About three weeks before the wedding, she and I were alone at their penthouse. I seduced her. She called off the wedding. We had one year together, and then she left me."

Ella blinked, drawing her knees up to her chest. "I thought…I thought you broke up with her."

"No," he said, clipped.

"But you said every word written about you was true."

"More or less. The important parts are true. And I may as well have ended things. I drove her away. I wasn't very much fun to be around, since I looked at her and saw the betrayal of my brother."

"Why did you…why?"

"Why?" he repeated. "Because I loved her, you know. At least that was my excuse. Love conquers all, yes? Even an engagement ring."

"You loved her?" A sharp tug of jealousy pulled at Ella. He had loved Marie enough to do anything to have her. She'd assumed, all this time, that he'd seduced her, maybe to get revenge on the brother who'd been raised in luxury while he'd been in Africa with his mother.

But love…she hadn't considered that. Her pirate, with all those walls around his heart, had been open with someone else. Had given his heart to someone else. Believing that he had been callous in his seduction of Marie had almost been easier.

"No. I did not love her. I believed it was love, and what a convenient excuse it makes, *non?* An excuse to be selfish, an excuse to have big, screaming fights, because love is so passionate and the heart wants what it wants. The heart is a wicked thing, Ella."

"I don't believe that."

"Because you have not seen it. Have not seen how far it can lead you from everything you believed you were. I prefer to use my mind now. That, I can trust." He looked out the window. "Do you know why I have this view? Because of her. She begged for a view of the Eiffel Tower, such status, and how wonderful for when she threw parties. One of the many things I did to prove my love for her, an easy way to prove it, because all I had to do was write a check. Tell me, Ella, is that love?"

"No."

"I thought not."

Ella's stomach was tight. Jealousy, sadness, anger, all rolled through her. She got out of the bed, not caring about her state of undress. Not even caring about her scars.

When she'd told Blaise about her family, she'd felt like a bond had been forged between them. She'd thought learning about his past would make it even stronger. But now she felt as if he'd just moved further away from him. As if the tenuous bond between them was fraying.

"I have to go to work," she said, stiffly. "I'll just… go home and use the shower there. I need new clothes anyway."

Blaise shrugged, tugging on a pair of dark blue jeans. "Have you heard back from Statham's?"

Ella shook her head. "Not yet."

"Let me know?"

Ella nodded, her heart feeling like it might be breaking in her chest. "Yeah. I'll call you."

CHAPTER THIRTEEN

"Hi," Ella said, stepping into Blaise's office. The view from there was just as spectacular as the view from his apartment. The thought made her stomach clench tight. She hadn't spoken to Blaise in twenty-four hours. Not since she'd left his penthouse after his revelation about Marie. And that was what the view reminded her of, the penthouse he'd bought for the woman he'd loved.

"What's your news, Ella?" he asked, his gaze barely flickering away from his computer screen.

"I just got a slot in a really big fashion show coming up next week," Ella said.

"Great," Blaise said, though he didn't sound shocked. "How did that come about?"

"There was a cancellation, and the organizers of the event called me. It's going to cost a bit to throw together so last minute, but I can show the line that Statham's is looking at, my collection for Fall of next year."

"You have models?"

"I have most of them. I suppose we could trawl your black book if I need any more."

That got his attention, a wry smile curving his lips. "If you need it, it's in the vault at my bank."

"I'm sure it contains State secrets," she said, smiling back in spite of herself.

"Possible incriminating evidence. Though I'm not sure much more could be done to damage my reputation."

Not likely. His reputation was well and truly damaged, and he seemed to revel in that. Seemed to wear it like a comfortable coat. She couldn't figure out why. And she wanted to, so badly. She wanted to know his heart, the heart that he saw as being so wicked. She wanted to know *him*.

"Probably not," she said, her throat tight. "You didn't… did you arrange for this?"

"No, Ella. I didn't arrange for Statham's to contact you, either."

A little bubble of satisfaction expanded in her chest. She'd appreciated Blaise's help so much along the way, but to know she'd done it on her own was huge. Because someday, she would be managing without Blaise entirely, both professionally and personally. She had to know she could do this alone. And the good thing was, now, she was sure that she could.

She didn't want to, but she could.

It was funny that not so long ago she'd been dreaming of the day she could pay him off as quickly as possible and get him out of her life. Now she didn't want to lose him. It would be funny if she didn't know it would hurt so bad when he walked out of her life. And he would. Because if he didn't love her, what would hold him to her? His sexual fascination with her would fade. It had to.

Although, she doubted the fascination she had for him would ever fade. Even now her body ached for him. Almost as much as her heart.

"I just wanted to tell you," she said. And she wanted to hug him. And kiss him. And tell him that she loved him.

"I'm proud of you, Ella."

Her heart stalled. It was the first time she could remember someone saying that to her, and it couldn't have meant more coming from anyone else.

"Thank you. I'd better go make some phone calls."

Blaise stood from his desk and crossed to her, putting his arms around her waist. He dipped his head and kissed her, his lips hot on hers, familiar and foreign at the same time.

"I'll see you tonight," he said.

She nodded. "Okay." It might be emotional suicide, but she was willing to take the chance.

Because some things were worth taking a chance on. Blaise was one of them.

The next week passed in a haze. Work filled up her day and Blaise took up each and every night, the passion between them only growing stronger each time they were together.

Ella's feelings for him growing stronger.

The night of the fashion show was chaotic, the backstage a blur of half-dressed models and screaming stage managers. Ella loved it. She was in her element. And tonight her confidence wasn't a show.

The woman she pretended to be had finally melded with the woman she was. She wasn't quite as outrageous as her persona had been, but she wasn't crippled by insecurity, either. She was happy now. Her makeup wasn't a mask, her clothes weren't armor. She was just Ella. And she was happy with that. And she was enough.

The voice in her head was Blaise now, telling her that she was beautiful, that she had talent. She wasn't bogged down by doubt anymore. She wasn't living in the tragedy that had happened eleven years earlier.

Ella watched on the monitor backstage as her line was paraded out in front of the audience. Listened to the applause. And, when it was time for Ella to walk out with her model wearing the finale piece, and she grabbed the other woman's hand and did her turn on the catwalk, confidence surged through her.

When she reached the backstage it was still in complete chaos. Another designer's work was going on in ten minutes and models and stylists were scrambling here and there in an attempt to get everything done on time.

Ella turned and saw Sarah Chadwick, the head buyer for Statham's, making her way through the throng of people. "Ella, that was fabulous."

"Thank you. I'm so glad I was able to participate."

"I'm glad you did, too. I think you make the kind of clothing that I want to see in Statham's. It's wearable, but it has an edge that I love."

"You want my line in your stores?" Ella knew she sounded a little bit breathless and shocked, but she was.

"I do. And I'm sure I won't be the only one. But if you can get us some exclusive pieces, I'm sure I can sweeten up the contract."

"I can…I can do that."

"I'll be sending over the paperwork later in the week and I…" Sarah checked the monitor behind them. "I'd better get back out there and watch the rest of this show. I'll be in touch."

Ella just stood there, letting the activity move around her. Statham's had been such a huge goal for her. To have achieved it was almost surreal. And the first person she wanted to share the news with was Blaise. He was the one who'd helped her get to this point, he was the one who'd really made it possible.

And he was the most important person in her life.

She turned and saw him, standing apart from the crowd of people. He was dressed in the suit from her line that she'd fitted to him, and he was holding a pink rose. The crowd faded away and she could picture him standing by a lake in Malawi, rose in hand. The night he'd traced her scars.

She walked over to him, her heart pounding in her chest. "I'm glad you're here."

"Well done," he said, handing her the rose. She touched it lightly, the texture of the velvet petals weaving sensual memories around her.

"I got the contract with Statham's. I just spoke to the head buyer."

He nodded slightly. "I knew you would."

"Only because you're too arrogant to admit otherwise."

He shrugged. "Or I have great confidence in you."

"I'll choose to believe that."

"When can you leave?" he asked, sensual intent threaded through his rich voice.

"I can leave now," she said. Because everything had been wonderful, and she'd just experienced a career high, and all she wanted to do was celebrate it with the man she loved.

"It's beautiful, Blaise." Blaise watched Ella's face as she surveyed the apartment. Candles were resting on every flat surface in the bedroom, except for the bed, casting a warm glow on everything the light touched.

"You don't mind candles?" He wondered if the fire might bother her.

She shook her head. "They're gorgeous. As long as we blow them out when we're done."

"Of course."

No, they wouldn't bother his Ella. She didn't hold on to her fear.

"Thank you. This is special. Tonight was special."

It had been. Watching Ella's clothes on the catwalk, seeing her come out and join the models, waving and smiling, taking ownership of her work, had made him feel like his chest was expanding.

And now, seeing her like this, bathed in the dim light, he felt as though he might explode with wanting her. With his desire to see her come to the peak of pleasure at his hands, but more than that, the desire to make her happy. To make her feel as special as she was.

"Come here, Ella."

Her blue eyes glittered with mischief in the flickering candlelight. "You come here, Mr. Chevalier."

And he did, because he was powerless to refuse her.

His blood ran hot and fast through his body, a fire raging out of control. He looked at Ella's body, skimmed his fingertips down the scar on her neck. That was the damage left by fire.

He tried to turn on his practiced seducer persona. He was a pro at it. He knew how to reduce a woman to a mass of quivering need while keeping his own desires in check, not taking his pleasure until the very last moment, after she had reached the peak several times.

But there was too much urgency in him, too much need. His body throbbed with it, his brain closed off to everything but the feel of her silken skin beneath his fingertips, everything but the ache in his hardened erection. Everything but the driving need to be in her. To make her his.

His woman. His Ella.

Ella did the seducing, her hands, her lips, her tongue.

His muscles shook with the effort of keeping himself from falling over the edge.

She was beautiful like this. Wild. Abandoned. Confident. Allowing her body to be bathed in firelight, unashamed, unafraid.

"Let me have you, Blaise," she whispered as he laid her back on the bed. "All of you."

The need in her voice, the desperation, pushed him past the point of return. If Ella hadn't placed the condom in his hand, he would have forgotten. Never, in all his life, had he forgotten about protection. He rolled it on with unsteady hands and thrust into her body, teeth clenched tight as pleasure poured over him like warm oil.

His mind was blank. Desire clouding everything, blocking out his usual reserve, his slow, practiced rhythm. All he could do was chase his satisfaction.

Ella arched against him, her tight nipples brushing against his chest. She gripped his butt, her fingers digging into his skin, soft, smooth legs locked around his calves as she moved against him, an active participant, as wild and out of control as he was.

"Blaise," she said hoarsely, her internal muscles clenching around him, pulling his own response from him.

He let out a harsh groan as he came, his body trembling in the aftermath of the intense release.

He rolled to the side, bringing Ella with him, his brain in a fog, his entire body heavy. Satisfied in a way he never had been before, and at the same time, hungry for more of her. He would always be hungry for more of her.

He was losing his control, could feel it slipping from his hands even now, the walls inside of him crumbling, leaving him exposed, allowing him to feel. He took a breath, and her scent filled him. His heart clenched tight.

It was unacceptable. He could not allow it.

Ella felt like she was walking on a cloud. The fashion show had been a success, her clothing line would be featured in one of the world's largest upscale department stores and she'd spent the entire night making love with Blaise.

Blaise. The man she loved.

She smiled as she pinned the sleeves on the jacket she was working on. She'd had to send some of her patterns out to sample makers since the workload was increasing, but there were a few key pieces she wanted to make sure she had a hand in, and her pink and gray trench was one of them.

The door to her studio opened and Ella turned sharply as Blaise strode in, his expression blank, his jaw tight. "You should lock the door," he said, his voice low.

"Sorry," she said, her stomach clenching. Everything about Blaise's body language spoke of intent, not of a casual visit. After last night, after the past week, she expected him to greet her with a kiss, not to stand with five feet of blank space between them, arms crossed.

"We have something we need to discuss."

Her stomach dropped. "Oh." It wasn't like she hadn't known it would happen eventually, wasn't as though she hadn't realized that a man who didn't believe in love wouldn't believe in commitment…but just because a prisoner knew the execution date was coming, didn't make it easier to bear.

And she'd thought…she'd thought it had changed. His walls had been coming down. He didn't treat her like an anonymous sex object; he treated her like a prize. Surely that meant something. She didn't say that, though. She didn't say anything. She couldn't.

"I'm ending our business association," he said tightly, handing her a stack of tightly folded documents.

She took them, fingers numb at the tips as she tried to grasp them. She was certain he could see her shaking.

"But…my business…my…I have contracts. The Ella Stanton label is poised on the brink of making it, *I'm* poised on the brink of making it."

"I am not calling the loan in. I am gifting you the amount of the loan, and the amount of the investment."

Ella shook her head. "I don't…I don't understand. Is it because we're in a relationship? Because that doesn't make it feel right, either. I can't just take money from you."

"You didn't seem to mind taking favors from me, connections, but if you've suddenly become above that, don't worry. We will end our personal association as well," he said, his voice flat, echoing in the expanse of the room.

She felt like the walls were closing in on her. "Why?"

"I've told you why. In truth I'm shocked you didn't end things when I told you about Marie. So now, I will do it for you."

"Why is that, Blaise?" she asked, her voice low, anger surging through her. "Because you couldn't chase me away with the revelation of what a bad, bad man you are? And now you have to do it by being more direct? Because you were counting on that to get rid of me, weren't you? Counting on your reputation to chase me away."

"It would get rid of anyone sane," he said, flatly.

"And this would, too? Right? This act you're pulling now, you standing there cold and flat when we both know how passionate you are." She could see it for what it was, she could see through him, and even though his words hurt, she knew they weren't real. She knew he was trying to protect himself. Because last night had cut deep, had forged a bond between them that was nearly frightening to her in intensity.

"I love you," she said. Why keep it a secret? Why lie when it was a truth that coursed through her veins, a truth that was in her, a part of her. Just like Blaise was a part of her.

He looked as though she'd struck him. "Stop."

"No. I can't. I won't."

"It's the sex, that's all. You were a virgin when we first made love and you're confusing lust with love. An easy thing to do, I know."

"Yes, yes, I was a virgin, thanks for the reminder. I also know that if this were only sex, the rumors of your reputation might have kept me at a distance. If it were only about sex then I would never have asked you about Marie. My heart wouldn't have bled for you, for the pain she put you through."

"The pain she put me through? It was a pain we brought on each other. One we both deserved."

"A pain you think you still deserve?"

He spoke through gritted teeth. "You don't know what you want. You don't want me, not for anything more than some fun in bed, trust me on that. I have nothing else for you."

"I do know what I want, Blaise. And I'm not going to be talked down to, and told that I don't. You can blame yourself for that. You're the one who helped me find my strength, who helped me see that I was taking half when I deserved whole just like everyone else.

And now, you're the one that's confused. You're the one that's afraid. It's so much easier for you to hold on to all of the stuff from the past because then you don't have to try, you don't have to take a risk. You don't have to put yourself out there again and take a chance on being wrong."

Blaise tightened his jaw, his eyes flat, void of emotion. A trick. One she'd seen him use before when she got too close, when he was feeling intensely.

"Are you really going to define your entire life by one mistake?" she asked.

When he spoke, his voice was low and hard. He didn't yell; he didn't need to. "That one mistake showed who I truly was. I thought I was such a great man, I had everything. A family that I was forging a new bond with. Position, power, wealth and honor. But none of it could stand up to my weakness," he said, his voice strained. "All the good I have done means nothing if I fail when it matters most."

Anger rose in her, along with desperation. Desperation to make him see himself. Really see himself, like she did. "Is that what bothers you most, Blaise Chevalier? The discovery that you're a man and not a god? That you're human, like everyone else? Well, I'm glad that you are. Because I needed a man to show me what I was missing. I needed a man to make me feel beautiful. I didn't need perfection. I needed someone who could understand *me.*" She put her palm flat against her chest. "And you did. You were there for me. You've made me see. You've made me see everything I deserve. Everything I spent the past eleven years denying myself out of fear. I'm not afraid now. And it's because of you."

"You're wrong, Ella," he said, his voice hard, unsteady. "Because you seem to think if you keep digging you'll find some hidden depth to me, but the truth is, this is it. I have nothing more for you. I have nothing more for anyone."

Images flashed through Ella's mind. The yacht. The rose. The night she'd taken him into her mouth and he'd trembled with ecstasy.

"You're wrong," she said. "You're afraid, and also wrong. There is so much to you, Blaise Chevalier. You're selling yourself short, you're selling both of us short."

"And you've bought into a fantasy, Ella Stanton. But a fantasy is just that. Fantasy. Nothing." A muscle in his jaw ticked and for a moment she saw a flash of blinding pain in his golden eyes, pain that ripped into her, echoed through her body. "There is no reason for you to see me again."

He turned and walked out of the room, closing the door behind him with a slam that was painful in its finality.

Ella set the papers down on the table, the words across the top blurring as her eyes filled with tears. She gripped the edge of the table, so hard that it bit into her palms, and felt her heart splinter, shatter, the pieces falling and blowing away. Out the door with Blaise.

He had her heart forever, and she knew she would never get it back.

CHAPTER FOURTEEN

BLAISE GAZED OUT the window of his penthouse, out at the view. The view he normally ignored. If he closed his eyes, he saw Ella, the bright lights of the city behind her, the silhouette of her curves much more enticing than any feat of man-made architecture.

He slammed his tumbler down onto the bar, whiskey sloshing over the side. When Marie had left, he'd gotten drunk. He'd called the last woman he'd dated and he'd lost himself in her body, using her to forget.

The thought of doing the same now made his stomach curdle, made him feel on the verge of physical sickness. He didn't want to forget Ella, he didn't want to touch another woman. He wanted to keep her essence on his skin, keep the feelings that he had for her at the surface. Even if all he had left was pain, he wanted to hold on to it.

Because there were feelings. Last night she'd torn down every defense he had, left him open and raw and bleeding.

He'd looked at her and seen everything she was. All of her heart and bravery. And he'd looked within himself and seen nothing. He wasn't afraid of heartbreak. He was experiencing it now in a way he'd never fathomed. As though a hole had been punched through his chest, leaving a bloody chasm where his heart had been.

He wanted to crumble from the pain. Even as the thought passed his mind, he found himself going to his knees, still staring out the window. He had thought he'd known love, and he'd been wrong, he'd realized that years ago.

What he hadn't realized was that love was very real, and that the power it possessed was much more than he could have ever fathomed.

You're wrong. And you're scared.

Damn right.

But the fear of a broken heart was nothing compared to the fear of Ella one day realizing she deserved more than him. To look in her eyes and see the disillusionment and pain he'd seen in his brother's eyes the day he'd found out about his betrayal.

To see the fire in Ella's eyes dim. To see the love there turn to hate, that was what he couldn't face.

He had always counted on his control to shield him from pain, to keep a buffer between himself and others. Playing the bastard was fine, because it meant no one looked inside him. He was afraid that if they did, the truth would be that he was nothing more than a bastard. Hadn't he proven it with Marie? Hadn't he proven it by betraying the brother who had welcomed him in France with open arms?

Ella made him want to try to be more. He didn't know if his best could ever be good enough.

He stood, pressed his palm flat against the cold glass. It would have to be good enough. Because he could not live without her.

"Ella."

Two weeks without Blaise and now she was hallucinating. She'd dreamed his voice so many times that she was hearing it while she was awake now. She was in a hurry to get out of the gray, Parisian weather, and she really wasn't in the mood to experience more time in her own personal hell.

Life without Blaise. A reality she had accepted, but a reality that hurt like an open, never-healing wound every day. She rested her head against the door of her studio, hand frozen on the key that she had jammed into the lock.

The touch on her neck was soft, familiar, as her hair was brushed back. It made her ache. The soft brush of lips on the scarred side of her neck. And she knew if she angled so he could reach the other side he would kiss her twice there.

She turned her head and saw him standing there in the rain, shirt collar open, no tie. He looked like a mess. Cheekbones too prominent, deep shadows beneath his eyes, black stubble on his face. And she'd never seen a more wonderful sight in her life. Or a more painful one.

"Why are you here?" she whispered, her voice thick with tears. "You said I wouldn't have to see you again."

He looked down, as though he couldn't meet her eyes. A first. "If you do not wish to see me, I will go."

"Why are you here?" she asked. Because she did wish to see him, no matter how cruel the pain, she wanted to see him for as long as she could, to drink in the sight of him, to feel the warmth of his caress. To just be with him.

"Ella," he said again, his voice gruff.

Her first instinct was to throw her arms around him and kiss him like she was love-starved. But she couldn't. Not until she knew why he was here.

If only she were love-starved, it might be better.

Instead she was filled with it. It colored everything she did, everything she saw. She would put on a dress and actually feel beautiful, and think of him, think of all that he had done to build that confidence within her. She would hear a joke and want to tell Blaise, would taste a new flavor of ice cream and want to share it with him. Alone in her bed at night, her body ached, and there was no relief. Because there was no Blaise.

Because he wasn't with her. Because he didn't love her.

"I could not stay away," he said, his voice rough. "Every night, sleep evades me. Every day my body aches, and I cannot eat. You…you are vital to me, and I did not realize it until I chased you away."

He took her hand in his, traced the scarring on the back of it with his thumb. "You were right about me, Ella. I was afraid. I am afraid. I said I was never nervous, but I am, shaking to my core, terrified that I have destroyed this thing between us. I have been a fool."

Rain was still falling, water spots darkening his white dress shirt. He didn't seem to care. Neither did she. The streets could flood and she wouldn't be tempted to move. Nothing could entice her away from Blaise, now or ever.

"You told me," he said, his thumb still moving over her scar-roughened skin, "that I was perfect once. That my body was perfect, and all that time, you saw yourself as damaged when you were more whole than I could have hoped to be."

She bit her lip and shook her head. "That's where you're wrong. I wasn't whole, I was fragmented, scared. That's how I recognized that fear in you, because I lived with it for so long. You helped me overcome it. You helped me realize that I was just sitting back waiting to live life when…I had nothing to wait for. You woke me up."

He kissed her then and her heart expanded. He wasn't here for work. He wasn't even here to tell her about his family. He was here for her. She kissed him back, slick lips sliding together in the pouring rain. Her skin was cold, but Blaise's hands warmed her, his lips on her neck lit a trail of fire that burned through her.

But this fire was different. It cleansed where it touched, burned away all of the debris that life had left both of them, so that there was nothing but Blaise and Ella.

"You've changed me," he said when they parted.

He traced the marks on her neck, reverently, his eyes never leaving hers. "I was afraid that if you ever saw past the walls I had put up, you would see nothing but a barren wasteland. I was afraid I could give you nothing."

"You've given me everything," she whispered. "You might not see it, Blaise, but you have. I was locked in myself, my body was my prison. And you set me free. When I look in you I see the world. Everything I've ever wanted or could ever want."

"I stand before you with no walls," he said, brushing his thumb over her lips, "I am not perfect, but I am a man who loves you very much, and I will do everything in my power to be all you deserve."

Everything in her expanded, filled, all of the love she had for him growing, rushing through her veins. "I didn't think you believed in love," she said, a smile on her face she could not hold back.

He pressed his forehead against hers, a smile curving his lips. "It was so much easier to believe that. Because as long as I believed everything had been a lie, I could pretend that I would never falter in that way again."

He took her hands in his, brought them to his lips. "I was wrong, again. Love is very real, Ella Stanton, and I know it because I love you with every fiber of my being. It's more than simple passion, more than lust. It is nothing I've ever known before. It's in every part of me. You are in me. The best parts of me. It isn't a facade for lust or selfishness, how can it be? If it were only my body that needed you, my heart wouldn't hurt every time it beat without you. If it were selfishness, you wouldn't have given me so much."

Tears were sliding down Ella's cheeks, mixing with the rain. And she didn't care. She didn't bother to wipe them away.

"I love you, too. I didn't even need you to do anything, to change. I just love you. All that you are, all that you've been, everything you will be."

Blaise's heart beat fast in his chest, without pain for the first time in two weeks, as Ella said the words that he had thrown aside that day at her studio. Words he'd been sure he would never hear from her lips again. Words he knew he'd done nothing to earn or deserve.

"I did need to change, Ella. You have changed me. You talked of being locked inside of yourself, and I had done that same thing, hiding behind my defenses. Defenses you wouldn't allow me to keep. You demand so much of me."

She nodded her head, blond curls swinging, flicking rainwater. "Because I needed all of you."

"You have all of me. I swear it. I will never hide from you again. And you will have my love, my body, my heart, for the rest of my days."

"How do you know that?" she asked, the tears clouding her brilliant blue eyes.

"Because being without you, losing you, was the lowest point of my life. There is nothing that comes close to rivaling it."

"Same goes for me," she said. "Never put either of us through that again."

"I won't." He reached into his pocket and pulled out a small velvet box. It was the ring he'd bought the night after he'd gone to his knees in his penthouse. Because he'd known that he had to have her back, that he had to do this. That he would lay down every shred of pride left and get on his knees before her if he had to, to try to convince her to take him back. To try to convince her to be with him forever.

Pride was nothing in the face of losing Ella. There was no room for it, not if it stood in the way of this.

"Be with me," he said, lowering himself to his knee. "Always. Be my wife."

She knelt down in front of him, the knees of her designer jeans on the wet sidewalk. She put her hand on his cheek, her eyes never leaving his. "Always."

He opened the box and delighted in the look on her face. "It's pink," she said, pulling the round cut, platinum-set bubblegum-pink diamond ring from its box.

"It's you." He slid it onto her finger, over the roughened patches that had been touched by fire. A hand uniquely Ella's and completely perfect in his eyes.

"It is," she said. "You know me so well."

"And you know me, and seem to love me anyway."

She leaned into him, her hands bracketing his face. "I love you because I know you."

He kissed her. He would never have enough of her lips. He would never have enough of her. He slid his hands beneath her shirt, felt the landscape of her skin. Felt the story of who she was with his fingertips.

"You are absolutely perfect, Ella Chevalier. In every way."

* * * * *

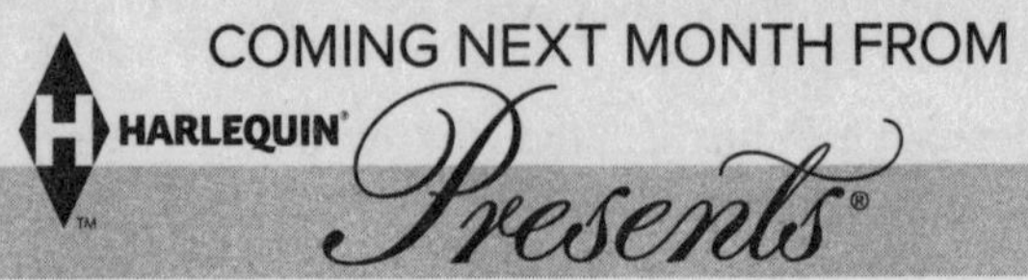

Available December 17, 2013

#3201 THE DIMITRAKOS PROPOSITION

Lynne Graham

Tabby Glover desperately needs Greek billionaire Acheron Dimitrakos to support her adoption claim over his cousin's child. His price? Marriage. But as the thin veil between truth and lies is lifted, will this relationship become more than in name only?

#3202 A MAN WITHOUT MERCY

Miranda Lee

Dumped by her fiancé *via text,* Vivienne Swan wants to nurse he shattered heart privately...until an intriguing offer from Jack Ston tempts her from her shell. He is a man used to taking what he wants, and Vivienne is now at his mercy!

#3203 FORGED IN THE DESERT HEAT

Maisey Yates

Newly crowned Sheikh Zafar Nejem's first act is to rescue heires Analise Christensen from her desert kidnappers and return her to her fiancé...or risk war. But the forbidden attraction burning between them rivals the heat of the sun, threatening everything.

#3204 THE FLAW IN HIS DIAMOND

Susan Stephens

When no-nonsense Eva Skavanga arrives on Count Roman Quisvada's Mediterranean Island with a business arrangement, Roman's more interested in the pleasure she might bring him. Perhaps Roman could help her with more than just securing her family's diamond mine...?

3205 THE TYCOON'S DELICIOUS DISTRACTION

aggie Cox

orced to rely on physio Kit after a skiing accident confines him a wheelchair, Hal Treverne has no escape from her intoxicating esence. But unleashing the simmering desire beneath her er-so-professional facade is a challenge this tycoon will relish!

3206 HIS TEMPORARY MISTRESS

athy Williams

amian Carver wants revenge on the woman who stole from him, d her sister Violet won't change his mind...until he needs a mporary mistress, and Violet's perfect! But sweet-natured Violet on turns the tables on his sensuous brand of blackmail....

3207 THE MOST EXPENSIVE LIE OF ALL

ichelle Conder

nampion horse breeder Aspen has never forgotten uz Rodriguez, so when he reappears with a multimillion-dollar vestment offer, Aspen's torn. She may crave his touch, but his ittering black eyes hide a deception that could prove more costly an ever before!

3208 A DEAL WITH BENEFITS

ne Night with Consequences

usanna Carr

ebastian Cruz has no intention of giving Ashley Jones's family's and back, but he does want her. He'll agree to her deal, but th a few clauses of his own—a month at his beck and call... d in his bed!

SPECIAL EXCERPT FROM

HARLEQUIN®

Presents®

Read on for an exclusive extract from THE DIMITRAKOS PROPOSITION, the sensational new story from Lynne Graham!

* * *

ABBY looked up at him and froze, literally not daring breathe. That close his eyes were no longer dark but downright amazing and glorious swirl of honey, gold nd caramel tones, enhanced by the spiky black lashes e envied.

His fingers were feathering over hers with a gentleness she ad not expected from so big and powerful a man, and little emors of response were filtering through her, undermining r self-control. She knew she wanted those expert hands on r body, exploring much more secret places, and color rose her cheeks, because she also knew she was out of her depth nd drowning. In an abrupt movement, she wrenched her ands free and turned away, momentarily shutting her eyes in gesture of angry self-loathing.

"Try on the rest of the clothes," Acheron instructed coolly, ot a flicker of lingering awareness in his dark deep voice.

Tension seethed through Acheron. What the hell was the atter with him? He had been on the edge of crushing that oft, luscious mouth beneath his, close to wrecking the non-exual relationship he envisaged between them. Impersonal ould work the best and it shouldn't be that difficult, he asoned impatiently, for they had nothing in common. She eaned up incredibly well, he acknowledged grudgingly,

HPEXP1213-1R

gritting his teeth together as his gaze instinctively dropp to the sweet pouting swell of her small breasts beneath clingy top.

He had done what he had to do, he reminded hims grimly. She was perfect for his purposes, for she had as mu riding on the success of their arrangement as he had. Tha fully nothing in his life was going to change in the slighte he had found the perfect wife, a nonwife….

Two hours later, Acheron opened the safe in his be room wall to remove a ring case he hadn't touched in yea The fabled emerald, which had reputedly once adornec maharajah's crown, had belonged to his late mother a would do duty as an engagement ring. The very thought putting the priceless jewel on Tabby's finger chilled Achero anticommitment gene to the marrow, and he squared broad shoulders, grateful that the engagement and marriage that would follow would be 100 percent fake.

* * *

Will sharp-tongued, independent firestorm Tabby Glov accept Greek billionaire Acheron Dimitrakos's outragec marriage proposal?

Find out in January 2014!